**Nobody could afford to be kind
if the war was going to start again.**

"They expect the business to fail quickly now that father is...is gone," said Enelle. "Before spring, they think. I...I would not like to live in the sort of house we would be able to afford if we sold this house."

"But..." said Jehenne, her voice trailing off as she found nothing else to suggest.

Nemienne drew a triangle absently on the polished surface of the table with the tip of her finger and fitted a smaller triangle inside it, and then another inside that. Then she looked up and said, since Enelle clearly could not bring herself to say it even if Ananda would let her, "Some of us will have to be sold."

Praise for The Griffin Mage Trilogy

"This book is like cupped fire, held in the hands: joyful and fierce and precise, painful and true beyond measure. It has the simplicity of poetry, the complexity of myth. I adored it."
— Daniel Fox, author of *Dragon in Chains*

"Very easy to read, filled with emotion and fluid writing."
— fantasybookcritic.blogspot.com

"Vivid, satisfying...most compelling is the world and its magical laws, which invite further related stories." — *Publishers Weekly*

By Rachel Neumeier

The Griffin Mage Trilogy
Lord of the Changing Winds
Land of the Burning Sands
Law of the Broken Earth

House of Shadows

HOUSE, of SHADOWS

RACHEL NEUMEIER

orbit

www.orbitbooks.net

Orbit
Hachette Book Group
237 Park Avenue, New York, NY 10017
www.HachetteBookGroup.com

First Edition: July 2012

Orbit is an imprint of Hachette Book Group, Inc. The Orbit name and logo are trademarks of Little, Brown Book Group Limited.

The publisher is not responsible for websites (or their content) that are not owned by the publisher.

The characters and events in this book are fictitious. Any similarity to real persons, living or dead, is coincidental and not intended by the author.

Library of Congress Cataloging-in-Publication Data
Neumeier, Rachel.
    House of shadows / Rachel Neumeier. — 1st ed.
        p. cm.
    ISBN 978-0-316-07277-9
    1. Griffins—Fiction. I. Title.

PS3614.E553H68 2012
813'.6—dc23

                                           2011033213

        10 9 8 7 6 5 4 3 2 1

                RRD-C

        Printed in the United States of America

For my sister-in-law, Astrid, who volunteers to sit up all night with newborn puppies so I can get some sleep. Thanks!

LONNE

NIJIADDE FALLS

King's District

Kerre Taum

Kerre Maraddras

Lane of Shadows

NIARRE RIVER

Docks

Candlelight District

KEMSENNES RIVER

Erhlianne

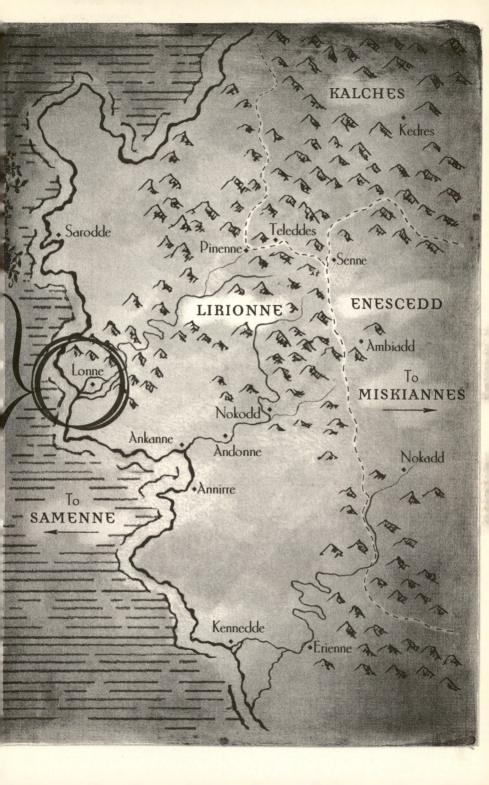

CHAPTER 1

In a city of gray stone and mist, between the steep rain-swept mountains and the sea, there lived a merchant with his eight daughters. The merchant's wife had died bearing the eighth daughter and so the girls had raised one another, the elder ones looking after the younger. The merchant was not wealthy, having eight daughters to support, but neither was he poor. He had a tall narrow house at the edge of the city, near his stone yard where he dealt in the blue slate and hard granite of the mountains and in imported white limestone and marble. His house had glass windows, tile floors, and a long gallery along the back where there was room for eight beds for his daughters.

The eldest of his daughters was named Ananda. Ananda was nineteen years old, with chestnut hair and pretty manners. She was not precisely engaged, but it was generally accepted that the second son of a merchant who dealt in fine cloth meant to offer for her soon, and it was also generally understood that she would assent. The youngest daughter, Liaska, was nine and as bright and impish as a puppy; she romped through her days and made her sisters and her father laugh with her mischief. In between were Karah and Enelle and Nemienne and Tana and Miande and Jehenne.

Gentle Karah, loveliest of all the sisters, mothered the younger girls. They adored her, and only Karah could calm Liaska on her more rambunctious days. Practical Enelle, with their father's broad cheekbones and their lost mother's gray eyes, kept the accounts for

1

both the household and their father's business. Tana, serious and grave even as a child, made sure the house was always neat. Lighthearted Miande sang as she went about the kitchen tasks, and made delicate pastries filled with cream and smooth sauces that never had lumps. Jehenne learned her letters early and found, even when quite young, that she had a feel for both graceful lettering and graceful phrases.

Nemienne, neither one of the eldest nor one of the youngest, neither the most beautiful nor the plainest of the daughters, drifted through her days. Her attention was likely to be caught at any moment by the sudden glancing of light across slate rooftops, or by the tangled whisper of the breeze that slid through the maze of city streets on its way to or from the sea. Though Nemienne baffled her father and puzzled her sisters, her quiet created a stillness otherwise rare in their crowded house.

For her part, Nemienne could not understand how her sisters did not see the strange slant into which light sometimes fell, as though it were falling into the world from a place not quite congruent. She didn't understand how they could fail to hear the way every drop of falling rain sometimes struck the cobbles with the pure ringing sound of a little bell, or the odd tones that sometimes echoed behind the sound of the wind to create a breathy, halfheard music pitched to the loneliness at the heart of the bustling city.

Even at home, Nemienne couldn't seem to keep her mind on letters of account or business—but then Enelle was the one who was interested in the prices of stone. Nor could Nemienne be trusted to take bread out of the oven before it burned—and anyway, Miande made much better bread. And when Nemienne went to the market, she seldom came back with what she had been asked to buy, returning instead with a flowering sprig she'd found growing out of a crumbling wall, or humming over and over three notes of a song she'd heard a street musician play. When sent to even the nearest noodle shop, just down the street and around the corner from the house, Nemienne sometimes got lost. She would find herself inexplicably walking down a street with no idea where she might be, so she had to ask strangers for the way home. But then, Tana always struck the best bargains in the market and the shops, so there was seldom a need for Nemienne to go on such errands.

The merchant looked proudly at Ananda, who would surely be happily wed by the turning of the year. He treasured Karah and would not look for a possible match for her even though she was nearly seventeen, for she was his favorite daughter—but then Karah was so sweet and good that she was everyone's favorite, so no one minded that she was their father's favorite, too. Practical Enelle was his greatest help in his business affairs; he called her his little business manager and joked that he should make his stone yard over into a partnership with her.

The merchant depended on Tana and Miande when he had his business associates to his home for a dinner, and always the dinners ran smoothly and comfortably, so that even the wealthiest merchants, who had wives and keimiso and children of their own, said they wished they had such a houseful of pretty and accomplished daughters. The merchant beamed smugly. He never told them that the invitations that brought them to his house had usually been written by Jehenne, whose hand was smoother than his. And on quiet family evenings, Liaska set her father and all her sisters laughing with her clever puppets, which she used in wickedly accurate mimicry of her father's associates.

Nemienne laughed at the puppets, too. But sometimes, especially on those evenings, she felt her father's puzzled gaze resting on her, as though he understood how each of his other daughters fit into his household but did not quite understand where Nemienne might exactly fit. Sometimes Nemienne herself wondered what kind of puzzle it might be, that had a Nemienne-shaped piece missing out of its middle.

Then one spring the merchant died, collapsing suddenly in the midst of his work and leaving his eight daughters alone in a city they suddenly found far from friendly.

There were business assets, but these were tied up in the stone yard and could not easily be freed. The assets could be sold in their entirety to the merchant's associates, but all of these men, whom the girls had thought were their father's friends, they now found had been his rivals. All the offers were very low. There were funeral expenses, and then there were the day-to-day expenses and the ordinary debts of business investments that ought to have yielded eventual profits if only the merchant had lived, but promised nothing but losses after his death.

"Must we sell father's business?" Ananda asked Enelle, after the cold edge of necessity had worn through the first dreadful shock of their father's death.

Enelle glanced down at the papers between her hands. They were all seated along both sides of the long supper table. None of the girls had taken their father's place at the head. Enelle, who had always taken the place at their father's left hand, sat there still. She was pale. But her voice was as calm and precise as ever. "We can't run it ourselves. We can't even legally own it," she said. "Petris could. Legally, I mean." Petris was the cloth merchant's son who had been expected to marry Ananda. "And we could run it with his name on the papers. But that is supposing he would be willing to marry a pauper. The business could be an asset to build on, but it isn't a . . . a fortune to marry into." Even her steady voice failed a little.

"We aren't paupers!" Jehenne exclaimed, offended at the very idea.

Enelle looked down, then lifted her gaze again. "It's strange about business. While father was alive, we operated at a profit. But now that he is . . . gone . . . we own a net loss. We are, in fact, paupers. Unless one of us can very quickly find a man to marry, someone sensible who will let me run the stone yard. Ananda?"

Ananda, across from Enelle, had her fingers laced tightly together on the polished wood of the table. She looked at her hands, not at her sisters. "Petris would still marry me. But his father won't permit the match if I don't have a dowry. A dowry up front, nothing tied up in future profit."

"We can't get you a dowry right now, without the stone yard," said Enelle. Her voice fell flatly into the room and there was a silence after it.

"But what shall we do, then?" Tana asked, and looked at Enelle, who seemed, uncharacteristically, at a loss for words.

"We must all think together," said Ananda.

"You already have an idea," observed Karah, studying Enelle. Faint lines of concern appeared on Karah's forehead—not worry about the difficulties they faced, but concern because she saw Enelle was distressed. "What is it? Is it so terrible?"

"It can't be *that* terrible," declared Miande, always optimistic. But even she sounded like she didn't have much confidence in this statement. They all understood now that sometimes things *could* be that terrible.

Enelle drew a breath without lifting her gaze, started to speak, and stopped.

"Enelle, no," said Ananda, firmly.

"We could sell parts of father's business?" suggested practical Jehenne, but doubtfully. "Or the house?"

Enelle glanced up. "The business would be worth ten times less broken up than it is intact. And if we sold the house to get a dowry for Ananda, we would have nowhere to live until the business begins to yield a profit, which will take years now, no matter what we do. None of our creditors will set favorable terms for us right now. Everyone expects trouble in the spring, you know. Because of the treaty."

She meant, as even the little girls knew, the Treaty of Brenedde. Its term would run out in the spring, and everyone knew that when it did, Kalches would immediately repudiate the peace and resume its war with Lirionne. Nemienne hadn't thought of how this would affect business in Lonne, but once Enelle pointed it out, she saw that her sister was right: Nobody could afford to be kind if the war was going to start again.

"They expect the business to fail quickly now that father is...is gone," said Enelle. "Before spring, they think. I...I would not like to live in the sort of house we would be able to afford if we sold this house."

"But…" said Jehenne, her voice trailing off as she found nothing else to suggest.

Nemienne drew a triangle absently on the polished surface of the table with the tip of her finger and fitted a smaller triangle inside it, and then another inside that. Then she looked up and said, since Enelle clearly could not bring herself to say it even if Ananda would let her, "Some of us will have to be sold."

The silence this time was fraught, but it did not last long. It was broken by Liaska, who leaped to her feet and cried, "No!"

"Or have you thought of another way?" Nemienne asked Enelle. She might be wrong. Nobody else seemed to think this was obvious except her. Perhaps Enelle was thinking of something else. But, surely, if Enelle had thought of some other way, she wouldn't be so hesitant to explain it.

Enelle looked up, and then down again. She was only sixteen, just a year older than Nemienne herself. It was a horrible decision for her to have to make. But it was not, of course, her decision to make. Not really. It was only her responsibility to tell them all that it was going to have to be made. Nemienne could see she had talked about this idea only with Ananda, and it was obvious Ananda had forbidden her to suggest it. Poor Enelle.

"How many of us?" Nemienne asked.

"No," said Ananda sharply.

Enelle didn't look at Ananda. She didn't look at any of them. She said to her tight-laced fingers, "At least two. Maybe three. It depends on the price we'd get, you see."

"Who would we—who would—who would be sold?" asked Karah.

"No one will be sold!" Ananda exclaimed. "We'll think of another way."

"I don't think there's another way," said Enelle, still looking at her hands, which had now closed into fists on the table. "And there's not much time to think of one."

"There is another way!" Ananda said fiercely. "There must be!"

"Me," said Nemienne, since that was obvious. "But who else?" She looked around the table. Not the little girls. Not Enelle, who was needed to run the stone yard and keep track of household expenses.

"No!" said Ananda. "No one will be sold."

"I am the most beautiful," Karah said simply, putting into plain words a truth they all knew. "A keiso House might be willing to give a large gift for me. That—that is an honorable life."

It wasn't that simple, of course. First Ananda and Miande and Jehenne had to argue bitterly that there had to be some other way. Enelle obviously couldn't bear to argue back, but her figures spoke for her. She had a whole long scroll of figures. She'd plainly tried very hard to find another way. It was equally plain that there wasn't another way to be found.

Jehenne looked at Enelle's figures and then ran out of the room in tears, because she knew Enelle was right but couldn't bring herself to argue for selling anybody. Liaska, who idolized the glamorous keiso and collected painted miniatures of all the most famous ones, was nevertheless outraged into a tantrum at the idea of losing Karah—and a little bit because she at least half wanted to be a keiso herself and knew none of her older sisters would consider selling *her*. In the end, Miande took the little girls away and the older ones looked at Enelle's papers.

Karah didn't examine Enelle's figures. She only believed them. She absolutely rejected any plan that involved selling the house. Nemienne saw that Karah's stubbornness surprised Ananda, though surely it should have been obvious that Karah would never agree to see the little girls forced to live in a violent, filthy part of the city.

Not that Karah argued. She simply continued to insist that she would do very well as a keiso, that it wasn't as if she was suggesting she might become an actress or an aika or anything disreputable. Then she announced that she would sell herself without Ananda's approval if she had to, and from this position she would not be budged. Ananda declared wildly that she herself could as well be sold as anybody, but of course that wasn't true. Nobody else had a merchant's son ready for a quick wedding and for the struggle that would follow to get the stone yard back into profitability.

Nemienne didn't argue either. She just waited for all the arguments to come to their inevitable conclusion. Two days later, she and Karah and Enelle took their father's small open carriage and drove to Cloisonné House, which all their cautious inquiries indicated was the very best keiso House in the candlelight district. Karah drove the carriage, with Enelle and Nemienne crowded close to either side of her on the high bench. None of them had wanted Tebbe, their father's driver, to accompany them on this particular errand.

Karah had cried. Then she had fixed her face and her hair very carefully. She was not crying now. Enelle was: Nemienne could see the sheen across her gray eyes. Enelle was gazing out at the city streets, one hand gripping the seat against the jouncing from uneven cobblestones, but Nemienne doubted her sister saw the city through which they drove or noticed the roughness of the cobbled streets.

Nemienne had not cried, though she felt a low, tight sensation in her stomach. She knew very well that Karah would make a wonderful keiso, but when Nemienne tried to picture *herself* learning to be charming and glamorous so that she might win honor and acclaim and eventually become a rich nobleman's flower wife . . . nothing about that future *fit*.

Lonne spread itself out around them, loud and busy. To Nemienne, she and her sisters seemed like ghosts, not nearly as solid and real as the cobbled streets through which they traveled, nor the mountains that loomed over the city. Nemienne stared up at the mountains, watching the low clouds that coiled and uncoiled in sinuous dragon shapes around their jagged peaks. The Laodd loomed among the cliffs, its sheer white walls and thousand glass windows glittering in the light, seeming from this distance no more a thing of men than were the mountains.

Yet keiso mingled freely with the powerful lords of the Laodd.

Many girls dreamed of becoming a famous keiso and being chosen as a flower wife by an important courtier. But Nemienne had never collected painted miniatures nor dreamed of glamour and fame. Now that the prospect lay before her, she found it...disturbing. She trusted Enelle's figures, and she also knew she was right to have argued that she herself should be one of those sold. But she wanted desperately to have the actual moment still ahead of her, waiting in some other day, not arriving in this one.

They came to the candlelight district and then to Cloisonné House far too quickly. The House proved to be an angular brick building, four stories tall, with wide balconies overlooking the street. Pink flowers and silver-variegated ivy poured down from the balconies despite the chill. The ivy did not exactly soften the look of the brick, but it made Cloisonné House look old and respectable and deserving of its good reputation.

At the same time, Nemienne thought that the shadow of the house and the edges of the bricks seemed to possess a strange, faint echo that she did not recognize. Then she blinked and looked again, and the house seemed perfectly normal. Servants quickly arrived to take the carriage away and welcome the sisters into the House, so there wasn't time to wonder about what she might have seen. But, as they passed under the lintel, a faint reverberation seemed to echo through the brick and the wood of the door. Nemienne tried to pause in the doorway, but Enelle was in front of her and Karah behind, and she went in after all without saying anything. Once within the house, the strange echo vanished, and as a tall woman approached them, she forgot about it.

The woman wore a gray overrobe, with a white and blue underrobe showing at throat and hemline. She took their names and their request to see the Mother of Cloisonné House. From her assured manner, Nemienne had thought this woman might herself be the Mother, but she only acknowledged their request, her eyes lingering thoughtfully on Karah. She left them in the hands of a servant girl and went away, carrying news of their arrival into the interior of the House.

Karah, nervous, glanced around with wide eyes that did not light on anything for more than an instant. Enelle was white faced, with a determined set to her mouth. She had her whole attention fixed on their purpose, with none left for anything beyond that necessity. Nemienne thought neither of her sisters even noticed the gracious warmth of the House's entry hall and parlor.

For, once inside, Cloisonné House indeed presented a gracious appearance. The walls of the entryway were paneled with wooden screens. Against the screens were little tables with mother-of-pearl inlay around their edges. Each table held some small object: the stylized pewter sculpture of a doe, a little finger harp with pearl knobs and silver strings, a decorative piece of cloisonné jewelry in muted colors. Each of these displays was framed by a washed-ink sketch of mountains or sea or sky. Looking at the grace of the hall, Nemienne felt a new and unexpected kind of sadness rise into her throat. She didn't truly expect—or even want—to remain in this House, but for the first time she felt that this might be something to regret.

They waited for the Mother of Cloisonné House in a small parlor that seemed made of sea and sky. Tapestries embroidered to suggest clouds and cliffs hung on the walls, and the chairs were upholstered in soft blue-gray fabric. Beyond the chairs, a cheerful fire burned in a slate hearth. A plump woman in robes of gray and blue brought hot spiced cider, assured them that the Mother of the House would attend them shortly, and went out again.

The Mother of Cloisonné House did not come in any haste, though servants brought iced cakes and dishes of sugared nuts and nikisi seeds. Karah had always loved sugared nuts. She only looked at these, clearly struggling against tears. Enelle turned away hastily, also blinking, and pretended to be absorbed in examining the fitted slate tiles of the hearth. Nemienne sat down in one of the chairs and looked into the fire. She felt numb, encased in a cold shell that stopped speech and thought and emotion.

The Mother of the House proved to be a stately woman with the dignity of a court lady, though her only crown was her own white hair braided into a coronet around her head. She was as richly dressed as a queen, though, with a sweeping blue-on-blue pattern washing down her overrobe like the waves of the sea from one shoulder to the opposite hem. Two little girls attended her, each carrying a covered tray. They settled gracefully by the door to wait for any commands she might give.

The woman's face was fine boned, with elegant cheekbones and shrewd dark eyes accentuated by violet powder. Her manner was reserved but not, Nemienne thought—hoped?—unkind. Her gaze moved quickly from one of them to the next as they rose to their feet. That gaze settled, unsurprisingly, on Karah. And widened slightly. That was surely promising.

The three sisters had risen to their feet. Enelle cleared her throat, and the woman at once turned her attention to her. She said, with a kind of brisk sympathy, "Welcome to Cloisonné House. I am Narienneh, Mother of Cloisonné House. May I hope for the opportunity to serve the daughters of Geranes Lihadde?"

Enelle blinked and lifted her chin. Karah and Nemienne exchanged glances, likewise understanding why the Mother of the House had kept them waiting in her parlor. She had had time to find out everything. Karah blushed and lowered her eyes, waiting for Enelle to speak. Color rose up Enelle's cheeks also, but she kept her gaze on the Mother's face. "Then you know why we have come—" she began.

"Yes," said Narienneh. "Please, sit. Accept the hospitality of Cloisonné House." She waited as one of the brown-clad girls quickly uncovered a tray and came forward to pour steaming tea. The girl served the Mother of the House first, then Enelle, then Karah, and finally Nemienne. Nemienne wondered what governed the child's decision to put the sisters in that order.

"Cloisonné is an exclusive House," said Narienneh. She spoke with dignified courtesy. "That is why you chose to come here, I presume. Any knowledgeable person advising you would certainly suggest Cloisonné." She sipped her tea, regarding them over the gilded edge of her cup. Then she set the cup down with a tiny *clink* of porcelain against glass. "You do understand, many keiso from this House become famous and wealthy. We flatter ourselves that their keisonne esteem their flower wives even more highly than they do their proper wives." She waited for their respectful nods; then, satisfied, went on, "We do not take on many girls." Her tone, though cordial, almost suggested that a girl ought to pay a dowry to the House for a place, rather than a gift being made to her family for the transfer of the girl's name to the House.

"Oh," said Enelle. She had never looked younger, Nemienne thought. None of the sisters could help but look young and naïve and, no doubt, vulnerable. They had certainly learned a good deal about vulnerability since their father's death. And about the willingness of people to exploit vulnerability when they found it.

Then Enelle, recovering, said in her best impersonal business manner, hiding any trace of their desperation, "We are sorry you have no room. Perhaps you might suggest a House that is less crowded. We understand that the House of Butterflies is also a fine establishment." She, too, put her cup down on a glass-topped table with a decisive little *click*. Karah and Nemienne exchanged glances. Karah looked genuinely modest and sweet. Nemienne tried to copy her manner, though she doubted she succeeded.

The Mother of Cloisonné slid a sideways glance at Karah. "Well, now, it is true that for an unusual beauty such as this, an exception might perhaps be made. If—that is, I presume you are suitable for a keiso House?" she added to Karah. "This is not an aika establishment, you know. Keiso are expected to be pure, ours more than any."

Karah, speechless, blushed fiercely. Narienneh, studying her carefully, gave a satisfied little nod.

"Of course Karah is pure!" Enelle declared, outraged.

Narienneh gave a second little nod. "I am confident of it. And here in Cloisonné House she will remain so, which is, of course, what you wish. Indeed, as a father desires his daughter happy and well settled, so you desire for your sister. If not with a husband who will be kind to her and respect her, then with a keisonne who will do the same. Naturally you wish this.

"There are few Houses in all of Lonne in which a truly discerning family would wish to see its sister placed in the flower life. But in Cloisonné House, your sister will be surrounded by accomplished women of good character, women who would enhance her honor and beauty by their example and company. However, keiso must be polished, you understand? And there is so much to learn." She glanced at Karah again, and then, clearly as an afterthought, Nemienne. "Even so, despite your sister's age, Cloisonné House might offer a gift of . . . a thousand hard cash to have the pleasure of counting such a lovely young woman among its daughters."

Enelle looked abstracted. Nemienne knew she was calculating sums in her head. Her sister would be afraid of losing this offer, Nemienne knew; they had put off this moment almost too long and now badly needed the offered money. But neither could they afford to take an offer that was too low. She said cautiously after a moment, "My family will be devastated by the loss of a lovely and accomplished sister. Though Cloisonné House is a beautiful setting for any—any flower, and we are overwhelmed by your generosity, still, I fear that even such a generous gift could not compensate us for this loss." She couldn't come right out and name a price that would, of course: One did not use the mercantile language of the stone yard to sell a member of one's family. That just one sister would find a place here was obvious. No one was raving about *Nemienne's* beauty.

They settled at last on what seemed to Nemienne the extremely generous sum of eighteen hundred hard cash, to be paid directly from Cloisonné House to the family's bank. The Mother of Cloisonné House made out a slip of credit and signed it with her name and her House name in a graceful flowing hand. Enelle read the House contract carefully and then signed it, her mouth set hard. She gave it to Karah with a nod. Karah's writing was also graceful, but her hand trembled as she signed the contract. She was not weeping openly but a single tear blotched the paper beside her name.

"Come, now, daughter," Narienneh said to her, not unkindly. "You are not boarding a ship for Samenne, you know. We are strict here, yes, but this is for your own protection. In time, you will be allowed to visit your first family, and you may send and receive letters on the ninth and eighteenth days of every month."

"Yes," whispered Karah.

Narienneh eyed her, and added, "I believe you will come to cherish your place with us. Cloisonné House does not in any way resemble a dock...establishment. We have no 'trash keiso' here." Her lip curled in elegant contempt.

"Yes," Karah whispered. "No. Of course. Forgive me. Only I had...I had so wished Nemienne at least would stay with me."

Everyone looked at Nemienne. Nemienne tried to look beautiful and suspected she only managed, at best, an unremarkable prettiness.

"You are not precisely a beauty," Narienneh said to her at last. "Keiso need not be extremely beautiful, but then have you a gift for music? For dance? Have you unusual skill for charm and conversation? No?" She paused, considering. "Your eyes are interesting, however. Very like smoked glass. They seem to me to have an uncommon quality. I do not think you will find a place at a keiso House, child, but I believe I have seen eyes such as yours once or twice." She gave Enelle a thoughtful look, then turned her glance back to Nemienne. "If I may be so bold as to suggest...you might go to the Lane of Shadows and look there for a place."

"At mages' houses?" Enelle said, startled.

After the first surprise, however, Nemienne found the idea somehow not astonishing. *Mages*, she thought, and then with an odd questioning note to the thought, *Magic?* She had passed by the Lane of Shadows from time to time on errands; it twisted along one side of the city, nearly lost in the shadow of looming Kerre Maraddras. She had imagined she could almost see magic rolling like mist down the steep barren slopes of the mountain and piling up behind the mages' houses.

Nemienne asked, "Which mage would you suggest?"

At the same time, Enelle asked, "Mages look for—" Their words tangled together and they both fell silent.

14

"As you ask for my suggestion... you might go to the third house on the Lane of Shadows and inquire there for Mage Ankennes. He is a generous patron of ours, and I believe he is quite a powerful mage. I think he may be interested in finding a young person with eyes such as yours. Mages do not, I believe, find it a simple matter to locate suitable apprentices."

"Apprentices?" Karah and Enelle said together.

"Your sister is a little old to begin such an apprenticeship, I believe, but then seventeen is quite old to begin as a deisa at a House. Mage Ankennes has mentioned, once or twice recently, his difficulty in finding a suitable young person. Perhaps he will make an exception as I have done. And," she added delicately, "I believe you will find your young sister will be safe in his house. His inclinations do not lie in that direction."

Enelle looked quickly at Nemienne and nodded, looking at least moderately reassured. Nemienne did not say anything. She was thinking of mages, and the Lane of Shadows, and magic rolling off the flanks of the mountains like mist.

"Well," said Enelle, rather blankly after she and Nemienne had left Cloisonné House. She gathered the reins of the carriage into her hands, but her hands were shaking so that the horses tossed their heads and sidled away sideways.

Nemienne took the reins away from her sister and started the horses moving toward the nearest bridge that crossed the Niarre toward the Lane of Shadows. She herself now felt a tremendous sense of relief. She had liked Cloisonné House. Or not liked, but *admired*. She'd wanted to stay with Karah rather than have either of them thrown out into the world completely alone. And yet... and yet... "Karah will do well there," Nemienne ventured, giving Enelle a sideways glance to see whether her sister was of any mind to hear an optimistic prediction. "That Narienneh is clever, don't you think? She'll want Karah to be happy."

Enelle gave a stricken little nod. "I hope so. I can't believe..." She fell silent.

How big a hole Karah left in their lives, and how immediately. And poor Enelle would have to leave Nemienne also and drive home all by herself. They should have let Ananda come. But none of them had thought ahead to Enelle's painful, solitary drive. "None of this is your fault," Nemienne told Enelle, as they had all been at pains to tell her over the past days.

"No," Enelle whispered. "Do you think...do you think she will be happy?"

"Yes," said Nemienne. And when her sister gave her a shocked look, added, "Why not? Everyone will love her. She'll be famous and wealthy. Girls all over Lonne will fix their hair the way she does and embroider their robes to echo hers. A hundred men will admire her and give her gifts. I'm sure dozens of them will want to be her keisonne." She gave Enelle a sideways look. "I know you were never interested in glamour, but you must know how many girls would like to be keiso, except they haven't the accomplishments or the beauty. Just think how Liaska admires keiso and always wants to follow the fashions they set."

"But—" Enelle began, too upset to admit the obvious.

"Karah might have preferred to stay with us, and of course we'll miss her terribly, but she'll be a wonderful keiso. She'll find a keisonne from among the men of the court—half the men who frequent Cloisonné House must surely be from the Laodd, don't you think? Some of them must be perfectly nice. She'll choose the nicest of them, of course, someone who loves her. Her sons will grow up with the children of princes."

"I...you're right. I suppose you're right," Enelle murmured doubtfully.

"Of course I am."

The Niarre River, running out of the shadow of the great mountain to the sea, seemed to carry the sound of magic with it as it washed around the bridge pilings. Nemienne glanced down at the water, her attention momentarily caught. Then they were across the bridge, and she tucked their little carriage behind a much bigger four-in-hand and turned down Herringbone Lane to the east, heading for the mountain's shadow.

"I...I never noticed anything about your eyes," Enelle confessed quietly. She was not quite looking at Nemienne, but rather off along the streets. It seemed to have caught up with her at last that she was on her way to losing a second sister, and in a way that carried less esteem and more—well, if not peril, then at least uncertainty.

Nemienne herself would have liked a chance to look at her eyes in a mirror. But there wasn't even a clear puddle of water on the street. "Probably you have to meet lots of mages before you'd see—whatever Narienneh saw. Look, there's the Lane of Shadows. Which house did she say?"

"The third." Enelle leaned forward to look for it. They had left the traffic behind them as they passed under the shadow of Kerre Maraddras, entering a district of quiet dimness that seemed only minimally connected to the city proper. "Is that it?" She sounded a little uncertain.

Nemienne could understand Enelle's doubt. The third house on the lane was a small, crooked structure, built of weathered gray stone. Set as it was into a fold of the mountain, the house looked less like a purpose-built structure than a natural outcropping. Light slanted obliquely across the glass windows—the house's one extravagant touch—so that the windows seemed blind, nothing anyone could look into. Or out of.

"It's a bit...it's rather...have you ever seen a less likable house?" Enelle asked. She looked appalled. "This was a bad idea. You needn't...we mustn't..."

"Oh, no," Nemienne said, her eyes on those blind windows. Light reflected from them, like light off water, so that anything might be hidden beyond sight in the depths. "No. We're here, and I know we still need more money. Though you did wonderfully well with the Mother of Cloisonné, you know you did," she added hastily. "But we're here. We must certainly ask." She drew the horses to the side of the lane, set the brake, wrapped the reins around the driver's bar, and jumped down to the cobbles, steadying herself with a hand on the near wheel's high rim.

"But—" Enelle began, her voice a little too high.

"Anyway," Nemienne said, as gently as she knew how because she knew her sister wouldn't understand this, "I rather like the house."

Enelle gave her an astonished stare. "You don't really."

"I think I do." Nemienne came around to the other side of the carriage and held up a hand to help Enelle down. If she would come. Her sister was actually shivering, Nemienne saw. Was it the house? Or had leaving Karah behind taught her to fear partings? Nemienne continued to hold her hand up, waiting for her sister to reach down and complete that grip. At last Enelle reached down her hand to meet Nemienne's.

The steps of the house were like the house itself: rough and oddly angled, with unexpected slants underfoot. The polished statue of a cat sat beside the door, gray soapstone with eyes of agate. Nemienne touched the cat's head curiously. The stone was silken smooth under her fingertips.

"There's no bellpull," Enelle said, stating the obvious because she was nervous.

"I think the cat is the bell," Nemienne said with an odd certainty, running her hand across the statue's head a second time.

Before them, the door unlatched itself with a muffled *click*. Enelle flinched slightly, but Nemienne put her hand out and touched the door. It swung back smoothly, showing them a dimly lit entry and a long hallway running back farther than seemed plausible. A gray cat sat bolt upright in the middle of the foyer. It was the image of the statue on the porch, except for one white foot and a narrow white streak that ran up its nose. The cat blinked eyes green as agates at them, then rose and walked away down the shadowed hallway, tail swaying upright, white foot flashing.

Enelle hesitated. "Do you think we should—"

"Of course," said Nemienne. She caught her sister's hand and stepped into the gray stone house after the cat. Stepping through the door was like stepping into the mountain itself: There was a sense of looming weight overhead. Unable to decide whether she found the unexpected presence of the mage's house oppressive or simply interesting, Nemienne almost hesitated herself. But if she retreated now, she suspected that she'd never get Enelle back inside this house. And if they paused for long here on the threshold, the cat would get too far ahead for them to see even its white foot.

The hallway did indeed run back a disconcerting distance before opening onto a landing. A stair came up from the left, turned on the landing, and went on up to the right. They passed no doors or windows along the length of the hall, only the occasional lantern hanging on a chain. The cat was just vanishing up the right-hand stair as they reached its foot.

"I hate this house!" Enelle whispered vehemently, staring into the bottomless shadows down the stair to the left. She glanced up the other way, after the cat, and shuddered. The tremor was too slight to see, but Nemienne felt it through their joined hands.

"It could be more cheerful," Nemienne conceded.

"We could go back," Enelle suggested, but not as though she expected her sister to agree. However reluctantly, she let Nemienne draw her forward and up the stairs.

There was a door ajar at the top of the stairs, friendly yellow light pouring through it to pool on the higher landing. Enelle let her breath out and went forward eagerly, so that this time it was Nemienne who followed her sister. The door was heavy but well-balanced. It swung wide easily at the touch of Enelle's hand.

The room behind the door was wide and warm, filled with light from lanterns and four generous windows on its far side. The windows did not look out into the Lane of Shadows but rather over the mountain heights. Nemienne, fascinated, went to the nearest and put her hands on the sill, standing on her toes to peer out. Cold struck, knife sharp, through the glass of the window. Mist blew across the jagged peaks, veiling and unveiling gray stone streaked with ice. Nemienne could almost discern the unfolding wing of a great insubstantial dragon in the shifting of the mist. Sunlight glinting from the ice was like the opening of a crystalline eye.

Enelle crossed the room and put a hand nervously on Nemienne's, as unhappy with the strange sharp beauty of the mountain heights as Nemienne was drawn to it. Her hand trembled. Nemienne put an arm around her sister, turning away from the windows. Indeed, once her attention had been pulled from the heights, she found herself looking with real fascination around the room in which they had found themselves.

An enormous table stood, surrounded by mismatched chairs, before an even more enormous fireplace that took up almost the entire wall behind it. The fire that burned in that fireplace occupied only a small area in the center, but it was intensely hot and very fragrant. Nemienne wondered what kind of wood the mage might be burning.

The entire surface of the table was cluttered with glass jars, piles of loose papers, angular metal objects that Nemienne thought might be a geometer's tools, and a tall stack of books that seemed likely at any moment to slide down and crush a spun-glass confection of no obvious purpose. A much smaller and neater writing desk sat to one side of the fireplace, its tall-backed chair pulled out and turned as though inviting somebody to sit down in it. At the moment, the cat was sitting in that chair. No one else was in the room. The cat groomed its shoulder, ignoring the girls.

Enelle let out a breath and gazed around with interest, looking much happier in the warmth and light. "Isn't this just *exactly* the workroom of a mage?" she said in a low voice to Nemienne. "What do you suppose that glass thing on the table is for?"

Both the comment and the question were so precisely what Nemienne had been thinking that she blinked and so missed the exact instant Mage Ankennes entered the room.

The mage was a broad man with powerful shoulders; he looked at first glance more like a man accustomed to earn his bread with the strength of his body than with his magecraft. But a second look found that his face was carved with lines of discipline and silence, and his slate-gray eyes were as secretive as the windows of his house. He looked at Enelle and Nemienne curiously, as he might have looked at two odd, foreign insects that had inexplicably turned up in his workroom, and Nemienne felt a shiver of disquiet run down her spine and lift the fine hairs on the back of her neck. She leaned closer to her sister, and Enelle simultaneously leaned toward her, so that their shoulders touched.

Then Ankennes smiled, and immediately the impression of chilly secretiveness vanished. His eyes met Nemienne's, and if the curiosity in them sharpened, this was offset by the warmth of his smile. He said courteously, in a deep smooth voice, "May I hope for the opportunity to serve you?"

"I—" said Enelle, with some confusion. "We—"

"The Mother of Cloisonné House suggested we might come to you," said Nemienne, quickly, to cover her sister's distress.

"Charming Narienneh!" said the mage. And added, his eyes still on Nemienne's, "Clever Narienneh. Yes, I can well believe she might. By all means, please sit. Will you have tea?" At the table, two of the chairs slid back, turning invitingly, and hot tea poured itself out of the air into a pair of heavy white porcelain mugs that had suddenly appeared amidst the clutter.

"I believe I may guess what has brought you young women to my house," said Ankennes, pulling a steaming mug out of the air for himself and dropping heavily into the biggest chair at the table. The cat leaped lightly down from its chair, wove its way among table and chair legs, and jumped up on the table to sit at his elbow. The mage made room for it absently, shoving jars out of the way. He said, "But you had better tell me, eh?"

Enelle sat down gingerly in a chair, mindful of a stack of papers weighted with a jar of round red marbles close by her left elbow. Nemienne took the other chair and breathed in the fragrant steam from her mug. The tea was spiced with something unfamiliar and not quite sweet.

Enelle cleared her throat. "Our father was Geranes Lihadde," she said. Her tentativeness was giving way again to her practiced businesslike manner.

"Yes," said the mage, both interest and sympathy in his tone. "I had heard of your father's untimely death. I sorrow for your loss."

"You see—"

"Yes, indeed; I understand. Thus your visit to Narienneh of Cloisonné House. Quite so. Did you then leave a sister in Cloisonné? Yes? Well, there is honor as well as beauty in the keiso life, and there is surely no better keiso House than Cloisonné. I am certain your sister is a flower that will flourish in that rich garden. And Narienneh, discerning woman, sent you on to me."

"We are sorry to intrude—"

"Not at all," the mage assured her. "Not at all." His attention shifted again to Nemienne. "Forgive the familiarity, if you will be so kind, young woman, and permit me to ask your age."

"Fifteen," said Nemienne.

"Hmm. And what do you think of my house, eh?"

Ankennes's tone was casual. But his glance was sharp, and Nemienne understood that this question was one that mattered—perhaps not the last of those that would matter, but the first, and perhaps the most important. She hesitated, afraid of giving a wrong answer. No one else ever saw the slantwise world that always seemed to show itself to her.

But she had to say something. She said hesitantly, "I think...I think your house is not really in Lonne at all. I think really your house is high up, among the peaks. That's why your windows are blind from the outside: They are looking out on rock and ice and don't see the city, and so the city can't see into them, either."

There was a brief silence. Both Enelle and Ankennes looked surprised, but not in the same way: Where Enelle was merely disconcerted, the mage was clearly pleased. Nemienne ducked her head and looked down into her tea, searching for patterns in the floating flecks of spice. If there were any, she couldn't find them.

"That is not quite correct," the mage told her. "But it is wrong in, mmm, an interesting way. Many young people make their ways to the Lane of Shadows, believing they might like to learn magecraft. Some greatly desire to study with me. A few have families willing to pay for the opportunity."

"But it doesn't matter what they want," said Enelle boldly, when Nemienne didn't answer. "What matters is what *you* want."

Ankennes smiled. "True." He leaned back in his chair, which creaked as it took the weight, and drank his tea, his broad hand almost engulfing the mug.

The cat, its tail curled neatly around its front feet, gazed into the empty air. It was purring, but very quietly, so that the vibration was more felt than heard.

"Narienneh was right to send you along to me," the mage said eventually. "I should hate to discourage her acuity. Perhaps...I might offer a gift of, shall we say, three hundred hard cash, if young Nemienne here will do me the favor of making a trial of the life of the mage. It is not an easy life, mind," he added. "But you may return that amount should she prove not to care for it, or I will triple that sum again to compensate her family for her lengthening absence by, say, midwinter, if we should mutually agree that the arrangement has proved satisfactory. Eh?"

It was a gamble, then, but not at all a dangerous one, Nemienne thought. It was indeed all to their advantage, and very generous if she suited the mage well enough for him to keep her. And she was determined that she *would* suit him, however demanding a master he should prove. Twelve hundred hard cash was a wonderful amount, without doubt more than Enelle had calculated in her sums of loss and hope. Twelve hundred, above the eighteen hundred Cloisonné had given them for Karah, was surely enough that they would be able to forget about selling a third sister.

And she could see that Enelle was comforted by the thought that Nemienne could get out of this apprenticeship if it turned out badly. But it wouldn't. Nemienne was determined it would not. She was sure of one thing amid the distress and confusion of the past days: She knew she wanted to stay in this house, to explore its strange angles and startling dimensions. To look out of its secretive windows and see the strange views onto which they opened. To find out what that odd glass thing on the table was for. She tried to communicate this to Enelle with a look.

Enelle returned a little sideways tilt of her head, understanding at least what Nemienne meant if not how she felt. She said to the mage, "A generous suggestion, and one I believe my sister welcomes. If she wants this, though we will be distressed to miss her daily company, how can we refuse her desire?"

Mage Ankennes did not trouble with contracts and drafts of credit but simply put out his hand. A heavy pouch fell, clinking, into it from the air. He gave this to Enelle with a little flourish and an air of bland satisfaction that somewhat called to mind the attitude of his cat.

Enelle seemed a little doubtful as she took the pouch, wondering perhaps whether cash conjured up in such a way might vanish when the light of the sun fell across it.

"Enkea will show you the way out," Ankennes told her. "I believe you will find the way back to the door briefer and less disconcerting than the route you took in. Though that depends rather upon Enkea's whim. She is a whimsical creature, I fear."

The cat gave Ankennes a wide green stare. Then it jumped down from the table and looked expectantly at Enelle, who rose quickly to her feet but then turned rather uncertainly to Nemienne.

Nemienne also stood. She went to Enelle, embracing her. "Go on," she whispered in her sister's ear. "Go on, and don't let anyone fear for me. This is a wonderful house."

"Is it?" Enelle asked a little wistfully. "Is it really?"

"I promise you," Nemienne assured her, glad she could speak with conviction.

"All right." Enelle returned her embrace with fierce, concerned affection and then stepped back. "If you change your mind—if you don't like it—if you get lonely—"

"She may write, of course. Or visit, if she wishes. At midwinter, perhaps." Mage Ankennes was patient, but clearly waiting for

Enelle to leave. The gray cat walked out of the room, its tail swaying gently upright.

Enelle hugged Nemienne once more, took a step after the cat, threw one more doubtful glance over her shoulder at the mage, and was gone. Though Nemienne had wanted to stay—though she far preferred this powerful mage and this magic-dense house to Cloisonné House, and though she was very grateful for the Mother of Cloisonné's suggestion that had brought them here—it was still hard to watch her sister step through the workroom door and vanish, leaving her behind.

"Well," said Mage Ankennes.

Nemienne turned her head and met his eyes. Light slid across them, as across the surface of opaque glass or deep water, hiding everything. He was smiling, an expression that was not unfriendly, but that told her nothing.

The mage said in a meditative tone, "Nemienne, is it, eh? And you like my house, do you? A satisfactory beginning, I should think. I wonder what we shall make of you?"

Nemienne wondered that herself.

CHAPTER 2

Though lively enough in its present incarnation as a keiso House, Cloisonné House was in truth made of silence and time. Leilis sometimes had trouble believing that the dozens of women and girls who dwelled within the house did not know that the echoing clamor of their lives and voices only masked the underlying silence. At its heart, Cloisonné House was a house of stillness, and there were places in it where even the most adventurous of the girls did not go—where no one went, where nothing was stored that anyone might want to find back.

One such place was the highest of the attics tucked up along the northwest edge of the roof. That attic had a narrow window that, set under the eaves, never admitted bright sun. Yet the diffuse light that came through the old glass always seemed to fill the attic—even in the evening, after the sun had set and there should have been no light. There was another quiet place in the deepest cellars, this one with a more perilous feel to it. Bottles of wine and casks of ale, barrels of pickles and jars of summer preserves stored in the far reaches of the cellars might last for months or years, as the cook's girls avoided going down farther than they must.

And the last bedchamber down the keiso gallery on the fourth floor, a small room that had a slanting ceiling and an old, enormous fireplace with three cracked hearthstones—that chamber was another such quiet place, as though it were surrounded by the musty solitude of a cloister rather than the bustle of a busy keiso

House. Fires set in its fireplace burned longer but with less heat than they should, and with a faintly greenish tint, or so it seemed to Leilis.

As none of the keiso desired this chamber, Leilis had been permitted to claim it for her own. She would lie at night on her narrow bed by the wall where the ceiling came down low, listening to the deep quiet beating softly through the darkness. Leilis liked the quiet, or had learned to because she liked the solitude it brought her.

Now she cleared the ash out of the fireplace and laid down new kindling and small logs. Then she carried the bucket of ashes out into the hallway and paused, listening. Whispers slipped through the quiet around her. She was not quite curious. But the whispers followed her down the stairs, tugging at the edges of her attention as she went out the barred service door that led to the alley behind the House.

Leilis tossed the ashes onto the midden heap, raising a puff of fine pale ash that tasted faintly bitter on the back of the tongue. The ash tasted of silence, she thought. Of silence and patience and the slow passing of time. It seemed strange that the memory of fire could taste of things so unlike the lively fire itself.

She turned back to the House, walking along the alley to enter this time through the small kitchen door.

Whispers instantly surrounded her. The keiso were all still abed, but two of the deisa, Lily and Sweetrose, were sitting at the cutting table, sneaking sugared nuts from a batch the cook had made. The girls had their heads tilted together. Their smiles were knowing, their voices smooth.

There was a new girl, Leilis gathered, attending at last. She must be a beauty, to judge by the spite she'd engendered so quickly in the deisa: Mother had paid a thousand hard for her, one of them murmured, and she already old, seventeen at least, and completely untrained. By the time she was bringing in a profit she'd be in debt to the House for twice what Mother had given for her. She wouldn't earn out until she was forty years old, if ever. Lily and Sweetrose shared the satisfied tone that came from the assurance that *they* were going to earn out their debts while they were still young and beautiful.

Leilis stepped past the deisa and began to clear up walnut shells. Sweetrose made room with an air that suggested she shifted out of Leilis's way only by chance; Lily gave Leilis a glance that combined wariness, resentment, and disdain and did not move at all. Only the cook gave her a welcoming nod. Leilis returned the nod and took the nut shells out to the midden heap.

Then it was back in and around to the banquet chambers where clients were entertained, to polish the low tables and the silverwork on the carved doors and, especially, the floors. Endless polishing: The women and girls of the House went softly shod, but clients wore boots on even the finest floors.

The whispers made their way to Leilis once more while she was in the last chamber. They had strengthened as the keiso at last began to come out of their rooms and join in the life of the house. The rumors were carried through the air along with the sharp scent of the wood polish, running along the keiso galleries and through the servants' narrow passages. The new girl had hair spun out of the dusky fall of twilight. Her skin was flawless, the soft color of the best Enescene porcelain. The curve of her throat... those fine delicate bones...Even her tears scattered like pearls, and her face did not blotch when she wept.

The new girl might well be tearful, thought Leilis. Though probably she feared the wrong things and for the wrong reasons. New girls always feared Mother, feared the senior keiso. But any new girl should instead fear the whispers that spread among the deisa. Those were the girls who would like to see a rival fail and sink into obscurity or mere servitude within the House.

Curiosity drove Leilis down from the keiso-trodden regions of the House to the laundry to see if the laundry maids needed extra hands, which of course they always did.

"Have you seen the new girl?" one of the laundry maids asked her. The maid was a tiny bit of a thing, too plain to dream of ever taking a flower name of her own. Her thin little voice was wistful.

"More beautiful than the stars over the mountains, they say. Mother paid two thousand hard cash for her and would have paid twice as much. You should go see if she's truly so beautiful and come tell us, will you, Leilis?"

The maid, tucked away in the laundry, could not herself run up to see the new deisa. Few of the residents of Cloisonné House moved as freely as Leilis between the public and private regions of the house, between the servants' areas and the keiso galleries and halls. Not that anyone but a laundry maid was likely to envy Leilis her unusual freedom. It was assuredly a poor enough trade for keiso glamour.

Leilis made a noncommittal sound and took a set of the very best silk sheets up to Mother's apartment.

Narienneh was speaking with the embroiderer, who was showing her an overrobe embroidered with a frothy lacework of white and pale pink. "She'd look like an apple blossom in this," Mother said, waving a dismissive hand at the froth. "Like an entire orchard. Something innocent is what we shall want, a clean design, something almost plain."

The embroiderer nodded, sketching quick patterns in charcoal for Narienneh to examine. Leilis slid past into Mother's bedchamber and made the bed, then came back out to the front room. She snipped the faded flowers off Mother's white roses and tidied away the clutter of discarded paper the embroiderer had produced. The embroiderer gathered up a rustling stack of sketches and went away.

Mother sighed and sat down at the table in front of the window. But she did not gaze out the window at the river. She lowered her head against her hand, pinching the bridge of her nose and looking, now that she was alone, uncharacteristically frail. Mother's hair, braided up into a crown on the top of her head, was flawlessly white, but her age was not what lent her this unexpected air of fragility. It occurred to Leilis to wonder for the first time how much Narienneh might really have paid for the new girl. Could it have been so much?

Leilis slipped quietly away. Going again by the laundry, she gathered up another armload of sheets. Thus armored, she went up at last to the deisa gallery, where the new girl would have a narrow bed at the end of the row where all the deisa slept.

The girl was there, sitting perfectly still in one of the straight-backed chairs by the window, her hands gripped together in her lap. The clutter of deisa belongings was scattered about: plain practice harps with extra strings coiled on shelves nearby, a kin-sana, sets of pipes. Scrolls for the poems the deisa were learning were pinned open on a low table by the window, the narrow pallets taking up the rest of that wall. There were half a dozen small chests, one at the foot of each pallet, for each deisa's personal possessions; the room's single large closet would hold all their daily robes and slippers, which they did not own themselves. Leilis wondered what, if anything, this new girl owned of her own. And whether she had the sense to guess she should guard her things, if she had any, from the other deisa.

None of the other deisa were present. Lily's doing? Or merely that none of them were free at this hour? It was true the deisa had their lessons and their other duties, but it was strange that none of them had slipped away for a look at this newest addition to their number.

If the girl had wept earlier—either tears like pearls or the more ordinary sort—she was not weeping now. Her eyes came up, tear-less, at Leilis's entry, and she sprang nervously to her feet. Her gaze, after a barely noticeable hesitation, steadied on Leilis's face.

Leilis, transfixed by a wide blue gaze as fathomless as the sea, stood motionless and looked back at the new girl across her pile of sheets.

No wonder Mother had purchased this girl. Leilis suddenly did not doubt that Mother had paid a great deal for her. Not for her beauty, though the girl was beautiful. For that priceless look in those eyes. That immeasurable trusting innocence was nothing you could get for any price in any House of the candlelight district. It was nothing you could expect to find, come to that, anywhere.

Leilis tried to imagine what kind of family this girl had grown up in to have a look like that.

Or else she was simple. That seemed likely, on a more collected assessment.

The girl said, in a faltering sort of voice, "Please, are you—are you—is there something I ought to be—what should I do?"

Leilis tilted her head to the side, oddly touched by this appeal. The artless manner seemed perfectly unstudied. Stepping across the room to the closet, Leilis put the linens she held away on a shelf. Then she turned and looked again at the girl, who was silent now, her amazing eyes wide with nerves.

"How much did she give for you?" Leilis asked abruptly.

The girl stared at her, deep-sea eyes wide and blank. Simple, after all, Leilis decided. It did seem a pity.

But the girl said then, "Eighteen hundred. She gifted us eighteen hundred hard cash." Her voice, though low and sweet, was not as shy as Leilis would have expected.

"Us?" said Leilis, tilting an eyebrow at the girl.

The girl blushed. It made her look more untutored and innocent than ever. "Them. My sisters. It was—we thought it was a good price..."

"It was. Very good." It was a *remarkable* price, especially this season, with an uncertain spring approaching and the city tense. Not that anyone doubted who would win if the war between Lirionne and Kalches resumed. Fifteen years ago, the Dragon of Lirionne had forced Kalches to sign the Treaty of Brenedde, ceding to Lirionne all the lands west of Teleddes and east of Anharadde. If war came again, then Lirionne would win again. All those disputed lands would belong to Lirionne forever, and after Kalches had been forced to accept its final defeat, everything would be fine. But still, at the moment, everything was more expensive than usual and every House hard-pressed. And yet Mother had paid so much for one girl?

But when Leilis studied the House's newest asset again, she could only shake her head. "You were worth every coin," she decided. "Mother is wavering a little now, I think, and small surprise there. But she is wrong to doubt her bargain. What is your name?"

"Karah," whispered the girl. Her fine slender hands closed slowly into fists at her sides.

"Don't worry over Mother," Leilis advised her, moved despite herself by the girl's uncertainty. "Don't fear the keiso. But be careful of the deisa. Especially Lily." She paused, studying the blank look in those exquisite eyes. "Have you met Lily? Or the other deisa? Do you *understand* me?"

"Yes," the girl said, dutiful as a child saying off a lesson she had learned by rote. "Or no. I have not met them. I will be careful of Lily. Thank you."

Maybe she understood and maybe she didn't, but Leilis could hardly stand behind her and coach her through the day. Besides, whatever happened in the deisa quarters was no concern of *hers*. Leilis gave a short little nod and turned to go.

"Wait!" said the girl, coming forward a half step. She was clenching her hands again, Leilis noted disapprovingly. "What is— Who are you?"

Leilis could feel her face set. "No one," she said, and was gone on that word, leaving the beautiful girl behind with a hand half raised and a stricken look in her sapphire eyes.

The deisa were gone from the kitchens, leaving the cook and her girls in peace to prepare for the coming evening. Preparations were now well along. A dozen plucked, headless ducks lay on the cutting table. Three fat red fish, so fresh they looked all but ready to swim away, lay on trays of crushed ice behind the ducks. Loaves of fresh bread cooled on racks alongside the ovens, and a large pot of broth simmered gently on top of the nearest oven. The cook looked weary but satisfied.

The cook was using a soft brush to coat the petals of flowers with beaten egg whites, then dusting the flower petals with fine sugar and placing each one on a wire rack to dry. Trays of brightly glazed pastries occupied the rest of the cook's huge stone table. Her newest girl, a solemn little creature with coarse black hair cropped short around her thin face, had come back from the market and now moved silently around the kitchens, putting butter and cream in the cold box and a sack of river mussels in the big stone sink.

Leilis leaned a hip on the edge of the cook's big table and used a fine pair of tongs to lift candied flower petals from the rack, laying a single one just so on each glazed pastry.

The cook nodded thanks to Leilis and said over her shoulder to her girl, "Start whipping the egg whites for the meringues." To Leilis, she said, "Do you think a red currant sauce for the ducks, or wild cherry? Did you go up and have a look at her, then?"

"Cherry," advised Leilis. "Her name is Karah. She's a lovely child."

"Ah," observed the cook wisely, "that won't last."

"Lily, you mean."

"Who else? And Tiarella, and that little fool Sweetrose."

The cook's girl brought the bowl of egg whites to the table and began to whisk them into a froth, listening covertly to the gossip of her superiors. Most of the residents of Cloisonné House passed through the kitchens several times a day, filching tidbits, so the cook was usually an excellent source of gossip. Leilis concentrated on laying candied flower petals delicately on top of the pastries and made no comment about jealous deisa or the risks this new girl might run among them. She said instead, "The true amount Mother gave for her was eighteen hundred. Hard."

"Ah. Mother won't care to have her interfered with, then," the cook commented, her eyes on the sugar she was dusting over flower petals. "Not paying as much as that. Especially this season, with expenses so tight. You wouldn't believe the price of butter and cream in the market these days." What the cook didn't add was that Lily was unlikely to be held back by concern over Mother's temper.

And, of course, Leilis, of all women, hardly needed to be

reminded of the grim possibilities inherent in deisa jealousy. "I warned her to be careful," Leilis said. Her tone had gone a little defensive, she found, and she shut her eyes for a second and hauled herself back toward the cool neutrality she'd thought she'd learned long since.

"Ah?" said the cook, meaning, *What good do you imagine that will do?*

Leilis had to nod. They both knew it would do nothing. But why Leilis should care... She was deliberately uninvolved in deisa quarrels and petty jealousies. For years she had held aloof from such concerns. Why should this new girl matter to her?

But, later, when most of the keiso and the deisa had gone out to entertain at Cloisonné's banquet, Leilis filled a covered tray with plates of duck breast in cherry sauce, pureed parsnips with butter and slivers of sea-urchin roe, and cream-filled pastries. Then she slipped through the near-empty living quarters of the House, up the back stairs, and along to the House's small dance studio.

The studio was, unsurprisingly, occupied.

Rue might have gone to the party, but large parties often took a raucous turn utterly unsuited to Rue's own gift. Rue was a connoisseur's keiso. Mother never asked her to attend the loud half-drunken parties that were the greatest pleasure of most of the younger keiso.

Instead, Rue was standing before the wide studio mirror, back straight and face blank, in an esienne stance, one foot on the polished floor and the other arched with just the toes placed delicately before the other foot. Leilis's entrance did not elicit even a flicker of attention from the keiso. The woman shifted slowly from the esienne stance through a floating cloud exchange and then to a kind of elongated cat stance, and from that back to esienne.

Rue repeated the steps again. Leilis sat down against the wall, set the tray on the floor beside her, wrapped her arms around her knees, and waited while Rue went through the sequence yet again. And then again, this time adding three gliding cat steps and a long dipping turn back into esienne. Leilis finally recognized part of the middle sequence of the Departing Swallows dance from the Autumn Lament. Evidently Rue was considering an adaptation for the dance. It looked fine to Leilis, but Rue continued rehearsing and adjusting the steps, her face calm and intent, until she reached some level of perfection perceptible only to herself. Then she stood still a moment longer, in the esienne stance once more, the tips of her fingers brushing the rail.

And then, at last, the remote intensity in her face slowly gave way to an awareness of the studio, and Leilis, and the tray. A smile broke into her dark eyes and she crossed the floor quickly and dropped down with a dancer's automatic grace to sit next to Leilis.

"Thank you."

Leilis uncovered the food. "It would be better hot."

Rue laughed. Though not beautiful, the woman had a beautiful voice and a warm, quiet laugh. "When do I ever have my supper hot?"

This was true. Rue spent most of her afternoons and many of her evenings either with the dance master or alone in the House studio, and even the more penetrating bells of the timekeeper seldom broke through her focus. She exclaimed in pleasure now, seeing the duck. "A cherry sauce? Wonderful!"

Leilis leaned back against the wall and watched the keiso eat.

Rue's father, a Samenian, had given her his narrow face and long bones; Rue was thus tall for a dancer, but she was not willowy. Her wrists and ankles were strong and her limbs muscular, so that she lacked the delicacy that made for true beauty. Her hair was Samenian black: not the desirable jet prized in the flower life, but muted with reddish highlights.

None of that mattered. Rue had left the household of her wealthy father to become keiso because her heart was given to dance. A wife must be a wife, and a mother a mother; a lady must be a lady; only a keiso could make art the center of her life. Rue had become keiso on her nineteenth birthday, had bought out her contract at twenty-three, and now, at thirty-four, was one of the great ornaments of Cloisonné

House and of all the flower world. Neither needing nor desiring to tie herself to a man, even the noblest or richest, Rue had no keisonne and would probably never accept one. Further, too secure within herself to concern herself with issues of status and rank, Rue was one of the easiest of all the House keiso for residents of lesser rank to approach.

"The House has gained a new deisa," Leilis told her.

"Yes, even I could not miss the word of it." Rue ate a slice of duck breast with concentrated pleasure and began to nibble the orange strands of urchin roe off the creamy mound of mashed parsnips.

"A lovely girl," remarked Leilis.

Rue made a perfunctory sound of mild interest without glancing up.

"Lily also thinks so."

Rue paused in the midst of her second slice of duck breast. She looked at Leilis, a searching look. "And so you bring me a tray?"

"With cherry sauce."

A slight smile crooked Rue's mouth. "I'm surprised you care."

Leilis did not know how to defend her own sympathy for the new girl. She said nothing.

"Does she dance?" Rue asked after a moment.

"Compared to you?"

Rue smiled again and went back to her duck. She knew, all possible modesty aside, that there was no likelihood that this new girl would even be able to perceive the distant heights of her art.

"Mother will want to protect her," said Leilis. "But she won't." She meant, *Not from Lily.* The faint, bitter edge to her voice surprised her, and she stopped.

The keiso, understanding, lifted an eyebrow in cynical agreement. "Children blind a mother. Even a Mother. Lily might have grown into a less selfish snip if Narienneh had fostered her out just as she'd have done with a boy." Even Rue would not have said anything that direct to just any servant, but then Leilis was not an ordinary servant. Rue simply went on, "But as she hasn't and won't, what do you think *I* will be able to do for this new deisa of ours?"

There was, of course, very little even an influential and well-disposed keiso could do for a deisa among deisa. Leilis lifted a shoulder in a tiny shrug.

Rue finished the duck and thoughtfully broke one of the cakes in two, exposing the thick cream filling. She ate the cake in two neat bites and licked cream off her fingers. "Very beautiful, is she?"

"She'll surprise you," Leilis promised. "Even though I tell you so now."

Rue made a skeptical little sound, ate the second pastry, and rose to her feet in one neat motion. "Will you take the tray back to the kitchens, or shall I?"

"I ought to leave it for you. Then at least you would have to leave the studio for half a moment."

The dancer only laughed, not at all offended at this impertinence. She glanced at the rail, at the mirror, but pulled herself away and strolled toward the door instead. She said over her shoulder to Leilis, who had picked up the tray and followed her, "I'm going out to the theater with Lord Nahadde soon. He gifts well, but he wishes an attentive companion, so I had better not be late. I must thank you for bringing the tray, Leilis. I would have noticed later that I had missed supper!"

Leilis watched Rue walk away, then turned and headed slowly back herself toward the kitchens.

Cloisonné's banquet would certainly continue into the small hours, leaving the House itself largely deserted until the keiso came wearily home to seek their beds. In the meantime, a deep quiet settled throughout the House. The young servants had already retired; they would rise early, while the keiso were still sleeping off their night. And the retired keiso who had never acquired property of their own and remained in the House were mostly elderly and abed with the sunset.

And, of course, the new girl would have been left to sleep in the deisa gallery, she being too new to the House to accompany the keiso to their banquet. Leilis wondered whether she had yet met the other deisa. Whether she had yet met Lily. Whether she slept, and whether her dreams troubled her.

Probably she was not asleep. Probably she lay awake in her narrow deisa bed and cried for her sisters. Especially if she had encountered Lily. She would be justified if she wept, then.

More important…more important, Mother would be in her apartment. Leilis changed her direction and quickened her step, realized she still held Rue's empty tray, hesitated, and turned back toward the kitchens after all.

The kitchens were dark, if still warm; they were never really cold, even in the depths of winter. Leilis put the tray down quietly by the nearest sink, lit a candle from a coal banked in a fireplace, and swung open the door to the cellars.

A sharp cold emanated from the stairway. Leilis's steps fell more softly than seemed reasonable, as though here sound itself became muted and tentative. Accustomed to this muffling of sound and sense and less given to fancies than most residents of Cloisonné House, Leilis did not pause but quickly went down another flight of stairs into the deeper, larger cellar beyond. There she found a bottle of straw-colored Enescene wine. The bottle was cold in the hand, and dusty. Leilis blew the dust off its label, holding the candle close to the cramped angular writing to make out the script. Then, satisfied, she went again through the small cellar and up the stairs.

Up in the kitchens once more, she dusted the bottle more thoroughly and set it and a tall goblet on a tray. She added a narrow vase of clear glass and a sprig of moonflowers from an arrangement chilling in the ice pantry, added a single cream-filled cake on a delicate plate painted with more moonflowers, and slipped out of the kitchens again without waking the girls.

Narienneh was awake; light showed in a narrow line beneath her door. Leilis was not surprised. She would probably be fretting about the new deisa she had bought into the House. Though probably she would not have framed clearly to herself any question about Lily in that connection, or Leilis would have no necessity to trouble her.

The door was shut nearly to, but not latched; a touch of Leilis's hand swung it inward. A small fire of rowan and mountain cedar was burning in the center of her large fireplace. A kettle of tea had been set to one side of the fire to keep hot, though Mother did not seem to have poured a cup. She was sitting at her small writing desk close by the fire, with the house ledger open before her and an abstracted expression on her aged, elegant face. Though she held a quill in her hand, she was not writing, but only gazing into the fire. But she glanced around as her door opened.

Her eyes traveled from Leilis's face to the tray she held, and she smiled a little. "Leilis."

"You seemed tired."

"I am, a little. Thank you."

Leilis walked forward, waited for Narienneh to close the ledger and move it aside, and laid her tray down on the table. "I presumed to open a bottle of the Enescene gold."

"That is thoughtfulness, not presumption. You have always," said Narienneh, with regret, "had a fine instinct."

Leilis said nothing. Even after so long, even spoken kindly, such a comment still had the power to wound. She refused, however, to flinch. Instead, she opened the bottle of wine and carefully poured, then set the goblet of wine down near Mother's hand, backed up a step, and settled herself on the floor by the hearth.

Narienneh lifted the goblet, sipped, sighed, and set the goblet back on the table again. She closed her eyes, leaning back in her chair.

"A pretty girl. A pretty naïveté," Leilis observed. "Doubtless she will ally the House with a most noble kisonne in her first keiso month, if she still owns such sweetness when she turns nineteen." Leilis did not stress the *if* by even so much as a direct glance up at Mother. Leilis, of all women of the House, did not need to.

"The deisa will help her. Lily will keep them in order," said Narienneh, with a peculiar and specific naïveté all her own. That she did not check Leilis for her impudence in offering an unsolicited opinion indicated clearly enough that she was worried, however. Possibly she even suspected her own blindness, around the edges of her conscious awareness.

Leilis modestly glanced downward and bowed her head, deliberately using a keiso trick to draw attention to herself, trying not to feel the irony of using keiso mannerisms to influence Narienneh when she would never in her life become a keiso.

Mother's eye was drawn by that movement, despite her own deep knowledge of all the keiso tricks. She shook her head. "I am quite certain that will not happen again."

Leilis bowed her head a little lower, to point up the irretrievable damage that deisa jealousy could do. If such damage could happen once, was Narienneh truly so confident that it could not happen twice?

Her own loss still bit deep; Leilis felt the teeth of it now more keenly than she had for years. Maybe she really *should* have left Cloisonné House and memory behind. But truly, even if she was forever barred from the keiso life, where else was there a place for her but in the flower world? She told herself, as she had a thousand times, and she knew it was true, that she was lucky Narienneh had made a place for her in Cloisonné House.

But the Mother of the House would not want to risk having to make such a place twice. Especially when her newest deisa had cost the House so dearly and showed such fine promise to win back her price doubled and redoubled. Leilis waited a moment, then murmured, "What a pity the girl is not already nineteen. A keiso is an asset to her House; a deisa merely an expense. If this girl must be too old for deisa, as well she were old enough to be made keiso at once."

Mother tilted her head, her fine-boned face going thoughtful. "Even if she were nineteen, I fear her elder sisters would resent such swift advancement."

Leilis did not let herself glance up, lest Mother should see the satisfaction hidden in her eyes. She could not have made a better opening if she had worked till dawn for it. She murmured, "Rue wouldn't," and rose, bowing gently to excuse herself, leaving that thought to mingle with the taste of the wine on the back of Narienneh's tongue.

CHAPTER 3

Taudde thought there was a fair possibility that he was going to find himself under arrest and on his way to some grim, silent dungeon within the hour. They had good dungeons in the Laodd, or so he'd heard. Prisons where a man could be locked away from light and music for a long, long lifetime...This situation must be due to some unrecognized carelessness. The wages of rampant stupidity, his grandfather would say. Bad enough to come to Lirionne at all, especially with the peace imposed by the Treaty of Brenedde so nearly at an end; worse still to dare Lonne itself; *beyond* foolish to be caught breaking the Seriantes ban. But *worst of all* and *proof* of blazing stupidity for a fool to completely miss whatever mistake had given him away!

Taudde could all but hear the old man's acerbic tone in his mind's ear, and at the moment he would have been hard put to refute a word of it. But—a poor saving grace—neither did he have leisure just now to indulge in recriminations. Taudde glanced warily from Lord Miennes to Mage Ankennes. If he'd merely had a lord of Lonne to contend with, he would have had more options. Lord Miennes knew that, of course. The mage's presence was hardly a coincidence.

Mage Ankennes, a big man with powerful hands and opaque gray eyes, looked deliberately into Taudde's face and smiled. That smile was not exactly a challenge, because a challenge would have invited opposition. There was no such invitation here. The mage truly believed that Taudde was going to yield. That he wouldn't even try to fight. Nor flee. That very confidence was intimidating. Taudde was afraid to reach for his flute, or even use perfectly ordinary tricks of tone and intonation.

Sometimes, aside from questions of intimidation and nerve, discretion was indeed the wisest course. Taudde put down the surging anger trying to rise into his eyes, his throat, and—dangerously—his voice. Instead, he smiled, lifted his cup, sipped, paused consideringly, and said casually, "Enescene, of course. A Tamissen gold, I think. From, oh, perhaps, the middle of the Niace regency? I don't think I can come closer. I did warn you I am not a connoisseur."

"Close, close," answered Miennes, smiling at this refusal to engage. The lord leaned comfortably back in his chair. His eyes, an ice-pale gray, glinted like cold stone as he watched his prey struggle on the hook. But his voice was as warm as his wine, and nearly as sweet. "You do yourself too little credit. For a young man, you have a most educated palate. Tamissen, yes, though from nearer the end of the Third Kesiande's reign."

Taudde made a vague gesture indicating polite self-deprecation. An extract of goldenthread would be undetectable in any sweet wine. So would Tincture of Esidde. Did the mages of Lonne know of that decoction? He tried to decide whether there was any trace of tingling or numbness in his lips or tongue. Any sudden flush of cold through his body. He could not detect any such sensations. Yet.

"Of course, both periods boasted hot, dry summers and long, lingering autumns," commented Miennes, still in that pleasant, mellow voice. "It tastes of autumn, this wine, I think. Rich and golden, apple scented and suggesting the merest hint of smoke."

Following this lead, Taudde murmured, "You entirely surpass me. I might agree with you about the apples. But I think only because you suggested it to me."

Mage Ankennes, too, was smiling. Unlike Miennes, the mage did not trouble to disguise the hardness under the smile. "Some men do not care for it. It is too sweet to suit every palate, even as an evening wine."

"Life holds enough that is bitter," murmured Lord Miennes, always ready to turn a courtly phrase. "Surely one should cherish the captured warmth of lingering autumns to remember through the long winters. Especially when the spring to come may be troubled."

Taudde said nothing. *Especially when the spring may be troubled*, indeed. He knew very well that Lord Miennes expected Kalches to resume its long war with Lirionne immediately after the solstice, when the Treaty of Brenedde at last reached its term. Everyone expected that.

Taudde knew, as few of the people of Lirionne would have believed, that the King of Kalches faced the prospect with resignation rather than bloody-minded enthusiasm. But Seriantes avarice was insatiable, and Geriodde Nerenne ken Seriantes certainly no less ambitious than his ancestors. No king of Kalches could possibly allow the Seriantes Dragon to keep his grip on the lands Lirionne had stolen from Kalches fifteen years ago. Those lands were too close to the heart of Kalches. One could indeed be quite certain that the coming spring would be *troubled*.

Taudde had expected to return home before the war resumed. He had even been glad to watch the solstice approach at last, except as the turning of the year would interfere with his studies in Lonne. He vividly remembered the field of Brenedde. That battle had ended with his father's body sprawled loose-limbed in the dirt before the Dragon of Lirionne. He had been a child, then. Too young to try for vengeance. And then the treaty had forced him to set the thought aside for fifteen years. Those years had seemed long to him. Now they were past, and the spring rushed toward them, and he was assuredly not the only Kalchesene who would be grimly satisfied to see the year turn.

Whether Lord Miennes or this mage of his was eager for the coming spring was harder to judge.

"Indeed, the winters in this city are long enough," Ankennes murmured. The mage glanced out the wide windows to the white clouds shredding against the jagged peaks. Then he turned his attention deliberately back to Taudde. "Though never so long nor so cold as those of ... your homeland."

"What, Miskiannes?" Taudde said, just for something to say.

Both of the other men smiled tolerantly. Neither bothered to state aloud that Taudde was not from Miskiannes. Neither one seemed at all concerned about any threat Taudde might pose to them. Or, evidently, to Lonne.

Miennes sipped more wine and sighed, shaking his head in mock wistfulness. "Every year when the mists come down from the mountains, I wonder why I do not move my establishment south. Yet how could one choose to abandon the civilized sophistication of the Pearl of the West? And, indeed, the cold teaches one to appreciate the warmth. Though, of course," he added without any change of tone, "as Ankennes said, you would know more of cold than we."

Taudde did not bother, this time, to deny it. It was too clear denial would not serve.

"Why did you come to Lonne in the first place? From, ah... Miskiannes."

Taudde lifted his eyebrows. "Does a man need a better reason than desire to see the Pearl of the West?" He paused for a heartbeat. "Does it matter?"

"Not at all," Miennes said, at the same moment that Ankennes said, "Of course it matters—" The two men glanced at each other. Miennes said, "My friend, I don't believe one must search over-diligently for reasons a young man from ... Miskiannes ... might venture to Lonne just in this season. Yes?"

The mage opened one broad hand, conceding the point.

Miennes said to Taudde, "As long as you abandon your original purpose, whether it was spycraft or assassination or some other manner of disruption—as long as you abandon that intention, I say, we needn't inquire too closely as to what it was. So long as you are amenable to the little task I—we have for you. You may even find our purposes run close coupled."

"Yes?" Taudde inquired, in his politest tone.

Miennes paused and held his goblet up to muse on the pale wine. "As you seem to approve this vintage, perhaps I will serve it with the sweet course tomorrow evening. You will join us for the occasion, I hope? There will be a guest we would particularly like you to meet."

"Of course I will attend. Your attention flatters me." Taudde set his cup down with a tiny precise *click* of porcelain against marble. The wine, he surmised, was not drugged. And an acquaintance with this guest was clearly the price of this forbearance. Not, he suspected, a lasting acquaintance. Miennes, unless he was very much mistaken, meant to make Taudde into something like his own private assassin...It was an ugly idea. But he suspected that such an ugly use was exactly what a man such as Lord Miennes would think of, for a Kalchesene sorcerer who had fallen into his hands.

And even that might be preferable to such use as Ankennes might intend. Everyone knew that what a mage would comprehend, he took first to pieces, as though by mapping out its constituent elements he would learn to understand the whole. Taudde did not want to imagine what a Lonne mage would do with a captive Kalchesene sorcerer and a free hand. Strange to think that Miennes might be an asset to him, under these peculiar circumstances.

At least, even if Miennes and Ankennes were both subtle men, probably neither was the type to set up this dance and counterdance merely as a ruse to trap a Kalchesene bardic sorcerer for the Laodd authorities. No. They could have done that more safely and surely in a dozen ways, mostly involving far less personal involvement. Taudde was surer by the moment that these two meant to keep their newest toy fast in their own hands. Taudde met Miennes's eyes. The lord smiled. Taudde smiled in return. Ankennes smiled. Everyone smiled. *Ah, yes, we are all fast friends here.*

"How fine a thing, travel," Mage Ankennes said warmly. "It broadens the mind and strengthens the will, I believe the saying goes. I am sure you will benefit from it, young man. And we here in Lonne will surely benefit from it as well."

That was the subtle way they delivered threats in civilized, sophisticated Lonne. Taudde wished he were back in Kalches, where both speech and threats were clear and straightforward.

The streets were indeed cold, Taudde found, once he was at last able to take his leave from Miennes's great gray house. The late sun shone forth with little light and less warmth, fading notes in the closing movement of the day's symphony. Even now the cold evening mists were creeping down the steep slopes into the city streets.

Taudde might have hired a conveyance, but it was not far to the townhouse he was renting, and perhaps the chilly air would help him clear his mind. He strode down the street, keeping well to the side to avoid getting afoul of the mounted traffic in the middle. Open carriages for wealthy merchants, closed ones for noble ladies, high-stepping horses for sleek young courtiers full of their own importance—very few of any sort would go to much trouble to avoid trampling a man on foot. But the streets were clear enough at this hour that Taudde could think while walking.

Taudde had spent considerable attention and effort on making sure he remained unnoticed by Lonne's mages. He'd thought he had succeeded. But it seemed that Mage Ankennes had discovered him somehow. No doubt both he and Lord Miennes were involved in some ridiculous conspiracy Taudde would not care about at all, but in which he was undoubtedly going to be forced to participate. He was quite certain that the conspirators would have some plan already in place to keep control of their newest tool. If that had not been so, there would have been a drug in the wine.

Miennes, Taudde was sure, would prefer something subtle and slow acting, a trap that a clever opponent would close on himself by being clever. Ankennes was perhaps more direct, or perhaps so subtle that he simply suggested directness. In either case, no doubt trying to leave the city tonight would be a mistake. Taudde only wondered what shape the trap would take, if he should try. If anyone followed him along the streets, he could not detect them. But then, Ankennes was a mage. No doubt he had some more subtle way to keep track of the conspiracy's newest tool.

Taudde rubbed his hands hard across his face. Why *exactly* had he come to Lonne in the first place? Beyond the satisfaction of defying his grandfather, a satisfaction that seemed at the moment rather trivial? Not, surely, to play games of politics and treachery with ruthless Lonne courtiers. Grandfather would laugh if he knew of this little predicament. Then he would stop laughing and say, *Fool boy, get out of Lonne and come home! Now is not the time for a Kalchesene to be caught in Lonne! If you'll only steady down, you'll find the bardic sorcery of your own country enough to hold your attention for a lifetime or two without adding in the treacherous, ungraspable magic of the sea!*

Those would be the very words. Taudde could hear the old man's exact tone: exasperated and affectionate and acerbic. But Grandfather wouldn't laugh if he'd seen the cold, clever avariciousness in Miennes's eyes, or Ankennes's calm intensity. Taudde shivered. It wasn't the chill in the air. He was, he admitted to himself, afraid. Lord Miennes was merely greedy or ambitious, he thought. Miennes had some ordinary, petty motive. He was dangerous, undoubtedly, but Taudde found he was much more afraid of Ankennes. Men who were absolutely certain of their own righteousness might do anything, and he thought, now he had time to think about it, that that kind of certainty was exactly what he'd heard in the undertones of the mage's voice. Taudde shivered again. He paused in his walk to make himself breathe deeply, dismissing fear. Whatever their plans, he would disentangle himself from them.

But, whatever he did, Taudde would have to do it carefully. If Miennes or the mage suspected that Taudde was going to slip whatever traps they'd prepared, what would stop them from sending word of Taudde to the Laodd themselves? Nothing, Taudde concluded, and thought, although he tried not to, of the soundless cells of the Laodd, in which a bardic sorcerer might be imprisoned in helpless silence.

He walked on after a moment, taking a faster pace as he neared his townhouse. Much of the traffic had died away, now. Smoke, tinged faintly red by the last light of the sun, rose in thin wisps from innumerable chimneys. Beyond the city, the great fortress of the Laodd brooded down upon the homes of lesser men, its glass windows throwing back the red light so that the fortress seemed to glitter with crystallized blood. Above it, ragged clouds tore themselves free of high mountain peaks and unfurled across the sky. Beneath and behind and beyond the city, Taudde fancied he could hear the sea itself calling, the waves breaking against the shore in a cadence older than time.

There would be snow three feet deep across Kalches at this time of year. Yet the chill of coastal Lirionne, at least here in Lonne, seemed to cut with a finer blade than any Kalchesene winter. The Lonne winter was altogether different from the brilliant cold that in Kalches drew folk out for skating parties on the frozen rivers. Taudde set his teeth as much against sudden, violent longing as against the wind. Yet for all he longed for his home, and for all the trouble in which he was now embroiled, he could not wish, even now, to exchange the drawing tides of the sea for the frozen rivers of Kalches. He bowed his head and tried to ignore the unfriendly bite of the chilly Lonne wind.

That was why he was taken by surprise by the young thugs of some street gang. There were three of them. They had taken advantage of an unlit part of the street, slipping out of a narrow side street to block his way. Two of the three had knives, the other a short, metal-bound club.

In Lonne, generally the threat of purse cutters was greater than the threat of plain violence, for the Laodd frowned on disorder. But foreigners were not permitted to carry weapons, so of course they attracted the city's predators. Wealthy foreigners such as Taudde were expected to travel by carriage, or hire local guards, or both. Taudde, not accustomed to thinking of petty threats, had carelessly let himself walk into danger and now was not certain he dared deal with it as he would have in Kalches. He glanced around, but saw no one on the street who might come to his aid.

"Not lookin' for trouble," the largest of the thugs said, smacking his club against his palm and grinning.

Taudde longed to smash the thugs to the cobbles. He was sure they deserved anything he might do to them. But he couldn't. There was no time for subtlety, not in this; yet any fast unsubtle sorcery he might do would give away his true nationality in a blaring rush of magic every little magelet in Lonne must perceive, never mind the skilled mages of the Laodd. Taudde shivered with the effort to contain his outrage. The thugs smirked, taking the tremors for terror. Their obvious self-satisfaction only fed Taudde's fury.

The moment he'd recognized the trap, Taudde had automatically slipped his flute from its special pocket in his sleeve. Now he almost brought it to his lips, despite the risk any hurried use of sorcery entailed, in Lonne.

Then he clenched the flute in his hand instead, and set his teeth as he forced himself instead to reach for his pouch. He thought he had enough script and hard cash to satisfy the street thugs. If they had the least sense, then they would indeed not want the trouble a wealthy foreigner might bring down on them—if he could stand to yield a little money to them, they should fade back into the streets that had spawned them. Ridiculous though it was that one of Kalches's dozen master sorcerers should be robbed by common thugs, striking them down was surely not worth the risk of drawing attention from Lonne's mages.

Then the thieves' leader smacked his club into his palm again and smiled, and the contempt and brutality in that smile simultaneously fed Taudde's anger and shook his presumption that the thugs had any sense at all. He took a step back—

A sound behind Taudde revealed the presence of another thug, and Taudde started to turn, knowing even as he moved that he might well have lost his opportunity to get away, that even if he were forced to a desperate sorcery, he might not now have time to play even a single note. The man behind him was huge, but cat footed for all his size; he'd come silently out of the evening mist—

Taudde hesitated, trapped between the thugs before and behind. But the big newcomer unexpectedly went right past him.

The big man strode right toward the leader of the thieves, who swung at him with the club, a short vicious blow. But the newcomer simply caught the club in one huge hand and wrenched it away from his attacker. He used it himself, three rapid blows that left the thug's leader moaning on the cobbles. The other two thugs stepped back, cursing, lifting their knives in threat and warning.

"Benne," Taudde said, belatedly recognizing his rescuer. The big man gave Taudde a quick look over his shoulder and then gestured with the club he still held, suggesting retreat back along the street.

"Yes," Taudde agreed. He felt shaky: shocked by how close he'd come to being forced to choose between alerting every mage in Lonne to his presence or being beaten to death on the city streets. He slipped his flute back into its concealed pocket and turned to go the way Benne had indicated.

But there were more thieves there, emerging from another alley: two—no, three—no, at least four, and how was it Lonne, which prided itself on its civilized ways, could prove so lawless? But there they were, four more thugs—at least four, and two of the first three still on their feet and dangerous. At least the one Benne had clubbed was groaning on the ground. And unlikely to get up without aid: Benne was a powerful man. Taudde had never been so grateful that his rented townhouse had come with servants attached.

"Well?" he asked Benne now.

The big man gave Taudde the club, smacked a massive fist into the palm of his other hand, and strode forward. Taudde, uncertain of the tactical wisdom involved in ignoring the knifemen at their backs, nevertheless followed in Benne's wake. The club felt strange and heavy in his hand. His flute would have been far more comfortable, or if not that, then at least a gentleman's sword rather than this street thug's tool.

From Benne's confident manner, Taudde half expected the thieves to give way and fade back into the shadowed alleys that had spawned them. But there were six of them left, after all, and they must have decided those odds were uneven enough to suit them. Two of the recent arrivals had the same sort of club Taudde now held. One of the others had a knife, like the two behind, and the other a wicked length of chain. That one seemed to be the leader, now that the other man was down. He looked brutal enough for the role.

"Nem, you get around—" that man began.

Benne didn't wait for the thug to complete his orders. He turned abruptly, smooth as a dancer, took a long step back, grabbed one of the knife wielders who had been edging forward, dropped him, half turned, stabbed the other knifeman in the stomach, completed his turn, and was back out in front of Taudde before any of the other four thieves or Taudde himself could quite comprehend what he'd done. The complete silence with which he'd performed this devastating attack, and in which he now faced the remaining thieves, lent a surreal quality to the whole performance. The man he'd stabbed was on his ground, curled up around his injury, making horrible small noises that served as an effective accompaniment to Benne's own silence. The man Benne had grabbed, from whom he'd taken the knife, wasn't making any sound at all. Or moving. Taudde realized, belatedly, that the big man must have broken the thief's neck in that first moment.

The other four thieves, understandably, were now hesitating to attack. One of them muttered an oath under his breath. Their leader stared in disbelief past Benne and Taudde at his three dead or injured companions, then shifted his gaze back to Benne's face. Benne simply stared back, apparently unmoved. He showed neither anger nor fear nor, really, anything much. After a moment, he gestured to Taudde and walked forward. He held the bloody knife in an apparently casual grip, as though barely aware it was in his fist.

It took Taudde a long moment to gather his wits and follow. He'd feared he wouldn't be able to give any great assistance to his servant in this little battle. Now he doubted he'd be called upon to render any assistance whatever.

The thief who had cursed before uttered another, more vehement oath. Then he turned and walked away. He didn't run, but he was moving briskly.

"Now, look," began the thug's leader, but Benne only continued to stride forward, and in another instant the remaining thieves gave way and followed their fellow into the shadows.

Ahead of them, a streetlamp cast its greenish light over Taudde's rented house, now just visible in the palely lit mist. Taudde followed Benne toward the house without uttering a word. He was seldom rendered speechless. But the cumulative effect of this evening had managed it.

The house stood in the heart of Lonne, less than a mile from Miennes's own graceful townhouse, if in a rather less exclusive district. Its rent was high, but nothing less would do for the wealthy man, son of wealthy merchants, whom Taudde was pretending to be. Had he instead presented himself as an ordinary man, even a poor one, would Miennes ever have noticed him? No way of knowing, without finding out how he'd given himself away in the first place. But it still seemed more likely the mage who had discovered him, and against that the trappings of disguise probably made little difference. At least he hadn't had to endure any sort of privation during his stay in Lonne. Yet.

The townhouse was a tall, narrow, sheer-walled structure, with no windows on the first floor and bars on those of the second floor: measures that would protect the house's inhabitants from the simpler sort of thief or thug. Taudde appreciated this design consideration far more now than he had previously. Though the house owned nothing at all, of course, to guard against the sort of thug who lived in a great stone mansion and gracefully served the very best wines to go with his delicate threats.

The lowest floor held the servants' quarters. Taudde took the angular stair that crooked around a corner of the house and led to an entrance directly on the second floor, beckoning Benne to follow. The long brass key he carried was stiff in the lock. Taudde could have unlocked the door almost as quickly without the key as with it, if he had dared use sorcery. But, of course, he did not.

again. "You know everything, Nala—let me ask your advice. I believe there may well be noble guests present. I may wish to invite one or more of these guests to a later function of my own. Do I correctly gather that a keiso House is considered a suitable venue for such an event?"

"Oh, yes, lord! Nothing could be more suitable."

After a moment Taudde managed to frame the sort of elliptical question preferred in Lonne. "As a foreigner, Nala, I am naturally not very familiar with the keiso of Lonne. But in Miskiannes, that, um, sort of establishment is not often considered proper for, ah, a high-class gathering."

"Oh, no, keiso Houses aren't *that* sort of establishment at all," the woman exclaimed. Her voice held underlying tones of both amusement at the foreigner's ignorance and shock at the suggestion he had skirted. "My lord is thinking of aika, not of keiso, and that's no wonder, I suppose, since no other city in the world has keiso. Not but that our aika aren't also the most glamorous anywhere. But, see, my lord, if a man wants more than elegant companionship from a keiso, he must handfast her as a flower wife, a keimiso. Then he must buy her a house of her own, and maybe a shop or restaurant if she wishes such a thing, and he must acknowledge any left-hand children she might bear him and set the boys up in a trade—the girls usually follow their mother's path and become keiso, of course."

"I can see," Taudde told her, "that you will need to teach me more of your Lonne customs, if I do entertain guests. But first we shall see how this dinner of Lord Miennes's goes. It is to be a formal occasion, I believe. Have I anything suitable to wear?"

Nala pursed her lips consideringly. "There are very good tailors in the Paliante, my lord. Benne can guide you."

"A man of multitudinous talents," Taudde murmured.

"Lord?"

"Never mind." Taudde went to find the big man.

Lonne, as befit the most refined city of sophisticated Lirionne, possessed many elegant treasures. Perhaps the queen among these was the Paliante, which lay immediately below the King's District. Farther back, the Laodd climbed the rugged cliffs. Immediately south of this fortress, the Nijiadde River flung itself over the cliffs and fell a thousand feet to shatter into diamond spume where it struck the stone below. Together, fortress and waterfall formed, as though by design, an imposing backdrop to the graceful Paliante.

Homes in the Paliante were faced with carved stone or expensive pale gold brick; the intricate wrought-iron work that guarded their spacious courtyards and windows was twisted into fanciful dragons or dolphins or eagles. Shops in the Paliante sold the work of the best perfumers and jewelers and woodcrafters to an exclusive clientele that, after dark, drifted across the Niarre to the theaters, aika establishments, fine restaurants, and keiso Houses of the candlelight district.

Far to the south of the Paliante, sprawling mercantile yards received overland trade from across the mountains—less trade than usual, in these tense times. Near the great tradeyards lay manufacturing districts where the dyers and coppersmiths, the woodworkers and stone masons had their establishments. And besides all this, street vendors held busy and crowded open-air markets down by the docks where they sold many odd and interesting objects.

This was where Taudde found himself an hour after dawn, in a morning that promised at least beauty if not clarity or confidence. The Paliante would be the place to purchase formal clothing for the evening, but it was the sea itself that drew Taudde. Slate gray where it washed up on the shale beaches, the sea turned brilliant sapphire farther out. The rhythm of its waves coming up against the shale formed a harmony with the clamor of the streets, the rattle of wheels across cobbles and the singing calls of vendors advertising their wares.

A fine three-masted ship had made its way out past the crowd at dock and was heading out toward the sapphire horizon. Taudde wished, suddenly and intensely, that he was aboard her—heading for Erhlianne perhaps, away from duty and peril and the hope or threat of vengeance. What would it be like to stand on the deck of a moving ship, surrounded by measureless blue fathoms? The music of the sea would not be a thin trace barely audible behind the clamor of the city, but all-enveloping. He half closed his eyes, listening for that music.

And heard an echo of it, captured and transmuted to a more familiar form.

The vendor was clearly an old sailor stranded ashore by age and infirmity. He had a thin bony face, deep-set eyes, and hands crippled by years of hard use. His booth was set low, tucked nearly out of sight under a dock, where the sea broke across the slate. It was a small booth and held very little, mostly rough objects made out of driftwood. But Taudde had been caught by the sound of a flute the man played.

The old sailor played with his eyes closed and his face tilted toward the sky. The flute was a crude instrument. But in it, the man had managed to capture an echo of the drawing tide. Intrigued, Taudde gave him a small silver coin for the flute. Then he spent an hour sitting on the rocks below the dock, sea spume dashing across his toes, discovering the little instrument's range and breadth and listening to the breathy echo of the sea hiding behind all its notes. It was a very simple flute, much plainer than Taudde's own, with no metalwork to increase its range or multiply its notes. But Taudde almost thought he might finally have found a way to begin binding the mysterious magic of the sea into a form he could actually understand and use. If he had time to work on it...time...what *was* the time? Taudde looked at the sun and jumped to his feet.

Lonne styles were set by law and by strict custom: Foreigners, no matter how wealthy or distinguished, were expected to comport themselves with modesty. The richest dyes were for Lonne nobility. Lavenders and blues were for wellborn or wealthy women, or for keiso. Flat red was for the military, black for the King's Own, and saffron only for the king's family.

As a foreigner, Taudde was expected to dress plainly. Yet he, as many foreigners who came to Lonne, was a man of wealth and breeding. Thus, many of the best and most expensive purveyors of cloth goods in Lonne were accustomed to providing the very finest clothing possible within the prescribed limitations. The tailor to whom Benne escorted Taudde brought out a rich brown outfit, accented with pale yellow, with a pair of calf-high boots with turned-down tops threaded with pale yellow ribbons. Taudde thought the ribbons excessive, but Benne so clearly approved of them that he allowed the tailor to add the boots to his purchase.

Then there was another complete outfit in charcoal gray with red accents, including soft suede boots that were clearly not intended for the winter streets. Taudde inclined his head. "I see I shall indeed need an equipage," he said to Benne, a touch drily. "Find one for me, nothing too extravagant. A single horse should certainly be sufficient."

The servant nodded quickly. Neither he nor Taudde had referred in any way to the incidents of the previous evening, but Taudde thought that the big man seemed, if anything, a little more wary and cautious this morning. Now he hesitantly sketched a saddle in the air with his hands, tilting his head inquiringly.

"Yes, both a small carriage and riding tack."

Benne nodded a second time as the tailor apologetically presented his bill. Taudde strolled out of doors to wait discreetly while his servant argued the bill up to an amount Taudde could properly pay.

Down the street toward the tailor's establishment came a black-and-red company: ordinary soldiers accompanied by half a handful of officers from the King's Own guard. Taudde turned with casual curiosity to watch the company pass, but found his eye unexpectedly caught by one man who rode in the midst of the guardsmen. A tall man, with strong, stark features and a face as cold and austere as the mountain heights.

Though he had not seen him for fifteen years, Taudde recognized the man at once, half from memory and half from the sheer sense of ungiving power that spread out from him like a river pouring down from a high cliff. This was Geriodde Nerenne ken

Seriantes, the Dragon of Lirionne himself, riding through the streets he ruled like any common court noble. Though, indeed, there was nothing common about the Dragon.

Taudde recognized the harsh, stark features of the king: the falcon-sharp bones, the ungiving mouth. But what he recognized first was the Dragon's sheer intensity of power. He had not been prepared to meet that power, not here or now, and took an involuntary step backward.

As though drawn by that movement, the king turned his head. The fierce gaze of his ice-pale eyes crossed Taudde's face. There could not possibly have been recognition in that glance, for a boy of ten can hardly be recognized in the man of twenty-five. Yet Taudde's breath caught with a conviction that the King of Lirionne *had* recognized him, that those soldiers would turn aside from their ordinary business to pursue and apprehend him. The Dragon's men would bring Taudde before the granite throne...He would be condemned and cast into the silent cells within the Laodde, or from the heights into the sea, which was how the Seriantes Dragon disposed of his enemies...Then the cold gaze passed on, and the King of Lirionne looked away indifferently.

The company clattered forward, iron-shod hooves ringing on the cobbled street, passersby hurriedly making way for it. Taudde put a hand out blindly, bracing himself against the door of the nearest shop and stood still, not because he intelligently resisted the temptation to give way to terrifying fancies, but simply because he found himself momentarily frozen by indecisive panic. It took every rational faculty he possessed to stop himself reaching for his flute. If the Dragon had indeed disregarded him, then flinching in terror and bringing a bardic sorcerer's flute out in plain sight would probably be a good way to get his attention. But Taudde found it impossible to stand quietly in the street and let the Dragon's company ride by so close, either.

Instead, and with a sharp effort, Taudde turned on his heel and plunged, without looking, into the shop.

"May I assist the noble lord in locating any poor oddment that may be offered in this humble establishment?" inquired a rather nasal voice.

Taudde, most of his attention still fixed on the sound of the passing horses, tried not to flinch noticeably at this unexpected address.

The horses' hooves clattered loudly in the street...They did not halt, but went on past. Taudde blinked and took a quick breath. He found his hand had indeed gone to touch the reassuring smoothness of his flute. He took his hand away, trying to cultivate a bland expression while his heart settled gradually back to a slower rhythm.

The shop, once Taudde glanced around it, proved to hold an interesting display of oddments: porcelain lamps, brass sconces, small glass bottles, mysterious confections of copper wire and glass bobbles, delicate bowls, and small musical instruments. The proprietor was an elderly man, but one who appeared prosperous. Despite the formal humility with which he had addressed Taudde, the man's attitude was far from humble. Taudde suspected he was of noble blood himself, perhaps the son of some lord's keiso mistress—no. His *wife*, he corrected himself. A keiso was not a mistress, but a *flower wife*. The mother of *left-hand* sons, who were, according to Lonne custom, recognized by their noble fathers.

"Ah—" Taudde managed. "Ah, I don't— I wasn't looking for any specific item." But his attention was caught by a diminutive finger harp strung with white fibers so fine they were all but invisible. Distracted from his urgent worries, Taudde bent to examine it. The harp was an exquisite instrument, made of some unfamiliar fine-grained red wood with pearl facing and pearl knobs. The strings did not seem to be silver wire. He touched one with a fingertip and frowned in surprise. It made an odd sound, not pure, but with a faint burring undertone, almost a buzz. Trying another string, he found a note not quite in tune with the first and affected by the same buzzing quality. Attempting to tune the second string to complement the first produced a flatter quality to its note and only accentuated the buzz.

"A pretty thing, but for display perhaps more than use," the proprietor murmured, correctly reading his expression. "It is from the great island of Erhlianne. The wood is poppy teak, which grows only in the far mountains of Erhlianne. Very rare and expensive. The strings are made from the feathers of a beautiful white bird called the miarre, which flies out at sea for all but three weeks a year, and comes inland for those three weeks to nest upon the branches of trees that stretch out over the sea from the cliffs of Erhlianne. Strings made from these feathers never break, for they have the endurance of the bird to which they once belonged."

"Ah," said Taudde.

"Or so it is said," murmured the proprietor smoothly. "Now, a connoisseur such as my lord...hmm. If my lord would care to step over here..." He guided Taudde toward the rear of the shop. Along the far wall were blanks of wood and sea ivory and bone and horn, racked in order of size; pegs and buttons of exotic wood or polished stone; spools of copper wire, or silver, or gold; tubes of brass and copper; delicate reeds oiled and curing in the gentle warmth of a lamp. A small table, lit by the lamp, was cluttered with clamps and carving tools, polishing cloths, and fine brushes.

"I believe my lord might prefer an instrument such as this," suggested the proprietor, reaching into the midst of the clutter and finding, apparently without needing to search, a set of pipes as broad as the palms of both hands. "Now these are meant for the hand of a skilled instrumentalist. They are made, as you see, of bone and copper. The inlay is abalone shell. The reeds are simple sea reeds, but treated with a special technique of my own to prevent warping or splitting and to purify their tone. Perhaps my lord would be pleased to try these pipes?"

The confidence in the proprietor's manner was sufficient that Taudde was not surprised to find the notes of the pipe unusually clear and delicate. The hum of the reeds lent a deep resonance to each note without harming its clarity. Taudde wondered how the effect had been achieved. He squinted into the pipes to see the thin reeds within each, noting their faint purplish sheen. Perhaps they had, in fact, been treated in some manner he did not know. "You made these?"

The proprietor gave a modest little bow. "My poor efforts are assuredly not sufficient to match those of the craftsmen with whom my lord is no doubt accustomed to do business."

Taudde played a quick set of trills, running through the surprisingly broad range of the pipes. They were not tuned to the familiar descene scale but to the far less common ioscene scale, every other note set half a step off.

"The pipes are not out of tune," said the proprietor, seeing Taudde's eyebrows rise.

Taudde returned a noncommittal nod. He lifted the pipes again and produced another brief ripple of notes, listening curiously to the odd catch and drag produced by the ioscene tuning. It seemed to him that the breathy resonance of these pipes was well suited to the sea. If he went down to the shore where the waves broke on the rocks, he wondered whether he might be able to capture the changeable sea winds in the reeds of this instrument. "Though I have traveled widely, I do not believe I have often seen better," he said at last. "And I see you are accustomed to such work." He gestured to the generous and varied supplies that occupied this part of the shop, the faint beginnings of a new inspiration murmuring at the back of his mind. He still would not claim to have a distinct *plan*, but he felt himself closer to one than he'd dared hope.

"I dabble from time to time," conceded the proprietor. "When an interesting idea occurs to me."

"I see. Well . . . I believe I will purchase these, if you are willing to part with them." Taudde began to turn back toward the front of the shop and unexpectedly found Benne at his elbow. He blinked. Benne flinched back slightly and dropped his gaze immediately.

Taudde hesitated for a moment. Then he said at last, "I will purchase this item," gave the pipes to Benne, and walked away, to wait politely out of earshot for Benne and the proprietor of the store to settle a price.

CHAPTER 4

The Mother of Cloisonné House, disposing of the iron custom of the flower world with a fine arrogance, made Karah into a keiso three days after the girl had been bought into the House. Leilis had hoped for exactly this, but the speed with which Narienneh made her decision impressed her anyway.

"You haven't the training, of course," Narienneh told the girl. "You will have to work very hard at your lessons." Karah could play the knee harp and sing some of the short gaodd poems that every keiso was supposed to know, but there was no pretending her accomplishments were up to Cloisonné's usual standards.

Karah bowed her head, looking young and shy. She made Leilis feel old.

Thirty-one keiso were present, sitting or kneeling gracefully on cushions all around the edges of the dance studio, which was the only room in the House large enough for the ceremony of adoption. The mirrors and the bar, along with all other utilitarian features of the room, had been hidden from sight behind tall color-washed screens.

Fourteen independent keiso had come to attend this adoption. They wore robes in restrained colors and few—but expensive—jewels. Meadowbell, her nature as sunny as her wheat-gold over-robe, was clearly amused and pleased by Mother's departure from tradition. On the other hand, though Celandine's mouth was set in a good-humored expression, her eyes were cold as the winter sea embroidered on her overrobe: *She* did not care to have a mere child handed special favors that had never come her own way. Nemienne knew Celandine bitterly resented Karah, with a steady, cold resentment that would wear down the years, but at least Celandine was not a resident of Cloisonné House, so Karah would not be thrown into her close company.

Silvermist, oldest of the independent keiso, would have far more influence than Celandine over the reaction of the flower world to Karah's too-swift advancement. Silvermist, her silver-shot hair braided with blue ribbons and fine silver chains, had been independent for better than thirty years. Her noble keisonne had long ago given her a house of her own and she had invested his gifts wisely; her wealth showed in her assurance as much as in the restrained elegance of her robes. Her daughters, Bellflower and Chelone, had settled near her. Each of them also had accepted a keisonne and acquired property of her own. Bellflower owned a restaurant near one of the bridges and Chelone a shop that made and embroidered keiso robes. Neither of them would feel in the least threatened by a child such as Karah, and fortunately neither liked Celandine. But what Silvermist herself thought was not obvious from her manner.

In addition to the independent keiso, seventeen resident keiso were present. *They* were the ones who had the most reason to feel personally threatened by Karah's early elevation—by her beauty and by the mere fact of her existence. They were the ones who would have to compete with her for attention. These women were bolder in clothing and jewelry and manner than the keiso of independent means, and yet even so accoutered, not one of them outshone Cloisonné's newest acquisition. They knew it. Most of them resented the knowledge. They knelt in pairs or small groups and murmured to one another behind their hands. Those who were aging pensioners upon the House would hate the too-young Karah for being given an extra chance to succeed where they had already failed.

Rue, aloof from the other resident keiso, had won a coveted spot near the studio's huge windows. From her patient put-upon air, she would rather have had the studio to herself and the mirrors uncovered.

Featherreed and Bluestar knelt nearest Rue, their heads tilted toward one another, murmuring together. But there was less of an edge to their whispers than to the rest; they were young keiso, kind-hearted and popular. Bluestar had no fewer than three potential keisonne currently negotiating with Mother for her favor, though Leilis suspected Bluestar would in the end accept none of them. The young keiso loved the son of a Laodd noble and intended to wait for the young man to come into property or a court appointment of his own. She, of any of the younger keiso, had least reason for jealousy and more inclination than any to support her newest sister. Or so Leilis hoped.

It would no doubt help that both Featherreed and Bluestar had been deisa with Lily and knew her intimately; they would be sympathetic to Karah's need to get out of the deisa quarters as quickly as she could. Leilis thought—hoped—that it would take very little management to be sure both Bluestar and Featherreed befriended the girl.

All six of the deisa, clad in black robes traced with blue around the hems, knelt by the door. Their faces were turned down and their mouths stubbornly set, as they took their common attitude from Lily. Lily herself had the sort of fine-boned elegance and striking presence that was most desired among keiso. Of all the keiso and deisa and servants in Cloisonné House, Leilis thought, only the Mother of the House was blind to the failings of her natural daughter.

Lily's temper was clearly in evidence at the moment, though subtly. She had beautiful sea-blue eyes, with fine arched brows and long dark lashes, but her eyes right now hid depths of anger. The other deisa took their cues from her, for to do otherwise was at best difficult and at worst dangerous. There was a stiffness to Karah's back, turned now toward Lily, that showed the girl had learned in her three days in the deisa quarters to be aware always of the older deisa. In just those three days, Leilis fancied, the precious, delicate edge of Karah's innocence had begun to be blunted. Even Narienneh must have seen it.

Thus, of course, this gathering.

Between Mother and Karah stood a low table of black wood with mother-of-pearl inlay. On this table stood a large bowl, surrounded by thirty-two small porcelain cups painted with flowers or reeds or dragonflies with opalescent wings. The bowl was filled with sweet berry liquor, so dark a red it was nearly black. Leilis had never tasted it.

The adoption ceremony was a simple one. Karah took a cup painted with blue columbines and golden butterflies and dipped it full of liquor. This she gave to Narienneh, offering it carefully in both hands.

Narienneh took the cup the same way, cradling it in her long thin fingers as though it were not only fragile but also infinitely valuable. She said to Karah, "My daughter, your name is Moonflower." Then she sipped the liquor and gave the cup back to Karah—Moonflower, now—who sipped in her turn and once more offered the cup back to Narienneh, who drained it.

Thirty-one more times, the newest flower of Cloisonné House filled a small cup with berry liquor. Thirty-one times, she shared a cup of liquor with a keiso, beginning with Silvermist, who was the eldest of them all, and ending with Bluestar, who was the youngest. Each time, the keiso who shared the cup murmured a word of advice or a suggestion to their youngest sister, from "Smile, my dear, your life will be beautiful," with gratifying warmth from Silvermist, to "You must improve your fretwork on the harp," from Celandine, in a disdainful tone.

At the end, Moonflower came back to place the last cup by the table and kneel on the cushion before Narienneh. She said in her soft little voice, her eyes downcast, "Mother."

A folded parcel of cloth had lain behind Narienneh. Now the elderly woman took this and formally offered it to her newest daughter.

Moonflower took this parcel and opened it out into a very fine keiso overrobe. Removing her deisa overrobe, she donned the one that marked her clearly as a keiso, her fingers lingering on the rich cloth as she tied the sash. Then she stood facing Mother.

A blue that matched Moonflower's eyes, the robe was embroidered from hip to hem with the fine-cut leaves and delicate white blooms of her namesake. White moths with long feathery antennae and green-traced wings fluttered in a graceful spiral from shoulder to hip. It was a robe that had once belonged to Mother herself, and a very generous gift—though also one that would enhance the beauty of the House by bringing out the beauty of its newest daughter.

Narienneh said gently, "My daughter, you need fear nothing, for you are part of Cloisonné House. All your elder sisters will teach you and look after you and you must respect them and always be courteous and guard the honor and dignity of the House. Of them all, you must have an Elder Sister to guide your steps as you learn the ways of the flower world." She sent a glance around the circle of keiso and asked, "Who will be Elder Sister to this youngest of our sisters?"

This had all been settled beforehand, of course. Rue straightened her back, and then bowed slowly and gracefully to the floor.

"Good," said Mother. "Well offered. Go to Rue, my daughter, and she will teach you the ways of the flower world and of Cloisonné House."

Moonflower bowed to Mother, straightened, went to Rue and bowed again, and then took her place behind the older keiso.

Mother rose, clapped her hands once, gently, and walked, her back straight, out of the studio. She did not seem to notice any of the keiso, and certainly not the deisa, though Lily sent her an angry sidelong glance as she passed her. The keiso left the room one at a time, in silence, in order of seniority—Rue neither early nor late in that precedence. Moonflower, though youngest in the House, nevertheless rose with her Elder Sister and went out with her; she would stay a step behind Rue for weeks, perhaps months, until she was ready to present herself on her own to the House and the candlelight district.

The deisa left after the keiso, Lily first among them. The line of her back was as straight as her natural mother's, but with anger and offended pride rather than Narienneh's effortless dignity.

Last of all—neither keiso nor deisa, nor quite a servant—Leilis rose from her place in the corner of the room. She gathered up the cups and carefully stacked them, six at a time, in the now-empty bowl. Then she threw a glance around the transformed studio. Drops of dark liquor marked the floor where each cup, dipped into the bowl, had scattered its own libation upon the polished wood. The floor would have to be cleaned and polished before the screens and cushions could be removed and the room restored to its ordinary function. Leilis would do this task, for it was not fitting that servants should so much as touch the liquor. And she was not, after all, quite a servant.

During the period of her keiso apprenticeship, Moonflower would sleep on a mat in Rue's room, as she would live every moment with her Elder Sister. But she came alone to Leilis's room even so, late that evening after most of the keiso and all the deisa had gone out about their duties.

"Rue said I should come," she said, in her soft, gentle voice. She had put aside her elaborate keiso overrobe, so she now wore only a simple pale-blue underrobe.

Leilis had been sitting by her hearth, one hand resting on the largest of the cracked hearthstones, watching a small fire burn in the depths of the great fireplace and thinking about nothing. Or trying to think about nothing, while memories she had thought long put aside seemed to her to flicker among the flames. Long inured to loss, long past any natural bitterness... so Leilis had thought herself. She'd watched more than a few deisa assume their keiso robes, but Karah—was it the special exception made for her, or was it the girl herself who had brought Leilis's half-forgotten anguish back to her so strongly? Looking up wordlessly at Karah now—at Moonflower—Leilis thought the girl's inherent sweet-ness must be responsible. But though the memory of her own loss had become so sharp, Leilis somehow could not regret Moonflow-er's ascension to keiso status, or the sense that she herself was in some way regaining a long-numbed capacity of feeling.

Moonflower slipped uncertainly into Leilis's room, though Lei-lis had not yet answered the girl. She drifted a step forward, with a natural grace for which many young keiso would have traded their toes. "Rue," she began, a little uncertainly, but then her voice firmed. She went on, "Rue said you persuaded Narienneh... Mother... to make me keiso. Even though I am only seventeen. She said I should come and thank you. I do thank you. I was afraid of Lily. The keiso... they are not truly like sisters, but even the ones who don't like me don't make me afraid."

"They have the sense to know that harming you would harm the house, and quite possibly bring them dismissal from Cloisonné House and the disdain of the whole flower world. Keiso are expected to be obedient and loyal daughters; keiso who are dis-missed find neither the flower world nor the outside world wel-coming." Leilis waited for a moment for the newest keiso of Cloisonné House to understand the point she was making, then added, "But you were right to be afraid of Lily. Did Rue tell you why?"

"She is—she is Narienneh's natural daughter. Rue said the, the flower world is hard on natural sons because there is so little place for boys or young men here, but usually daughters do well, except that Narienneh—Mother—is blind to Lily's faults and has indulged her too much." Karah sounded a little doubtful.

"Narienneh believes that once Lily has become keiso, she will have no need to be unkind," explained Leilis. "Not all the deisa become keiso. Did Rue tell you that? If they do not receive the command to change their robes—" or were unable to do so for other, stranger, reasons "—then in the end they will become merely servants."

"But keiso never become... become servants?"

Leilis shook her head. "If a keiso is dull or timid or lazy, she may find herself obscure, dependent on her House for everything, and finally forgotten. But keiso are never demoted. So the deisa fear and hate their rivals, where keiso merely dislike and resent theirs. Mother hardly sees what Lily is, and then when she cannot close her eyes, she believes it is merely the natural deisa rivalry that makes Lily cruel."

Moonflower came a step or two farther into the room. "Lily is beautiful. I don't—I don't understand why she should be so—so unkind to—to everybody. To the other deisa."

"Do you think beautiful girls are always kind?"

Karah flinched a little and dropped her eyes.

"Ah, well." Leilis found herself relenting a little. "Lily is different from even the most petty failed keiso. It is her nature to be vicious. She was a sly and cruel child and no doubt she will be a cruel and sly keiso. Some wealthy man will beg for her to be his keimiso, and he will regret it."

Karah looked shocked, and Leilis found herself adding, "Men are often fools, and to their lasting grief choose wives poorly, flower wives as well as true wives. Surely you have seen this. Lily will find a keisonne whom she can handle as a jeweler handles wire, and she will make his life miserable."

"Oh," Karah said in a faint voice.

"At least then she will leave the House. That will be welcome. Though Narienneh believes that one day Lily will inherit Cloisonné House from her and be Mother here in her place." Leilis allowed her tone to express a certain doubt of that possibility. "But certainly you'll have time to establish yourself before Lily changes her robe. Rue will help you. She doesn't care for rivalry and won't put herself forward, but she will take her responsibility as your Elder Sister seriously."

"Yes," said the girl, with a pretty little downward glance, naturally modest. "And Mother will help me, Rue says. And you. I am grateful for your kindness."

Leilis said nothing for a moment. Impatience with the girl's naïvety warred within her with a much more surprising inclination to be gentle. She said at last, her tone only slightly edged, "I'm seldom *kind*. Ask anyone. Anyway, there's little enough I can do for you. Moonflower is your name. You are a keiso now. Look to Rue for support."

"That's not...Rue said..."

"Oh, yes," Leilis said bitterly. "Sometimes I manage to nudge a keiso—if she's already inclined to go the way I think she should. Occasionally I nudge Mother. But I have no authority in this House. Only the merest scraps of influence. Rue didn't tell you about me?"

Moonflower glanced up. She was as appealing when she steeled herself to be direct as when she was diffident—a rare gift. "She told me only a little. Rue said you understood the danger of deisa rivalry. And that the deisa who...who hurt you was sent away. You are—you are beautiful. She did not tell me what the other deisa did to you."

And she was, of course, curious. Leilis wordlessly held out her hand to the child.

Moonflower, looking very serious, took Leilis's hand between both of hers. For a moment she looked only puzzled. Then surprised revulsion came into her face and she jerked away, holding her hands out from her body as though they were contaminated. Confusion came into her expression next, and embarrassment. She held her hands up and looked at her palms, then rubbed them on her thighs and looked in even greater embarrassment back at Leilis.

It took a moment for Leilis to steady her voice, to speak with some semblance of her customary flat indifference. True indifference was not, right now, within her reach. But she was too proud to make a show of loss, of grief. Of the bitterness of failure. She said, "The effect is even stronger when a man touches me." She had to cut the last word off short, or she would have lost control of her tone.

Moonflower cried, with intense sympathy, "But that is horrible! Couldn't Narienneh—couldn't Mother make it better?"

Again, it took a long moment for Leilis to flatten her tone. She said, her tone colder than she'd intended, "All the mages of Lonne tried, one after another. None of them could remove the spell. None of them understood exactly what Blueflax had done, or how she had done it so—powerfully. One of them tried Blueflax as an apprentice, but she had no aptitude. Another said I—said I was myself at fault, that there was some kind of intrinsic magic in me that had got slantwise to the magery in the curse. He thought if he could get rid of the curse I might have aptitude myself, maybe because of my father. But he couldn't, so it didn't matter."

"Your father?"

"He was a mage, a king's mage, from the Laodd. He never had much interest in the left-hand daughter whose birth killed her mother. I didn't know him." Leilis waved an impatient hand. "He's dead now—it doesn't matter." It didn't. No girl born to a keiso was likely to think overmuch of her *father*. In the flower world, mothers and sisters were everything. And, of course, as she was not keiso, Leilis did not truly have those, either. She set her teeth against sharp anger Moonflower surely did not deserve.

"Oh," Moonflower said in a faint voice.

"But even though Mother wouldn't send me away, of course I was ruined for the flower world." Despite everything she could do, Leilis's voice shook a little at the end of this explanation.

"This is *terrible*!"

"I'm accustomed to it," said Leilis. But she had to wait a moment before she could go on smoothly. "It was years ago. But what happened to me made Mother guard you more carefully." Though Leilis had had to work hard to make sure of it, and now found herself even doubting whether anything she'd yet managed could even begin to guard this innocent girl *enough*. Or whether she could stand the burden of Karah's gratitude or trust or whatever it was the girl was offering . . . Suddenly desperate to recover her solitude, Leilis said, "You will be very busy. You have a great deal to learn. So you had best go back to Rue and rest while you have the chance." She knew her tone had gone sharp, even savage.

"Yes," Moonflower said, earnestly, without either apparent offense or fear, and bowed herself gracefully out of Leilis's room.

She would, Leilis thought, make an unforgettable keiso. If only that would be enough...Narienneh might have required prompting to change the girl's robe straightaway, but she shouldn't regret her decision. Though Leilis had no authority or official reason even to consider such questions, though nothing about running Cloisonné House could ever legitimately be her business, Leilis couldn't help but find satisfaction, cold though it might be, in that conclusion.

And if Narienneh remembered that the initial idea had come from Leilis...well, naturally it wouldn't matter, because Leilis could never be anything more than she already was: not quite a servant, yet truly nothing more, either. She threw a knot of wood violently into her fire, scattering burning twigs out onto the hearth. She left them there, guttering on the hearthstones, and went to gaze blindly out the room's small window.

CHAPTER 5

Nemienne sat cross-legged on cold stone, her hands resting on her thighs, her back very straight, surrounded by a heavy, ungiving darkness that pressed down upon her. It was not quite silent: A slow drip of water somewhere far away broke through the otherwise impenetrable boundaries of the dark.

She was trying to call light.

"It is a simple magic, and a necessary one," Mage Ankennes had told her. "You learn the theory of magecraft quickly and this is good. You understand some of what you are taught, which is better still. But what I will begin to teach you now is the foundation of true magic. The featureless dark resists any form a mage tries to give it. It crushes the heart and muffles the mind. You will find that darkness may of itself smother light. Magic requires light and clarity. You must learn to strike through the dark and send it back to hide in its shadows so that you will be able to work."

So far Nemienne had proved unable to do any such thing. She wondered how stupid she would have to be at summoning light before Ankennes would give up on her and send her home. Well, but it didn't matter, she told herself firmly. Because she *would* learn how to do it.

She knew, though she could not see it, that a fat white candle sat on a saucer at her feet. "You may find it helpful to use fire to remind yourself of light," the mage had explained. "Light the candle if you wish. Then, when you have reminded yourself of the heft and quality of fire, blow it out and try again to summon a purer light."

Nemienne had not yet reached for the candle. She had never been frightened of the dark in her life, yet she thought she could become afraid of this darkness. That didn't help. It made her angry. That wouldn't help, either.

Light. She needed to think of light . . . There was the pearly light of the early morning before the sun had quite risen above the mountains; there was the light of the morning sun that glittered on the waves of the harbor. Flames leaping in fireplaces drove away the chill. Slender tapers with tall narrow flames created a mysterious flickering light so sisters could huddle close and tell stories in the dark.

This darkness did not seem to invite companionable stories. Nemienne held her hands in front of her face, opening and closing her fingers. Her hands were completely invisible.

In summer afternoons, heat poured down into the narrow streets of the city and ran, heavy as gold, along the cobbles. At home on those afternoons, she and her sisters would go out onto their balcony to sleep at night. Miande would let the fire in the oven go out, and Father would send out for cold soups or chilled noodles.

Nemienne closed her eyes, fiercely homesick. It was the fault, she thought, of this featureless dark. She could almost believe that when she opened her eyes, she would find herself in the familiar gallery, with the voices of her sisters echoing up to her from the house below.

She opened her eyes to darkness and cold, and the sound of the distant slow dripping of water onto stone. The candle sat before her in its saucer. She reached out to find it, ran a fingertip over the smoothness of its wax and the stiff little wick reassuring at the top. Yes. The mage had shown her how to light a candle: pulling a little fire from the air to light a candle was not difficult. She had done it seven tries out of ten only the previous afternoon. Only now, though she tried and tried, fire refused to bloom along the candle's wick. Nemienne took her hand away from the candle, grimacing.

In the distance, water dripped from some unguessable height into an unseen pool.

Abruptly, the darkness folded back around her, and she found herself sitting on the floor of the mage's workroom. The room was flooded with light and heat, from wide windows and lanterns and a fire roaring in the great fireplace. The darkness, so heavy and impenetrable a moment before, immediately seemed a distant, weightless thing. Nemienne blinked in the light, feeling half drowned by it, wondering how she could have failed to summon such a powerful substance.

Mage Ankennes sat at his writing desk, one elbow propped on its surface. Enkea perched on his knee. He leaned his chin on his palm and regarded Nemienne with a thoughtful expression very like the cat's. "Can you light the candle now?" he asked.

Nemienne blinked again and lowered her gaze to the candle sitting on the floor by her knee. The heat of the fire beat against her face. Looking into the fire, Nemienne borrowed a little of its fierceness. Reaching out, she brushed the wick of the candle with the tip of her finger and, as he had taught her, let the fire run through her mind and into her hand. The candle burst into flame.

"Yes," said the mage thoughtfully.

"It's easy," Nemienne said. "I mean, here it's easy. I don't know why it's different in the dark."

"Hmm. Tell me, what disturbed you most, in that dark place?"

Nemienne thought about this. She said finally, "The dripping water."

"Mmm." The mage studied Nemienne, seeming taken a little by surprise. "The water. Not the dark itself."

"The sound of the water seemed too far away. Hearing the drops fall made the dark seem to stretch out too far. As though there was no end to it anywhere. And the sound seemed too loud for its distance."

"Ah. A good observation. You are a perceptive child. Ordinarily one would expect insight to lead to practical achievement." His tone gave her no hint whether he valued insight more than practical achievement or the reverse, but he offered Nemienne a hand up without apparent disapproval, lifting her effortlessly to her feet. His grip was firm and impersonal, his hand almost fever hot, as though fire burned behind his skin. He said, "That is water that falls from one darkness into another without ever being touched by light. It carries power into the depths of the mountain. You felt that. Were you afraid of that darkness?"

"A little," Nemienne admitted.

"That will pass," said the mage. "You may read, hmm, Kelle Iasodde, I think. The fifth section, where he discusses the eternal darkness and contrasts it with the simple darkness of the ephemeral world. Write me, shall we say, a five-hundred-word essay? About the symbolism of glass and iron and their use in allowing a mage to shift between the worlds of the ephemeral and the eternal."

Nemienne nodded, brightening. Iasodde was hard to understand in places, but that sounded interesting.

The mage smiled a little more widely, missing nothing. He said, "Good. You may try this again tomorrow, then. Or the next day, perhaps. Tonight, the essay. And you may practice calling fire to light candles even in the dark, eh? The ordinary darkness of your room, for now. And practice putting them out again. You're clever enough with fire. Fire is sympathetic to light. Work with the one and the other should come to you more easily."

Nemienne nodded again. "You mean, light and fire are in sympathy with one another because they are similar things? Fire is ephemeral, isn't that what Iasodde says? And light is eternal. Fire brings light, but it isn't really the same thing at all." She had been reading about the principles of sympathetic magic, and finding the theory not quite impenetrably dense.

"Precisely so," said the mage. "Very good. Read the fourth passage of the second chapter of Iasodde—yes, I know you have read it. Read it again. Write a second essay for me comparing fire and light, heat and fire, and sympathy and similarity. You will enjoy that, I think, and you may find that understanding the underlying theory will lead to smoother application in practice. You will learn to hold both light and fire in your mind, a defense against any dark, though it stretches out infinitely far."

Nemienne tried to imagine this. She would far rather write difficult essays than try to summon light into impenetrable darkness, but she didn't say so. But she thought she understood why it was important to learn how. She asked, "Why *did* you build your house in the shadow of the mountain, stretching back into the mountain, if darkness is an enemy of magic?"

Ankennes smiled. "A good question. Your answer?"

"So you would remain familiar with the dark, through continually dealing with it? So you would be constantly reminded of light, through having to keep it in mind against the dark?"

"Both good answers," said the mage approvingly.

As Nemienne had already learned was his habit, he did not give any suggestion whether either guess was actually correct. But he seemed happy with her, so she was tentatively pleased with herself despite her inability to summon light into darkness. Anyway, she would learn that. She would learn *everything*. She already knew— she had known from the first moment in the mage's house—that she belonged here in this house of magic, in the shadow of the mountain and the shadow of magic. She wasn't sure Mage Ankennes was perfectly confident of it; she never knew what the mage was thinking. But she meant to prove it to him by midwinter.

"I am going out this evening," the mage told her. "You will be well enough here alone?"

Nemienne blinked, recalled to the moment. This was a question that should have seemed condescending or insulting, the sort of question you would ask a much younger child, not a girl Nemienne's age. But this house *was* a little confusing, sometimes. Parts of it were even a little frightening—sometimes. Nemienne said firmly, "Yes, of course. I'll be perfectly fine."

"Of course. Besides, Enkea will be here," Ankennes assured her, stroking the cat, who half closed her green eyes and sat up straight on his knee. He picked her up and handed her to Nemienne.

"Of course," said Nemienne, taking the cat and stroking her throat. She was pleased. The cat could always lead Nemienne wherever she wanted to go in the house, although sometimes she wouldn't leave a comfortable chair for any coaxing. Mage Ankennes had commented, shortly after Nemienne had become his apprentice, that Enkea had already been in this house when he'd purchased it. This had startled Nemienne, who in the back of her mind had assumed the mage had lived in this house forever. But no. Less than fifteen years, he'd told her when she asked. So Enkea was an old cat—older than she looked—but not as old as Nemienne's first startled assumption. Though surely it had been a mage who had built this house, mages who had always lived here—she was sure Enkea had always been a mage's cat.

She wandered through the house after the mage had gone, Enkea on her shoulder. The house itself seemed in some ways a test of aptitude for magecraft, like lighting a candle with the memory of fire. Navigating it took practice and a certain amount of luck. Nemienne liked the challenge of it. She thought she could feel herself stretching to meet this challenge, as she had somehow never seemed to meet the ordinary challenges of day-to-day life in her father's house.

Nemienne shifted uneasily at this thought. Was it disloyal to her family to be glad she was in the mage's house, to like the strangeness of it? The solitude? She felt the occasional twinge of homesickness, yes; she missed her sisters, yes. The knowledge that her father was gone was a constant ache at the back of her mind. And yet . . . and yet, it seemed to her that she had fallen into the mage's house as a fish falls into the sea. Already she could not imagine living anywhere else, and though she read them avidly, letters from her sisters seemed like messages from another country.

Ankennes's house always struck Nemienne as oddly outsized, but now, with the mage absent, it seemed even larger than usual. Nemienne had accepted halls that stretched out for surprising distances and turned at odd angles. On the uppermost floor of the house, besides the workroom, she was aware of only two small libraries and a musty scriptorium. Well, *usually* these were all on the uppermost floor. She had never been down to the lowest level of the house because the door at the bottom of the stair was always closed.

On the main floor, Nemienne could almost always find her own room, though occasionally she had to hunt back and forth for its door. The room was small, but she had it all to herself. Nemienne liked her room's small size; it felt very private and enclosed. The quiet of the room, in which she might think or read or study without interruption, had quickly gone from seeming like extraordinary luxury to seeming natural. She found her room now without difficulty and wandered in, glancing around possessively.

The room had a soft rug, tawny gold and brown, on the floor beside the narrow bed, and walls painted in dusty green and taupe. Above the bed was a shelf on the wall, which held the half-dozen books she was reading. Including the dense Iasodde, from which she was to write her essays. Nemienne opened the volume, thinking she might start that at once, but then, finding herself for some reason restless, closed it again and set it aside.

Karah's letter lay on the table. Karah had written with descriptions about lessons and clothing and small details of daily life in a keiso House. Nemienne had read her sister's letter eagerly, but found it hard to write back; she found her own lessons and the details of her own life difficult to put into words.

The kitchen, almost as stable as the workroom or the scriptorium, could usually be found along the hall and down a short flight of stairs from her room. It was a large, friendly room with a heavy iron stove capable of producing prodigious heat. Enkea was often to be found stretched out in the chair nearest the stove, luxuriating in heat that seemed as though it should have been too intense for any reasonable creature. She jumped off Nemienne's shoulder now and leaped up on her chair, purring.

Exploring the ice pantry, Nemienne found cold roast chicken and noodles dressed with a spicy brown sauce and pink pepperberries. Nemienne, wondering where the mage might have gone—

the possibilities seemed endless, and endlessly exotic—ate her supper and fed bits of chicken to Enkea. The cat accepted them with the air of one conveying a favor.

Nemienne washed her supper dishes, but found herself abruptly consumed, as happened at odd moments, by the memory of doing such homely chores in company with Tana and Miande. Tears prickled suddenly behind her eyes. Nemienne put the dishes to drip by the sink and, lifting Enkea back to her shoulder, hastily left the kitchen. She turned into the long hallway that led to the stairs. She meant to go up to one of the libraries and distract herself by looking at the books there, but when she came to the main landing and began to turn to the right, Enkea leaped from her shoulder and disappeared instead down the stairs to the left. The slim cat blurred at once into shadow, save for her white foot, which flashed in the dim light as she moved. She looked back at Nemienne once. Her eyes caught the light of the landing and cast it back like smoky green lanterns.

Nemienne hesitated on the landing. When Enkea did not return, she slowly went down the stairs after the cat. They were not quite level; each step was worn a little in the center where traversing feet had fallen for many, many years. Nemienne wondered whose feet those had been, before her master's. It seemed impossible that ordinary folk had ever dwelled in this house.

The walls held tall candles in sconces, none lit. The walls, like the stairs, were stone. Cold rolled off them in almost visible waves, so that Nemienne was shivering before she had gone halfway down.

At the bottom of the stairs, there was a small landing and a great oaken door bound with brass. Nemienne had seen this before. But this time, the door was standing ajar. Beyond the door was the featureless dark. Enkea was nowhere to be seen.

For what seemed a long time, Nemienne stood on the lowest step and simply looked into the darkness. She *was* afraid of it, and yet...if she learned to call light into the darkness tonight, then tomorrow she could impress Mage Ankennes with her confident skill. She liked that idea. And there was the door, right here, so if she couldn't summon light, she could always back up a few steps and find herself again in the safe—well, familiar—well, sort of familiar—house.

At last she took a candle from a wall sconce and drew fire from the air to light it. This time the flame came without difficulty. It rose off its wick long and white and nearly smokeless, casting a pool of light that poured across the steps and the landing and accented every unevenness and roughly mortared crack in the stone. But the light somehow seemed reluctant to press beyond the door.

Slowly, Nemienne stepped down to the landing and put a hand against the door. It was cold. Even the wood was cold, and the brass almost seemed to *burn* with cold. But the instant she touched it, the door swung wide open to the darkness beyond. Nemienne jumped back. Then she scolded herself—what, did she think the darkness was going to leap out at her?

But the idea didn't seem as silly as it should have. Her heart pounded. But the thought of impressing Mage Ankennes kept her on the landing. And besides...it frightened her, that open door, but it drew her as well: She wanted to run away, but she also wanted to accept the door's invitation. Or challenge. It almost seemed like that. Like a *dare*.

Well...and there was nothing in the darkness but more darkness, and was she a baby, to be afraid of that? Besides, she *did* have a candle—already lit, this time. Lifting it high, Nemienne edged forward, not quite through the doorway. Light, forcing its way into the dark, showed her a floor of stone and walls of fitted brick running featurelessly back as far as she could see. Which was not very far. But far enough to see Enkea. Nemienne felt a rush of confidence at the sight of the slim little cat sitting in the middle of the floor, at the farthest extent of the candlelight, staring ahead into the darkness. When the light touched her, Enkea turned her head and looked at Nemienne over her shoulder, her eyes shining in the dimness.

Then the cat rose to her feet and walked away into the darkness, her tail swaying with evident satisfaction and her white foot flashing as though she carried a tiny lantern of her own. She looked back once more before she vanished, straight at Nemienne. Then she was gone. The cat might as well have spoken aloud: *Follow me.* Surely Enkea, however whimsical she might be, wouldn't try to get Nemienne into trouble?

"Well," Nemienne said aloud, and stopped, startled by the echo of her own voice. She stood hesitating on the threshold between dark and light, between the cold that rolled through the great doorway and the warmth that waited in the friendlier places upstairs. She did not know what drew her, in the end, to step through that doorway: the cat who had gone before her, or simple curiosity, or a wish to impress Mage Ankennes, or some stranger impulsion.

The candle created a small pool of light around Nemienne's feet without in any way seeming to trouble the darkness beyond the door. The darkness itself seemed, in a very few steps, to grow infinite, as though Nemienne had found her way out of the mage's house entirely and into the measureless places within the heart of the mountain. When she turned, she could not see the open door behind her. When she moved experimentally sideways, she could not find the brick wall she had seen close to the door. Indeed, she could not find a wall of any kind, but only space that opened out and out before her as she went on. In the far distance, she thought she might be able to hear a slow dripping of water, falling from stone onto stone.

The candlelight illuminated an area perhaps an arm's length on each side of her, not enough to gain a sense of the place in which she stood. The light she carried with her seemed to create, not a rival for the darkness, nor even a contrast to it, but only an accent that clarified its sweep and power. There was no sign, now, of the cat.

Nemienne had never been afraid of any ordinary dark. But *this* darkness pressed down upon her with the weight of the whole mountain behind it. Even the candle flame seemed to burn lower and flatter and with less light than it had out on the landing. And this time, there was no mage waiting to pull her out of the dark if she could not break it herself. Nemienne found herself setting her teeth against fear. She deliberately tried to relax the tense muscles in her back and neck, with little effect.

Holding the candle before her in both hands, Nemienne looked into its long white flame and tried to think about light. As earlier, however, nothing she did brought more light into the darkness. All she had was the candle she had carried with her.

And then the darkness, pressing ever more heavily and coldly against the fire she carried, put out the candle.

Nemienne made a small sound, not quite a scream. More an embarrassing little squeak of terror. The silence came down on her like a mountain falling. In her alarm, she dropped the candle she held, and then fell to her knees and scrabbled across the stone for it. But it was as though the candle had fallen away into some place more amenable to light, for though she felt all around, she could not find it.

She sat back on her knees after a moment, clinging, barely, to the last remnants of her self-control. Worse than being stuck in the dark was surely being *panicked* in the dark. Even *thinking* about panic made her want to leap to her feet and race into the darkness, and just knowing how foolish that would be didn't help *enough* . . . She realized she was gasping in short, frightened breaths and tried to make herself breathe more slowly. Telling herself she was being stupid helped a little. Stubborn pride helped more.

Nemienne thought of light as hard as she could. She was no longer trying to call light into the darkness, she realized. She had given up on that. She was thinking instead of the warmly lit life she had left behind when she had stepped through the mage's doorway. Getting to her feet, Nemienne thought hard of light and stepped forward blindly into the dark.

CHAPTER 6

In Lonne, dusk was invariably the correct time for an evening engagement to begin, though this meant, naturally, that the actual proper hour changed as the length of the days waxed and waned through the year. Taudde knew this. However, obeying Lord Miennes's instructions, he deliberately aimed to arrive a little late. Around him the lamps of the city, massive globes atop tall iron poles, were flickering to life. The lamps glowed with a pale green light through the long hours of the night. The mist that curled slowly down the mountain's flanks and threaded through the city streets took on an unsettling greenish tint in that light. Taudde would have preferred the natural light of the moon and stars, but that silvery light was masked by the city lamps.

Benne drove because in Lonne it was considered horribly inappropriate for a man of quality to touch his horse's reins himself. The big man had found a small but rather fine carriage, dark gray, with silver scrollwork on the doors. The horse was a young gelding, dappled gray, with high flashy action and a seafoam-white mane and tail. At first inclined to think this display excessive, upon arrival at Miennes's house Taudde saw that any less showy an equipage would have seemed altogether shabby in the company the lord was keeping this evening.

Three other carriages waited along the drive. Two were large, elaborate affairs. The doors and window frames of the first carriage were inlaid with gold and pearl. Four matched chestnut horses stood before it. The second was plainer but had the sleek look of quality; the blood bays harnessed to it were finer than the chestnuts. The last carriage, of the same style as Taudde's new acquisition, appeared to be made entirely of rare, expensive ebony from southernmost Miskiannes. Complicated mother-of-pearl inlay spun a delicate pattern across the black doors, and the fine black mare that drew it had pearls set into her harness and dripping from her bridle. Against such display, the silver on the doors of Taudde's carriage no longer seemed quite so extravagant.

Normally comfortable making an entrance into any company, tonight Taudde could not help but feel self-conscious. A servant, blankly oblivious to his tardiness, admitted him to the house and then to a small dining chamber. Here, Miennes, Ankennes, and six other men lounged at their ease around a carved table.

All of the men looked up when Taudde entered the room, some amused but others clearly annoyed. Taudde had the impression that they had been arguing about some issue that had tempers running high. He also guessed that, though some of them were happy to have an interruption, others were not.

Oddly, although it was his house, Miennes had not taken the place at the head of the table, but rather the first place to the left. He said with sleek satisfaction, "Come in, come in—my lords, this is the foreign lord whom I had mentioned."

Taudde took a step forward and paused. The place at the head of the table was occupied by a young man with a thin, strong-featured face and elegant hands. He had dark, serious eyes under straw-pale brows and a rather arrogant mouth; his hair, a shade lighter than his brows, was long, straight, and caught back at the base of his neck with a clip of jet and gold. He wore black cut through by an abstract pattern of saffron.

It was that particular saffron shade that allowed Taudde to recognize the young man: This must surely be one of the princes of Lonne. A son of *Geriodde Nerenne ken Seriantes* himself, and some remarkable tide of chance had cast *this* young man at Taudde's feet? For this prince of Lirionne must, without doubt, be

Miennes's intended target. It was impossible that a Seriantes prince should be at this table, and yet Miennes's target be some other man. It seemed likely that Miennes would demand Taudde do murder upon a son of the very *Dragon of Lirionne*. The prospect all but stopped breath.

Taudde had once promised his grandfather, swearing on his own father's grave, that he would never seek personal vengeance against the King of Lirionne. The Treaty of Brenedde specifically forbade such acts, and Taudde, of all men, was surely required to abide by its terms. In the note he'd left for his grandfather, he'd sworn again that vengeance had no part in his reasons for coming to Lonne.

But now this. This.

And Miennes had arranged for Taudde to walk into this room blindly. Taudde fought to set a mask of grave apology over the storm of anger and grief that shook him—it felt like trying to hold back striking lightning with a silken veil—and walked forward to make his bow to the company. He ended, however, by dropping to one knee and bowing his head to the prince. "Forgive me, eminence," he said, in his best court tone, layered with bland respect and apology, "I see I am behind-hand in my arrival. I am, as Lord Miennes has said, a foreigner, and I regret I did not realize Lord Miennes meant to specify so precisely the hour in the invitation he did me the honor to extend. I am devastated to have put so noble an assembly to any difficulty."

"My fault entirely!" Miennes exclaimed, smiling. "I should have taken greater pains to be clear, knowing I spoke to a foreigner. Especially given the distinction of my guests. I fear I did not warn Lord Chontas Taudde ser Omientes of the company to which he would be made known this evening."

"What can I be but grateful of the honor Lord Miennes affords me?" Taudde said at once.

The prince glanced at Miennes and then back at Taudde. An eyebrow lifted, and then his disapproving expression eased toward a smile, so that he looked suddenly both younger and far more welcoming. He said, "Of course, Lord Chontas. We have not been discomposed by any such small error. We are glad of your company. Please, sit." His voice was a rather light tenor, but with a barely discernible harsh edge behind it, whether temper or simply tension Taudde could not tell.

Taudde rose to his feet, bowed, and took the open place at the end of the left-hand curve of the table. A boy in a brown robe brought him a bowl of clear broth scattered with pink pepperberries. Taudde tasted it, pretending absorption in the broth while he studied the assembly. There was something...something about the way everyone present oriented toward the prince...

Ah. In fact...in fact, this prince was, Taudde guessed at last, not merely just *one* of the princes. He must be Tepres Nemedde ken Soriantes, the only *legitimate* son remaining to the King of Lirionne. The *heir* of the Dragon of Lirionne was Miennes's target. Taudde much doubted Miennes had ever made so fraught a demand of any of his other blackmail victims, though they were no doubt many.

Taudde shut his eyes for a moment, trying not to let anything of the storm within show on his face. At least any oddity in his expression or manner would surely be put down to shock at finding himself in such exalted company.

He had intended to find some way to evade whatever trap Miennes and Mage Ankennes had laid for him. He'd meant to find a way to punish the arrogance of both lord and mage if he could, or simply to slip quietly out of Lonne if they proved too clever and well-guarded. Now...well...well, perhaps Taudde might bring himself to perform this one little service for them after all. He drew a slow, steadying breath and opened his eyes, re-orienting himself to the company he had found himself so unexpectedly keeping.

The three younger men were, Taudde guessed, companions of the heir. To the prince's right there was an older man in the black of the King's Own, but with deep purple embroidery across the shoulders of his overrobe: a personal guard of the prince, of high family himself, Taudde guessed. Taudde suspected that the other older man was the prince's tutor. He had heard the man's name, though he could not at once recall it, and he was almost certain he had heard that the prince was much inclined toward his tutor's company. Opposite Taudde was Ankennes, in the black underrobe and long white overrobe of a Lonne mage. Taudde gave him a wary nod.

"You are from Miskiannes, we understand, Lord Chontas," one of the young men near Taudde commented. "So, tell us, what does Miskiannes think of the coming spring? Does Miskiannes await the solstice with eagerness or with dismay? And whom does Miskiannes support in the conflict?" The young man asked this question with a raised-eyebrow look directed not at Taudde but toward another of the young men. Clearly it was a continuation of the earlier argument.

"Ah..." Taudde did not dare declare that he favored Kalches, but he could not bring himself to pretend support for Lirionne. "Miskiannes awaits the spring with trepidation, I believe, my lord, and with relief that we are widely separated from any possible field of battle and thus need not declare partiality." There: That was both true and unobjectionable.

"Why trepidation? If you're so far removed from battle, why should you care at all?" the other young man demanded.

"Why, whoever might win or lose, war disrupts trade," Taudde pointed out as though surprised, borrowing for a moment his favorite uncle's opinions and manner.

"Well, whatever else you may say of Miskiannes, it is above all a nation of *tradesmen*," commented the first young man, a trifle snidely.

"All nations are founded on trade," Taudde said, a very Miskiannes opinion. "Do you yourself await the coming spring with eagerness, then, my lord?" He didn't add his uncle's opinion, from time to time forcefully expressed, of excitable young nobles who considered adventure more important than profit.

"The treaty merely deferred hostilities," began the young man.

"A welcome deferral," murmured the prince. Everyone at the table naturally quieted to hear him. "Fifteen years without open violence; half a generation for tempers to settle...Most likely they have not settled enough. But it was the best that could be won, at the time."

"And hard won at that," one of the older men rebuked the snide young man. "You young men don't know what those days were like, or how hard the Dragon worked to force that treaty upon the ice-hearted Kalchesene people, or you would be far less ready to decry Miskiannes's elevation of trade above warfare."

"Kalches can't possibly *win*, however dedicated they may—" began the young man, his tone hot.

The older man cut him off. "When we have spent another generation or two of young men's blood winning one stony field after another, you may find yourself less inclined to pursue victory!"

"Those fields, however thin and stony, rightfully belong to us!" snapped the young man. "Would *you* pursue *defeat*?"

Taudde set his teeth, lifted his goblet, stared intently into the straw-pale wine, and pretended hard to a neutrality he was far from feeling.

"Better, perhaps, to pursue a quiet spring," murmured the prince, cutting off what had promised to be a sharpening argument. "Though there seems little hope of it."

There was a tense pause. Taudde certainly did not break it, though he could not prevent himself glancing in surprise at Prince Tepres. He would not have expected the Dragon's very *heir*, of all men, to express a wish for peace. The Seriantes Dragons had always considered that the lands to the north should by rights belong to Lirionne.

Enescedd might be protected by its wide enchanted forests, through which armies could not march; and Miskiannes by wealth and distance and most of all by the fortunate chance of having Enescedd between itself and Lirionne. But Kalches was protected only by its mountains, and those had never been enough. However hard the kings of Kalches fought to defend their people and their lands, they had nevertheless been forced to yield and then yield again, until now, since the Treaty of Brenedde, Kalches was able to claim less than half the territory it had once possessed.

And now the Dragon's very *heir* wished for peace? If any Seriantes had ever wished for anything but conquest, Taudde could not recall his tutors mentioning it.

"So," the third of the young men said at last, breaking the tension, "such interesting weather we're having this year!"

Everyone laughed, the unpleasant young man a trifle reluctantly. The prince gave the humorist a slight nod of approval and sealed the change of topic by adding with dry amusement, "Whoever would expect cold breezes in the winter?" He turned deliberately toward Taudde. "Though in Miskiannes, perhaps, one would not?"

"Certainly not as you have here, eminence," Taudde agreed. He set his goblet down again, gently.

"Oh, well, it's not bad yet, but I promise you, Lord Chontas, plenty of snow will shortly come down off the mountains!" said the friendly, outspoken young man. "Ice will freeze down all the walls of the Laodd; it will glitter like the purest diamond. It is a most imposing sight."

"Oh, imposing!" The remaining young man waved a dismissive hand. "Yes, the Laodd is *imposing*, if that pleases you. But for beauty in the winter, one must ride through the candlelight district. All the keiso Houses and aika establishments sculpt ice into flowers and birds and fantastic creatures. At night the theaters hang out lanterns bright as the moon, and the keiso have the mages make them streamers of colorful fire to float in the wind—is that something you do, Ankennes?"

The mage smiled. "I have been known to make such toys." He had not seemed disturbed by the previous argument, and seemed equally comfortable with the present flippancy. His voice was smooth and deep, rich with humor, with very little trace of the coldness Taudde had heard in it the previous day. "It pleases the keiso, and is that not greatly to be desired?"

The other men laughed and agreed with this comment. A second course, of doves cooked with leeks and cream, was brought in on small copper-colored plates.

"But we have neglected all the courtesies!" the young man with the sense of humor said to Taudde as the course was served. He bowed with a hand over his heart. "Lord Chontas, I am Koriadde. To my constant embarrassment, this is my younger brother, Kemes Haliande ken Nemelle."

His brother, the man who had mentioned the candlelight district, aimed a mock blow at him, which Koriadde blithely ignored. He continued, "Allow me to make known to you these others of this gathering: Jerinte Naliadde ken Miches—" He indicated the third of the young men, the aggressive one who thought all lands belonged to Lirionne. "And this is Jeres Geliadde, the prince's foremost bodyguard, and Liedde Masienne ken Lochelle, his tutor. Miennes informs us you are acquainted with Mage Ankennes, who is pleased to do small favors for the flowers of Lonne."

Taudde bowed gravely to them all. "Most often I am known as Taudde. 'Chontas' is a very common name in the south. There are five other scions of my house named Chontas, which I fear leads to some confusion. I am," he added, lying blandly now that he had laced sufficient truth through his lies, "as perhaps Lord Miennes has informed you, traveling on behalf of my uncle's interests. As I seem likely to spend this winter in Lonne, I hope I will have every opportunity to witness firsthand the beauty of Lonne's famous flower world, of which I have heard tales all my life."

There was a general murmur of gratification. The heir himself looked mildly amused. "So, though you have traveled a good deal, you have nowhere else encountered a custom comparable to our flower world?"

Taudde heard in this query, which indeed everyone quieted to hear, a faint undertone of mockery. He answered seriously, "I have not, eminence. Not in Miskiannes nor Enescedd nor even in southern Lirionne, where I lived for a time several years ago. I suppose only the wealth and age of Lonne is able to support such a custom."

"We say in Lonne that we are simply accustomed to appreciate beauty."

There was, Taudde thought, definitely a trace of mockery in the prince's voice...but he almost thought it was self-mockery. He was surprised. He had not expected, well, depth, from the Dragon's heir. But there were undertones layered all through the young man's voice, and not all of them suggested simple hauteur. Taudde wanted to make the prince speak again and listen to those under-tones. But Prince Tepres did not seem much given to casual talk.

"Surely you do not spend all your time making ornaments for the keiso, however," Taudde said to Mage Ankennes, to fill the pause. "There are no mages in Miskiannes, you are aware. Lord Jerinte is right to say that Miskiannes is a country of tradesmen. I would add, it is a land of farmers and country gentlemen. Perhaps we have less need of magic there."

"The land itself contains less magic," the mage said, smiling. To a bardic sorcerer, his tone contained suggestions of fraught acquaintance, but less-trained men would hear nothing. Taudde noted the mage's smooth deceptiveness for future reference. "For powerful magic, one cannot do better than the wild heights or the wilder sea."

"Then Lonne is ideally situated," Taudde observed. "And yet I should not have thought either the mountains or the sea would yield amiably to the will of men, even mages. What is it you call that great mountain of yours? Kerre Maraddras?"

"The Heart of Darkness," said the mage. "Yes." There was an odd note to his tone; Taudde wasn't quite able to decipher the undertone. "Kerre Maraddras is strong, but difficult," the mage went on. "Its darkness lies very close to Lonne. But then, darkness always lies behind all that mages do, ready to engulf and ruin our works. Yet, is that any less true of the ordinary works of men than of magic?"

"A grim view," protested Koriadde.

"Not at all—it was well said!" exclaimed the prince's tutor. "Indeed, the sweep of history clearly shows us how eager men are to tear down what their own ancestors before them built with such effort."

There was a slight pause as everyone avoided looking at Prince Tepres. However, if the prince connected this comment with the recent deaths of his brothers, there was no sign of it. Even in Kal-ches, everyone knew that tale of rebellion and suspected usurpation, of treachery and death. But the prince merely leaned his chin on his palm. His eyes had narrowed a little, but he listened with no sign of disapproval.

It occurred to Taudde that the young heir was by no means unacquainted with death and grief. He wondered if this might go some way, perhaps, toward explaining the prince's surprising desire to pursue peace rather than victory.

When he had heard the tale of the elder princes' executions, Taudde had felt only righteous outrage and horror against their father. Now he was forced to think of Prince Tepres as well. This was not comfortable. He ate a bite of creamed leeks, grimly.

"Ordinary men seldom think of what they do in those terms, I suspect," Ankennes answered the prince's tutor. "I believe the exigencies of magecraft are more clearly evident. At least, men who are not mages seldom appear to see the darkness hiding behind their actions until it is very late in the day—too late, indeed, to remedy even the most grievous error." But, as the third course was brought in, the mage smiled and turned to welcome it, dismissing this bleak observation.

The course consisted of a whole fish stuffed with bread crumbs and minced vegetables, its scales replaced with parchment-thin slices of white radish. Miennes greeted the murmurs of approval with a deprecating wave of his hand and the information that his kitchens were run by a woman who had been a keiso in her youth and had then managed a restaurant for several years.

"Oh—that would be Disanna, who was Starlily and then owned the Crested Dragon," said Koriadde in startled recognition. "She is a friend of my mother's—I had heard that she had taken private employ! I hope for your sake you are paying her a very generous wage, my lord, as otherwise I shall feel tempted to hire her away from you and I surely cannot afford such a lavish expense."

Miennes assured the young man he was paying the woman very generously, at which Koriadde pretended to be extravagantly disappointed.

"A friend of your mother's?" Taudde asked, before he could quite prevent himself. It did not, however, appear to be a difficult topic, for Koriadde seemed perfectly comfortable.

"My mother is keiso, of course," he said, and his brother Kemes—half-brother, Taudde now realized—leaned over and said something to him in a low voice that made Koriadde laugh.

Prince Tepres had said nothing through any of this. But Taudde caught a faintly wistful look in his dark eyes and wondered whether possibly the heir of Lirionne sometimes wished that he, like his surviving brothers and like Koriadde, was keiso-bred rather than a legitimate son of his father. That was *another* uncomfortable thought. Taudde tried not to grimace. He did not *want* to like, or approve of, and certainly not *pity* the prince. Especially as he had no doubt Miennes meant to use him as a weapon against the young heir.

But it was better not to think about such possibilities. Not just now. Not when he needed to pay attention to the present moment. The future would hold what it held. For this moment, Taudde set to studying and deliberately courting the company. He didn't dare use even the merest trace of sorcery, but he didn't scruple to use all his bard's tricks of tone and attitude; this was a courtship at which he meant to succeed.

Of the men his own age, Koriadde was the friendliest, and his brother Kemes also easy-natured. The prince himself spoke seldom, and yet Taudde suspected he might be courted through his friends and be inclined to favor someone whom Koriadde liked. Taudde rather suspected Koriadde was probably more discerning and a good deal less casual than his easy manner suggested.

"I have," Taudde said at last, over a course of mussels and the finest Enescene black rice, "lived in Lonne for some weeks now, and yet I have not visited the candlelight district in all that time. All this talk has made it clear to me that I must repair this oversight. I have heard mentioned the name of Cloisonné House as perhaps the finest of all the Houses of the flower world. Perhaps some of you would do me the kindness to accompany me there as my guests?"

Only a foreigner, Taudde suspected, would have had the presumption to thus issue an invitation to the heir himself and his companions. The young men might have accepted easily if they had been alone; now they all looked, cautiously, to their prince.

The heir of Lirionne leaned an elbow on the table and studied Taudde, evidently bemused. Jeres, on his right, touched his arm and murmured to him. Whatever he said, the prince dismissed it with a small gesture and a frown.

Taudde, shamelessly trading on his foreign status, said, "Eminence, if I have offended, I can only plead unfamiliarity with the customs of Lonne and ask forgiveness."

"We are not offended," the prince said at once. "Indeed...I am even inclined to accept your generous invitation." He slid a glance toward his bodyguard, met Jeres's scowl, and half smiled. "Perhaps as early as the evening after next, if that should please you. You might make the reservation in your own name. You might perhaps fail to mention mine."

Taudde, judging that the prince did not care for a fulsome show, acceded to this suggestion with restrained gratification.

Mage Ankennes, naturally, declared that he would certainly attend. The tutor begged to be excused on the grounds of a prior engagement. Jeres Geliadde scowled and said nothing, but once the prince had granted his approval, his young companions all seemed genuinely pleased by the plan.

Miennes gave Taudde a look of heavy satisfaction. Later, when the gathering dispersed, he held Taudde back with a glance. Mage Ankennes, too, lingered while the younger men and the prince's tutor departed. "You understand what you are to do? You have sufficient skill?" Miennes said to Taudde once they were safely away. "I fear it will not be easy. The heir does not trust lightly."

Taudde inclined his head in acknowledgment. "His trust, fortunately, is not specifically required for his death by sorcery. I presume that is what you want from me?" He waited, curious to see whether Miennes, consummate courtier that he undoubtedly was, would be willing to confirm so bald a statement.

The Lonne lord in fact hesitated. But Mage Ankennes said, unsmiling, "Of course. You are young, but surely your...uncle... would not have sent an incapable man to Lonne on his behalf. You are indeed capable?"

Taudde looked at the mage with dislike. He answered deliberately, "Despite my youth, you may accept my assurance that I am not unskilled. My grandfather began teaching me bardic sorcery hardly later than my grandmother began teaching me to talk." This was true, but Taudde meant the strong undertones of arrogance he laid beneath his words to disguise the *extent* of that truth. He thought this strategy worked to deceive Miennes, but Ankennes... he thought Ankennes might have heard the truth Taudde had meant to conceal. Taudde saw the covetousness behind the mage's opaque eyes. He would not allow himself to flinch, but he had to suppress a shudder.

"Well, skill and strength are exactly what one would expect in a young man sent here in this season," Miennes said, slyly pleased. "And was our aim indeed your own, first? You must have had *some* such aim, I should think, to enter Lonne on the eve of the coming solstice."

"It was not," Taudde said, and continued smoothly, "Though I should hardly object to your immediate goal, to be sure. I might wonder what purpose you have, however, in sowing confusion and disorder in Lonne... on the very eve, as you say, of the solstice."

Lord Miennes only smiled. "My young friend, you needn't concern yourself with our motives. I assure you, they are sufficient."

Taudde inclined his head. He wondered whether Miennes might be so close to the throne he thought he might seize power himself. More likely he was closely attached to one of the left-hand princes. Or possibly Lord Miennes meant to sow disorder in order to quell it and thus gain the favor of the people, or the king, or both. He might be inclined toward such subtle maneuvers.

Taudde certainly assumed the lord meant to use the heir's death, in one way or another, to gain power in Lonne. What Mage Ankennes hoped to gain was much less clear. *His* goal seemed unlikely to be simple political power.

He said, keeping his tone calm and flat, "Well, I care little enough, to be sure, and I must confess that your goal pleases me. Save, of course, that it seems quite likely you mean to use me to lay the blame for the prince's death on Kalches. I am not so certain *that* pleases me."

"Indeed, you mistake us!" Miennes exclaimed. His smile widened. "No, no, my friend! Far better if no one knows the manner in which the prince comes to his, ah, fate. Indeed, *far* better!"

Taudde, looking steadily at Mage Ankennes, made a noncommittal sound. He already guessed that Miennes wanted to keep his new pet bardic sorcerer for future use, not spend him all at once. But he wanted the *mage* to speak. Almost anything would do: a protest, a reassurance, even a threat. It was the deep-buried undertones of his voice Taudde wanted to hear. He doubted even an accomplished mage of Lonne would understand how his voice might reveal deceit and offer hints of his true intentions.

"We do not wish to prompt a wide outcry," said the mage, responding to Taudde's silent pressure. "Nor to encourage violent reprisals against anyone. We wish merely to end the dominance of the Seriantes line. The quiet death of the Dragon's last remaining legitimate son should achieve this aim. What replaces Seriantes power hardly seems your concern."

"Save that, I assure you, young man, *we* have no interest in furious acquisitions to the north!" Lord Miennes added. "A waste of gold and blood and time, all far better invested elsewhere! Indeed, the attitudes of Miskiannes have much to recommend them!"

Taudde inclined his head as though reassured. In fact, though he thought Lord Miennes meant what he said, he was almost certain that Mage Ankennes... Well, he did not precisely suspect Ankennes of outright lying. But an underlying hard resolve beneath the mage's words made him wonder whether, when Ankennes said *end the dominance of the Seriantes line*, he really meant *destroy every root and branch of the Seriantes line*. And that implied a hatred that went beyond what even *Taudde* felt for the Seriantes Dragons. Except he could hear no such depths of hatred in the mage's voice. But what save deep loathing could lead to such a broad and brutal goal?

But he did not have time or leisure to consider that question now. He said, in a neutral tone, addressing both men, "If I do this for you, I will be free to go about my own business? You understand, I will not under any compulsion stay in Lonne beyond the solstice."

"Of course. I—we—should never expect that of you," Miennes assured him, deceit so clear in his voice that he might have simply said out loud, *No, you are mine, I will never release you from my hand.* "You are perfectly correct. You did very well, setting up that engagement of yours to follow this one," the lord concluded. "Very clever." He patted Taudde on the arm, a possessive gesture that made Taudde set his teeth. If he noticed Taudde's distaste, it didn't trouble him. He went on smoothly, "I presumed even the heir himself might find himself vulnerable to a man of your…heritage and training. I surmise I was correct."

Taudde nodded. The Dragon's heir indeed seemed vulnerable to a creative sorcerer, a vulnerability that was one reason for the Seriantes ban against bardic sorcerers. However—"The ban," he began.

"You need not concern yourself with the ban," Ankennes murmured in his deep voice. "I will craft a protection about you and above you. Other mages of Lonne will find it far more difficult to perceive your workings than would ordinarily be the case. You understand?"

"Certainly that will make this task far more straightforward," Taudde murmured. "I thank you for your shield. Ah—difficult, you say. But, I surmise, not—"

The mage smiled, an expression both amused and cold. "Not wholly impossible, no. I recommend a continuing discretion."

Taudde inclined his head. So Mage Ankennes would set protections round about to ensure that he'd be able to do the sorcery they required. No doubt the mage would take other precautions to see to it, and to prevent his escape afterward. But the conspirators were sure he would do their murder, first. A Kalchesene bardic sorcerer? Of course they were sure. The heir's death would leave the Dragon himself without legitimate sons…grieving, if Geriodde Nerenne ken Seriantes was actually capable of grief, which Taudde personally doubted, given what he had done to his own elder sons. But even so, the death of his last remaining heir would unquestionably deliver a devastating blow to the King of Lirionne. Taudde could hardly accustom himself to the idea that he himself could be the one to deliver such a blow to the Seriantes Dragon. It was a vengeance he had never looked to gain, and it had not merely fallen into his path but had been forced into his hands.

He said slowly, "I will do this." He said it with conviction, though he had not yet actually decided whether he would do it or not. But already he had an idea of how he *could* do it. And he truly thought he might, the treaty and his vow to his grandfather notwithstanding. Could he truly claim these conspirators had forced him to break the treaty and that vow? Or would he act, if he did, simply because he chose to, for himself and for Kalches? He felt a little ill with the uncertainty.

Satisfied, unaware either of the deceit or of the confusion, Miennes gave Mage Ankennes a sideways glance and then nodded to Taudde. "I am confident we all understand one another." He lifted a hand, adding, "Allow me to escort you to your conveyance, my young friend."

Taudde's carriage waited merely a dozen steps down the drive. The wind came gently from the sea and over the city, carrying the scents of salt and sand and the myriad close smells of the city. It ruffled the horse's white mane. The moon shone palely overhead, muted by the greenish magelight that illuminated the city.

Taudde stepped into the carriage, settled into its well-cushioned seat, tipped his head back, and closed his eyes. He longed for the midnight skies of Kalches, where in the winter the brilliant darkness of the sky came so close to the endless snow that each star sounded a clear and separate note on the theme of the night. He almost told Benne to drive on, along the Kemsennes River and up into the mountains that framed the city. There in the heights, the stars would at last become visible.

But he knew very well that the chance of such an easy escape was purely illusory. If the conspirators were not confident they had a leash on him, they would not have let him go.

Besides, if he fled Lonne tonight, he would never know whether he might, after all, have struck a sharp blow against the Dragon of Lirionne. Though in some ways...in some ways, in fact, never having to know the answer to that question was a greater temptation to flight than getting away from Miennes. Or even from Ankennes.

But regardless of the pull of the sea, how could he leave Lonne without at least *considering* whether he might rather comply with rather than avoid the demand Miennes had set on him?

Taudde allowed Benne to drive him back to his rented house, but he found he could not bear its close confines. Not tonight, of all nights he had spent in Lonne. He opened the shutters of his window and stood gazing out into the night. It seemed to him he could hear the ceaseless murmur of the sea, though this far from the shore no sound of the waves should have been audible.

Though he was bone weary, Taudde found himself unable to be still. His flute was in his hand, though he had no memory of reaching for it. He hesitated a moment to recover prudence, and another moment to try at least for good sense. But then, he had a murder to arrange...at least to consider arranging. He had every reason, indeed nearly a requirement, to dispense with good sense.

So he allowed himself to lift the flute to his lips. He played himself into the shadows and the night breeze and the mist. He did not trouble overmuch with subtlety. If he would test Ankennes's protection, why not at once? So when he clambered out the window, he did not fall, and when he reached the cobbles of the street at last, his boots on the stone made no sound. Turning away from the house, back into the dimly lit streets, he strode toward the sea.

As Taudde walked west toward the sea, the streets became gradually narrower and rougher, and the residences that lined them smaller and more crowded. Wealth ran like water down from the mountains toward the sea, so the people of Lonne said, growing shallow as it neared the docks. Taudde bent his steps north of west, not quite toward the sea but toward the Niarre River.

By this time of evening, the candlelight district had come to graceful life. Aika establishments had hung out blue paper lanterns shaped like flowers and silver ones shaped like crescent moons, and theaters were lighting the elaborate candelabra fixtures that arched over their doors. One restaurant after another was putting back its shutters and setting out lanterns—plain ones—to illuminate its sign, and the keiso Houses were alight with round, white porcelain lamps.

In contrast to the flower world, the Paliante was somnolent. Nearly all the traffic across the bridge was moving toward the candlelight district and the residential areas of the city farther south. But Taudde thought there were as yet enough late travelers through the streets of the Paliante that his presence there should go unremarked.

Taudde found the shop of oddments and instruments with less trouble than he'd expected, for all he'd been there only once. It was closed and locked. More than locked: shut fast with some mage-crafted spell that wove back and forth across its entire façade. For a moment, Taudde considered trying to unweave the guarding spell. But it was complex and powerful. He suspected that any attempt he made in that direction would fail of Ankennes's injunction in favor of "continuing discretion."

Instead, Taudde coaxed open the simpler lock of the neighboring tailor's establishment with the merest whisper of melody and stepped in among racks of finished clothing and bolts of cloth. The shutters at the front of the shop were closed fast, so he felt it should be safe to play a soft fall of moonlight through the tailor's shop—enough to find his way among the racks to the back of the shop. Here, he paused and studied the wall that separated the tailor's shop from the neighboring shop of oddments and instruments.

The wall was plaster, painted a pale bird's egg blue. Laying a hand upon it, Taudde let his awareness settle into and past the paint and the plaster. He found no web of magery within the wall, only timbers and stonework, and then on the far side more plaster.

Taudde withdrew his awareness and paused again, considering. He might yet leave the Paliante—return to his rented house, even make a real attempt to slip the conspirators' chain and get out of Lonne entirely.

Instead, he took out his flute once more. From it, he drew a music that melted through the plaster and wove among the interstices between the stones of the wall, that made at last a way through the solid wall that he might follow. Then he stood for a time on the other side while the sorcery faded, until he could remember how to move muscle and bone.

He waited another long moment, listening. He heard nothing. He perceived no sign that any Lonne mage had noticed the whisper of bardic sorcery through their city. Would he, if any did? And was there any point to asking himself such questions after he'd already chosen to risk this trespass? That last question, at least, answered itself.

Taudde made his way carefully to the rear of the cluttered shop. Yes, there was the table he recalled, with all manner of tools and fittings ready to hand for a craftsman. He got out his candlelighter, lit the waiting lamp to illuminate the table, absently pulled the nearest chair over to the table, and sat down to look over the materials available. He could already hear, in his mind, the instruments he wanted to make. Pipes—two sets, of course: one set pitched to open the way and the other to follow. He already knew their tones and voices, pure as the crystalline air in the high mountains . . . He reached, not even consciously looking, after a suitable blank for the first pipe, and then for a blade that would let him turn the ivory blank he'd selected into the pipe he already held, whole and perfect, in his mind.

Lost in his craftworking, Taudde found himself surprised by the dawn. He glanced up at last, surprised by the dazzle as the rising sun found its way through chinks in the shutters of the high windows and fell across the table. Reaching up, he pushed the shutters back. Then he looked down at the work of his hands, revealed by the vivid light of the sun.

He had worked through the night with intense concentration abetted by the occasional lift of sorcery. This was not the first time he'd lost himself in craftwork, but the resulting instruments nevertheless astonished him. He thought he had never made finer instruments. Ironic, that *these* should be a masterwork. What would his grandfather say to the use of uncommon skill toward such an end? Though...given the approaching solstice, he might actually say something on the order of *Good work, boy.* Probably *Good work, boy, considering you're a fool.*

Taudde let his breath out and steadfastly turned his attention toward more immediate matters. Two completed sets of twin pipes lay before him. Each set was composed of six pipes, three matched pairs per set. The smallest were the length of a man's forefinger, the longest perhaps twice so long. Taudde examined his work by the morning's clear light. The craftsmanship, he judged, evaluating the instruments with an objective eye, was indeed very fine. And the sorcery threaded through the instruments...He let it resonate through his hands and his heart and thought that the sorcery, too, should prove adequate.

The table was littered with bits of cut wire, shavings of ivory and horn, discarded fittings, and the odd blank that had not proven amenable to the crafting. Taudde tucked the finished pipes into a belt pouch and began to clean up all this random debris. The shop's proprietor had seemed shrewd. Probably he knew his shop as he knew the fit of his own boots. Even so...the supply of craft materials in this shop was so generous that possibly the proprietor would not realize some of his blanks were missing. Or at least not at once. Even a little delay would be sufficient. Or at least helpful.

Taudde swept the last of the shavings into a different pouch for later disposal and tried to remember precisely where the chair had been resting before he'd pulled it over to the table. And had the table lamp always been at this exact angle?

He had no time to decide, because at that moment—defying the general rule that late nights in the candlelight district should be

followed by late mornings in wealthy districts such as the Paliante—
the mage spell that guarded the door and front wall of the shop
suddenly dissolved, and Taudde heard the simultaneous metallic
clink of a key being inserted into the door's lock.

Taudde didn't panic. Not exactly. But for one shocked instant,
he froze. For that instant, he was certain that the shop's proprietor
was going to step into the shop and find Taudde still standing there
like a fool, speechless and motionless.

The door swung open and the proprietor came in. Taudde, duck-
ing sideways and down, got just enough of a glimpse to recognize
the man. He dropped to his knees, out of sight behind a bank of
shelves that held more blanks and a large collection of clay jars
and opaque glass bottles. Some of the bottles rattled gently as his
abrupt motion rocked the shelves, and Taudde held his breath, listening intently. He could hear the proprietor moving unhurriedly
about the shop and began to believe that he was, for the moment,
undiscovered. This was good, although it did not answer the larger
question of how he was going to get out of the shop. Bardic sorcery
was out of the question; he certainly couldn't play a single note
without the proprietor hearing, and any suggestion of sorcery connected with this shop...No. It would be very bad to have anyone
make *that* connection.

Taudde silently uncorked one of the bottles on the shelf in front
of him and sniffed at its contents. Something sharp, astringent...
familiar. He identified the smell after a moment: a cleaning solution
used to remove glues and waxes from a craftsman's hands. He put
the cork back in the bottle and set the bottle back on the shelf, then
picked up a second bottle. This one contained a heavily viscous oil
used to cure certain kinds of reeds and light woods. He hesitated
over this bottle, but then put it back and selected a third.

There were mysterious scraping sounds, wood against wood,
which after a moment Taudde identified as the sound of shutters
being opened...It occurred to him, belatedly, that he had forgotten to close the shutters over the window above the table. He

cursed inwardly, listening to the approaching steps. And the pause in those steps. The man had just noticed the open shutters, Taudde surmised. Either the proprietor was asking himself how he'd managed to forget to close them the previous evening, or else he was asking himself *whether* he'd forgotten. Probably he was also noticing the smell of burning lamp oil; possibly he was even reaching out to touch the lamp and confirm that it was still hot from recent burning... Who knew what else Taudde had altered and then forgotten, which the shop proprietor would instantly notice?

Taudde uncapped the third bottle. The scent of this one's contents was heady and strong: rosemary oil, used to keep the skin of an instrumentalist's hands supple. Perfect. Taudde splashed the oil generously across two wooden blanks, set them alight with his candlelighter as the scent of rosemary rose around him, and threw both blanks high over the shelves toward the back of the shop.

The clatter and alarmed gasp that resulted was gratifying, but Taudde did not stay to listen. It wouldn't take the man long at all to put out the fires; unlike the curing oil, rosemary oil wouldn't burn with any great vigor. He ducked low around the other end of the shelves and sprinted for the door.

It was locked. Taudde, not expecting this, was momentarily too startled to do anything but jerk on the handle. Ominous sounds behind him indicated the shop's proprietor might already have dealt with the little fires and be heading through the clutter toward the front of the shop. Taudde found his flute in his hand. The temptation to simply use sorcery to slip across distance and out of peril was overwhelming.

But if he used sorcery here, and the shop's proprietor realized it—and if the man knew his own stock well enough to guess what Taudde had made—he might even be perceptive enough to put the pieces together after Taudde's pipes were put to the use for which he'd made them. The risk was impossible, but the heavy door wasn't going to yield to any simple blow, either. From a table near the door, Taudde swept up the heavy brass statue of a rearing horse, spun back toward the door, took the one long step required, and slammed the statue end-on directly against the lock. He hid a short, whistled, precisely calculated melodic phrase in the crash the statue made as it struck the door, and the lock shattered. One more blow and the door was open, and Taudde was through it on that instant and sprinting down the wide street.

Twenty feet, thirty, forty and he could at last cut sideways down a different street—he threw a look over his shoulder as he ran and glimpsed the proprietor just emerging from his shop. Not likely the man had gotten much of a look at Taudde—he thought—and in the wide, empty streets of the early-morning Paliante, he now had the space he needed for proper sorcery. Though hardly the breath he needed to play himself out of the Paliante and across Lonne, straight back into the safety of his rented house. Relative safety. Taudde played the merest whisper of inattention and invisibility as he slipped past Nala and Benne and up the stairs into his own room. Then, shivering, he dropped his flute into its pocket, closed his shutters against the brilliance of the morning, and collapsed to sit on the floor next to his bed. For a while, he did nothing but sit there, his head tilted back against the mattress and his eyes closed. Then, eventually, he took out the two sets of twin pipes he'd made—at such unexpected hazard, and carrying worse hazard within their seeming innocence—and laid them out on the floor next to his knee.

The pipes were beautiful. A fine example of the bard's craft. Taudde had made too many sets of pipes to recall, but he couldn't remember when he'd made better. But he could see the death they carried within their craftsmanship, and he could hardly stand to look at them.

CHAPTER 7

Stepping out of darkness, stepping into remembered light, Nemienne found herself in the middle of the long gallery that ran along the back of her father's house. She turned in a bewildered circle, for that first moment not trusting that she had come home. Her eyes were dazzled by the light that filled the gallery from the eight lanterns that hung on hooks from the ceiling.

Then Jehenne, sitting beside Miande on the next bed over, screamed with startled joy and jumped forward into Nemienne's arms. Nemienne reflexively caught her little sister and held her tightly. Lifting her eyes, she met Miande's wide bewildered gaze, and then found Liaska and Tana, equally astonished, clinging together and looking not quite certain whether they should be happy or alarmed.

It was Miande who came forward after that brief pause and took Nemienne's hands, exclaiming at how cold they were. It was Miande who sent Tana to bring Enelle, and who fetched a blanket from her own bed to toss around Nemienne's shoulders, and who pulled Nemienne over to the fireplace at the far end of the gallery. Jehenne clung to Nemienne's hand through this, and then sat on the floor nestled up against her when Nemienne, shivering with cold and reaction, sank down by the hearth.

"Go bring some mulled cider," Miande told Liaska, who clearly needed a job to settle her down. Then Miande knelt down next to Nemienne and looked anxiously into her face. "Are you well?"

She did not ask, *Where did you come from?* Or, *How did you come like that out of the air?*

Nemienne, though she had known her sisters loved her, had somehow not expected such evidence of it. She felt almost over-whelmed by affection for Miande and Jehenne—for all her sisters, but perhaps especially for these two, who had so clearly missed her. Guilt at how little she had missed them in return scored her heart. She missed them now, retroactively, as though their absence in the past days echoed suddenly forward into this startling present. She put an arm around Jehenne and hugged her close. "I'm well—I'm happy—except I miss you, love. All of you," she added, reaching out to pat Miande's arm. "And have *you* been well? I know you've been busy. Have you been helping Enelle?" she asked Jehenne.

"Yes, I wrote out all the invitations," Jehenne answered, with shy pride. "And Miande is making these amazing cakes for the wedding."

Enelle came up the stairs and into the gallery, not running, but at a very dignified adult pace. She had Liaska with her and the same questions Miande had not quite asked in her eyes. But Enelle didn't ask those questions either. She said only, as Liaska pressed a mug of cider into Nemienne's hands, "Ananda is with Petris. They're drawing up plans for their wedding. I didn't want to alarm Petris. If you don't need to see Ananda, I think we oughtn't disturb them. I left Tana with them to preserve propriety."

The care and thoroughness with which Enelle always approached every task was exactly as Nemienne remembered, but the edge of bitterness was new. Nemienne put her hands up for Enelle's and drew her sister down to sit with her by the fire. Enelle resisted the tug for a moment, but then yielded and sank down. Jehenne pressed in from the other side and held Nemienne's hand. The fire, burning with a somehow more ordinary kind of heat than Mage Anken-nes's fires ever seemed to, warmed their backs.

"Everything is very well," Nemienne told Enelle—told them all. This reassurance tasted oddly ambiguous on the back of her tongue, and she hesitated for a second. But it was perfectly true, after all. "Mage Ankennes is kind and generous, exactly as the mother of Cloisonné House said. His house is strange but not—not generally alarming. I took a . . . a wrong turn, I suppose, and got . . ." She edited her explanation hastily. ". . . lost."

"Lost? In the *house*?" Liaska seemed more intrigued than alarmed by this. "I'd like to see a house you can get lost in!"

"It's . . . well, it's a strange house. But beautifully strange," Nemienne assured her youngest sister. "Usually. I like it. And I love what I'm learning—Mage Ankennes is teaching me wonderful things." She tried to think of some things she'd learned that seemed charming and harmless and didn't have anything to do with frightening reaches of heavy darkness. "How to find small things that have been lost. How to read words in a language you don't know. How to call a fire out of the air to light a candle."

"Is that better than lighting a candle with a candlelighter?" Miande asked, baffled.

"Well," Nemienne said, laughing a little at this practical question, "it's different. I like it." She met Enelle's eyes as she said this, and Enelle gave a little nod, her tight expression easing a little.

"It would be really splendid to be able to read languages you never learned," exclaimed Jehenne, who had recently begun learning the languages of the far islands, Erhlianne and Samenne, and found them heavy going.

"I'll try to teach you someday, after I know the way of it better myself," promised Nemienne. "But the house can be, well, difficult. I got lost tonight, and when I thought of light and warmth and . . ." She did not want to say *safety*. "Anyway, I came here." She looked around the gallery where her bed still stood, at the interested, bewildered faces of her sisters and the cheerful fire. "How nice it is here!" she exclaimed. "I have my own room in Mage Ankennes's house, you know . . ."

"Your own room," Liaska repeated enviously. "Is it pretty?"

"Yes, and I love it, but I hadn't realized I miss all this warmth and crowding. Tell me—tell me everything. The wedding plans are nearly finished, Enelle, surely? Jehenne, will you find one of your invitations to show me? Miande, have you decided what you'll serve the guests? Are you keeping out of trouble and helping Enelle, Liaska?"

Everyone, even Enelle, tried to answer at once, and for an hour Nemienne lost herself in the familiar warmth and chatter. She tried not to talk about herself or Mage Ankennes, for nothing about the mage or his strange house seemed quite real here in the noisy company of her sisters. But Jehenne brought Nemienne a book from Samenne and listened, fascinated, as Nemienne tried to explain how you could read a new language without learning it first. And then Liaska wanted to see Nemienne light a candle without a candlelighter.

"That's enough, now, Liaska," Enelle said firmly. "If Nemienne wants to, and if she thinks it would be all right with Mage Ankennes, she can show you that in the morning."

"Oh," Nemienne, startled, and looked at the hourglass on the fireplace mantel. She said reluctantly, "I had better go back."

"Already?" said Miande.

"But you just came!" protested Jehenne.

"You have to show us all the other magic things you've learned!" cried Liaska.

"Is it so urgent you should go back?" asked Enelle, cautiously. "Is Mage Ankennes so strict?"

Nemienne stood up, drawing Enelle up with her. She embraced her sister and smiled at her, around at them all. All the brief terror of the strange darkness seemed distant and much less disturbing in this familiar place. She said—and was relieved to hear no unexpected ambiguity in the statement—"I'm happy being apprenticed to Mage Ankennes. I am happy." She paused to appreciate this thought, still odd to her, especially in these familiar surroundings. "The mage is kind to me, and he is teaching me so many things I never knew—never knew I wanted to learn. I've loved seeing you all, but look at the glass! Time's passed so fast! And I don't want to be gone when Mage Ankennes looks for me in the morning."

"He'd be angry with you?" Enelle asked doubtfully, clearly wondering again, or still, whether the mage was really the best teacher and master for her sister.

"Oh, no. I mean, I don't think he'd be angry if I came back in daylight, after breakfast—but why risk his displeasure when I didn't have his leave to come here? Besides, it's embarrassing to have...gotten lost. I think I should go back right away."

"Oh," said Jehenne, looking downcast.

"Perhaps that would be best," Enelle said reluctantly, undoubtedly thinking of the extra nine hundred hard cash that depended on Mage Ankennes not being displeased. "If you truly think so, Nemienne. I'll send down for the carriage." She looked sternly at the little girls. "Time for bed! Liaska, Jehenne, it's rather late for you, isn't it? Don't fuss! I'm sure Nemienne will come visit soon. During the day, even. And she'll write you a letter tomorrow and tell you all about the mage's house and about reading languages without having to learn them first, won't you, Nemienne?"

She gave Nemienne a look on this last, and Nemienne promised meekly. "I meant to write...I was waiting for more to happen."

"Well, I'm sure enough has happened now."

Nemienne had to agree with this, and did, as gracefully as possible. "*You* are all well?" she asked Enelle, very specifically, as they left the littler girls and walked from the gallery toward the front of the house.

Her older sister gave her a tense smile. "Oh, yes. Ananda will be married next week—we will send an invitation to Mage Ankennes, of course. Jehenne did a wonderful job on the invitations; no scribe in Lonne has a nicer hand. Even the announcement has helped, and we'll do much better after the marriage has actually taken place. Petris seems quite sensible." Meaning he still intended to let Enelle run the stone yard.

Nemienne nodded. "Have you heard from Karah? She wrote me about becoming a keiso."

Enelle managed an almost natural smile. "Two years early, we are told. Yes. *She* writes."

"I'll write! I'll write! Anyway, I told you that woman, Narienneh, would be too clever to let Karah be unhappy," Nemienne said, allowing a little smugness into her tone to cheer her sister. "I told you everyone would love her and she would be happy. And there she is, made keiso two years early!"

"And happy, I hope. Well, she has a gift for happiness...I wish she would come visit! Though not *precisely* as you have done."

Nemienne laughed and peered out the door to where the carriage already waited, with Tebbe standing at the horse's head with the reins in his hand. "Tell Ananda I am sorry to have missed her. And Petris, if you think it wise."

"Neither of them is able to keep a thought in mind for more than a moment." Enelle was amused and exasperated at the same time. "Ananda has the attention span of a butterfly, and Petris trips over his own feet and can hardly speak to her without stuttering. It's sweet, really, except it *is* hard to persuade them to settle down when I need them to go over contracts. Well. I'll tell them you stopped by. They will think nothing of your visiting at night for a scant hour." She embraced Nemienne. "Write and tell me you are well."

Nemienne promised, and drew herself away into a night that was no more than normally dark. She had never, she reflected, appreciated the streetlamps properly. She appreciated them now. Nodding to Tebbe, she jumped up into the small carriage and dropped onto the bench with a sigh of mingled relief and sadness.

What she had not expected was that, arriving in the middle of the night at Mage Ankennes's house, she would not be able to open the door.

Nemienne leaped down from the carriage, ran up the walk, jumped up the stairs onto the porch, and waved to Tebbe, who nodded and turned the horses back the way they'd come. Nemienne stood watching him out of sight, then turned and stroked the cat statue outside the front door. But the door did not click open. Nonplussed, she stepped back and regarded the mage's house. It had an unaccommodating look to it tonight. Its rough stones and blind windows could not be said to look friendly. But she'd thought she had reached an understanding with this house, because it seldom hid important rooms from her, and usually when she meant to go to, say, the smaller library, she got there without too much trouble.

Mage Ankennes would, of course, return eventually. Nemienne had not expected to hide this evening's adventure from him, but she had also expected to tell him about it in a civilized manner. In the morning, for example, over sweet cakes and tea. She had not expected and did not want to meet her master on the porch of his house because she couldn't get a stubborn *door* to cooperate.

The door itself yielded nothing to Nemienne's exploratory touch. Certainly it did not simply swing open as she set her hand on it. She had not really expected that it would, but this was still disappointing. She sat down on the house's top step—she could feel the cold of the stone even through the heavy robe Enelle had lent her—and studied the door. It looked heavier and more unyielding than ever.

Nemienne sent her thoughts into it, as Mage Ankennes had begun to teach her. She meant to coax the tumblers to drop in its lock, but she discovered that she couldn't find the lock at all. Her mind was caught instead in the grain of the wood, so that she wandered in ragged circles that led one into another but never resolved. Baffled, she drew herself out again into the ordinary night.

Perhaps mages did not trouble with ordinary locks. Perhaps they spelled their doors shut and the keyholes were only meant to puzzle thieves ignorant enough to try to rob them. Perhaps all their doors were made to confuse apprentice mages, if the apprentices were foolish enough to get locked outside in the middle of the night.

It was growing colder, too, and Nemienne shivered despite the warmth of her robes. She supposed that, if the night continued as it had begun, she would manage a little too successfully to summon fire and set the house aflame. If it would burn. Probably only the neighbors' houses would burn. That would . . . probably not be the best thing for Mage Ankennes to find when he got home.

But it *was* cold. And Tebbe was long gone with the carriage. It would be extremely embarrassing if she were forced to find a conveyance to take her home again simply to avoid freezing because she couldn't get the mage's door opened.

Nemienne was fairly certain she had at least learned to tell the difference between fire and light. Taking the precaution of settling down in the middle of the bare stone of the porch, she thought about light. Warm light. Indeed, warmth alone would be fine. Better, even. Less, well, eye-catching. Not the warmth of a fire, no. The warmth of stone that had been lying under a blazing sun all during a long summer afternoon, say, and was now giving back the sun's heat into the night. That kind of gentle warmth from the stone would be very welcome. She laid a hand on the stone beside her.

It was warm to the touch.

This was the only thing that saved her from dying of embarrassment when Mage Ankennes found her waiting on his porch when he arrived home at dawn.

Nemienne was sitting on the warm stone in the center of the mage's porch, her arms wrapped around her drawn-up knees. She had continued to try, from time to time, to open the door. It had resisted all her attempts, though she thought some of them had been rather clever. She had even tried to *make* keys that would fit the lock on the door. She had made one out of moonlight and, when that one had melted away when she tried to turn it in the lock, another out of a chip of white stone from the walkway. That one had seemed to fit. It had even turned. But it hadn't opened the door.

At least the warm stone was sort of comfortable to sit on. Though not really for an *entire* night. She was so stiff Mage Ankennes had to give her a hand up, which, looking bemused, he did.

Then he opened the door with a look. It simply clicked and swung inward, just as though it had not spent recalcitrant hours refusing to open for Nemienne.

She followed Mage Ankennes into the entry and stopped, startled. The hall, which had always been dim, was filled with light. There were windows all down its length, some with the pearly dawn light coming through them and others blazing with brilliant sunlight. Silver moonlight pooled on the floor by the nearest, and through it Nemienne could see the full moon riding high among the mountain peaks.

Among the windows were three doors. The first was of beech wood, carved with an intricate border of interlocking beech leaves all around its edges. The second, carved of what she thought was red cedar, had fantastic animals twining together in sharply jagged patterns that linked each of its panels to the next. The third door was absolutely plain, made of some ink-dark wood she did not recognize, with no carving at all.

"Ah," said the mage, looking at her face. "How many doors do you see in this hall?"

"Three," said Nemienne, hoping this was good and that the appearance of the doors would make up for her stupidity in getting locked out. She described each one in turn when he prompted her. The mage looked pleased when she described the beech door, interested when she described the cedar door with the carved animals, and a bit startled when she described the black door.

"You won't want to open that one just yet," he said, and waved her ahead of him toward the kitchen. Every window they passed looked out onto the mountain heights. Through one, dark with night, she glimpsed distant lights and wondered whether she might be looking down on Lonne. If that was Lonne, it was very far away. She touched the glass of the windowpane. It was very cold.

"Come along!" Mage Ankennes called, and Nemienne jumped and hurried to follow him, tearing herself away from the windows.

The mage made breakfast for them both while she told him about her night. The kitchen, at least, was unchanged. Nemienne found this reassuring. She sat near the iron stove, for once enjoying its furnace heat. Even her toes and the tips of her ears felt like they were finally getting warm. She could feel every tight muscle unknotting while the reassuring heat wrapped around her. She did miss Enkea. She'd half expected to find the slim little cat sleeping peacefully in the chair near the stove, but there was no sign of her this morning.

The mage did not interrupt her on that first recounting, but then he made her go back over everything again once she was finished.

"The door was standing open?" he asked, handing her a plate of rice porridge and eggs scrambled with tiny shrimp. "And Enkea went through it before you?"

Nemienne nodded to both questions.

"You should never have gone into the darkness—"

Nemienne, who agreed completely, apologized.

"No, indeed," the mage assured her. "You should have been safe following Enkea. One does wonder what the creature was about." His expression became speculative, contemplating the absent cat. "And, of course, you *were* safe," he added. "If uncomfortable. I would have found you, eventually. But you did well to find your own way through the darkness and back into the ordinary night." He paused, contemplating Nemienne. "You do show interesting sparks of unusual talent. I believe Narienneh did well, sending you to me. You will clearly make a mage."

Startled and very pleased, Nemienne stared back at the mage. She found herself smiling suddenly. "Even though I couldn't open the door?"

"Child! *I* locked the door."

"Oh!" Nemienne was embarrassed. "Of course." Though she *did* wonder whom the mage might have locked his door against, and whether mages usually guarded themselves so carefully from other mages. She was too tired to think about it, though. She was surprised by a yawn, and put a hand hastily over her mouth.

"You are very tired," Mage Ankennes said, amused. "So am I, as my night was also eventful, in its way. Finish your breakfast. Have a bath and a little nap. Come find me when you have rested and had a look through the beech door and the door with the carved animals. Not the other, just yet. Yes?"

"Yes!" Nemienne said, and flushed at the eagerness in her voice, but the amusement in the mage's face only deepened. He left her in the warmth and she heard his heavy tread going...she listened carefully...up the stairs, toward his workroom. Or perhaps whatever else might be upstairs for him. She wondered whether the upper hall had also sprouted wonderful new doors for her during that long night.

Nemienne wanted very badly to go peek through the doors right away, but she *was* very tired. After having to be rescued from the porch like a stray kitten, she thought she had better be dutiful. So, a bath and a nap. Nemienne yawned her way from the kitchen to her small room and slept for five hours.

When Nemienne at last opened it, the beech door opened into a forest of leaves. Nemienne blinked. The smooth gray boles of trees crowded into her sight; the pale jade green of leaves fluttered overhead. Roots tangled beneath a carpet of golden leaves from past autumns. Here and there outcrops of white stone shoved up from the black earth. A thin silvery stream meandered gently across the wood, from an unknown source to an unguessable destination, and a warm breeze, smelling of green growth and damp earth, made its tentative way through the trees.

Charmed beyond words, Nemienne almost stepped into the wood and went looking for the source of the little stream. Only the memory of the last door she'd stepped through and immediately lost kept her from this adventure. She did not want Mage Ankennes to be forced to rescue her from an enchanted beech wood in some unknown country of dark earth and gentle streams.

Nemienne closed the door gently, half expecting it to vanish softly back into the paneling of the hall. But the smooth gray door simply shut with a gentle *click*. She almost thought she saw its carved leaves flutter in an unseen breeze. But when she touched one, it was only quiet wood under her fingers.

Nemienne was almost reluctant to go down the hall to the next door, feeling that whatever that door opened onto must surely be less amazing than the beech wood. And that, well, if it opened to reveal something disturbing or ugly, it would somehow soil the memory of the leaves and the woodland breeze. But at the same time she was very curious.

The carved animals contained within the sharp, jagged patterns on the second door were not ordinary creatures, she saw upon closer inspection. There were slender, elongated creatures a little like deer, only with longer legs and necks and a far greater delicacy of bone than ordinary deer, and with smooth straight horns instead of antlers. The jagged patterns surrounding them suggested cliffs, as though they leaped from ledge to ledge across the stark landscape of a mountain. Scattered among the deer were animals like dogs, longer legged and more graceful than ordinary dogs, but Nemienne could not tell whether they hunted the deer or not. On the uppermost panels there were birds like eagles, only everything about them was sharp edged, as though their feathers had been made out of slivers of glass and the edges of knives.

The eyes of the carved animals were set with jewels: agate and lapis and amethyst. Traceries of alabaster and mother-of-pearl and abalone shell had been inlaid here and there, along the elegant arched neck of an animal or weaving through the feathers of a bird. The light glittering from this inlay suggested movement, giving Nemienne the impression that in a moment the carved creatures might leap away or turn to look at her.

Nemienne opened this door cautiously. She did not know what she expected, only something exotic and amazing. What she found was a music room. As this did not seem as fraught with possibility as the beech wood—indeed, it seemed a little disappointing— Nemienne stepped through the doorway. An ornate floor harp stood in the center of the room. A dragon was carved all down its face—not the more familiar sea dragon, but a serpentine creature with a long elegant head. Its talons were of opal, its throat and spine edged with mother-of-pearl. Delicate antennae tipped with lapis nodded above its eyes, which were as dark as the winter sky. Above the dragon were set three beads, one above the next: a bead of smoky glass, a bead of hematite, and a silvery pearl. Nemienne at once thought of the book by Kelle Iasodde, of his discussion of the ephemeral versus the eternal. She resolved to search for what meaning the pearl might have when balanced against glass and iron.

Symbolic meaning aside, she could not begin to imagine what such an elaborate harp must have cost. She touched a harp string, but gently, not sounding the note.

Besides the harp, there were three sets of pipes and a plain flute of bone or ivory on a stand. A more complicated flute, made of rosewood, with stops and a mouthpiece of brass and thin adjustable reeds in its throat, rested on a stand of its own. A scroll was clipped open beside it to show a strange spidery musical notation. An ekonne horn carved of black wood occupied another stand, and an unstrung kinsana stood in a corner, its strings coiled neatly on a shelf beside it.

With a last glance at the dragon carved on the harp, Nemienne left the room. She closed the door gently behind her and stood for a moment, studying it. On impulse she opened it a second time and looked in, but the music room was still there. She could hardly believe it was just an ordinary music room, but what else could it be? Did Mage Ankennes come here to play these instruments? Nemienne had never heard music in this house, but if he didn't play, why have a music room at all? She shut the door again, questions unanswered, and went thoughtfully toward the mage's workroom.

She could not help but glance sidelong at the plain black door when she passed it, but she didn't touch it. She felt somehow that if she so much as brushed it, it might open, and she found she was afraid of it. It might be on the main floor of the house, but it *looked* like the sort of door that would open on infinite depths of darkness. She went past it hastily and up the stairs.

The mage was indeed in his workroom, doing something mysterious with an unidentifiable object of spun glass and copper. Nemienne perched on a tall stool on the other side of the table and watched him.

The mage glanced up, but did not speak. He was measuring a glittery white powder into a glass bowl held aloft by a ring of copper. Mage Ankennes made a fire burn in the air below the ring with a gesture. Then, apparently satisfied, he grunted and flung himself into a chair that whisked over to catch his weight.

"Well?" the mage asked her.

Nemienne told him about the music room first, at his prompting describing each instrument she'd found in it. "Are they magical?" she asked. "The harp *looks* like it ought to be magical."

The mage half smiled. "It might be. It's meant to be. I didn't make it, though I had it made by Erhlianne craftsmasters. That harp isn't really a thing of magecraft at all, but meant for a different kind of magic altogether, more akin to the sorcery of Kalches. Did you try to play it?"

Nemienne shook her head, hoping she hadn't been expected to. Probably sending her to that room had been one of the mage's subtle tests, but whether she'd done well or badly by not trying to play the instruments she'd found there, she had no idea. Watching the mage's face gave her no clues.

"I'll show you a book that describes dragon magic and bardic sorcery," he told her. "You'll find it on the table of your room. Kelle Iasodde wrote this one also. He wrote it several hundred years ago, so you may find the style difficult. Also, not everyone can perceive the words he set down in this book. You may be able to read it; if you can, I'll ask you to tell me something useful about that harp in . . . shall we say, a month or so. Now, the beech door?"

The book sounded fascinating. Nemienne wanted to go look at it right away, make sure she was one of the people who could see the writing in it. She was sure she would be, only not *really* sure. She wanted to go find out. She wondered if the spell that let you read a language you had never learned would work on language you simply found difficult . . .

"The beech door?" the mage prompted patiently.

"Oh—" She described the beech wood. Mage Ankennes leaned his chin on his palm and made little *hmm* noises to show he was listening, but she couldn't tell what he thought.

"It isn't *really* a wood?" Nemienne asked him after a moment, when he didn't seem inclined to speak. "If you go through that door?"

The mage smiled. "Oh, yes. It really is. That's part of the enchanted forest of Enescedd. Enescedd possesses a strange sort of magic, different from any other I've encountered and less, hmm, tractable, than one might expect. Men there don't, mmm, *employ* magic in any sort of craft. The magic is simply *there*. You come upon it unexpectedly, at the oddest times and places, and it seldom takes any form you would expect…" The mage rubbed his chin, studying Nemienne. "You didn't go through that door. Did you want to?"

"Yes," Nemienne admitted, wondering whether that was good or bad.

"Yes," murmured the mage. "Hmm. Probably it would be better if you resisted the urge for the next little while, eh? Even if Enkea should go through the door ahead of you, yes? It's easy to lose yourself in that wood, and not entirely safe. Although I would find you eventually."

Nemienne nodded, relieved that she had resisted the impulse to step into the wood. "If that door leads to Enescedd, does that mean there are other doors in the hall that lead to Miskiannes? Or even…" She hesitated and then completed the sentence: "Even Kalches?" She wasn't sure she even *wanted* a door to Kalches sharing this house with her, fascinating as the idea might be. Maybe that was why Mage Ankennes had a music room and had ordered the harp made—because he needed to be ready for Kalchesene magic? As soon as this occurred to her, it seemed not only plausible but likely.

Mage Ankennes paused, lifting an inscrutable eyebrow at her. "Perhaps," he said maddeningly.

"Is Enkea here?" Nemienne asked, changing the subject.

"No," said the mage, sounding doubtful. "I think not. She is sometimes a difficult creature to keep in one's eye. I am, in truth, a touch surprised at her. But she is an unpredictable creature."

"Do you…know why she wanted me to go through that other door? Last night?"

Mage Ankennes regarded Nemienne dispassionately. Instead of answering her question, he said, "I will be going out again, not tonight, but tomorrow evening. There will be a gathering at Cloisonné House."

"Oh?" Nemienne couldn't quite decide whether she would like to see Karah in her new role as a keiso, or whether that would be too strange.

"Your presence at a keiso banquet would not be quite suitable, apprentice." The mage sounded mildly regretful. "Besides, you haven't been invited. However, it's not likely your sister will be attending the banquet either. Deisa sometimes do, but she's very new to the flower life. However—"

"Oh," Nemienne said, a little startled he didn't know about Karah, though there was no reason he should. "Karah's already a keiso—she was made keiso early. So maybe she will be there, do you think?"

Mage Ankennes paused. One eyebrow lifted, giving his heavy features a look both quizzical and sardonic. "Was she? Well—she might, then, I suppose. *However*—" and here he lifted a hand sternly, preventing a second interruption "—I am afraid your presence at the banquet would still not be suitable. You will have to visit your sister later, and not, hmm, during the candlelight hours, eh?"

Nemienne, disappointed but not surprised, nodded.

"So I'll leave you here. Do please remain in the, hmm, I was going to say more ordinary, but let me say, instead, more *traveled* parts of the house. However swift your sister's rise in her new world, *you* are still a very new apprentice. There are much more uncomfortable places to end up than my front porch. Understood?"

Nemienne was sure there were. Lost in an enchanted forest in some far distant country probably didn't begin to cover the possibilities. She was surprised at the pang of regret she felt at the injunction not to explore, stronger even than the regret at the missed banquet, but she suppressed it firmly and nodded.

"Now," Mage Ankennes said, picking a candle out of the clutter on the table without looking and reaching across the expanse of the table to set it in front of Nemienne. "Melt it, if you please," he told her. "Without lighting it."

CHAPTER 8

Taudde liked Cloisonné House immediately. It was a large, formal building of pale gold brick and weathered white limestone. Ivy crept up the brick to meet vines that dangled from long balconies, dotted with delicate pink flowers. Surely the flowers would not last through the coming winter, but they had not yet been withered by the chill in the air.

Girls came out to hold the carriage horse while Taudde stepped down onto a clean walkway of crushed limestone. He turned to face Cloisonné House, and paused. He still liked its graceful proportions. But even so, somehow the long shadow the house cast in the late sun seemed darker than it should. Or fell, perhaps, at an odd slant. Or into a place that wasn't quite the same evening in which he stood ... He shook his head slightly, not sure what he was perceiving.

One of the girls, not more than seven or eight years of age, ran ahead of Taudde to open the door for him. The other girl, a little older, jumped lightly up onto the driver's bench beside Benne to show him where to take the carriage.

Taudde laid a hand momentarily on the door as he passed through it. The wood was smooth and unexceptional, yet he felt a faint echo behind that ordinary surface, as though his hand might have passed through the door by some measureless fraction to touch something else entirely. Something old beyond age. He lifted his hand, disturbed, and glanced at the girl, who seemed perfectly ordinary. She bowed him into the House. Taudde wondered what the building might have been before it had become a keiso establishment.

"It was a noble's house, before the Laodd was built," the girl explained when he asked her. "That was ever so long ago!" When she saw he was genuinely interested, she went on, "It was Mage Lord Meredde Rette Danoros Uruddun who built this house. He built lots of houses, all over Lonne, but this was his best. They say he had island blood, but they don't mean Samenne when they say that! They mean Anaddon. The invisible island, you know, the island in the west, beyond the sunset. It's a way," the girl confided, "of saying he was a kind of mage without just saying so, because when Lord Meredde built Cloisonné House, mages weren't really respectable the way they are now."

Taudde wasn't surprised that a mage had built this house. He was more surprised that this detail was still remembered. The era to which the girl referred was more than two hundred years ago. A long time, by the energetic standards of Lirionne.

From what he could see, the residents had reason enough to be proud of their House, whoever had built it. The entry hall, spacious and serene, held no echo of the strangeness he had felt before he entered. It was decorated with little tables that each held a single pretty object. Taudde admired a little finger harp with silver strings and a frame of bone; the string he touched gave back an ethereal note, and he smiled.

The banquet chamber was intimate, meant for a small party. Decorative screens of fine wood and sea ivory closed off the balcony against the chill of the evening, but the room was well lit by a dozen ornate porcelain lamps hanging from the ceiling. A fire burned cheerfully within a broad fireplace.

In the banquet chamber, the girl turned Taudde over to a grave-faced young woman with remote storm-gray eyes and robes of subdued slate blue. The woman's hair was so dark it was almost black, her nose small and straight, and her mouth stronger than the rigid standards of Lonne preferred—though certainly by Kalchesene standards she was beautiful enough. From the plainness of her robes, she must not be a keiso—a little surprising, given her beauty. Well, despite the pretty picture of keiso life Nala had drawn for him, no doubt many women preferred a less, well, flamboyant life. But there was something else about this woman...something...

The woman offered Taudde a small, formal bow, interrupting his puzzlement. "I am Leilis," she informed him, almost as though this was a title rather than her name. Her voice was low and a little husky. It was a good voice: attractive and compelling. Taudde thought she would sing alto, probably base alto. But there was something else in her voice, as there was something odd about her physical presence...some unexpected undertone he couldn't quite understand.

"I have prepared lists of the courses that will be served and the keiso who will attend," the woman continued, unaware of Taudde's curiosity. "Please inspect these lists. If my lord does not approve of any dish, I will be happy to suggest substitutions."

Taudde noticed that the woman didn't offer substitutions if he didn't care for one or another of the keiso. He smiled and shook his head at the lists. "I've no doubt everything provided by Cloisonné House will be perfectly suitable and of the highest quality."

Leilis inclined her head in graceful appreciation of the compliment. "We have arranged for Bluefountain, our premier instrumentalist, and Rue, the finest dancer in the whole of the flower world, to attend your banquet. And we shall send in the youngest of our keiso. It will be her first banquet. She is a sweet child. I am certain she will please my lord's guests."

Taudde inclined his head in acknowledgment, though he couldn't concentrate on the woman's words. He was thinking instead of his...guests. The thought of approaching vengeance should have been satisfying, but in fact tension made him feel slightly ill. And the need to conceal everything he felt made the tension worse. He touched the small, heavy packet he carried in an interior pocket of his robe, wishing he found the weight of it reassuring. He only wanted to be rid of it.

"As I believe my lord is not from Lonne—" Leilis added, and paused for him to return his attention to her.

Taudde, glad to be interrupted from thoughts tending darker and darker, looked up, met her eyes, and made himself smile. "I would certainly welcome any advice you might offer."

The woman gave him a calm nod. "It is the custom in Lonne for the host of a gathering such as this to present each of his guests with a small gift. If my lord should not have provided himself with suitable items, Cloisonné House would be honored to supply appropriate, tasteful gifts for the occasion."

Taudde again touched the package he carried and answered, only a little too grimly, "Indeed, I thank you, but fortunately I was aware of the custom and I am thus fully provided with small gifts."

The young woman accepted this assurance with graceful approval, though with a slight reserve that suggested she might have heard and wondered at the harshness in Taudde's tone. But she did not, of course, comment. She nodded instead toward a sideboard of polished wood and said, "If my lord would care to place these items in the accustomed location?"

Taudde hesitated for a bare instant and then nodded in return and held the packet out to the woman. A slight hesitation before she put out a hand to take it suggested, a heartbeat too late, that she'd expected him to take the package of gifts to the sideboard himself. Distracted by his own dislike of what the packet contained, he hadn't noticed her expectation. Then, as Taudde gave her the package, he brushed the woman's fingers. At once, a powerful echo sprang up between them, wholly unexpected.

Leilis jerked back, dropping the packet, which Taudde caught, barely. With his other hand he caught hers, firmly, resisting her sharp attempt to wrench herself free.

An ugly dissonance echoed and re-echoed, splintering Taudde's perception of light and sound. He set his teeth against a strong desire to let the woman go…for a beat and another beat of time, and then released his grip. Their hands sprang apart as though propelled by some independent force, and they each took a hasty step to recover their balance.

Then Leilis took a hard breath, collected her dignity—no wonder she moved and spoke with such reserve, yes, that made sense now. She said with frozen disdain, "Your guests shall be shown in as they arrive, my lord," and began a measured retreat. Not a rout, Taudde thought: nothing like it. "Wait," he said hastily. "Please— wait only a moment. Allow me to beg your pardon. I had no idea—"

The ice thawed just a little. Though the woman didn't turn back to face him, she at least paused.

"Cloisonné House itself has a strange depth to it. Have you felt this?" Taudde said, speaking not quite at random. He let his words come quick and unguarded. He wanted to hold the woman a little longer; he wanted a chance to perceive that strange blended enchantment more clearly. "As though its shadows are darker than the shadows of other houses, and its light clearer? As though in this house, voices and music and the slam of a door resonate in more than one direction? I think this may be in some way related to your—your—"

"Curse?" Leilis did turn, now. She gave Taudde a steady, neutral stare.

"Is that what it is? I haven't...It's some sort of...echo, or interaction, isn't it, between a mageworking and something else..." His voice trailed off. *Something of the sea.* Or, if not of the sea, at least something similar, or allied. It was a unique sort of working, whatever blend of magery and other ensorcellment had created it...No wonder he found the woman so compelling. He himself was trying to achieve just such a blend. Though not for so cruel a purpose... He regarded the woman with redoubled fascination, wishing for the time and opportunity to examine the strange curse. He might learn a good deal if he could unravel it, see how it had been made...It would be a kindness to unravel it, if he could...

"You are a mage, then?"

"I?" Taudde was startled to realize how much he had given

away to this woman. "More a theorist than a practitioner," he said, since he didn't dare deny it entirely. "But I cannot claim great skill, and you are no doubt aware that Miskiannes lacks strong magic."

"But—" began the woman.

"Leilis?" a servant leaned through the doorway, saw Taudde, and instantly assumed a more formal manner. "My lord—the first of our keiso is ready to attend you, if I may announce her?"

Leilis, her manner a perfect mask of impersonal calm, withdrew. She left Taudde merely with repeated declarations of Cloisonné House's desire to meet any wish he might discover, but clearly did not include her own presence among wishes she was willing to fulfill. As soon as she had departed, the first of the keiso entered.

Taudde tried to collect himself. His part this evening was surely sufficiently complicated without adding the distraction of even the most compellingly ensorcelled woman. There would be time *later* for less urgent matters, if he could first break free of Miennes's leash, free of the threat Mage Ankennes posed to him. Those concerns *must* come first.

The keiso who had come into the banquet chamber was not as young a woman as Taudde had expected. Though beautiful, hers was a mature beauty. She was a good deal older than he—at least his mother's age. Her face was delicate in bone, but with an assured set to the mouth and a slightly sardonic tilt to the eyebrows. Violet powder extended the line of each eye and blended on the left side of her face into an intricate tracery of violet and blue that reached from the outside corner of her eye halfway along her cheekbone. This was a style Taudde had not seen before, and he blinked—and then smiled, for despite his nervousness the good-natured, ironic glint in the keiso's eyes instantly put him at ease.

The keiso was wearing a blue overrobe traced with a complicated pattern of lavender and blue that echoed the pattern on her face. There was a comb of sea ivory in her hair, and she carried a knee harp in the crook of her arm. She set this on a small table near the door and swept into a low bow, her hands pressed together before her heart. "I am Summer Pearl," she said. Her voice was warm and lovely, with a slight burr to it, like the deepest tone of a set of alto pipes. "Welcome, my lord, to Cloisonné House."

Smiling, Taudde returned her bow. Gesturing to her harp, he said, "You are an instrumentalist?"

"I play a little," Summer Pearl answered, with a glint of humor in her dark eyes that mocked the modesty of her words. "Of course I will not match my lord's skill."

"Of course not," Taudde said drily. He took his place at the table, to the left of the table's head. He tried a nikisi seed from the bowl on the table. It was excellent, with under the sweetness an unexpected trace of heat that lingered on the tongue.

Summer Pearl came and knelt on a cushion across from him, on the inside of the *U* made by the table. "In Lonne, it is customary for the host to take the most honored place," she said, with a nod toward the head of the table. She offered this explanation with a modest, diffident air, pretending mild embarrassment at proffering advice to a valued guest. Again, there was a touch of humor in the curve of her mouth, as though she invited him to share a subtle joke at her own performance.

It occurred to Taudde that the skills of keiso were more comprehensive than he had expected. He could not keep from smiling. "Not this evening," he said, and rose to his feet as Prince Tepres entered the banquet chamber.

The prince was accompanied by Koriadde and by Jerinte Naliadde ken Miches—Taudde would have preferred Koriadde's brother to the less-courteous Jerinte, but no one had consulted him—and of course by the dour Jeres Geliadde.

Taudde bowed, stopped from kneeling by the prince's slight gesture. He caught a sudden reverberant echo of the earlier strangeness as the prince entered the room but could spare no attention now to consider the phenomenon.

Summer Pearl, clearly startled by the prince's arrival, had risen gracefully and now began a deep bow of her own, saying warmly, "Eminence, we had no expectation—"

Koriadde, stepping forward, caught the keiso's hands and prevented her from completing her bow. He said, "We are not formal this evening," and kissed her hands, smiling down into her beautiful face.

"Cloisonné House is lovely tonight," the prince said, also smiling at the woman. Summer Pearl smiled in return and bowed her head, taking the compliment as directed at herself, and the prince nodded to her. They were fond of subtle compliments in Lonne, as well as subtle threats.

The prince nodded to Taudde and walked across the room to take the place of honor at the head of the table. He wore an over-robe of black and jewel-dark purple. His fine hair was back in a single braid, bound off by a plain black band. The stark colors suited the prince's rather angular features, making him appear both older and more authoritative than so young a man would likely otherwise have managed.

Though the authority, at least, seemed a natural quality. This young man had been the heir for... only for the past year, surely? The Dragon's ruthless execution of the latest in his string of rebellious sons—which one had it been? Rette?—hadn't that execution taken place only this summer just past?

The past year must have been a difficult time, surely, for Prince Tepres. A harsh education in power and its uses. There was something about him that suggested he'd grown very fast to meet the demands placed on him. Taudde felt his mouth tighten. He kept finding himself inclined to admire or like the young prince, which was disconcerting and not at all welcome.

He turned, a little too stiffly, to greet the prince's two young companions and bow slightly to Jeres Geliadde. The young men bowed in return, hands over their hearts; the prince's bodyguard inclined his head minutely, frowning.

"Do cease this sour manner," the prince said to his bodyguard, frowning quickly in his turn. "I vow, you tire me with this refusal to be agreeable, Jeres. This is Cloisonné House, not some disreputable dock establishment."

"Sit down and smile," Koriadde advised the older man, following his own advice. "We are all friends here."

Taudde tried to find the young men's confidence amusing, but could manage only a biting sense of irony. He nodded to a servant to pour tea, which was of the kind most admired in Lonne: a pale crystalline green with a complex floral scent and no discernible taste. It was served in fragile cups like lacquered eggshells. Taudde lifted his cup, smiled, and nodded at the girl to pour for the other men. He meant to say something to Koriadde, something light and humorous. But Miennes arrived just then, smiling and affable, and Taudde lost the flow of his thought in his struggle to hide his revulsion at the man's presence.

At least he now found it very simple to focus purely on the urgent concerns of the moment. Lord Miennes was clad in the best style of a Lonne nobleman, in a fine amethyst overrobe, matching amethysts in the rings on his fingers. Miennes, Taudde thought, would have been greatly amused to hear the prince chiding his bodyguard for unnecessary wariness.

He forced his expression into an easy smile.

Miennes made his bow to the prince and took a place at the table.

Two more keiso entered the chamber. They bowed to the prince, then to Taudde, and finally to the rest of the gathering, smiling with what appeared to be unfeigned delight. Both were younger than Summer Pearl. The first was a young woman with pleasantly rounded features and a dimpled smile; she wore an overrobe embroidered with autumn leaves, in rust and copper, from bodice to hem. Her blue-black hair, falling down her back in a thick plait, was gathered into five descending clips of amber and gold.

This keiso carried a white bowl in which floated a single exquisite pale-lavender flower. She set this bowl in front of Taudde with a small bow that suggested she was particularly delighted to find him, specifically, present at this banquet. A light, spicy fragrance rose from the flower. "My lord, I am Meadowbell," the keiso said, in a cheerful tone. "Welcome to Cloisonné House. May this visit be the first of many!"

"Thank you," said Taudde. Deliberately emulating the prince, he reached out a finger to brush a delicate lavender petal and said, glancing at the keiso rather than at the bloom, "A beautiful flower."

The keiso smiled delightedly as though she were not accustomed to being paid such compliments, or at least not by men she admired as she admired Taudde. Taudde, amused at this flattery, concluded that, unless the men of Lonne were blind and deaf, this keiso's cheerful manner and softly rounded figure must surely make her a favorite even among all the beauties of the candlelight district.

Koriadde declared, "Well said, my friend! We shall count you an asset to the flower world!" and lifted a tiny cup in salute.

Taudde put his hand over his heart and bowed slightly in his turn to acknowledge the compliment.

"And do you have a mistress in Miskiannes upon whom you practice your graceful manner?" Miennes inquired.

"I have forgotten," said Taudde, offering another slight bow, this time to the keiso, who laughed and slyly bowed her head, turning so as to glance at him over her shoulder in a teasing, deliberately seductive gesture.

The other keiso, the youngest of the three, said in a light, bantering tone, "Meadowbell has a keisonne, my lord, so all other men must be wary lest she break their hearts! Now, *I* am still free. My name is Featherreed." She looked at Taudde through downswept lashes. "You are from Miskiannes? How exciting! Is it true snow never falls in Miskiannes? Do flowers bloom all through the winter?"

This keiso was as tall and slender as her namesake, fine-boned, with delicate features and a graceful way of moving. Her hair, golden as wheat, was pinned up with small ivory combs. Birds as golden as her hair flew in a spiral from throat to waist around her overrobe.

"It snowed at my uncle's house once when I was very young," Taudde told her. This was even true. "We thought it very pretty, but the snow did wilt the winter lilies, which would otherwise have bloomed straight through until spring."

"So an unexpected snow may rob us untimely of our last blooms," Miennes said, smiling warmly around at the keiso. "But in Lonne, of course, we are fortunate to have other flowers we may cherish while we wait for spring."

"A sharp winter is perhaps the price Lonne pays for possessing the greatest and most splendid mountains in the world," remarked Taudde, though in fact he thought the stark mountains of Kalches more beautiful. He wished, suddenly and intensely, that he was home among his own mountains now, but hoped that long practice kept this yearning from showing in his face.

"Ah, Kerre Maraddras!" said Koriadde. "I tried to climb it once, you know."

The prince, accepting a tall slender glass of straw-pale wine from Featherreed, turned his head at this. "Did you? I didn't know that. How far did you get?"

"Hardly past the first shoulder," Koriadde replied. "I was young and foolish and had neglected to wear spiked boots. Fortunately, you will say. I hardly like to think of the mountain's response, had I had the temerity to lay a hand on the stone of his face."

"We should have been robbed of the pleasure of your company," agreed the prince. He had relaxed visibly and now lounged comfortably back on one elbow, holding his glass of wine with his other hand. "I went up Kerre Taum once, where the rock is broken, beside the waterfall."

"A good climb," Koriadde agreed.

"Surely not to the very top? Can one climb so high?" asked Featherreed admiringly. She offered the prince the bowl of nikisi seeds.

"Almost all the way." The prince's dark eyes had gone quiet with memory. He stirred a palmful of seeds with one fingertip, but did not taste any. He said softly, "There is a great hollow there, cut into the rock where the spray breaks against the cliff. One can see halfway to Ankanne. The Laodd looks small under your feet, like a townhouse, and the townhouses look like toys. From that height, the bridges across the rivers might be made of quills and golden thread, and the ships coming into the harbor of gull's feathers and paper."

"I would be afraid to be so high!" exclaimed the young keiso. "But you describe it so well I can see it from this very room. How beautiful it must be!"

"The Seriantes princes make that climb when they are twelve years of age," said a deep voice from the door. Taudde saw without surprise that Mage Ankennes stood there. He felt he had known of the mage's arrival before Ankennes had even laid a hand on the door, if not quite consciously. It seemed to him now that the whole of Cloisonné House reverberated with the mage's arrival. That Ankennes's words fell as he spoke them into the ordinary world and yet echoed as well into a different world lying just aslant of the visible and ordinary. Yet, in this house, the mage himself seemed somehow more ordinary and less threatening than ever before. Taudde eyed him covertly, trying to decide whether the mage was doing something himself deliberately to create this impression or whether it was caused by something about the house itself.

Then the mage's words distracted him completely, for the mage was continuing, "The hollow of which Prince Tepres speaks is not merely a natural hollow. It is the tomb of the kings of Lirionne. Young princes make that climb in order to become acquainted with mortality. There are steps carved into the face of Kerre Taum, but even so that is not an easy climb. Customarily, a prince's father or an older brother will accompany the boy. I believe it was Prince Rette who escorted you, was it not, eminence?"

"So it was," the prince said equably, showing no visible reaction to the mention of the Seriantes tomb or his deceased brother who now occupied a niche within it. Yet, though his outward tone was calm, there was a sudden tightness to the undertones of his voice. Everyone else in the room had gone noticeably still.

"Sometimes the thoughts prompted by Kerre Taum are dark ones."

"So you have said to my father," Prince Tepres said, his tone at last acquiring an edge. "On more than one occasion, I believe. If *his* answers do not please you, Mage Ankennes, do not look to me for satisfaction."

"The heart of the mountains is the heart of darkness, as I think the dead on Kerre Taum would tell you. Though the dead have no speech, their bones speak a language more true than any that passes the tongues of the living—"

"Enough, I say!" snapped the prince, straightening. "That is all past. Do not speak of the dead."

The mage stopped, bowing his head in what appeared perfectly ordinary and polite apology and acquiescence.

Taudde did not understand why Ankennes should make such strange and daring comments. He did not believe for a moment that the mage had so little self-control that he could not resist baiting the Seriantes prince. He was certain Ankennes did nothing without reason.

Did Ankennes wish to draw attention to himself and away from Miennes? Or perhaps away from Taudde? Or perhaps…it occurred to Taudde that if Ankennes wished to encourage the prince in fear or bitterness or hatred of his father, he might do worse than refer to his dead brothers. Though Taudde could not guess why the mage should bother, when he expected the prince to very shortly follow his brothers to the Seriantes tomb…perhaps he intended to achieve all those results, or something else entirely. Taudde could easily believe the mage subtle enough to have half a dozen goals in mind for every word he spoke.

Summer Pearl said gravely, with a practiced grace that suggested keiso also learned to smooth over incipient quarrels, "Memories at times clamor as loudly as the Nijiadde River crashing over the cliffs. And the approach of winter draws out memories we should perhaps rather let sleep."

The prince gave the older keiso a sharp glance and, after a moment, inclined his head. He did not smile, but he leaned an elbow on the table, his manner easing. He said, "'The season of falling leaves, and falling winds, and falling mists; memories, too, come down and linger with the cold.'"

Summer Pearl evidently recognized the quote, for she responded, "'Memories deepen as the snows deepen; they drift over our hearts; our hearts, frozen in ice, wait for spring.'" She poured a tiny cup of fragrant tea for the prince and lifted her own cup to him. Taudde found himself wondering whom the keiso had loved and lost.

Mage Ankennes, evidently willing to allow the keiso to ease away from the difficult moment, quietly took a place toward the foot of the table and nibbled nikisi seeds. Taudde studied him discreetly, but came to no further conclusions.

Two more keiso came into the room. The first was a young woman with the look of a Samenian, coarse boned and over tall. Despite her lack of beauty, she had the confident air of one who sets her own worth very high. She wore a blue overrobe with falling leaves and rising birds embroidered in rust.

However, the second girl, once she came into sight, utterly eclipsed the first. She was a truly lovely girl, with beautiful creamy skin, clouds of twilight hair, and the most exquisite eyes Taudde had ever seen. She wore a rich blue overrobe with white moths fluttering in a spiral over the great blossoms of moonflowers.

She was also, Taudde realized slowly, extremely young. Everything showed this, but most especially the girl's obvious nervousness. Her shyness, however, did not detract from her beauty. Quite the reverse. Glancing around, Taudde saw that every man in the room was as captivated as he. Even Jeres Geliadde appeared to have been charmed. The prince set his wineglass down, making no attempt to disguise his interest.

The other keiso, Taudde saw with some amusement, were unsurprised by the effect the girl had produced. Summer Pearl had a tolerant, humorous curve to her mouth; her eyes were alight with gratification. Meadowbell and Featherreed were exchanging glances filled with enjoyment that approached hilarity.

The girl bowed shyly and said in a soft, timid little voice, "I am—I am Moonflower, my lords. I beg my lords' indulgence. I don't— I— This is my first week as a keiso and I know nothing. I beg my lords will permit me to—to merely observe their banquet."

There was a general murmur through the room that encompassed, Taudde thought, disappointment and approval and resignation. The prince gave young Moonflower a nod and then looked deliberately away. Compelled by this royal example, the other men sat back on their cushions and also turned their attention elsewhere.

Moonflower's companion murmured to her, and the girl found a place at the end of the table and settled there with her eyes cast down and her hands folded in her lap.

The other keiso then made her bow to the prince, who rose and took her hands with obvious warmth. He said, "Rue, my beauty. You will dance tonight?"

"Of course, eminence, if it would please you," agreed the Samenian keiso, and went to murmur with Summer Pearl and Meadowbell while Featherreed poured tea and wine for the men.

There was suddenly movement both within and without the banquet chamber, apparently on some signal Taudde had missed. Servants served broth in bowls painted with waving sea grasses, and, on small plates painted with dragonflies, translucent noodles sprinkled with chopped abalone.

Summer Pearl settled herself with her knee harp and began to play, with confidence but without seeming to give much attention to the music she made. Another older keiso who had entered quietly joined her, playing the kinsana. This newcomer played with great skill, but also with feeling that transcended skill. Taudde assumed that this was Bluefountain, for it was only natural that anyone should think of this woman when music was mentioned. She found the heart of the demanding instrument effortlessly. Taudde refrained, with difficulty, from showing excessive interest.

Koriadde told a story of sledding down the Laodd road and nearly into the churning basin where the Nijiadde Falls came down onto the rocks. "Only Lord Geriente drove his horse sideways and knocked my sled into the snow beside the road. I broke my arm and his carriage wheel and my father nearly threw me into the river himself."

Everyone laughed. Meadowbell, who had taken a place next to

Koriadde at the table, said cheerfully, "Sledding below the Laodd! Only you!"

Jerinte Naliadde ken Miches said unexpectedly, "Oh, no. I was there." He was smiling, for the first time Taudde had seen. "There were several of us who stole trays from the kitchens for sledding, but only Koriadde broke his arm."

"The ending to every tale," Koriadde said wryly. "If someone must break an arm, it always seems to be me."

Bluefountain and Summer Pearl brought their song to an ambiguous close, as though the music might continue if one listened for it, or might at least be meant to continue. Taudde tilted his head, intrigued. But Summer Pearl set her harp on the floor beside her cushion and went around the table to pour more wine for anyone who nodded, ending by pouring a glass for herself. She settled on a cushion between Lord Miennes and Mage Ankennes and said, "Oh, tales of our foolish youth. Mine are modestly lost in the distant past, which is fortunate for my present dignity."

To Taudde's surprise, Mage Ankennes removed a thick ring of braided gold and silver wire from his thumb and offered it as a gift to whoever told the best story of misspent youth. Koriadde instantly tossed an armband of copper set with fire opals onto the table and suggested that everyone tell a story and then the entire gathering could decide upon a winner, everyone else paying a forfeit to this fortunate person. The young men and the keiso agreed enthusiastically.

Summer Pearl poured more wine for everyone to toast this decision while the servants brought in new dishes. Featherreed began a story from her first year as a deisa of climbing over the rooftops of the candlelight district on midsummer night to meet a boy from Maple Leaf House—the son of a keiso and a wealthy ship merchant. Taudde lost the first part of this story because Leilis led in two servants with trays of some complicated tidbits and he found himself at once trying to trace the workings of the ensorcellment that surrounded the woman. Without touching her again, he couldn't quite grasp the edges of the spellwork…She went out again, leaving him once more frustrated and distracted. And worried. What if she told the Mother of Cloisonné House that she thought the foreign Lord Chontas might be a mage?

"I made it to the rooftop of the Sea-Dragon Theater much later than we had agreed to meet there," Featherreed was saying when Taudde finally managed, with some difficulty, to bring his attention back to her story. "It was nearly the hinge of the night when I arrived, and raining gently. That night the Riembana were performing the 'Four Seasons of the Heart,' by Geselle Maniente, you know. The music came up and mingled with the rain. I thought I had never heard anything so beautiful. It seemed to me that every drop of rain chimed like a bell as it hit the rooftops. So I made my way around to the western side of the theater where the rooftops nearly touch and jumped across the last gap—"

"And found the boy there with another girl," guessed Ankennes, smiling. "Girls mustn't trust the promises boys make at noon; so few last till dawn."

Meadowbell and Rue both laughed knowingly, clearly familiar with this story.

"You're wrong," said Featherreed, laughing and blushing at the same time. "He was there. So were four other couples. Even in the rain! But it was midsummer night, and there was 'Four Seasons of the Heart,' so everybody had had the same idea. Including Mother and her keisonne!"

Ankennes exclaimed "No!" and laughed freely. All the young men were grinning or laughing. The prince smiled.

"The Mothers of all the Houses knew perfectly well somebody ought to be there," finished Featherreed. "I was so embarrassed! But the boy—it was Hedderes, son of Kedres ken Miriedd, and he'll tell you it's all true—anyway, he'd very bravely remained to stay by me if I came. We both swore on the mountains and the sea that we'd just meant to listen to the music—all the young people swore the same oath, I believe—and fortunately Mother didn't take the adventure very seriously."

"A good story," approved Koriadde, and immediately began to

try to outdo it with a story involving his father's favorite horse, half a dozen of his evidently wild friends, and the terrible time they'd had getting the animal into the uppermost story of his father's country house in Kenne.

The youngest of the keiso had remained at the edge of the gathering, her intense sapphire gaze drawn first to one and then another of the company as the stories were told. She was eating only a little and drinking nothing but tea, Taudde had noticed with approval. But the girl's shyness had eased as the men's attention was drawn elsewhere. She laughed freely at Koriadde's story and then at Meadowbell's, looking young, happy, and extremely beautiful. And the prince, though he laughed dutifully at Meadowbell's story and then Jerinte's, was clearly enthralled by her. His captivation was, in fact, rather charming. Taudde, not wanting to be charmed, looked away.

The keiso, too, were aware of the prince's attention. After Jerinte's story, Rue murmured to her young protégée. Moonflower looked first surprised and then pleased. Truly, she was not shy by nature, Taudde saw, only she had been uncertain at first in company she did not know.

Now she thought for a moment and then began, "Now, this happened when I was only fourteen. One cannot expect good sense from a child of fourteen, so what happened was not my fault."

Around the table everyone was settling back with anticipation. The keiso shifted around the table, Meadowbell settling next to Miennes and Featherreed by Jerinte. Rue settled to a cushion beside Taudde. Servants had brought a pale liquor, and Rue poured him a small cup. Taudde tasted the liquor cautiously. It was very sweet, with a tart aftertaste that lingered on the tongue. The prince distractedly waved away the cup Summer Pearl offered him, his attention all for Moonflower.

The girl clearly wasn't *trying* to captivate the prince. There was nothing studied or artificial about her manner. But her natural warmth and innocence was delightful. And, Taudde judged, glancing around the table, every other man present agreed, even

Miennes, whose close attention to the young keiso Taudde read as ugly and lascivious. Ankennes, in contrast, had an air of rather paternal interest. Koriadde and Jerinte had noticed their prince's fascination and had taken a slightly distant attitude.

Rue and Summer Pearl both looked wry and amused and a little resigned at the men's reaction to their young companion. Meadowbell and Featherreed had their heads tilted together, and Taudde suspected this evening would itself become a story. Bluefountain was playing a quick rippling melody with an intricate descant behind the melodic line. Her expression was closed, intent. Taudde thought the older keiso might not even have noticed the general male focus on Moonflower.

"We had taken ship for Ankanne," Moonflower explained. "My father had business with the stone yards there. Why he thought he should take all eight of his daughters along I can't say, except we begged to go and he did not like to be parted from us. And then I suppose he thought a little travel would be good for us—we had never been out of Lonne, except for Ananda once." There was a touch of sadness when she spoke of her family, which only added to her charm.

"You have seven sisters?" asked Prince Tepres, seeming much struck by this detail. He had had seven brothers, of course, before the various rebellions three of them had attempted against their father.

"Yes, my lord. Eminence. My lord," answered the girl, with pretty confusion. They had been very informal all through the evening and yet she knew this was a prince of Lonne. A little confusion of address was not exceptional, but in this case the prince seemed charmed by it. Again Taudde found himself drawn to like the young prince, and again he flinched from that impulse.

"By no means regard my interruption," Prince Tepres was saying warmly, and gestured for the girl to continue. "And, indeed, we are not at all formal this evening."

Blushing, Moonflower lowered her sapphire gaze. She said softly, "Well, then, my lord, we took ship for Ankanne. My sister

Miande learned to make a horrible kind of porridge with fish and hard cracker, and all that next year she would make it sometimes, to tease us. My sister Enelle learned to figure the ship's heading from the stars, and the captain of the ship gave her a compass of crystal and brass when we left the ship. Does one say 'disembarked'? Is that the term?"

"One might," said the prince. He rested his chin into his palm, regarding the young keiso with a serious expression, but the corners of his eyes had crinkled with laughter.

"Well, disembarked, then. But before that, my poor sister Nemienne was ill and hid below in our cabin, so we took turns nursing her. She thought it was very unfair and complained until she was too ill even to grumble."

Jerinte, a little too far into the liquor, sat up and declared, "I'm always ill at sea! I go overland all the time now."

"Yes, Jerinte, we all have great sympathy for your affliction," said the prince sharply, and then much more kindly to the young keiso, "But by all means continue."

"Well, my lord, so Nemienne was ill, and Tana a little, but not so much. And my sister Liaska, who was only just seven years of age, learned to climb in the rigging like a ship's boy, even though everyone tried to prevent her, and she learned to curse like a sailor, too. It took months to teach her not to."

There were chuckles around the table and Moonflower smiled in return and continued, "But I am the only one of us in all that voyage who laid a hand on the nose of a sea dragon."

The prince sat up straight, exclaiming. From the reactions of the keiso, Taudde realized that none of them had heard this story before either. He realized that this girl must be a newcomer to Cloisonné House. Mage Ankennes blinked and cocked his head at her, deeply interested, and even Jeres leaned an elbow on the table and looked sincerely intrigued for the first time in the evening. Miennes had a faintly skeptical look in his eye, but said nothing.

"It came out of the sea on a day so quiet the water was as still as the sky," Moonflower said. Her voice dropped, creating a new sense of intimacy as everyone was forced to hush and lean forward to listen. "The sea is dark there off Monne, where the bottom falls away and the sea is deep. There is a different look to the waves there, as though they hide all their power in the depths and so there is less to see on the surface.

"Birds had been with us all the time, flying after the ship and perching on the ropes: That kind with the long white wings, and the small kind that darts in and out of the waves as though it were half fish and only half bird. But there were no birds with us that morning. I think they saw it far below, a shadow in the blue, and it frightened them because it was so much greater than they."

She was a natural storyteller, Taudde thought. There was music in the cadences of her voice. Despite everything, he found himself genuinely interested in her story. Bluefountain had begun playing an accompaniment, picking up the rhythm of the girl's voice with her kinsana and adding a dark burring underneath that rhythm, as though something great swam below Moonflower's words.

"Fish came before it, leaping on the surface of the water. The light turned them to silver and pearl as they leaped. There were hundreds of fish, thousands maybe, so many the whole sea seemed alive with them. If someone had leaped over the railing, I think he would have been able to walk on their backs as though on cobbles.

"I remember the captain shouting to us to get away from the railing. At the time, I did not hear him. I was looking at the dragon. My father and my older sisters were busy with the little girls, and Nemienne, who would have given her toes for a chance to see a dragon, was below in our cabin. So there was no one by the railing but me when the dragon came up out of the sea.

"It might have been made by a Paliante jeweler." The girl's voice dropped even lower, taking on a dreamier cadence. "Its scales were enameled in jet and citrine. Its ivory tusks looked like crescent moons, and its horns were jet spiraled around with gold. It seemed to rise up as high as Kerre Maraddras. Its head seemed the size of the Laodd, its eyes larger than whole oxen. They were sapphire traced with nets of gold, and they had slit pupils like a cat's.

"I thought it would fall down on the ship and crush it, as an avalanche will crush a cart, and with no more malice. It seemed to me a force of the sea, like the wind and the waves. But then it dipped its head to the railing and turned to look across the deck with one sapphire eye, and I saw it knew we were a ship and not really a thing of the sea, and that it was curious. By then I knew that I should back away, only it was too late. And it was so beautiful. It was near enough I could reach out my hand and touch it. So I did. It was cool, but not cold, and not slippery as a fish is slippery. Touching it was like touching glass.

"Then it lifted its head again and went down into the sea, and the water closed over it, and it was gone. And I cried," the girl finished simply. "My father thought it was because I had been afraid, but really I cried because it had been so beautiful."

There was a brief, awed pause. Bluefountain drew her accompaniment to a conclusion, letting the burr underlying the melody sink down and disappear, like something great slipping slowly from sight. She did not lay a hand across the strings to still them, but let the last notes ease imperceptibly down into silence.

Then Koriadde, without a word, picked up his arm ring and tossed it to the table before Moonflower. It nearly slid off the edge, so the girl had to put a hand out to steady it. She looked at Koriadde in surprise, and Taudde knew she had not expected to win any prize for her story—that she had not been thinking at all of the terms the young man had proposed for the game.

Ankennes gave the young keiso his ring, murmuring, "Beautifully told, child." Jeres Geliadde gave her his thumb ring of plain polished hematite, and Rue leaned over and murmured to Moonflower that this ring meant she could request aid from any of the King's Own guardsmen. Moonflower looked suitably impressed. Taudde observed the glance the prince and his bodyguard exchanged, and the resigned nod Jeres Geliadde gave the prince, and the prince's small smile, but he thought Moonflower missed this exchange.

The prince's friend, Jerinte, presented Moonflower with a more costly ring, gold and set with an expensive black opal, though presumably this one came without valuable attachments. Taudde had guessed this would be a rich party where every gift given would be expensive. Now he saw he had reason to be grateful he'd prepared for it. He gave the girl one of his own rings: silver wire woven to encage a single fine pearl.

Miennes's smile held an element of smugness, no doubt because he could well afford this game of generosity. He gave the girl an earring that held a sapphire precisely the color of her eyes and was certainly worth more than all the other rings together. Jerinte glanced at the older man with dislike, but Koriadde only looked amused.

Moonflower stared at these gifts and blushed.

"Take them," Summer Pearl said to her, in a kind tone. "You won them fairly."

"But—"

"You did," Rue said, smiling, and patted Moonflower's hand, which the girl had put out cautiously to touch the sapphire earring. "No one will tell a story to rout that one. Never tell me if it was not true. I will like to think of you on the deck of that ship, with the dragon rearing up out of the sea as high as Kerre Maraddras."

"But it *was* true," the girl said, blinking. "I thought all the stories were supposed to be true?"

"A well-told tale has a truth of its own," commented the prince. "But of course yours would be unexaggerated." He was smiling. He seemed both pleased and a little proud, as though he took the young keiso's shining performance as a credit to himself.

Moonflower looked up at him and dropped her gaze again at once, blushing in delightful confusion.

The prince laughed a little. He plucked a single hair from his head and threaded it around a simple ring of gold wire before presenting the ring to the young keiso. The pause this time was rather fraught. Koriadde and Jerinte exchanged a swift glance, appearing both pleased and uneasy. The prince's bodyguard merely looked resigned.

Summer Pearl had the indulgent look of an older person watching young love blossom. Meadowbell and Featherreed looked amused and a touch envious. Rue had a slightly calculating expression in her dark eyes.

Servants brought in sticky nut candies and bowls of rose-scented water so they could wash the stickiness off their fingers, and Bluefountain began to play again, a warm, light melody that broke the mood and made everyone smile. Rue rose to her feet and went out into the center of the room. She moved with a new kind of grace, and there was a general settling around the table as the company prepared to watch her dance.

The music lifted suddenly and Summer Pearl and Meadowbell both joined Bluefountain. Summer Pearl's knee harp drew a light, ethereal descant about the deeper, burring sound of the kinsana, while Meadowbell's pipes tossed glittering notes out at seeming random and yet fit perfectly into the piece. It was a variant of a Miskiannes dancing song, Taudde realized, doubtless chosen in his own honor. Rue was preparing to dance, and Taudde was suddenly ashamed that he'd assumed the subtle calculation he'd seen in her face had been due to Moonflower's success.

The dance Rue performed did not use the set of strict forms Taudde would have expected from a Lonne-trained dancer. Instead, Rue seemed to float through the dance, always on the verge of drifting into a form and yet never quite letting her steps resolve into the expected pattern. This lack of resolution created a tension that was wound tighter with every form Rue did not quite carry through, and in only a few moments no one in the room was looking anywhere but at the dancer.

Rue drew the dance to an end that did not conclude and yet somehow was still satisfying. At that moment, while she made her bows, every man in her audience would have sworn that Rue was the most beautiful woman in Lonne, little Moonflower notwithstanding. And this, Taudde thought, with no deliberate effort on her part to beguile. She had only given herself to the dance.

The prince began the applause, a soft tapping of fingertips

against the polished surface of the table, and the rest of the gathering joined him.

"Beautiful. Very lovely and unusual," Taudde said to Rue. He added sincerely, "Indeed, I do not recall anything I have ever seen to rival it," and went on, "Truly it is said that one must come to Lonne in order to live! I hope you will accept a small token of my regard, forgiving any imperfections of taste a foreigner might have shown in its selection."

Bringing out the packet he had set aside on the sideboard, biting back a sharp reluctance to do so, Taudde unwove the cord that bound it. He set out on the table the items he had brought, each wrapped in its own fine suede cloth and bound with a little cord.

Not being personally acquainted with any of the keiso, nor even being certain how many keiso would be present, Taudde had simply bought a selection of small gifts for them. Understanding that ostentatious generosity was expected—indeed, a keiso House, almost as much as high-class but ordinary prostitutes of other cities, must surely depend on the generosity of its patrons—he had made certain the gifts were expensive, for all their small size. He chose for Rue a bracelet of copper and amber, judging that it would set off her coloring well. She accepted this gift as her due, with a slight inclination of her head.

To Summer Pearl, he gave a ring of silver and Enescene jade, and to Meadowbell and Featherreed combs of mountain cedar inlaid with abalone shell. To Bluefountain, with a bow to acknowledge her skill, he gave a deceptively simple little flute of black wood that he had found at the Paliante and loved immediately: He had expected at least one of the keiso to be a true instrumentalist. All the keiso accepted their gifts with graceful exclamations of happiness, and Bluefountain blew a soft trill on the flute and closed her eyes in pleasure at the clean, pure sound.

To Moonflower, he gave a fortuitous trinket: a finger-high sculpture of a sea dragon carved of expensive red inda wood from Miskiannes. To Koriadde and Jerinte, Taudde gave graceful thanks for the pleasure of their company and small practical knives with sharkskin hilts and deadly edges. The sheath of one was set with small cabo-chons, the other with tiny pearls. Both young men seemed pleased.

To Jeres Geliadde, he gave a completely unadorned knife, of the kind meant to be carried unobtrusively in the boot for emergen-cies, and received in return a curt nod.

To Ankennes, Taudde gave a drinking cup whimsically carved to resemble a mage's scrying ball, and the mage laughed and claimed he would see more truth in a cup of liquor than any true crystal. Taudde only hoped his own smile looked unforced. He had used a triple-bladed tuning rod to weave deadly sorcery into the cup, so that any wine poured into it would become inimical. Lest someone other than the mage might fall victim to the poison, Taudde had also limited the sorcery so that the enspelled malice of it would wear away over the course of a few weeks.

He would be shocked if the mage actually drank from the cup in the meantime. That spell was not very subtle. But, though Taudde would be delighted if Mage Ankennes did drink from it, its "loud" ensorcellment was meant merely to drown out the far more subtly enspelled items Taudde had brought to this banquet. Ankennes would, of course, know these, too, carried sorcery. But Taudde hoped to prevent him from determining the exact details of how that sorcery would work.

To Miennes, with a significant look, Taudde gave a set of twin pipes made of horn and bound in silver. To the prince, with a deep bow of extravagant gratitude for the honor of his presence, and with a deepening reluctance he worked hard to conceal, he gave an even more beautiful set made of sea ivory and bound in gold. As the prince touched his set, Taudde felt the familiar whisper of sor-cery waking. He found himself gripped by a sudden intense urge to snatch the ivory pipes back, break the waiting enchantment, render the pipes harmless. But it was far too late for second thoughts. Taudde slowly lowered his hand to the table.

"How lovely!" Bluefountain explained, turning to study first the pipes made of horn and then the set made of ivory. "What exqui-site work! Are these from Miskiannes?"

The prince smiled and offered his set to Bluefountain so she could examine them more closely. Several of the other keiso peered over her shoulder as she turned them over in her hand and then, with a glance at the prince for permission, brought them to her lips and played a single note. It swelled in the room, mellow and pure, and Bluefountain closed her eyes and lowered the pipes again, smiling with delight.

The note seemed to Taudde to echo with shadowy grief, and he had to pause a moment before he could lie smoothly. "I bought them in Miskiannes. But I believe they were made across the sea, in Erhlianne. They do fine work there." They did, but not as fine as the work Kalchesene bardic sorcerers could do. But he did not say that.

"Lovely," agreed Mage Ankennes, smiling blandly. "Certainly more than the equal of my cup. May I?" He leaned forward to examine the prince's set more closely, then sat back again with a murmured, "Masterful work indeed. Lord Miennes, yours are very fine as well. If I may?" He took the horn set and examined them curiously.

Taudde tried to match the mage's bland smile, but suspected he'd failed.

The mage gave the set back to Miennes and nodded to Taudde. "Lovely work, indeed," said the mage. " I commend your . . . taste, indeed I do, and the craftsmanship that went into this piece."

Taudde murmured appreciation, wondering just how much of the complex working Mage Ankennes had perceived. That the mage had given the pipes back to Miennes was surely a good sign . . . probably a good sign . . . Just how subtle *was* the mage?

"They are so beautiful, and such a pure sound! I have never seen anything to match them," murmured young Moonflower, putting out a tentative finger to brush the carved ivory of Prince Tepres's set. Her glance rose, Taudde thought by chance, to catch the prince's, and she blushed and looked away. The prince smiled. The rest of the company hid smiles of their own, or in the case of the prince's bodyguard, a frown. But at least the young keiso had drawn everyone's attention away from Taudde. He took the opportunity to covertly trade the plain ring Jeres Geliadde had given Moonflower for a narrower ring of his own that was roughly similar. At least it seemed unlikely the child would have any call to try to use it to solicit aid from any guardsmen. At least not soon.

Miennes accompanied Taudde to his carriage, of course. On passing out of Cloisonné House into the night, Taudde felt again that odd jarring dissonance he had perceived on arriving. The sensation startled him. He had almost forgotten his earlier feeling that the keiso House was a fraction aslant of the ordinary world. He hesitated in the doorway, half inclined to go back into the house and see whether he might find Leilis, compare the dissonance that clung to her to the sensation that occupied the doorway. Study, even unravel, the strange spellwork that had been imposed on her...She had at least seemed a naturally reticent woman. He would have to find an excuse to see her later. He would have liked to find her now.

But Miennes, of course, was present. Interfering in small ways and great. Miennes, at least, deserved the fate Taudde had crafted into those pipes. But Taudde found his angry regret growing only sharper. He had needed Miennes to step into his own trap, and the lord was dangerously perceptive and clever. So Taudde had baited his trap with truth, and Miennes had taken that bait. And yet...

Taudde knew he could have thought of a way to deal with the Lonne nobleman that would touch no one else. Or at least, a way for himself to get free of Lonne. Well, he hadn't wished to leave Lonne and he had been seduced by the vengeance forced into his hands, and it was too late to regret his choice now. Taudde told himself that he was glad to comply with Miennes's demand. What was the saying in this city? Something suitably coastal: to catch two fish on the same hook? Something of the kind.

But at the moment he could not be glad of anything. Even thinking of Geriodde Nerenne ken Seriantes's coming grief and despair brought him no pleasure. Taudde tilted his face up to the sky. It was very late, not in fact far removed from dawn, and the air was crisp with the approaching winter. But lights glowing all about the candlelight district drowned the darkness, and no stars were visible. Music played somewhere nearby, and a girl sang...a long slow lament that somehow seemed to contain in its cadences the rhythm of the tides and winds. The music rose above the girl's voice, crying like the voices of seabirds.

The prince and his close companions had departed first, the prince giving young Moonflower back into the care of her elders with obvious reluctance. Koriadde and Jerinte had implored Meadowbell and Featherreed to accompany them to a nearby theater, a plan to which the two keiso had acceded with pleasure. The prince had not opposed the idea, but also had not shown any sign of wishing to join them. He had headed back toward the Laodd, his bodyguard trailing at his heel. Taudde hadn't seen Mage Ankennes go, but the mage, too, had departed, thankfully without seeming to want to examine Miennes's pipes more closely.

Miennes himself, of course, had lingered. He drew Taudde a few steps from their waiting carriages. "Well?" he demanded, his low, mellow voice edged, to Taudde's ear, with a hard and ugly undertone.

"He took the pipes," Taudde said shortly. Then he stopped and took a breath. Needing Miennes to believe him and doubt nothing, he layered truth and impatience and arrogance into his tone over the anger he felt. All of it was real, so there was no reason for Miennes to doubt anything he heard. Taudde continued, "Play the set I gave you, and you will draw his life from his body and leave only a husk. What you do then, or whom you do it to, or for, is your business. I have no interest in the politics of Lirionne." Which was decidedly not true, but he layered sincerity through the statement.

Miennes smiled as though he believed it. "I'm sure not. So. The pipes. I see. How *fitting*." Then he frowned. "When *I* play mine? *You* will play them, of course."

Taudde tipped his head slightly back in refusal. "You are the one who wants him dead. You play his death. I promise you, no one will be able to charge you with it; the mages of Lonne know nothing of true sorcery."

"I have said, *you* will do it," the Lonne nobleman said, low and dangerous. "I am astonished you object—being what you are."

He had no idea what Taudde was. "I will not," Taudde answered. "Indeed, I cannot. You took the other set of twin pipes as a gift and they became yours. No one now can use them for their intended task but you. I have accommodated your desire. But I am not a murderer. I will not play the pipes myself." Though, he thought bleakly, he had become sufficiently a murderer when he had *made* those pipes. It was a weak claim he made now. But he needed Miennes to believe it, and so he worked hard to at least half believe it himself, at least for this moment. He added a sharp and bitter truth to anchor his deception, "But you are correct: I have no love for the Dragon of Lirionne. If this blow strikes through *his* heart, that is very well."

There was a brittle silence. Miennes broke it at last with a sharp laugh. "Well, if these pipes work as you say, I suppose you are murderer enough for me. But do not," he said, his tone again affable, "mistake me for a man who will tolerate defiance."

Taudde did not. He was certain Miennes was already considering ways in which he might punish his new tool's insolence. He bowed his head and answered, this time with a far easier truth. "I do not want you as my enemy, my lord. I promise you, the pipes will do your will."

This drew a smile of renewed confidence, a warm expression that went oddly with the cold note in the Lonne nobleman's voice. "Well, if I am to choose my own moment...perhaps I may at least do so with purpose. Not tonight, then, I think. But in a day or two, when...circumstances align most favorably. What does one play, to make them do their work? A mourning dirge?"

"Any music will do, lord—a springtime melody as well as a dirge. Nor does the skill of the piper matter: Death resides in the pipes and not the player. Play them at your will, my lord. You may play those pipes at any moment you desire." Taudde set smooth confidence under his tone to encourage the other man's confidence. "I will hope——" and he tried fiercely to hope it, "——to hear shortly that the Dragon of Lirionne is bereft of legitimate sons and all Lirionne in mourning."

"Yes," Miennes said, with a nod that combined both threat and dismissal, "I hope that, too, and for your sake as well as mine."

CHAPTER 9

The striking success of Moonflower's first appearance as a keiso annoyed some of the less-generous-hearted keiso. But it delighted Rue, pleased Mother, and—most satisfying of all—completely justified Leilis.

"I think perhaps it might be best to withdraw the child from the public view for a time," Mother mused, studying a chart of tentative keiso engagements for the coming weeks. Some of the more popular keiso refused to commit to any specific engagement very far in advance, so keeping up the chart was a complicated task, as Leilis knew from personal experience.

Mother tapped a stylus on her desk and frowned. "Moonflower has received twelve invitations already. But sometimes fame grows best where it is not actively encouraged. Men desire most fiercely what is farthest from their reach."

Leilis, who was carefully rearranging flowers in Mother's collection of crystal vases, discarded a few that were on the verge of becoming overblown. She glanced sidelong toward Mother and murmured, "Some flowers are best in the bud; once fully opened, though still pleasing to the eye, they have already lost their special loveliness."

Mother's frown deepened. "Perhaps." She set down her stylus and set the chart aside, lifting instead a roll of fine parchment with an embossed seal of saffron wax. After a moment of consideration, she offered this across the table to Leilis.

The letter did not require more than a glance. Leilis brushed the ball of her thumb lightly across the seal, set the letter back on the table, and murmured, "Cloisonné House is favored above all keiso Houses by the attention of the heir."

"Of course," agreed Mother, in a rather perfunctory tone. She was still frowning. "And profitably so. All of our keiso, not merely Moonflower, will receive many rich gifts if the heir and his companions become regular visitors." That consideration was nothing to dismiss. Keiso Houses must always be extravagant, yet the continual generosity of their patrons could not be assured. In tense times, men hesitated to spend hard coin on luxuries and the entire candlelight district suffered, but the keiso Houses suffered worst because their daily expenses were highest, and hardest to reduce. The approaching spring would make this winter decidedly tense. "This will require careful management, however," murmured Mother.

"Young people often prefer romance over practical sense," Leilis said thoughtfully.

Mother half smiled, an expression that held more thought than humor. "So they do. And you?"

Leilis hesitated. Romance? Or practicality?

The girl might well fancy herself in love. But to send a keiso into a royal family was perilous. Prince Tepres had no true wife, yet. But soon enough he would, and eventually his wife would be queen. A queen was unlikely to be pleased to share her influence with a mere keimiso. She might object, strenuously. And a queen would have influence of her own, which did not depend on her lord husband. As the king would likely have married her for political advantage, even he might find her influence difficult to counter, lest he lose that advantage.

A queen who resented her lord's flower wife might pursue a persistent feud against her. Possibly against all keiso. Such feuds had occurred before in Lonne's long history. Sometimes they ended with the death of the king's keimiso. Sometimes they ended with the entire destruction of one or more of the keiso Houses. That, too, had occurred before.

The pause lengthened as Leilis realized that she was setting concern for Karah's personal happiness against the good of the House. How strange that she had become so sentimental! She said after a moment, "A keiso from Cloisonné House would be a very respectable keimiso for Prince Tepres, but the king may well wish his son to first take a wife and secure a right-born heir of his own for the succession, before getting children on the left. A wife whose child is the king's eldest born might well be less offended by her lord's taking a flower wife. Cloisonné House might best win the Dragon's favor by slowing his heir's rush—and Karah's age provides every necessary reason to resist haste."

"A gentle courtship," murmured Narienneh. She tapped the letter with the tip of one finger. "Perhaps. We do not want the heir's interest to wane, but your suggestion may be wise. Profit and prudence combined. A slow and gentle courtship...that may serve our purpose well. Write out an acceptance to this, Leilis, if you please. I think it best if Moonflower does not see the prince anywhere save within the protection of the House, but the prince is welcome to engage her company here. We will all be very respectable."

Leilis bowed her head.

"You are quite correct," added Mother. "We do not wish the bud to lose its fresh purity. If Rue is not available to accompany Moonflower, then someone else may chaperone her. No one who resents her. Bluefountain has sense. But I will want two women with her. Hmm. You may stay with her, perhaps."

Leilis acknowledged this with a nod, though chaperoning young keiso was not ordinarily a part of her duties. But she did not dislike the idea, in this case. With Moonflower in the room, Leilis doubted that she herself would even be visible to the prince's eye. And if the prince happened to bring with him the foreign lord, Lord Chontas...She did not permit herself to consider whether she either wanted or did not want a renewed acquaintance with that one. She had not described the prior encounter to anyone. It had seemed too complicated. She did not know how to frame it even to herself, much less to anyone else, even if she'd been inclined to confide in anyone. Or had anyone in whom to confide.

Round white lanterns glowed in the slender branches of graceful trees along the river. The lanterns echoed the moon, which could be glimpsed now and then through long streamers of apricot and dusky-violet cloud.

With the lighting of the lanterns, the flower world itself came to life: Graceful keiso strolled along the riverside walks, accompanied by musicians and players of the candlelight district or by their patrons or keisonne. The musicians were often loud and the players flamboyant, but it was the keiso who drew the eye. It was neither their elegant overrobes nor their grace that produced this effect, or not wholly. It was that air of confidence they wore that proclaimed their quality as clearly as a herald might have announced it.

Leilis had had years to become resigned to the hopelessness of herself ever joining their privileged company. She no longer repined over the impossible. Now she stepped deliberately back into the intimate dining chamber and drew the curtains across the balcony entrance, shutting out the evening.

Prince Tepres had come alone to Cloisonné House. Well, as nearly alone as his father's heir could manage. Only the dour Jeres Geliadde had accompanied him. Leilis did not allow herself to feel disappointment at the absence of the foreign lord.

Prince Tepres wore an understated dark overrobe that was almost as plain as his guard's, with only a tracing of saffron and purple embroidery across his shoulders and on the cuffs of his sleeves. He had chosen well, Leilis admitted to herself. The severe plainness of his robe accented his pale hair and brought out his dark eyes. She suspected he knew it, too. Well, a king's heir must learn such things, she supposed. A prince was surely as much on display as any keiso.

Moonflower wore a simple blue overrobe embroidered around the hem with leaves and dragonflies, and a jeweled dragonfly in her hair. Mother had, of course, chosen the robe and the jewel, and very appropriately. Though Leilis privately thought it would have mattered very little to the prince whether the girl wore a keiso robe or drab servant's brown.

This evening Prince Tepres had chosen to soften his image to suit his company: He had brought Moonflower a kitten, which he was just now releasing from its basket. The creature was a soft silver color, with ripples of smoke-dark stripes showing through the silver when it moved and eyes as green as willow leaves.

The kitten had been a clever choice. It instantly gave prince and keiso a common source of merriment. Moonflower exclaimed over its soft fur, then set it down on the floor and laughed with delight as it pounced on her toes. Leilis was certain its claws had been carefully blunted before the prince had presented it; she knew from personal experience how easily sharp claws would go right through light house slippers.

"What is her name?" Moonflower asked the prince, kneeling down and wiggling her fingers in invitation. The kitten, accepting this enticement, flung itself flat on its side and tried to wrestle the girl's hand into submission. Moonflower laughed.

"Moonglow," answered Prince Tepres, leaning his hip against the table and smiling down at this charming picture. "For she so delightfully captures the soft beauty of the moon."

Moonflower glanced up to meet the prince's eyes. If she'd been in doubt about his implied compliment, his smile banished that doubt. She blushed and laughed at the same time, scooping the kitten up into her arms as she rose. "She's—" She paused, because any compliment she paid the kitten now would sound like vanity. "Thank you," she finished simply. "Um—eminence." She blushed again, most becomingly.

"We are not at all formal tonight," the prince assured her. He moved to the head of the chamber's small table and knelt on the cushion there, opening a hand in invitation for Moonflower to join him. His bodyguard took a place against the wall, effacing himself with a practiced air. Leilis, with deliberate humor, took a precisely similar place on the other side of the room.

Servants—Birre and Kaerih—brought in the first dishes of the evening: rounds of soft bread with a delicate mousse of smoked fish on sea-green plates, and mussels in saffron broth in small black bowls. Bluefountain slipped in after them, carrying her kinsana. She gave Prince Tepres a thoughtful glance and knelt on the floor by the door with only the sketchiest bow. He returned a slight nod, looking amused and, beneath the amusement, faintly annoyed.

Bluefountain began a soft rippling melody that did not press itself on the attention, the sort that could spin out for a long time without ever really being noticed. Clearly she intended to stay for a while. An additional chaperone, and this one a respected keiso, would certainly ensure the unimpeachable respectability of the engagement. Wise of Mother, given the speed with which the prince seemed inclined to move in this courtship. He leaned closer to Moonflower and murmured something, gesturing toward the kitten, which was playing with a ribbon the girl had taken from her hair. She laughed and answered, "Oh, I'm sure Mother won't mind—doesn't everyone love kittens? What kind is she? I've never seen one like her."

"There are few of this breed in Lonne," agreed the prince. "They're called Pinenne Clouds, but they're rare even in Pinenne, I believe. My mother brought them with her. This one is a Cloud silver, the rarest color in the breed."

"All the way from Pinenne!" Moonflower marveled.

Well, it *was* a little marvelous, Leilis acknowledged privately. Pinenne was a town of the northern border. If a devotee of the late queen, one would say that Pinenne lay on the border between Lirionne and Enescedd. But if not an admirer of the queen, one might say just as accurately that Pinenne lay on the border with Kalches. Certainly the town had a reputation for more than pretty cats. But young Moonflower didn't seem to know anything of this.

"And a kitten from your mother's home," the girl was saying. "How kind of you to bring so special a gift. I have very little to remind me of my own mother. But I will think of her now, as well as your mother, when I see this kitten."

"Ah." Prince Tepres lifted a hand to prevent the kitten stealing mussels out of the broth, then absently stroked the little animal. "Your mother has also gone beyond? I am sorry. I did not know."

Moonflower glanced down. "When I was eight. I am fortunate to remember her well."

"That...may be harder," said the prince in a low voice. "To remember clearly what one has lost." His own mother, of course, had died when he was much younger.

"But not so hard, after the first grief, as having no memories to hold in the mind and the heart," Moonflower said gently, and moved a hand to touch his in uncalculated sympathy. "It must be a comfort to you, that you still have your father, at least." Her grief for her own father, still immediate, was very clear in her soft voice.

Realization had dawned: The prince saw that this was why the girl had become a keiso. Yet he could hardly proclaim his delight at this outcome. He said instead, "You loved your father? Then I'm sorry for your loss."

Something in the prince's tone drew Moonflower's attention. She said after a moment, "You don't love your father? Or, no... you aren't certain of his love for you? I'm so sorry."

"My father is the Dragon of Lirionne, first," Prince Tepres answered, a little too quickly, as though this was an idea he had spent his life rehearsing. "Of course, he must be so. And he's had poor fortune with his sons..."

"Poor fortune" was not the term Leilis would have used to describe the brutal sequence of treachery, suspicion, trap and betrayal, and counterbetrayal that had led, in the last few years, to the executions of the Dragon's three older legitimate sons. For as little acquaintance as the two had, the conversation had become remarkably intimate. And with no noticeable effort. What a keiso the girl would make! Leilis thought the prince himself was surprised. She pretended very hard she wasn't present, since undoubtedly Prince Tepres would have preferred she not be. Near her, his bodyguard was echoing her I'm-not-here invisible attitude.

Servants brought in new dishes, increasingly elaborate. Leilis suspected neither the prince nor Moonflower really noticed the food. They fed tidbits to the kitten, which finally curled, purring, onto a corner of the prince's overrobe, and fell into a replete slumber. They did not discuss their fathers, but Moonflower told Prince Tepres a bit about her mother, and coaxed him to respond with small details he remembered about his—from a faint crease across Jeres Geliadde's forehead, Leilis thought this was unusual. Moonflower told the prince stories of her seven sisters, and he told her a few from his childhood about his seven brothers, including the brothers who had rebelled against the king their father and been executed for it—and, from the look in the bodyguard's eye, this was *strikingly* unusual.

Moonflower listened with flatteringly close attention and heard possibly more than the prince had meant to tell her. "You were closest to Prince Rette, of all of your brothers, weren't you?"

"I was," agreed Prince Tepres, glancing down. "He was only eight years older than I—not that eight years is so little, but from the time I could walk, he was patient with a younger brother tagging at his heels. He seemed to me everything a prince should be: brave and strong, quick of tongue and hand. Good at everything. I idolized him, I suppose."

"Why—" Moonflower began, and stopped.

The prince lifted his eyes to hers, searching for—what? Leilis wondered. Signs of pity, of hidden condemnation, of fear? What would a highborn girl of the Laodd court think about Prince Rette, about the older two princes whom he had followed into treachery and then death? What did Prince Tepres fear to find in Moonflower's eyes?

Whatever that might be, he didn't seem to find it. After a moment, he relaxed a little. "My brother—" he began, and halted. "I—you have to understand—" He stopped again. Finally he said, "My left-hand brothers are all much older than I am, you know. You did know that? They all hold high places in my father's court—well, not Mieredd, but he's never been interested in politics or power or anything to do with court, only in ships and sailing. But my father... You understand, kings don't share power easily. My mother—" He stopped abruptly. Then he began again. "They—I mean, Gerenes and Tivodd and Rette—they were never...um."

Leilis guessed that the prince was trying to explain, without condemning either his father or his brothers, that the king had never allowed his right-hand sons the authority that was their due and that they had bitterly resented their father's tight-held rein. This was fairly common knowledge in certain circles, but nothing that anybody would be comfortable putting into words. Moonflower obviously didn't understand anything he was trying to say, but her attention to Prince Tepres was close and sympathetic.

"Gerenes and Tivodd were both high-tempered. Hard-mouthed on a tight-held bit, as they say. Impatient..."

And neither one half as clever as he'd thought himself, as Leilis recalled. A bad combination, arrogance and folly. A combination that had led to the downfall of plenty of young lords. And young keiso, for that matter.

Moonflower, probably still not following much of the prince's meaning, nevertheless made a sympathetic sound.

"But Rette...I've never understood why he..."

"I'm sorry," Moonflower said softly, responding to the pain in the prince's tone however little she understood.

"Neither did my father, I think," Prince Tepres added. Hidden behind the flatness of his tone was deep feeling, but clearly nothing he intended to volunteer. Grief for his brother and rage at his father, Leilis guessed, and neither emotion safe to express. Shock at the events of the summer, still not wholly accepted; resentment of the brother, for embroiling himself in that last disastrous plot; both terror and pride at becoming his father's heir? Leilis wondered if the prince himself had ever recognized, ever let himself untangle, all the wild knots that must have been created in his heart this past summer.

"Couldn't your father just, just, I don't know, have...just sent him away, or—"

"No," Prince Tepres said, with finality.

Moonflower was silent for a moment. Then she said, "How simple my father's death seems! We all grieved for him, we still grieve for him, but...it's not a complicated grief. Except...Poor Enelle felt so awful for being the first one to understand that some of us would have to be sold into contracts. Nothing any of us could say could make her really feel that it wasn't any fault of hers, even though she really knows that it wasn't."

She offered this comment delicately, with a downcast glance. Not by even a glance did she suggest explicitly, *Just as it wasn't your fault about your brother.* But the implicit suggestion was clear, if subtle. The prince drew a breath, but Moonflower added, "It was hard, leaving my sisters. But we—we keiso, we say we are sisters, too, did you know? There are things—things here that I wouldn't have wanted to miss." And she looked up quickly to meet the prince's eyes for an instant.

Prince Tepres leaned an elbow on the table, relaxing. "Tell me about your sisters," he invited.

The supper stretched out about twice as long as was usual for such an engagement. Even then, Prince Tepres quite clearly had to compel himself to rise and bow and take his leave, and Moonflower was equally clearly sorry to see him go. The prince offered Bluefountain a plainly set sapphire ring for her company, appropriate but in no way remarkable. But he offered the younger keiso no jewel on his departure. Rather, with surprising diffidence, he opened out a cloth-wrapped parcel to show Moonflower a set of twin pipes of sea dragon ivory and gold. "I believe these pleased you the other evening," he explained. "I thought you might like them, because of your tale of the sea dragon. The ivory makes me think of that."

"Oh," Moonflower breathed, touching the pipes with one tentative fingertip. "I do love them—but they're so beautiful—are you sure you want to give them away?"

"Ah, well—it's not such a generous gift. I don't play pipes, you see, but I thought you might, as you are a keiso." The prince tipped the pipes into her hand and gently folded her fingers closed around them. "You would please me very much if you would someday play them for me."

"I don't play pipes *yet*," the girl replied earnestly. "But I will learn, so I can play these for you. I will have to learn to play *very* well, so I do not insult your beautiful gift."

"Your touch, even inexperienced, will surely draw only beauty from them," Prince Tepres assured her, and took his leave.

"Well, that was a resounding success," Leilis said to Bluefountain later, after settling Moonflower back in the room she shared with Rue. Bluefountain, long secure in her own worth to Cloisonné House and to the flower world, found no threat in Moonflower's swift rise. That was why Mother had sent her to accompany and chaperone the girl's engagement: Narienneh was too wise to put the newest of her daughters in company that would resent her. Now Leilis helped Bluefountain unstring and put away her kinsana. "She's exhausted. And thoroughly charmed. She has the kitten on the foot of her pallet, and the pipes next to her pillow."

"They're a matched pair. As much as those twin pipes. Ah, young love," Bluefountain said nostalgically. She was rubbing a perfumed ointment into her fingertips, lest extended playing ruin the softness of her fingers. "She will be flying through the clouds in her dreams tonight, I'm sure."

"It's all quite genuine, you know."

"Oh, I know! There's not a stitch of cunning anywhere in that child, is there? Not that she's foolish—"

"No. Just candidly charming," agreed Leilis. "No wonder the heir is falling for her—how much candor do you suppose comes his way? Though I'm sure plenty of charm," she added.

"Well, if she's charmed you, Leilis, she may certainly warm the heart of a young man. You suppose his father—"

Leilis shrugged, honestly unable to guess. She wondered whether Bluefountain was right: Had she herself been charmed by the innocence of the girl? She supposed she had. It was a strange realization. Uncomfortable when Leilis thought about it, and yet not entirely unpleasant. She said merely, "That's Mother's task, to judge that." Her tone was a little sharper than she had intended.

"Well, if the Dragon doesn't care for the notion, Narienneh's the one to work him around to it, if anyone can," Bluefountain commented, unoffended by the sharpness. She yawned hugely, covering her mouth hastily as she took even herself by surprise. "Sorry! I'm not so young as I used to be."

Leilis smothered a yawn of her own and withdrew, allowing the older woman to retire. Then she hesitated. Now that she was alone, weariness dragged at her as well. More than weariness. Jealousy, like bitter ashes on the tongue. That was merely foolish. There was nothing new about solitude. Leilis turned toward the stairs and her own small private chamber with its huge fireplace. The warmth of a fire would be welcome tonight. Since she could not personally curl herself around the warmth of a dawning—or burgeoning—or remembered, for that matter—rapport with a lover.

Well, that *was* bitter. And bitterness was a gall that would eat out a woman's heart. Where was the cool acceptance of loneliness that Leilis had striven so hard to win? Tonight that coolness of mind and spirit seemed as distant as the child she had once been, who had entertained such dreams... At the moment, even a large fire would likely be inadequate to warm *her* chamber. But at least Leilis could have the fire.

Though that thought was not amusing tonight. Tonight, Leilis was in no mood to find amusement in anything.

Entering her own chamber, Leilis shut the door firmly behind her, as though she might shut out both the crowded galleries of Cloisonné House and her own bitter mood.

An insistent hand on her shoulder shook Leilis out of drowned sleep far too soon. A voice said urgently, "Leilis! Leilis!"

For a long blurry moment Leilis thought she must have overslept and someone had been sent to rouse her, but the urgency in the voice meant there was something else, some trouble—some trouble someone thought *she* ought to deal with, instead of Mother or Terah or anyone more official. A deisa or servant had got into trouble, somehow, probably, and now wanted Leilis to help her get out of it again.

Leilis hauled herself up to sitting, rubbing her face hard to try and wake up. There was a low red glow from the smoldering coals in her own fireplace, and a very faint pearly light glimmering around the edges of the closed shutters. Not enough light from either source to make out who had woken her.

"Are you awake?" asked the voice anxiously.

Leilis placed it at last. "Rue," she said. And, not gently, "Rue, it's *barely dawn*. Do you know what time I went to bed last night? What can possibly be so important?"

The keiso ignored this. "Karah's missing."

"What?" Leilis woke up the rest of the way. "Tell me."

"She was asleep when I came in, but then I woke up and she was gone. I thought she'd just stepped out to the necessity, but she didn't come back, and, Leilis, I was afraid to wait."

Because she'd thought at once of Lily, yes. Leilis could think of several things Lily might have done. Persuaded the girl to go outside, trying to make it look as though she'd gone out to meet a lover—that was an old deisa trick. Had Rue warned her about that?

"I looked outside," Rue said anxiously. "She's not right outside any of the doors, and anyway I showed her how to get back in if she should be locked out. No little sister of *mine* is going to be caught that way! I looked in the kitchens, in case she'd just wanted something to eat, but she wasn't there, either. Then I didn't know where to look."

Leilis nodded, stood up, felt her way over to the fireplace, and lit a candle from the coals there. Then, thoughtfully, another. It would be some time before the gray dawn brightened enough to be useful, and much of the House was unlit at night.

"If Lily set this up, Karah will be somewhere she wouldn't want to be found," she said. "If she's in the House, she'll be somewhere she could be locked in, to make sure she's found there. What places in the House lock?"

Not many. Rue and Leilis started at the top of the House and checked the attics, which were sometimes used for storing expensive things. Lily might have lured the girl up to the attics, if she meant to make it seem that Karah had been trying to steal from the House. But Karah was not in the attics.

Leilis and Rue worked their way with increasing grimness down through the House. "She can't be in any of the gallery chambers," Leilis decided. Those chambers didn't lock. "Nor in any of the banquet chambers or other public areas of the house." She rubbed her face hard with the tips of her fingers, trying to think. "We should skip from here down to the servant's areas. The laundry..." Light dawned, as though the rising sun had brought inspiration with it. "You checked the kitchens, Rue. But did you check the cellars?"

Rue stopped. "Oh. Even Lily wouldn't have..."

They both knew she certainly would have. "Last night was a late one for the cook and all the kitchen girls, too," Leilis said grimly. "It will be hours yet before anyone opens the cellar doors." She stalked past Rue, heading for the stairs. But the dancer passed her, took the stairs three at a time with an assured grace Leilis couldn't match, and reached the kitchens first.

The bar was indeed across the cellar doors, as it always was—sometimes some of the kitchen girls slept in the kitchens, and without discussing the matter the doors were barred. No one was comfortable sleeping with the cellar doors unbarred.

Rue crossed the kitchen with half a dozen long strides, jerked the bar up, and flung the door wide. Then she hissed with mingled satisfaction and outrage and offered a hand to the girl sitting at the top of the cellar stairs.

Karah accepted the hand and came out of the stairwell into the warm kitchens, where Leilis was lighting the lanterns and setting water on the coals for tea.

"Oh, yes, please," Karah said gratefully. "Hot tea would be wonderful! It was so cold down there! Thank you so much for coming to find me." She was barefoot and wearing only a light sleeping robe, but though she was shivering, her voice held only a normal relief. She held her new kitten in her arms, but it jumped down at once as Karah carried it into the kitchen. It shook each of its feet in turn as though it had stepped in a puddle, and purposefully hopped up onto a bench by the oven.

Leilis gave Karah a long look, and then exchanged a glance with Rue. Leilis tossed a few pieces of charcoal and a handful of kindling into the oven to encourage the fire and said, keeping her tone casual, "You worried Rue, when she woke and found you gone. How did you come to be down in the cellars?"

"Oh, well…" Karah looked embarrassed. "Sweetrose told me Moonglow had gone down there and she couldn't coax her out from under the wine racks. There's fish in the ice cupboard, and who knows what else Moonglow might have gotten into, so I knew I'd better get her." She sat down gratefully on a cushion Rue put on the edge of the hearth for her and accepted a cup of tea from Leilis with a nod of thanks.

"You ought to have woken me," Rue told her severely.

The girl looked even more embarrassed. "I knew that as soon as Sweetrose shut the door behind me and dropped the bar. I'm sorry, Rue. But it was just a silly prank. I knew Cook would open up the cellar door eventually, and really it was only a little cold on the stairs."

"You didn't feel… you weren't… weren't you frightened?" Rue asked at last.

"Frightened?" Karah looked puzzled. "Well, I was a little uncomfortable when my candle burned out," she conceded. "But after all, I knew someone would come *eventually*. And Moonglow was there to keep me company, of course."

Rue and Leilis exchanged another look. Purity of character as a shield against the unnatural cold of the cellars? Leilis, for one, could not believe this. Plenty of girls were sweet-natured. Leilis did not know of any who could have spent hours in the cellars, in the dark, without being more than *a little uncomfortable*. Or was it the kitten that had somehow protected Karah? Pinenne Clouds

171

were supposed to be lucky, somehow, weren't they? Just what did that reputed luck comprise?

"I could tell Mother about this," Leilis said at last. "But you ought to, Rue. Karah is *your* little sister."

"Yes," agreed Rue, looking grim. She, too, knew how easily the girl might have been ruined by this *prank*. "But, Leilis—"

"I'll come, too," Leilis promised her.

"Wait, wait!" Karah stared from one of them to the other. "It was only a joke—I'm sure Sweetrose didn't mean anything by it. Why can't we all simply...simply go back to bed and forget all this silliness?"

Rue, who hated any sort of fuss and hated it worse if it touched her in any way, looked tempted. Leilis crossed her arms across her chest, gave the dancer a stern look, and said, "This particular prank went well beyond silliness. As Sweetrose knew as well as Rue, or I. You're a keiso, no fit target for deisa mischief. Oh, I'm sure *Sweetrose* didn't mean much by it. I doubt she had two thoughts in her head beyond placating Lily. But, unfortunately, she's the only one you can honestly claim to have seen—is she?"

"Well...yes," Karah admitted. "You think Lily made her take Moonglow and put her in the cellar and bar the door behind me?" She looked disturbed. "Sweetrose ought to have told me. Or you. She could have thought of something to tell Lily, if she'd tried. But even so—"

"No," Rue said, suddenly decisive. She stood up, looking like the whole matter had settled at last in her mind. "Leilis is right. No, hush, child. She is. You've taken no harm from it..." Her voice trailed off in doubt, and she inspected the younger girl with a long stare. "No harm from it, seemingly," she repeated, more firmly. "Even so, this was an assault. On a keiso."

"Mother will be outraged," Leilis predicted, with a kind of grim satisfaction. "*You*," she added firmly to Karah, "had better go to your room and go to sleep! This isn't for you to deal with. Keiso shouldn't be up at dawn anyway. How will you stay lively through your late evenings? Rue, tell the child to go to bed."

"Yes," said Rue, nodding. "Go to bed, child. Take your kitten and go to sleep. Leilis—"

"I'll wake Mother," said Leilis. "You'd better warn Sweetrose and give the stupid girl a chance to get herself together."

"Yes," said Rue. She gave Karah a little push toward the room they shared and strode away toward the deisa rooms.

"This was an assault. An *assault*. On a keiso." Narienneh was exactly as outraged as Leilis had predicted. She fixed the unfortunate Sweetrose with an unforgiving stare. "You have never been the most clever girl, Sweetrose. But this!"

Besides the Mother of Cloisonné House, only Terah, Rue, and Leilis were present. Rue would be, of course, and Terah was the retired keiso Narienneh most depended on in managing household affairs, but there was no obvious excuse for Leilis's presence. Nevertheless, Narienneh hadn't sent her away. No one seemed to find this surprising.

Sweetrose, an exquisite girl of sixteen with dazzling huge eyes and a pretty, artless manner, was close to tears. Leilis knew that the girl's artless manner actually rose from a wit too dim for artifice. But the girl could manage a certain basic charm. Easy tears were part of this.

Narienneh, of course, was not impressed by girls' tricks with tears. She said now, both impatient and regretful, "Well? You thought I would take no notice of this jealous attack on a *keiso*?"

"But . . . she's not even *really* a keiso," Sweetrose protested, eyes brimming. "Truly, I never meant . . . and Lily said . . ."

The *crack* of Narienneh's hand on the surface of her desk was as sharp as the crack of a whip, and nearly as alarming.

Leilis hid a sigh. She could have warned Sweetrose not to bring Lily into this. In fact, she should have. Mother was now, if possible, even angrier.

Mother leaned forward, her fine-boned elegant face rigid. "Do not *dare* throw guilt for your own acts on the other deisa!" she snapped. "Do not *dare*!"

Sweetrose, thoroughly quelled, shrank in the face of this rage.

Narienneh straightened, drew a slow breath, and let it out again. All her anger seemed to go with it, leaving only a weary regret. "You'll have to leave this House, child," she said at last. "There's no way else. No. Stop that weeping, foolish girl. You should have thought twice and three times before that outrageous trick of yours! Only great good fortune spared my newest daughter a ruined spirit or spoiled disposition." The phrase *my newest daughter* emphasized Sweetrose's lack of that status. "It's quite plain you haven't the sense to make a keiso in Cloisonné House. Go fetch your things, girl. Terah will help you gather them. Out. Go."

Narienneh watched the former Sweetrose stumble from the room, then turned a hard glance on Rue. The dancer, with a streak of ruthlessness few would have guessed at, only returned a short nod and strode out after the unfortunate girl.

The Mother of Cloisonné House stared after them, expressionless.

Leilis, surprised by an unexpected impulse toward sympathy, bowed her head a little to make Mother notice her.

Narienneh, her eye drawn by that gesture, glanced toward Leilis. After a moment, she nodded permission to speak.

"A foolish, weak-willed child," murmured Leilis. "But so many girls are foolish, no matter how pretty! How fortunate there are keiso Houses willing to shelter such girls, so long as they are earnest and industrious, or the flower world would never have enough young deisa coming up."

Mother glanced thoughtfully after the departed Sweetrose. "Earnest and industrious, I will allow. Sweet tempered and willing to please, ordinarily. But such an ugly resentment of our newest keiso, and such poor judgment!"

"Foolish talk in the deisa quarters should never be encouraged," Leilis agreed.

The glance Narienneh directed toward Leilis was sharp. "You believe I should write her a reference?"

Leilis widened her eyes just a little. "That would be very generous, Mother. With such a reference, one of the lower-tier Houses might take the child as a deisa. Riverreed House, perhaps. That would spare Sweetrose being forced into an aika House, or worse, some dockside establishment."

"I am surprised you should concern yourself with her," Narienneh commented, but the Mother of Cloisonné House clearly liked the idea of providing at least a small boost to her rejected deisa. She sat down at her desk, pulled out a formal roll of parchment, and set quill to it. She wrote quickly for a moment, then held the resultant note out to Leilis.

Leilis, wondering herself about her own generous impulse, took the parchment by the edges, careful of the drying ink, and scanned the delicate clear script. She glanced up.

Narienneh sat back in her tall-backed chair and tapped the feathered end of the quill gently on the surface of her desk. "One would not wish to be too easy."

"Generosity is a certain sign of nobility of heart," Leilis commented, in a slightly dry tone, because though this was always true in the theater and in dances, anyone who lived in a keiso House knew better than to believe artistic truths.

Mother made a faint gesture of disdain, but at the same time her mouth crooked into a slight smile.

"I shall suggest appropriate Houses, then," Leilis said, with a small formal bow of acquiescence. "And I shall advise her to dry those tears of hers and try each one smiling. Resilience and a bit of spirit will do better for her than piteous tears. Have you other advice I should convey?"

"If advice would make a fool wise, there would be no fools in the world," Mother said tartly, and sighed, the sadness in her face belying the sharpness of her words. She added in a lower tone, "Perhaps I should make Lily keiso at once. Perhaps that would..." She did not complete the suggestion.

Leilis bit back an exclamation of dismay. She lowered her eyes instead, and murmured, "Cloisonné House may surely set the style for lesser Houses. But yielding to foolishness among the deisa may not end their envy." *Rather the reverse*, she did not say. It was hardly necessary to point out the obvious. Mother was already waving away her own suggestion. She said merely, "You may deliver that reference, Leilis."

Leilis bowed obedience and rolled up the parchment. It was only a pity, she thought, that she was not delivering this reference to Lily. Except she doubted that any reference, no matter how generously worded, would open a place for Lily at any house other than Cloisonné... at any house where the Mother was not so blinded by partiality that she could not see that Lily's malice was not the ordinary jealousy of any deisa.

Well... at least Sweetrose's dismissal should make even Lily cautious. For a while. So for that little while, Karah should be safe. Leilis tapped the parchment against the palm of her hand and lengthened her stride down the stairs, hurrying to be sure she would catch Sweetrose before the girl left the house. There was a pleasure in the hurry, a kind of pleasure Leilis had almost forgotten. Not the cold satisfaction of settling the affairs of Cloisonné House properly, but a warmer feeling, born of unaccustomed kindness.

And yet Leilis did not think she had ever been deliberately unkind toward the girls and women of Cloisonné House. Indifferent, perhaps, to the concerns that moved them and were so often so petty. But unkind? Surely mere lack of interest was not the same as unkindness? And if she had for years been unmoved by the small troubles of keiso and servants and, especially, servants, then... why now should those troubles move her? She turned a corner and went down a flight of stairs, frowning.

CHAPTER 10

Nemienne woke up out of unremembered dreams with a sharp thrill of terror and a conviction that she had almost heard a scattering of delicate musical notes. She understood the terror only after she felt it. It woke her, and she sat up with a sharp gasp. Only then did she realize that she was not in her bed at home alongside her sisters, nor in her small, pretty room in Mage Ankennes's house. Instead, she sat on cold stone. She was surrounded by stone, enclosed by a great, heavy darkness. It was the darkness that smothered light; the darkness that seemed as though it might smother breath as well. In the far distance, Nemienne could not hear music now, but only the slow, distant dripping of water.

There was stone under her hand when she pushed herself to her feet, stone above her and all around her. She couldn't see it, but she knew it was there: a crushing weight above and to every side. This heavy darkness was the shadow the stone cast, she understood suddenly. That was why it weighed so heavily, because there was so much stone . . . She understood as well, and just as abruptly, that she was still dreaming.

Over the past days, Nemienne had learned to summon first warmth and then light into the commonplace darkness that lay in an ordinary unlit room or outside under the high stars. But she had never yet been able to break through the heavier darkness that lay under stone.

She was embarrassed by her failure, though Mage Ankennes

was patient. Nemienne was grateful every day for his patience, but she resented the fact that he needed to be patient. Mage Ankennes said she would learn. He said she had been born to be a mage. Nemienne was determined to make sure he was proved right. But still she could not learn to summon light into the darkness.

But it seemed unfair—silly, even—that she should not be able to summon light in a *dream*. In a dream, you should be able to do *anything*. In the dream, then, Nemienne lifted her hands and tried again to call light. Or not call, exactly. She found she was more searching for light that might already be here, light that would not do battle with the surrounding darkness, but would exist in companionable peace with it.

And light came. But not any familiar light. Not the clean white light she'd wanted. This was a pale greenish light that clung to her hands and illuminated...well, very little. Nemienne knew she stood on stone because she could feel it underfoot. She knew that somewhere far away water was dripping into a pool from somewhere very high above. But the light she had found did not press back the darkness very far, and she could see nothing else.

Then a glimmer, up ahead of her, turned out on a second glance to be Enkea's white foot. The cat was just visible, standing like a statue at the farthest boundary of Nemienne's light. She turned her head and looked at Nemienne over her shoulder, and her eyes flashed green as the light—greener: green as the shade under beech leaves, green as the light that filtered through the sea...The slim cat turned again and walked away into the dark.

Nemienne walked forward, following the cat through her dream. The pale light that clung to her hands trailed behind her as she moved, ribbons of light that undulated through the dark like waterweed through the moving sea. Nemienne felt that she herself drifted like that through this dark, as though it had as much substance and body as water and she almost swam through it rather than walked.

It occurred to Nemienne, as she followed Enkea, that behind the dripping of the water, she could once more hear the breathy, delicate sound of pipes. The music was not loud, but the pipes possessed a pure fragile voice—no, two distinct voices. One was pitched low, to match the weight of the surrounding darkness. The other was pitched high...to match light? No, of course not, she realized at once. The higher voice of the pipe was pitched to lay a path through the dark, but not a path into light...Nemienne hesitated, drawn to follow that strange harmony and yet doubting suddenly where that path might lead.

Ahead of her, Enkea turned her head again and mewed, a thin sound that slipped through the dark without disturbing it. Nemienne hurried forward after the cat. In the way of dreams, she was suddenly running...She no longer felt the stone under her feet, but the sound of each water drop striking into whatever pool hid in the darkness echoed around Nemienne like the stroke of a brazen bell.

Ahead of her, she suddenly saw someone. In the way of dreams, she knew at once who this was. As though this knowledge brought her through all the darkness and across all the distance that separated them, she found herself immediately at her sister's side, reaching out to grasp Karah's hands. She was only tangentially aware of someone else, another presence, a man, a stranger...but whoever he was, she did not know him, and while she clung to her sister's hands, he walked away from them both, following the music of the pipes into the darkness.

Karah, Nemienne knew, had also been following the voices of the pipes. And, without understanding why, Nemienne knew her sister must not follow that music. That neither of them dared follow it, or like the stranger, they would vanish along the path the music laid down into the dark. As though the very realization broke some strange spell, the sound of the pipes faded into the distance...faint and fainter, and then gone. And as though the vanishing sound of the pipes took confusion away with it, Nemienne realized that she was awake.

In the greenish glow of light clinging to Nemienne's hands, Karah blinked, shook her head, and blinked again—much as though she herself was waking from a dream. A shape half hidden by her hair stirred, and Nemienne saw that her sister carried a kitten on her shoulder. The small animal seemed made of silver and smoke. Its eyes were green as water. It peered down from Karah's shoulder toward Enkea, who sat with her tail coiled around her feet and blinked up at it in calm disdain.

"Karah?" Nemienne said, and was surprised by how self-possessed she sounded. Almost as if she spoke with someone else's voice, someone older and much more experienced. She could not, after all, decide whether she was dreaming or awake. She pinched the skin of her wrist between her fingernails, blinking at the sharp pain.

"Nemienne?" Karah said in return. She gazed, bewildered, at her sister and the greenish light, and then around at the powerful darkness that surrounded them both. Then she scrubbed her face with her hands, shook her head again, and asked, "Where are we? What is this...place?" The last word sounded doubtful.

The kitten leaped down from Karah's shoulder, dashed toward Enkea, flung itself flat on its side, slid across the stone, and wound up nearly underneath the adult cat, reaching up with one little paw to bat at her nose. Enkea drew herself up to her feet with an affronted hiss and stalked away, pausing only to glare back commandingly over her shoulder at Nemienne.

"Um..." Nemienne did not know how to answer her sister. Instead, she drew Karah around, never letting go of her hand, and tugged her after the cat. The kitten dashed after them, making little forays out into the dark but always circling back to the girls. Several times Nemienne nearly tripped on it, until Karah finally picked the little creature up and put it back on her shoulder. Then it hid itself in her hair, peering out with eyes that reflected the green light like emeralds.

"Where did you get the kitten?" Nemienne asked at last, because that was a question that might actually have an answer.

"Oh, she was a gift," answered Karah, and blushed—actually blushed, visible even in the strange light, which made Nemienne laugh. Karah laughed, too, a warm chuckle that invited her sister to share her delight not only in the gift but also in the fact of the giving.

"You're already receiving gifts! And from whom? Is he wonderful?" Nemienne asked, teasing.

"He might be. Maybe he is," Karah said, laughing again, seeming both happy and embarrassed. But then she at once turned the subject: "And your cat? Where did you get her? I think Moonglow is special, I mean really special, not just special to me. But your cat must be special, too, don't you think? She certainly seems to know where she's going."

"Oh, she's not mine," Nemienne said, and started to say that Enkea belonged to Mage Ankennes. But then she was not sure this was exactly true, either, and so she said instead, "She always does seem to know where she's going—and she always seems to think I should follow her, usually into uncomfortable places!"

"As long as she leads us out again," Karah said, glancing around once more at the surrounding darkness that pressed in on all sides.

Somehow Nemienne didn't think this was the right time to explain that the last time Enkea had led her into the dark, the cat had not in fact led her back out.

Trails of green light rippled behind them where they had passed, brightest near at hand and trailing out to invisibility about twenty steps behind them. "That's so strange," Karah said, glancing back, and echoed Nemienne's own thought: "That light of yours looks like undersea plants stirred by the current. But a current through, I don't know, darkness instead of water. Where *are* we, exactly?"

Nemienne began to say that she didn't know, but what came out was, "I think, beneath the mountain. Kerre Maraddras, I think." She paused, hearing this answer echo away into the dark. Hearing the truth of it. She said, exploring that truth, "I've been here before—there's a way into this place from Mage Ankennes's house. At least one way. But this time I only woke up and I was here. I think I came here this time because you were here. But however did *you* come to be here, Karah?"

Her sister answered slowly, "I was asleep, too, I think. I think, in my dreams, there was piping."

"Piping!" Nemienne almost thought she might have heard pipe music, too, just as she had woken into the darkness here, but she was no longer sure.

"Yes. I followed the music. I didn't walk through darkness, not then. It seemed I walked through a marvelous place, but I can't remember anything of that place now. Or maybe it only seemed that the piping was leading me somewhere marvelous... Then you caught my hands and I... woke up." She glanced around doubtfully, probably wondering whether she was truly awake after all.

Nemienne had no doubt of that. Not anymore. She only wished she knew exactly what it meant, to be inside the mountain. And she wished she knew how to get out again. She had a sudden, vivid idea that she might perhaps walk with her sister, through the dark, forever. How long would it be, if they could not find their way out, before they left their bones here, surrounded by stone, to whiten in the dark where no one would ever see them?

The sound of dripping water had become much louder, and the sound had gained a reverberant echo that was somehow disturbing. They were going toward it, Nemienne realized, and for no reason that she understood, she felt a jolt of terror at the thought. She stopped in her tracks.

Karah, still holding Nemienne's hand, perforce drew to a halt as well. "Nemienne?" Karah asked, not frightened herself. Or not yet.

Nemienne, unable to explain her own fear, stood wordless.

Ahead of them, Enkea turned and gazed back over her shoulder at them, her green eyes glowing like small lamps. Karah's smoke-and-silver kitten slipped out from Karah's hair again and jumped down to the stone. This time the kitten didn't dash about and play but stepped solemnly forward to join the older cat. She looked like a puff of silver steam next to the nearly invisible Enkea, but her eyes were the same glittering emerald, and her air of not-quite-patient waiting was the same as well.

"We don't have to follow them," Karah pointed out, "if you'd rather not, and if you know another way out."

"They're not leading us out of the dark at all," Nemienne answered, though not knowing how she knew this. "They're leading us toward something else..."

"Really? What?"

Nemienne only shook her head. She remembered perfectly well the homely, everyday light she'd held in her mind previously, when she had stepped out of the dark and into that remembered light. She could do that again, probably. Probably she could even bring Karah with her. She was sure she could. That kind of ordinary light glimmered around the edges of her mind and memory in implicit invitation. But if she took that way out, she'd never know toward what goal Enkea and the kitten were leading them. And she was curious as well as frightened. What was it that lay beneath stone, within Kerre Maraddras, at the heart of darkness?

"I'm not sure we should follow them, if they're not showing us the way out," Karah said. Her tone was still reasonable, still matter-of-fact, as though this were some practical decision they had to make. "It's terribly late, I think—or terribly early. I'm sure I should be back in Cloisonné House by the time everyone's stirring. And you..." Her eye fell worriedly on her sister.

Nemienne shook her head, though a moment ago she had been the one frightened, the one who had wanted to turn aside. "It's not a question of what we *should* do. It's a question of what we *need* to do." This came out more confusing than she'd intended, but she didn't know how to put what she felt into words. She took a step forward again. Ahead of them, both cats immediately started forward again as well. Enkea's white foot flashed with her steps, and the kitten's pale form flickered at the older cat's side like a silver fish swimming through dark waters. Nemienne had not released Karah's hand, and so her sister was drawn after her.

Ahead of them, the endless darkness was in fact ending at last. Uneven walls of pale stone became visible before the girls, glimmering with a subdued light that seemed to pass through them, as the light of a candle might pass through a translucent screen. Like the light that clung to Nemienne's hands, this light was green tinged. The green light seemed less to push back the darkness than...*accent* it, somehow. Nemienne suspected that this was not the sort of light Mage Ankennes had in mind when he tried to teach her to summon light as a defense against the dark.

And yet, now that they were able to see them properly, the caverns were unexpectedly beautiful. On all sides, glistening pale stone folded into curtains and pillars. Powerful stalactites and delicate spines descended from unseen heights, each beaded with moisture that slowly gathered at its tip before dripping to the moist stone beneath. But these drops of falling water were not what had haunted Nemienne through this darkness.

What she had heard...what echoed through the caverns here... was the sound of fat drops of water falling into a deep pool of black water that, as they came around one last curtain of stone, lay unexpectedly before them. Though the water was black, it seemed to glimmer with a light of its own, and each drop of water that fell into the pool glowed like a live ember. And when each drop fell, it seemed to Nemienne, it struck the black pool with a reverberant liquid chiming, as though a bell was somehow ringing under the water.

Beyond the pool...and this took time to grasp, for it was so unexpected and so vast that at first the eye did not focus on it...but beyond the pool lay, carved in deep relief from the pale stone, a dragon. Nemienne at once recognized the long serpentine form as the dragon from Mage Ankennes's harp. In the book by Kelle Iasodde that Mage Ankennes had given her to study, Nemienne had found images of dragons like this one, drawn in fine black inks and illuminated with gold and crushed pearl.

But *this* dragon had been carved in more detail than any little image engraved in ink. Indeed, it was so detailed that it might have been living, except it was half embedded within the stone of the cavern. The dragon was enormous. If it could have torn itself out of the mountain and taken to the air, it would surely have shaded half of Lonne with the shadow of its outspread wings. But here, within the mountain, those wings were folded.

Water gathered, drop by drop, along the carved edge of one great wing and fell, glittering, into the black water: *plink*. Ripples spread out on the surface of the pool every time a drop fell, and each ripple seemed to run up against the shallow edge of the pool with a not-quite-audible sound of its own, like the vibration that lingered in the air after the note of a plucked kinsana string had faded. This was the sound that had so troubled Nemienne, and now that she saw its source, she could believe she would hear that sound in her dreams forever, that she would never be beyond the reach of that persistent vibration.

The dragon was curled in a loose half circle against the vast wall of the cavern, with the pool of black water spreading out between it and the girls. Nemienne felt a strange relief that the pool was there, as though the water was somehow a protection or a barrier between them. As though they needed that protection.

The dragon's head and part of its neck had been carved free of the far wall. Its head, huge enough to engulf a small house without difficulty, was nevertheless surprisingly graceful. Stone antennae rose in supple curves above the dragon's eyes, more delicate than even the finest cave formations. Behind the head, the dragon's sinuous neck melded imperceptibly into the wall of the cavern. Some distance farther back, the great muscled bulk of its shoulder swelled again out of the wall, leading in turn to the suggestion of a deep chest. Far away along the wall, the dragon's tail looped in and out of the stone of the cavern like a reiterated melody, disappearing and reappearing as though the stone carvers had wanted to suggest infinite length.

"*Oh*," Karah breathed.

Nemienne knew how her sister felt. She herself felt half dazed by the size and beauty of the carving. A king must have commanded it done. Several kings. Surely this dragon was too vast to have been the work of just one king. How many generations had it taken to carve this dragon in the heart of the mountain?

"How beautiful," Karah whispered. "How splendid."

Nemienne glanced at her sister. Karah was transfixed, her hands gripping each other, her head tipped back, staring at the dragon as though she would never be able to look *enough*. She did not seem frightened at all.

Nemienne, in contrast, felt as though they stood on the edge of a great height, where a sudden gust of wind might press them forward and send them tumbling through clouds to the unseen rocks far below; or as though they stood underneath a vast avalanche that was poised to roar down toward them. Stunned by the dragon's magnificence, she was also frightened of it, though she could not guess what peril it might pose to them. "We . . . I don't think we should be here," she whispered. She was afraid to speak too loudly, as though too loud a voice might loose the avalanche.

Karah put an arm around Nemienne's shoulders and hugged her close. "You'll find the way home," she said, not as though she was offering reassurance, but confidently, as though she sincerely believed this.

Nemienne shook her head. She was flattered by her sister's confidence, but she didn't know how to explain that she wasn't afraid because she thought they were lost. It wasn't even *fear* she felt, exactly. Not really *fear*. It was more like awe. She thought there were depths to the darkness here that her sister didn't see. But *she* saw those depths, or at least guessed they were there. She said again, almost in a whisper, "We shouldn't be here." Then she added, "This isn't a place for men at all."

"Well, then—"

"Yes," said Nemienne. "Shh." She looked at the cats, who both sat at the extreme edge of the black pool with their tails wrapped around their feet and gazed back at her with pale light glimmering in their unreadable green eyes. *We've brought you here*, their eyes seemed to say. *Now it's up to you to understand what this place is, and why you needed to see it.* And if Nemienne had no ideas about that, well, she should learn to think like a cat, she supposed.

In fact, though she had no idea why Enkea should have brought them to this place and had never felt farther from the ordinary places of home and hearth, Nemienne was somehow becoming increasingly confident that she could indeed find a path for Karah and herself from this uncanny cavern to that ordinary world. She almost thought she knew how to do that right now. The other time she had been trapped in the dark, she had drawn herself back into the world by remembering ordinary light. Now, in this place where nothing was ordinary, she shut her eyes in favor of the more familiar darkness behind her own eyelids, and searched within that personal darkness for some place more recognizable than the dragon's cavern. The sound of water droplets falling from the dragon's wing intruded, each musical *plink* echoing across the next until the reverberations of sound crept into her bones. That reverberation was almost familiar, but not quite.

Beside her, Karah murmured, "Nemienne, what are you thinking? You're frowning."

"Am I?" Nemienne whispered. It still seemed to her—she couldn't quite decide why—that it would be rude or imprudent, even dangerous, to speak aloud in this place. "Karah, does this cavern remind you of somewhere else?"

"Remind me—" Her sister's answering whisper seemed incredulous. "No! What place could possibly be like this?"

"Not *like*. Just…you know…not similar, but in sympathy?" Nemienne didn't know how to express what she meant, and stopped. Without opening her eyes, she turned toward her sister. There was a faint greenish light that trailed out behind Karah and wavered away into the dark. It did not precisely illuminate a path, but perhaps, Nemienne thought, the echo of a path. She stepped sideways through the dark after that rippling light, drawing her sister after her into the echo of some other place, she did not know quite where…Karah made a surprised sound, but let herself be tugged along.

Nemienne's foot came jarringly down on a surface that was not the stone of the cavern floor. She found gritty, dusty stone under her palm, in a tight-cramped space that pressed her down to her hands and knees. She would have lost her grip on Karah's hand, except that her sister also clung tightly. The air in this place was nothing like the chill damp air of the dragon's cavern. This place, whatever it was, smelled of ash and unfamiliar musky incense and, most strangely, flowers. Nemienne coughed. Ash rose around her, chokingly. She coughed again and couldn't stop.

Then a voice exclaimed, and a strong, slim hand closed around hers, and Nemienne was dragged forward, hard. She crawled into a strange room. There was something strange about that grip as well, but Nemienne did not have time to consider what this oddness might be before she was released again. She was coughing, and her eyes were tearing, but there was suddenly space and air and light. Karah crowded forward after her, also coughing, their hands still linked. Nemienne, frightened despite herself, was glad her sister was with her in this... Where *were* they?

"*What* is this?" exclaimed the voice, and Nemienne blinked her sight clear and found herself on her knees, on the wide hearth of a great fireplace, in an unfamiliar chamber. She was facing a stern-faced young woman about Ananda's age.

The room was a bedchamber, plain but painstakingly neat. The bed was narrow; in fact, the chamber itself was narrow and small. The coverlet on the bed, a good heavy one, was a rich blue, but dyed unevenly so that the blue was streaked all down one side. There was a slim vase on a small table at the foot of the bed, which held in this season only a few plumes of dried grass. There was no ornament in the room but this single vase.

A single long window was placed high on one side, beneath a slanting ceiling. Morning light came in through the window, rose and gold. It was later than Nemienne had thought—breakfast time, at least. Her heart sank. Mage Ankennes would certainly realize she had gone before she could get back. She didn't exactly think he would be angry, but she also didn't look forward to explaining that she had got herself lost beneath the mountain *again*. Well, at least this time she could say truthfully that she hadn't deliberately gone through any doors into the dark.

Nemienne hoped *Karah* wasn't in trouble. The young woman who had helped her clamber out of the fireplace looked angry. She was as austere as the room. She wore a plain overrobe of slate gray over an underrobe of a yellow so pale it was almost cream. Her hair, quite straight, had been put back into a severe knot at the back of her long neck. The comb that held the knot in place was not much of an adornment; it was a simple dark brown that almost vanished against the color of the hair itself. The woman's eyes were a dark storm gray, their expression reserved. Her strong mouth was set in an unamused line.

Then it relaxed in astonishment. "Karah?" the woman said.

Karah said, in a voice only a little choked with ash and bewilderment, "Leilis? But—" and stopped again.

Nemienne said, "Oh, is this Cloisonné House, then?" That explained the scents of incense and flowers. The ash was self-explanatory. She began to make movements toward getting up off her knees, though she felt oddly insecure in her balance. Perhaps being dragged forcibly from a hidden cavern and back into the ordinary world of men through a fireplace was inherently unsettling. Why a fireplace, anyway? Though at that the taste of ashes in her mouth was a little like the taste of shadows and limestone...

Leilis did not offer a hand up. Instead, the young woman stood with her arms crossed over her chest and looked, to Nemienne, to be growing ever more severe. She said to Karah, "Rue told me you'd vanished again. This time I was half minded not to help her look for you—I thought Lily had lured you out again, and was once not enough? But I did. Only this time, neither of us could find you. Did you slip out to find your sister? You never should, not without permission; you may be new to the flower life, but you should know *that*."

"Yes—no—I know—I didn't—" Karah stuttered to a confused halt. Nemienne wanted to pinch her. Couldn't her sister put a reasonable sentence together?

"Well?" said Leilis, sternly.

Nemienne did pinch Karah on the arm, but gently. Karah gave

her a flashing look of mingled affection and exasperation, but she also took the time for a deep breath. When she answered Leilis, she spoke steadily, although not actually very sensibly. "I didn't slip out. I wouldn't do that, Leilis! I heard music and I woke up in the dark, under the mountains, Nemienne said, and at first I thought I was dreaming, but I wasn't. Nemienne was there, and we—there was—well, Nemienne brought us out." She left out the dragon. Nemienne understood: That great carven monster did not lend itself to any kind of casual description.

Karah finished her abbreviated account by giving the fireplace behind them a doubtful look. "I don't know why we came back through your fireplace."

"It's an interesting fireplace," Nemienne said, realizing this was true. She turned to give it a more careful examination. "It's deeper than it looks, isn't it? And that white stone it's made of, that's not ordinary quarry stone." In fact . . . in fact, Nemienne rather thought that that stone had been carved out of the depths of some deep cavern at the heart of a mountain. The cracks in the hearthstones looked odd, too: strangely precise, almost like—well, like—she could not quite remember what those jagged lines reminded her of. She wanted to crouch down by the hearth and trace those lines, make them familiar to the tips of her fingertips in the hopes that this would shake loose her memory. But Leilis didn't look like the sort of woman who would be patient with any such examination.

The woman tapped her foot. "The dark under the mountains," she repeated, her voice edged with sarcasm.

"Yes!" said Karah.

"Yes," said Nemienne, wondering how anyone could possibly doubt her sister's obvious sincerity. "Really. Or how do you think we got into your fireplace? Surely people don't spring out of it every morning."

To Nemienne's surprise, Leilis's mouth crooked at this bit of impudence. "Not *every* morning," she admitted. "Bespelled under the mountains by music! I suppose Lily hired a bit of odd spell-work from some dock mage. How very creative of her."

"Lily?" Nemienne asked.

But Leilis only shook her head, impatient and wary and dismissive all at once. "Never mind. I'll speak to her. In the meantime . . ." She looked the girls up and down and then shook her head again. "You," she said to Karah, "need a bath! You won't have time for sleep now, not before you're supposed to be up properly, which only punishes you as you deserve for springing out of my fireplace and frightening me to death. Go tell Rue you are back even before you bathe!"

"Yes, Leilis." Karah slipped away in immediate obedience.

Nemienne didn't think Leilis looked much like she had ever been frightened by anything. Despite her youth and her plain room, she was obviously someone important in Cloisonné House. So, although Nemienne wanted to ask again about this Lily who might have bought a spell to throw Karah into the dark, she held her tongue.

"Now, you are no one Lily has ever heard of," Leilis said to her. "You're the sister who was apprenticed to Mage Ankennes, of course? Yes. You must have a bath, too, but first I want you to tell me again, in a little more detail, if you please, where and how you found your sister." She sat down on the bed and looked at Nemienne expectantly.

Since there was nowhere else to sit, Nemienne folded up her legs and sat down on the hearth. She surreptitiously traced a fingertip along one of the cracks that ran through the hearthstones while trying to decide what to tell this woman. The odd resonance the fireplace produced was much stronger along the crack. There was a sort of half-felt draft of cool air through the fissure, as though the great caverns beneath the mountain lay only the width of this stone away . . . which they did, in a way. Cloisonné House was a house of shadows, no less than Mage Ankennes's house, Nemienne realized. She wondered who had originally built this house and laid the stones for this fireplace . . .

Leilis made a small, impatient sound.

Nemienne, recalled to the moment, explained hastily, "Karah

191

said she heard music and found herself in the dark. So did I. I dreamed of piping in the dark and woke up under the mountain. It was…well, it was…I don't know if a dock mage would know about that place, or how to make a spell that would take you there." This in fact seemed very unlikely. Nemienne frowned, thinking about it.

Leilis frowned at her. "Piping. Not just music, but specifically piping."

"…yes?"

The woman stood up. "Come along," she said. She led Nemienne out of the room and strode purposively down the gallery, so that Nemienne had to hurry to keep up with her. Leilis led the way along the gallery—all the doors were shut, the women of Cloisonné House evidently all still asleep—and down a flight of stairs to a second, shorter gallery. She strode along this hall to the room on the far end, and here she tapped gently and entered without waiting for an answer.

The room was another bedchamber, this one twice as large and far more handsomely appointed than Leilis's. Two small tables, each with its own dainty little chair set before it, held respectively brushes and combs and pins in neat racks, or little pottery bowls filled with ointments and waxes. A well-used kinsana was set against the far wall, a flute and three sets of hand pipes occupied an ornate stand next to the kinsana, and a scroll filled with musical notation had been pinned open on a stand of its own. The bed was set so that its occupant could catch the breeze from the room's one window, though this was shuttered now against the morning's chill. A pallet was lying across the room from the bed. The pallet was occupied only by Karah's silver kitten, which had evidently made its own way back from the deep places beneath the mountain and was now curled up asleep on the pillow. Karah herself, Nemienne supposed, must already have gone on to her bath.

But another woman was sitting on the bed. Like Leilis, this woman was fully dressed, which Nemienne had begun to guess from the quiet of the House might not be customary at this time of day. Past the first bloom of youth, and with the narrow features and reddish-black hair of a Samenian, this woman looked more interesting than beautiful. Right now her expression combined weariness and exasperation and relief all at once.

The woman—she must be Rue—looked up as Leilis entered and gave a little nod. "So you found our little strayed bird—again. Honestly, Leilis, what are we going to do?" Then she saw Nemienne and stopped abruptly.

Leilis gave a little brusque wave of her hand toward Nemienne. "Karah's sister. She's the one who found her." Leilis stepped aside and impatiently gestured Nemienne forward. "You surely know that your sister has charmed Prince Tepres? Your sister must have said so?"

Karah somehow hadn't thought to mention this. Nemienne knew she must look shocked, but she couldn't help it.

Disregarding Nemienne's amazement, Leilis was going on, "He gave her a set of twin pipes. Where did she keep them, Rue? Oh, under her pillow? Ah, the romance of the young!" From her tone, she might have been a grandmother rather than maybe in her mid-twenties. But Leilis *did* just seem older, somehow. She said, crossing the room to Karah's pallet, "Well, let's have a look, then." The kitten twitched an ear as Leilis lifted the pillow, cracked open one eye, hissed halfheartedly at the intrusion, and went back to sleep.

There was indeed a set of twin pipes under Karah's pillow, a set carved of ivory and bound with gold. Clearly the set had once been very beautiful. Even now an echo of that beauty remained. But the ivory was cracked and yellowed, and the gold blackened and twisted. The pipes looked like they had been thrown into a fire and left there to smolder. Rue, eyes widening in surprise and dismay, silently took them from Leilis, holding them cupped in her hands as though the pipes were some small injured creature.

"Well," said Leilis to Nemienne, "now I believe you did hear piping." She took the pipes gently back from Rue and turned them over curiously.

193

"Prince Tepres...the prince *himself* gave these to her? And she sleeps with them under her *pillow*?" Nemienne remembered Karah blushing when she thought of the man who had given her the kitten. *Is he wonderful?* Nemienne had asked. And her sister had said, *Maybe he is.* Karah was in love with *Prince Tepres.*

Nemienne shook her head in amazement. She reached to take the pipes from Leilis, half expecting the ruined pipes to leap with fire and life in her hands—either because they'd clearly been bespelled or because they'd been a royal gift, she did not quite know which. But they lay quiescent in her hand. But the brush of Leilis's hand against hers was another thing, and not so quiet. Nemienne pulled back and gave Leilis a wide, surprised stare.

Leilis took no notice of Nemienne's reaction. She said, still focused on the pipes, "I much doubt the Dragon's heir knew what he gave her. He knew only that she would be pleased to have them as a gift. He saw as much when he received them himself, a few days past, at that foreign lord's engagement..." Her voice trailed off, and then firmed: "At that engagement, where the foreign lord gave these pipes from his own hand to Prince Tepres."

CHAPTER 11

The pipes Taudde had made were finally brought to life a few days after the keiso engagement, very early in the morning, before the sky had yet begun to lighten toward dawn. Taudde, lying sleepless in his bed, had been listening to the rhythm of the waves that sometimes seemed to permeate Lonne in the long hours that preceded the dawn. He could not quite tell whether he actually heard the music of the sea—his townhouse, set well back from the shore, should have been too far from the sea to hear its voice. But if the music of the sea did reach him even here, the voice of the pipes drowned it.

He had been waiting for the sound of that music—dreading it, but fearing even more that he would never hear it. But Miennes must have decided at last that the time had come to destroy the Dragon's heir.

The inexpert playing set Taudde's teeth on edge, but he was so glad to have the waiting resolved that he welcomed even that. He lay awake and motionless while the delicate web of sound drew tight and then faded slowly, drawing its victims, he knew, along the path that led from the world of ephemeral life into the country of eternal death.

Only when the music had entirely passed beyond hearing did he rise. He went to the window of his room, putting back the shutters so he could gaze out at the chill night. The streetlamps below glowed like pale sea jewels, drowning the light of the stars and the early dawn. In the mountainous heights of Kalches, the stars would be brilliant. On crisp, cold nights, they would seem so close one might reach out and brush them from the sky. Tonight, both Kalches and the stars seemed very far away.

With the fading of the piping came, perhaps, other possibilities. The time for timidity was surely past. Taudde went to his writing desk. There he took out the note Miennes had so recently written to invite him to that fraught dinner. He studied the graceful, slant-ing letters. Then he sat down and penned a letter of his own in that same graceful hand, with ink the azure of the sunlit sea, on the fin-est pale-cream parchment. *If I am dead, know that it was sorcery struck the blow*, he wrote. *But it was not a Kalchesene made this spell: There is treachery 'twixt mountain and sea. Look to the mages of Lonne for this crafting; one of them has betrayed the Dragon and made it seem as though I were false myself.* Would Miennes have used that phrase? Taudde decided that he would, and continued. *Look to the prince; if I am dead, he must be the next target of Lirionne's enemy. If you read this, let my death prove my faithfulness and warn of betrayal from one who has been trusted.* When Taudde wrote the name *Ankennes*, he wrote it in blood-red ink. And when he signed Miennes's name, he signed it in gold ink and with a practiced flourish so like the original that he hoped Miennes himself would have been unable to tell it from his own true signature.

Then he stood waiting for the last words to dry so that he could roll up the parchment and bind it with a black ribbon. And at last he took out his flute once more, and the ring he had stolen from little Moonflower. He let his awareness sink into this ring and found himself playing a low circular melody that wound around and around, smooth and hard and filled with the name of a cau-tious, dour man, but not, Taudde found to his surprise, a man entirely without humor...He spun out a line between himself and this man, and dropped the letter, he hoped, straight into the private room of the prince's bodyguard, Jeres Geliadde. In the early pre-dawn hours, he had every hope no one would see it fall out of the air into that chamber. Though if someone did...that would certainly guarantee the letter would be read immediately.

This was an attack he hoped Mage Ankennes had not anticipated: an attack that hardly used sorcery at all. Taudde did not necessarily expect it to be decisive, but he hoped it would at least prove distracting. Thus he might find his next opportunity—to strike a sharper blow against the mage, or if he could not find a way to do that, at least to get out of Lonne. As soon as the prince's people found him dead, Taudde's letter would be taken very seriously, and once suspicion fell on Mage Ankennes, the mage would undoubtedly find himself answering close questions in the Laodd. Taudde meant to act the moment word of the prince's death made its way down from the Laodd into the city.

After a moment of hesitation, he walked again to the window of his chamber. It was just past dawn, now: the hour of pearl and mist in which the city was most hushed. When *would* the death of the Dragon's heir be discovered? Not long, probably. News of it should rush down from the heights as fast as the Nijiadde Falls and smash into the city as forcefully as the falls smashed into the lake below the mountains. But until the Seriantes Dragon moved against Ankennes, Taudde must expect his own peril to be considerably heightened.

Despite his own danger, Taudde had expected to feel triumph at this moment. Not joy, no, but at least satisfaction at vengeance achieved. He did not know how long he stood by his window, waiting for the rush of triumph through his blood. But he felt only a cold, creeping dread. Not at his own danger. He thought not. He had claimed a victory, but it unexpectedly felt to him like a defeat and he could take no pleasure in it.

The sky in the east brightened, and the wisps of cloud around the jagged peaks turned to rose and gold in the light of the hidden sun. The light poured past the mountains, illuminating their high traceries of ice to jewels and flame. Then the sun rose over the mountain peaks, and the magecrafted lights that lined the streets of Lonne flickered and went out. The sea and sky turned from gray to blue, and the roofs of the city reflected that color back again so strongly that the tiles almost seemed to be made of lapis rather than slate.

Shortly after dawn came the first of the street vendors, calling out their wares: fruit and pastries, bread and fresh-laid eggs. There was nothing in those mingled voices to suggest any unsettling news from the Laodd. Yet.

The morning went forward. No word of death and disaster came down from the Laodd. The palace-fortress of Lonne only loomed as quietly as always above the city, which went on with its customary business. At first Taudde wondered whether the news was simply not being made public. But he realized gradually that this public calm could not possibly mask private disaster: If the Dragon's heir had died in the night, word of it could not possibly have been so completely withheld from the city. Whispers of the loss would have come down on the wind. No matter how quiet or distorted, the unease would be felt in the streets.

The only possible conclusion was that the heir had not died. It was simply not possible that he had died. This knowledge should have carried with it disappointment, rage, a grim sense of failure. But instead, Taudde felt a shocking, unexpected relief: He had failed to do murder. He was not a murderer.

As a boy, staggered by grief after the death of his father at Brenedde, Taudde had longed for vengeance against Geriodde Nerenne ken Seriantes. As a youth, he had dreamed of facing the King of Lirionne across a sharp-edged blade; later, he had dreamed he might someday make a harp of bone, string it with sorrow and rage, and play vengeance for Kalches and for his own father out of its music. But it seemed now that leading the king's son out of life with pipes tuned to the paths of death had never been part of that dream.

On the other hand . . . on the other hand, whatever had happened, or failed to happen, to the prince . . . well, if the prince had not died, was it possible Miennes also still lived? Taudde dispatched Benne to Miennes's house, requesting the favor of an appointment. He was surprised, relieved, and grimly pleased when the big man arrived back with the news that the household of Lord Miennes was in great disarray following the sudden death of the lord in the night, presumably of an unsuspected weakness of the heart. So Taudde's spell had gone only half astray. This was all very well and good, but what then of the other half of the spell?

Taudde dismissed Benne, who went stolidly away. He himself went up to his room to think. If Lord Miennes was dead, that was very well. Taudde did not regret *that* death in the least. But now?

If Ankennes had not already moved against Taudde...what did that mean? Taudde took a deliberate breath, trying to calm himself and think. Had the Laodd not taken his sorcerously delivered warning seriously? Or had the prince's bodyguard not discovered it yet? Or was Mage Ankennes even now answering close questions, and Taudde merely did not know it? Or was the mage merely, like Taudde, considering what he might do next? The urge to do something was very powerful, and yet Taudde feared to act before he knew more clearly what had happened.

Another question occurred to Taudde and at once assumed considerable urgency: If Miennes had indeed played the pipes—as it now seemed he must have—then who else had been caught in the music besides the scheming Lonne lord? Because it was very clear that the second set of pipes had gone astray.

Taudde found that creeping sense of dread again slipping through his veins, as though the chill of it moved right along with his blood. He had tried to be glad, and then had been at least *willing*, to murder the heir of Lirionne. That this murder would also rid him of Miennes had in a way become a mere advantage and not the object of the exercise. After giving the ensorcelled pipes to the prince, he had found himself increasingly horrified by what he had done, but then it had been too late to reconsider his act.

But Prince Tepres had not died. So someone else had possessed the ivory pipes when Lord Miennes had lifted his set of horn and silver to his lips. Someone to whom the young prince would have given them freely. Some young friend of the heir...not a noble, or word of that death would surely have come down from the Laodd. Perhaps the cheerful young Koriadde? Taudde liked Koriadde. He did not want to wonder whether the prince had perhaps given the ivory twin pipes to that young man. But the prince must have passed them on to someone. Koriadde was as likely as anyone else, surely.

The sensation of creeping cold grew worse. Why—*why?*—had Taudde not warned Miennes that he should play the pipes at once, the very night Taudde gave them to him, to ensure the heir would not have time to give the ivory set away? Taudde had not guessed he might do so; in Kalches, such a gift would never be re-gifted within the same year it had been given. But in Lonne, clearly this was not the custom. What would his grandfather say if he knew how extraordinarily careless his grandson had been? Actually— Taudde winced—it was altogether too possible to imagine precisely what that stern old man would say, and every word would be justified.

To whom had the pipes gone? Who had died because of Taudde's carelessness? Koriadde? Another of the young men? Possibly worse, if there was such a thing as *better* or *worse* in this situation: could the prince have given his pipes to a true innocent—a favored servant? A woman?

Taudde had a sudden, horrible sense that he knew exactly to whom the prince had gifted those pipes. On that thought, and as he must wait on events in any case, he went to have his carriage made ready.

Though this interminable day had crept by on slow, clawed feet, it was well past noon. Yet the hour was still early for the candle-light district of the city. But Taudde could not bear to wait for the sun to sink low above the sea—and dared not wait, anyway, lest he find Ankennes taking some unanticipated action against him. He thought perhaps he should try to leave Lonne immediately. Yet...it was always better to act knowledgeably rather than blindly. And he thought he knew where he might get news about Miennes and Ankennes, about Prince Tepres and unusual activity in the Laodd, and most particularly about the little keiso to whom, he now suspected, the prince might have given those pipes.

Benne had the carriage waiting almost before Taudde could make ready for his visit to the keiso district. It was a silent drive: The thronging streets seemed, today, only to point up the depth of the silence that underlay their clamor.

Cloisonné House was indeed quiet at this hour of the afternoon. But, though the House might be quiet, it was not actually asleep. Voices were audible through open windows. Music drifted down from those windows as well: Most clear was a kinsana accompanied by girls' voices chanting gaodd poems. Thankfully farther removed, an inexpertly played ekonne horn was also audible. Voices, blurred by distance and walls, mingled in conversation, and somewhere close at hand a rich alto voice laughed.

It all sounded very peaceful. Taudde, though he was listening carefully, heard no underlying dissonance of grief or distress beneath the cheerful sounds of the keiso House.

He was as much surprised by this as relieved. He had been so sure...but perhaps Prince Tepres had gifted his ivory pipes elsewhere, to someone Taudde had never met. This did not, of course, lessen his culpability in that person's death, whoever it might have been. But Taudde found that he was nevertheless relieved that his unintended victim had evidently not after all been that lovely keiso child.

The peace emanating from Cloisonné House was immeasurably reassuring. Taudde descended from his carriage and went toward the house. As he passed into its shadow, Taudde thought that the edges of that shadow seemed a little less distinct than they should, and that the ivy that climbed the walls seemed to tremble very slightly in a breeze that did not blow from quite the same direction as the breeze that whisked through the street itself. He had nearly forgotten the strange echo that clung to this house, and now he paused, distracted anew, before he collected himself and touched the bellpull.

For all the relatively early hour, servants came quickly to

welcome Taudde and show him to a small parlor. The Mother of the House herself came to greet him there and inquire with grave courtesy what small service Cloisonné House might have the pleasure of offering him.

Taudde said diffidently, "Indeed, I may hope for a kindness to a foreigner, perhaps."

The woman's eyebrows rose.

"If I may ask: That young keiso, I believe she is called Moonflower? A most charming girl. I wish to impress a business associate of my uncle's and I had wondered whether she might be available for engagements?"

"Alas, Cloisonné is as yet strictly limiting Moonflower's engagements. However, if you wish to engage another of our keiso, I believe several might be available..."

Taudde was so relieved that little Moonflower was evidently perfectly well that he nearly forgot to seem disappointed. "Of course I understand, a girl so young," he said quickly, with a downcast look. "Naturally you would wish to guard her well-being. And her future, to be sure. She will be a lovely addition to the, ah, flowers in Cloisonné's garden. I should not imagine there are two such girls even in Lonne. If you see fit, you might pass on to her my admiration."

"Indeed," agreed the Mother of the House warmly, clearly pleased by Taudde's praise. "I will indeed, as you request it. Too much praise can spoil a young keiso's good nature, but I doubt that is a concern in this case. Moonflower is a modest child. No doubt she will only assure me that there are at least seven girls in Lonne who surpass her, as she has so many sisters."

"Seven sisters!" Taudde murmured, raising his eyebrows, as the woman evidently expected some such exclamation.

"Oh, yes." The Mother smiled at his surprise. "Natural sisters, I mean; not the many keiso of the House. Indeed, one of her sisters is apprenticed to one of your guests of the previous evening: Mage Ankennes. A family that owns diverse gifts, one surmises."

Taudde thought he managed some appropriate, vacuous phrase. He hoped he had. He was momentarily too stunned to know what he said, or even to be sure he spoke at all. Moonflower's *sister* was Ankennes's *apprentice*. Pieces of a puzzle he had barely glimpsed fell suddenly into place, like an unforeseen harmony resolving a long-standing discord. *Thus* Moonflower still lived, though Miennes was dead. Though was it the sister or Mage Ankennes himself who had protected the young keiso?

Taudde took a deep breath, collected himself, and since he was still in Cloisonné House made himself turn to the remaining part of his purpose. He rapidly found that he had been quite right: The keiso House was an excellent source of information. Through a few moments of inconsequential converse, Taudde discovered that Miennes was known to have died, but that there was no rumor of sorcery tainting his death; that there was a slight stir within the Laodd but no one knew precisely what had caused it; that only an hour previously Prince Tepres had sent a request for Moonflower's company for an engagement the following evening.

Taudde could not, unfortunately, manage to discover anything useful about Ankennes's current activities or future intentions, but then he had not really expected to. The slight disturbance in the Laodd was promising, however. He thought he might try to get out of Lonne as soon as he left Cloisonné House and discover by that trial whether or not Ankennes was currently otherwise occupied.

"If I may," he murmured at last, as he took his leave. He tried to give the impression of a man struck by a sudden thought—since he was just that, it was not difficult. "The other evening, the keiso were all extremely charming—all that I had been led to believe, I assure you. But I know the servants of this House also worked very hard to make the occasion a success, as you'll understand was very important to me. In Miskiannes, it's the custom for a man of means to offer a gratuity to servants who render good service. Of course, I understand that Cloisonné House cares well for all its dependents. But I wonder whether you might permit me to indulge my custom, even if it is not the custom of Lonne."

The Mother of the House appeared surprised but approving—indeed, she was probably accustomed to being charmed by most of the desires and eccentricities of Cloisonné's clients. He continued, as though casually, "The head of the servants on that evening seemed to me to be a young woman. I believe her name is Leilis? I would like... that is, I wonder if I might impose upon a moment of her time, on behalf of all the servants who assisted on that evening?"

"Yes," the Mother of the House agreed readily. "That would be Leilis. She is a very competent young woman; Moonflower is fortunate to have gained her good opinion. I'm sure Leilis would be pleased by such a request. I shall pass on to her your intention, and any gratuity you should kindly offer, but I regret that Leilis herself is not within the House this evening."

Taudde's heart sank even before he'd ever consciously realized what Leilis's absence from Cloisonné House on this particular day might mean for him—especially if she was a particular friend of the young Moonflower. Then, as he truly understood what the Mother of the House had said and what it might mean, he paused, reordering his immediate plans once again. Then he extricated himself with careful haste from the Mother's company and from Cloisonné House entire and called for Benne.

Benne brought the carriage up as Taudde emerged from Cloisonné House, and leaped down from his high driver's seat to place the step. Taudde took his place within the carriage and leaned forward to say in a deliberately absent tone, "Let us go down to the shore, if you would, Benne. Where the cliffs come down to meet the sea, near the Nijiadde Falls."

The big man nodded and touched the reins, and the horse tossed its head and started forward.

The streets were crowded at first, but shortly Benne turned the horse down less-traveled ways that took them away even from these travelers, toward the sea. Even from this distance, the sound of the waves crashing against the broken shore was clearly audible.

The cliffs where the mountains came down to the sea were gray as wet slate. The sheer white walls of the Laodd loomed over the city, powerful and cold as ice poised for avalanche. Beside the Laodd, the Nijiadde River plunged down from the heights and shattered into roaring spume in its broad lake; then the river poured in wild haste from that lake along its narrow channel to the sea. There, where the incoming waves battled with the river's powerful current, the rugged rocks were black as charcoal. It was like no other shore Taudde had ever seen. It possessed, poised between the steady roar of the Nijiadde River Falls and the constant ebb and flow of the sea, a unique music that he had never yet been able to capture, though he had tried repeatedly during his time in Lonne.

Now Benne drew the horse to a halt on the edge of this shore. They had come out farther than the road led, but not very much farther, for the harsh rocks here were not easily navigated by wheeled vehicles. The horse sidled and tossed its head, restless in the cold salt-laden wind that broke against the cliffs and came down along the shore from odd directions. Benne set the brake and slid down from his seat to stand by the horse's head. The big man took hold of the animal's bridle and patted it reassuringly, then turned to look inquiringly up at Taudde.

Of course Benne had come before with Taudde out to this shore. Taudde had come down to the edge of the sea half a dozen times, covert and solitary, compelled by the rhythm of the waves against the rocks and the slow receding music of the outgoing tide. When he'd come here with Benne, he'd thought it was safe enough. He'd believed any man from an inland country might reasonably be expected to find the sea compelling. Now...now Taudde bent to fetch a packet of papers and a good-quality quill pen out from their packet in the carriage. The quill was magecrafted, inelegantly but with some attention to detail; one might use it to sketch for an hour without the ink needing renewal. It was not the sort of item bardic sorcery could make, and Taudde had already purchased a good many such quills to take home with him when he finally quitted this city.

He tossed the papers to the rocks at Benne's feet and followed this with the quill pen. The wind tried to snatch the quill away and send it spinning out over the sea, but Taudde checked that errant gust with a low whistle. The quill fell straight and struck the papers point down, with an audible little *shick*. It stayed there, its sharpened tip embedded in the packet like a miniature dagger.

Benne watched the quill fall, then lifted his gaze.

Taudde took out his small wooden flute and turned it over in his fingers. He did not look at the instrument he held, but only at the other man. When he spoke, his voice was not loud but pitched to carry over the sounds of sea and wind. "I wondered how it was Lord Miennes came to discover that I am from Kalches. Then I wondered if perhaps Ankennes had discovered it. Then at last I realized I should wonder how it was that *you* discovered it."

Benne straightened his shoulders and stared back at Taudde in, of course, silence. Yet neither did he shake his head or otherwise try to deny the accusation. It occurred to Taudde that Benne, voiceless, was almost as helpless in the face of disaster as the horse would have been: No more than an animal could a mute offer excuses or plead for mercy. His broad, coarse face had set in the blank expression of a man preparing to endure whatever a harsh fate might mete out.

"How did you discover me?" Taudde asked him.

There was an almost imperceptible pause. Then Benne went to one knee and bent to retrieve the packet of paper. He pulled the quill free and took out a single leaf of paper, supporting it on his other knee to write. Even under these straitened circumstances, the man wrote a quick neat hand. Finishing, he held the paper out toward Taudde.

Taudde took it and read, *My lord, you were not subtle enough. I saw a Kalchesene sorcerer once, and heard him speak. I heard that quality in your voice, lord, and sometimes I heard you play. I watched you listening to the sea.*

Taudde looked again at the other man, lifting an eyebrow. He crumpled the paper absently in his hand and tossed it into the wash and ebb of the wave that broke on the rocks. Quickly waterlogged, the bit of paper sank into the water and followed the retreating waves out to sea. Taudde let his eyes follow the path of the waves for a moment, then turned back to Benne. "I knew perfectly well a mute need not be deaf. And yet I see that sometimes I forgot this. I am sure many others have made the same mistake. Miennes owned the house I have been renting, yes? And placed you there to spy on those who might rent it?"

Benne gave a curt nod, and waited.

"Yes," Taudde repeated. He studied the other man. "Was it Miennes, then, who cut your tongue?"

Benne hesitated, then nodded again. He extracted a second leaf of paper from the packet and wrote quickly, then offered the paper to Taudde. It read, *Lord Miennes desired a servant before whom men would speak freely. He bought me from the stone yards and had me taught to read and write. When I had nothing, Lord Miennes gave me everything. Then he told me why he had purchased me. He offered me a choice: to have the cut made in my tongue or to return to the stone yards.*

"A hard choice." And a cruel one. Taudde absently tossed this paper after the other and wondered how many big, simple-looking men had been offered the choice Benne described before Miennes had found one who chose as he desired. And whether any of the ones who had chosen to return whole to the stone yards had actually survived their choice. And further, considering the hidden cleverness in the man before him, whether Benne, too, might have guessed that his only real choice most likely lay between mutilated life as Miennes's servant and death. He asked, "And Nala?"

Benne gave an emphatic shake of his head.

"No?" If Benne had been able to speak, Taudde might have listened for truth or deceit in the tones of his voice. Miennes had made a better spy than he had probably realized with that mutilating knife. Even so, Taudde believed the man was telling him the truth. He asked curiously, "What is she to you?"

Not by so much as a flicker of the eyes did Benne reveal the calculations that passed through his mind as he wrote his response: What answer did Taudde expect? What would be the best answer for Nala, or for Benne himself? But the subtle shift of the big man's breathing suggested to Taudde that those calculations were there.

He took the paper Benne held out to him and read, *Nala is just as she seems: a woman hired to keep the house in order. Lord Miennes ~~has~~ had woman spies, but Nala never even knew that the house was his. She has been a friend to me. I beg my lord will not harm her. I swear she does not know the truth about me. Nor the truth about you.*

"Well, I think that is probably true," Taudde allowed, looking up. He watched a little of the tension leave the man before him. In fact, he thought Benne had not tried to deceive him, not at any moment since Taudde had made his accusation, which spoke well of his courage. Or at least his sense.

"What would you do now that Miennes is dead," Taudde asked him, "if I opened my hand at this moment?" Then he answered his own question: "You would go immediately to Mage Ankennes, or to the Laodd—that might even be more likely. You could inform some lord there of the bardic sorcerer who had the effrontery to come into Lirionne. Into Lonne itself, no less. You would surely be well-rewarded for that information. You would gain the favor of a powerful man—most likely a place in his household—"

A forceful jerk of the head denied this scenario. Benne wrote quickly and offered the paper to Taudde with a sharp gesture. The note read, *I swear I would not. I know what place any great lord would give me: He would make me again into a spy. I would sooner find a place with a scribe in the Paliante. Or down by the docks, where the ships come in from the islands. I understand the speech of Erhlianne, of Samenne, of the outer islands, I write those languages, I could find a place with a reputable scribe. I beg my lord will permit me to seek such a place. I swear I will not reveal you to anyone.*

On consideration, it did indeed seem possible that Benne would prefer the role of scribe to spy. It even seemed likely. Taudde thought about what the big man's life had been since his tongue had been cut: Able to write but forbidden to reveal this skill, he was twice separated from the normal discourse of men. By Lord Miennes's order. Surely he could not have loved his master. Could he? Taudde said slowly, "A man under threat will make any claim. From what you tell me, you served Miennes for years. Would you wish me to believe you would not desire vengeance for his death?"

Benne's wide mouth crooked a little at this. He shook his head and made a deliberate gesture of negation, of denial. Taking another leaf of paper from the packet, he wrote briefly. The words, when Taudde took the note, were very clear: *To Lord Miennes, I was a tool to be fashioned as he wished. His death frees me. I beg my lord will free me also. I swear I will not trouble you again.*

Taudde crumpled this paper, too, and dropped it into the surf after the others. Then, absently, he ran the smooth length of his flute through his hands, fingering its stops and frets. He said slowly, "Bardic sorcery is not without its limitations. But the limitations of sorcery are not the same as those of magecraft. You say you wish to find a place with a scribe? I offer you better: You may accompany me to Kalches, if you wish. Where we shall see whether sorcery will stretch so far as to restore your voice."

Benne had been looking at the little flute. Now the man lifted his gaze to Taudde's face and stared at him, motionless.

"What I ask in return," Taudde told him, "is that you place service to me above any other loyalty you may owe elsewhere, until we depart Lirionne. I cannot guarantee I will be able to restore your voice. But I swear to you, if you pledge me what I ask, I will try."

It took Benne a long moment to extract a paper from the packet, and when he did at last, his hand was shaking so that he tore it. When he wrote, he tore the paper again with the point of the quill pen.

The note read simply, *For that chance, I will do anything.*

Taudde shook his head immediately. "In Kalches, we hold that it's perilous to make so broad a promise to anyone, and ill done to accept it. Make a narrower pledge, man. I ask only for your service and loyalty while I am in Lirionne. Can you promise that, above any other loyalty you may owe elsewhere?"

Benne gave Taudde a long, unreadable look. Then he took another paper out, this time more carefully. He wrote for a moment, hesitated, then added a few more words. When he offered this paper to Taudde, his expression was once more restrained, his mouth set and steady, his eyes unrevealing. But his hand still trembled, just perceptibly.

I owe no loyalty to anyone in Lonne. As Lord Miennes has died, I owe no service anywhere. I wish nothing but to accept what you offer, my lord. If you can restore my speech, my loyalty is yours, and I am glad to offer it. But I would ask, if my lord will permit me, what is your purpose in Lonne?

Taudde read this and nodded. This was much better, implying as it did a limit to the pledge Benne was willing to make. He said, truthfully, because it would be an ill thing to bind falsehood into an oath of loyalty and fidelity, "I am neither a spy nor a saboteur nor an assassin—I have no leave to be here at all, from my own people. I came to Lonne to strive to understand the sea, nothing more. Kalches has no coast, and I...there is a deep magic in the sea, especially perceptible near Lonne, that I desire to understand." Though *desire* seemed a weak term to describe the heart-deep compulsion that had driven him to this coast. But he knew no words to describe the goad that his dreams of sea magic had become. "Now that my nationality has become known, I intend to leave Lirionne as soon as I may. But Mage Ankennes blocks me. Would you then be willing to stand out of the way as I move against Ankennes?"

Benne's face hardened. This, he did not need to think about: He nodded sharply at once.

"You dislike the mage?"

Another nod, as decisive as the first.

"Why?"

But this seemed difficult to explain. Benne started to write, paused, crumpled up the paper and began again, but with no better result.

"Never mind." Satisfied that the other man would not warn or assist Ankennes, even if he knew of Taudde's move and found the chance, Taudde dismissed the question. "That will do."

Benne made a gesture of acceptance and followed it with a deep bow: the bow of a man offering fealty, his palms flat on the rocks and his face touching the damp stone.

"Well," said Taudde, moved even though he had expected the man to accept his proposal. "I will be glad of your service. As it happens, you may be of use to me at once. There is a woman, a servant in Cloisonné House. She has, I believe, evidence that links me to Miennes's death. I believe she has taken it to the Laodd— she may have done so as early as this past dawn. Perhaps she might go to Prince Tepres, perhaps to someone else. You will understand that I wish to intercept her before she can make this evidence known to anyone there. Can you assist me in this, Benne?" Laid out like that, it scarcely seemed likely that anyone could help.

But the big man looked thoughtful. He wrote quickly.

Taudde read, *This woman is not a keiso, but House staff? I know where in the Laodd she will wait.* Taudde finished reading and looked up, cautiously hopeful. "This seems promising."

Benne nodded, and got to his feet. He nodded toward the Laodd and looked at Taudde, clearly meaning *That way.*

If there was anywhere Taudde less wished to find himself than the Dragon's fortress, he could not immediately think of it. He made himself nod in return and lift a hand for Benne to precede him.

CHAPTER 12

Nemienne, returning to the Lane of Shadows from Cloisonné House rather later than she had hoped to, laid her hand on the door of Mage Ankennes's house and then touched the head of the cat statue by the door. Of course, the door didn't open. After several minutes, Nemienne gritted her teeth and rapped hard on the oak panels in the center of the door.

A moment later the lock clicked, and Ankennes swung the door open. His eyebrows rose as he looked down at her. Nemienne tried to look as though she was perfectly at ease, but didn't think she managed it very well.

"I've had apprentices now and again in the past," the mage observed at last, his tone mild. "Each had unique strengths and odd weaknesses. But I don't recall any of them having precisely the idiosyncrasies you are displaying, Nemienne. Come in. Have you had breakfast? No? Well, then, perhaps while you do, you can tell me where you have been this time."

Nemienne meekly followed Ankennes through the stubborn door, trying to decide just how displeased he might be with his current apprentice's, well, idiosyncrasies. There were no new doors or windows in the hall, this time. Most of the current row of windows looked out into morning light high in the mountains, but the nearest showed a sharp-edged night that glittered with stars. The beech door and the door with the carved animals were both shut fast, but the black door was standing a little ajar. Mage Ankennes gave it a look and pulled it shut as he passed it, with a swift glance at Nemienne. Nemienne flushed under that glance.

The mage made her rice porridge for breakfast, taking fresh bread out of the cupboard and butter out of the ice pantry while they waited for the rice to cook. Nemienne sliced the bread and spread it with butter. Since Enkea was asleep on the chair nearest the stove, Nemienne sat down on the stove's hearth to eat the bread. The heat of the stove beat pleasantly over her, driving away the memory of cold. Nemienne bit into her bread and tried to decide how to put into words the thin piping and heavy darkness and great carved dragon.

"Did you go through the black door?" the mage asked her. He had sat down himself on the bench by the long table, where he could keep an eye on the porridge. His tone was not unkind, but his slate-gray eyes were chilly.

"No!" said Nemienne. The look in his eyes frightened her. She was relieved she could deny it. "I..." She paused, trying to make sense of the night's events, conscious of how strange any explanation must seem to anyone who had not been there. Her family, despite the best will in the world, would not have really been able to understand the... the *feel* of the heavy darkness and the dragon's cavern. But Ankennes was a mage, she reminded herself. *He* would understand. And yet, although this ought to have been true, she could not overcome a visceral reluctance to explain what had happened.

But that was silly. It was *stupid*. What, so far, had Mage Ankennes failed to understand? When had he ever been anything other than kind and patient? She said, trying for a firm tone but sounding hesitant even to herself, "I woke up in the dark—well, that is, I thought I was dreaming, but after a while I knew I was awake. There was music—at least, I'm sure there was, but it was very faint. I couldn't really hear it—I don't think it was really meant for me—but I found my sister Karah following the music. She stopped when I caught her hand, and then the music stopped, too. It was after that that I knew I was awake. I thought—I knew—we were deep under Kerre Maraddras, but I don't know how I knew. Enkea was there, and a kitten someone gave Karah. They led us..." Her voice trailed off. She found herself somehow reluctant to describe the cavern with the black pool and the great white dragon carved into its farthest wall.

"Music drew you into the dark?" murmured the mage. He got up briefly to stir the porridge, then sat back down and looked thoughtfully at her. His eyes were no longer cold, but they held a strange, predatory glint. He seemed to have found this account perfectly plausible, for some reason. He asked, "What kind of music?"

"Pipes," answered Nemienne. "I don't know—someone showed me a set of twin pipes Karah had been given, but they were ruined. But it might have been those I heard. I think it was."

"Interesting," said the mage, but though Nemienne waited hopefully, he did not explain anything of his thoughts. He merely waved a hand at her: *Go on*.

"Well..." Nemienne tried to organize memories that now seemed jumbled and uncertain. "There was the sound of dripping water. Of water falling into a pool. You know, the sound that's always there in the dark..."

"Yes. And?"

"Well, Enkea led us to a place, a cavern, really big. There was a pool there, and water dripping into it, and...there was this carving..."

"The Dragon of Lonne." Mage Ankennes leaned back in his chair and regarded Nemienne as though she had just this moment magically appeared in his kitchen, next to his iron stove, eating his bread. As though he had never really seen her before and wasn't entirely certain he was pleased by the sight. "You found the dragon's chamber."

A shiver went down Nemienne's spine, but she could not tell whether this was because of the memories of the cavern under Kerre Maraddras or because of the mage's cool tone. She asked cautiously, "Do you know what...what any of that means, any of the things that happened last night?"

The mage lifted an eyebrow and served them both porridge without answering. The rice was perfectly cooked, but Nemienne, finding herself with little appetite, only stirred hers around in the bowl.

"You saw no one else under the mountain?" Ankennes asked.

"No," Nemienne answered, and then paused. "There might have been somebody else. Right at the beginning. He wasn't there later. I'm not . . . I'm not certain he was there at all."

"He was," the mage said, a trifle grimly. "Briefly." He tapped the tips of two fingers against the table, lost in thought. After a moment, he added, "Your sister is fortunate that you have the inclination toward magecraft. And that you love her. Or I suspect she, like the man you so briefly perceived, would have followed the music you heard into a darkness deeper and more constant than even the darkness under Kerre Maraddras. I gather Enkea did not lead you out?"

Nemienne admitted the cat had not, and the mage sighed. "She has her own inclinations, that creature. How did you find your way out, then? Sideways as before, back to your sisters' house? No? You emerged in Cloisonné House?" The mage was momentarily surprised by this, but then went on after a moment, "Well, that was one of the other houses Meredde Uruddun built, I believe, and its cellars delve perhaps a little deeper among the mountains' roots than is wise. And your keiso sister might have pulled you toward her House, I suppose. One would not have expected her bond with Cloisonné to be so strong, but clearly she has been swift to make a place there for herself."

Nemienne hesitated. They had not found themselves in Cloisonné's *cellars*, and she didn't think Karah had had anything to do with drawing them toward Cloisonné House. But she didn't know how to say so. "I don't—" she began.

"But it was well done of you to find a path out," the mage added, and rose, collecting the empty bowls and dropping them in the sink. Then he offered Nemienne a hand up. "Come along, Nemienne. It may be as well to show you the ordinary method by which most of us find our way into the heart of the mountain. I believe you may have rather an affinity for the dark after all, and possibly a natural inclination toward the Dragon of Lonne. That might be useful."

Nemienne's heart tried to leap up and sink at the same time. She discovered that she simultaneously feared and longed to look again at the dragon. She was sure Mage Ankennes meant to take her back to that cavern. Every detail of the dragon, every shift of the pale light across the powerful shoulder and elegant head and delicate antennae, was engraved in her memory. At the same time, she wanted to see it again and assure herself that her memory was indeed accurate and true. Distracted by this intense confusion of feeling, she let the mage draw her to her feet without speaking. Behind them, Enkea lifted her head and blinked after them with her emerald eyes, but did not volunteer to accompany them.

The black door, when the mage led her to it, was ajar again. A cold draft came through the crack, redolent of water and stone and, Nemienne thought, the subtle scent of darkness itself. She shivered.

The mage frowned as he studied the door. "Hmm." He transferred the frown to her. "You didn't . . . No," he answered this question, whatever it had been, himself. Then, leaving this ambiguous negative unexplained, he reached out with one powerful hand to lift a tall lamp, its oil already alight, out of the air. Then he shoved the door wide.

The caverns beneath the mountain lay immediately beyond the black door. Light from the lamp streamed through the doorway to reveal white stone formed by the pressure of time and darkness into graceful draperies and tall pillars and fragile needles.

Mage Ankennes summoned a lamp for Nemienne, too. She took it gratefully and edged after the mage into the caverns. He strode out briskly, with the air of a man who knows his path well.

Nemienne followed with rather less confidence. She knew she should have felt safe in the mage's presence, and she did, in a way. But in another way, and though she didn't understand why, she would almost have preferred to come here again on her own, or with the unpredictable Enkea.

Though she listened carefully, Nemienne could hear nothing now that resembled piping. If Karah's pipes had been used last time to draw a path into the dark, clearly Mage Ankennes did not need such a tool to make his own path. He continued to walk quickly, his lamp held high, its light pouring out to reveal fantastic structures of stone. Nemienne paused to admire a fragile stone needle, longer than she was tall and yet not half so wide at its widest point as her smallest finger. A drop of water clung, trembling, to its tip.

Feeling her absence at his back, Mage Ankennes glanced around and said, "Nemienne!"

She jumped, and hurried to catch him up. "I'm sorry. It's beautiful," she said humbly at his impatient look.

After a moment, the mage's mouth crooked a little. "It is," he conceded. He held his lamp a little higher, and the light it cast forth brightened, shoving the dark farther back, and farther still, until they could see the vastness of stone through which they walked. Nemienne stared around with awe.

The mage, watching her, smiled more freely. "I had forgotten what it was like to see this for the first time. More impressive in its way than any of the works of men, is it not? This is a living water that runs here. I believe the water itself is what shapes the stone, through ages unmeasured by our ephemeral kingdoms."

Nemienne nodded, though she didn't understand exactly what he meant.

"Listen!" said the mage. "Do you hear? There is the black pool. These caverns are like my house: unpredictable in distance and arrangement. But the dragon's chamber is not far now."

They passed between two great pillars and stepped over a sharp-edged ridge of stone laid like a blade across their path. The light of the lamps swung around them, never steady, so that shadows rose and stretched out and subsided again as they moved. Then they turned around the edge of a rippling curtain of stone and found, at last, the wide black pool before them, with the white dragon curving in and out of the cavern wall behind it. The mage walked to the edge of the pool and paused there, holding his lantern high as he stared across the water.

Nemienne came up beside the mage, looked at him uncertainly, then turned back to gaze at the dragon. It was just as magnificent as she had remembered. Nemienne had known exactly how it would look, and yet she was almost frightened to see the truth of her memory.

"Geriodde Nerenne ken Seriantes is called the Dragon of Lirionne," commented Mage Ankennes, holding his lamp high and gazing without expression at the stone monster before them. "After his great-grandfather, Taliente Neredde ken Seriantes, who was first given that title by the peoples he conquered."

Nemienne nodded, her eyes wide.

"This, however, is the true dragon: the Dragon of Lonne. It has slept here beneath Kerre Maraddras for years unto years, curled into the stone, the living stone growing around it. Its breath forms the high clouds that are torn to shreds by the knife-edged peaks, and the mists that creep into Lonne on winter nights. Its heart is cold, and its fire colder. When it shifts in its sleep, the mountains tremble and crack. Its blood is black and powerful."

"It—it's not—" Nemienne's voice shook, and she closed her mouth and swallowed.

Mage Ankennes looked down at her, his expression somber, but not unkind. "It is alive. Merely quiescent."

"I—I thought it had been carved—"

The mage's mouth crooked. "The Dragon of Lonne could never have been made by the hands of men, no matter how masterful their craft. No. It is allied with stone and stone protects it, but it is not a *made* thing." He turned back to contemplate the dragon again. "I have been trying for years, with all my arts, to destroy it."

"You—" Nemienne stared at him in terror and amazement, both distraught that he might destroy so splendid a creature and awed by his temerity.

"The darkness of the dragon's heart has crept into the heart of Lonne." Passion had entered the mage's tone; his voice shook with it. "Taliente Seriantes was the first of the kings of Lirionne to find it here. Its power drew him into the dark. He used to come here simply to gaze upon the dragon. It seduced him—the mere awareness of its presence seduced him, and the slow seeping of power from these caverns. It was why he founded a city here, and why he made Lonne the capital of his kingdom. But dragons are creatures of darkness, antithetical to the bright, vigorous world of men. My studies have made it clear to me that the power that flows from them cannot be turned toward the service of any great good."

Nemienne didn't understand what he meant. Or she did, she thought, but it didn't seem to agree with the things she'd been reading. She said tentatively, "But Kelle Iasodde says—"

"Iasodde never understood what he studied," Mage Ankennes said impatiently. "Or more likely he did not wish to accept it. Men, even mages, even kings, have a great desire to believe what they wish to be true. Especially kings." His mouth had tightened, and he bit off his words more sharply. "They will not make the hard choices, and they will never turn away from power. No more than Iasodde himself has any Seriantes ever accepted the inherent corruption that flows from the dragon. Not even when the corruption of the Dragon of Lonne crept into their very hearts. Or the hearts of their sons."

"Corruption?" Nemienne repeated uncertainly and grasped after his meaning. "You mean—you mean, Prince Rette? And before that, Prince Gerenes and Prince Tivodd?"

"That is exactly what I mean." Mage Ankennes gave a short little nod. "Yes. The ill-considered and inevitable betrayals and treacheries of the elder princes were obviously—and predictably—a consequence of the dragon's baleful influence, increasing through the generations in the family that most depends upon it."

Nemienne stared at him. This was awful, and yet something about it seemed wrong to her. At first she did not know why she should feel that way. It wasn't just what Kelle Iasodde said . . . Then she remembered about Karah and Prince Tepres, and realized she didn't believe her sister could possibly have fallen in love with the prince if he had really been corrupted by the dragon. But she did not know how to say so to Mage Ankennes.

The mage was not looking at her. He went on, but he was now clearly speaking almost to himself. "The Seriantes of Lirionne have been deaf to all warnings I could give them. They will not set aside this dark draught. Anyone not blinded by the love of power and the ordinary shortsightedness of men could see what the consequences of this must be. I have *warned* them. They will not hear me. The entire Seriantes line has become inextricably corrupted."

Nemienne opened her mouth, but then closed it again without protesting. She did not know what to say. She was afraid to say anything. Mage Ankennes was different here within the mountain: He seemed darker, more gripped by purpose, somehow dangerous.

She stared again at the dragon, trying hard to see the evil that Mage Ankennes said was in its heart. Yet she found she could not make herself view the dragon with horror. She might feel terror of such a magnificent creature, at the thought of it waking and lifting its great head, spreading its splendid wings—but not horror. What she felt was still, despite everything the mage had said, something more akin to awe.

"But even quiescent, the Dragon of Lonne is extraordinarily difficult to destroy," Mage Ankennes concluded. "I had arranged a method that seemed to hold promise, but unfortunately the necessary sacrifice appears to have failed." He contemplated this failure, eyes hooded and dark.

"Oh," Nemienne said faintly.

As though this whisper made him suddenly recall her presence, the mage turned his head to look down at Nemienne. "Well," he said after a moment, his tone once again ordinary and kind, "that is a heavy load to set on small shoulders. Never mind, Nemienne. The dragon and its effluence is a puzzle and a problem for me, not for you. We shall go back to the light and warmth, yes? And you shall tell me again of your night. I should particularly like to hear in more detail your description of the music you believe you heard." He lowered his lamp, shadows swinging around them in disturbing confusion, and turned back the way they had come.

Nemienne flung a glance back over her shoulder at the supine form of the Dragon of Lonne stretching back and back along the cavern wall. She could not imagine any work of men, even mages, that could destroy such a . . . creature.

But what she truly found beyond her to imagine, despite all Mage Ankennes had told her, was that anyone, even a mage, *ought* to destroy it. Such an act seemed somehow . . . somehow beyond the right ambition of men. "Mage Ankennes understands these great things," Nemienne whispered to herself, trying to find this thought comforting, and hurried to keep up.

"Tell me again about this music," Mage Ankennes asked Nemienne, for the sixth time. They were in the mage's workroom, facing each other across the enormous cluttered table. Mage Ankennes lounged in a large ornate chair of wood and leather. He no longer seemed strange or frightening. Nemienne perched on a high stool that was exactly the right height to let her prop her elbows on the table and tried not to think of how he had seemed while in the dragon's cavern. She tried instead to think of new ways to describe the piping she'd heard under the mountain. She had no idea why the first five times she had described it hadn't been adequate; she'd even tried to hum the melody she remembered, though it escaped her best efforts. Now she dredged through her memory for details she might have missed previously.

Mage Ankennes frowned even after she had done her best, but only thoughtfully, not as though he was angry or disappointed. "A low line and a high one," he mused, but more as though he spoke to himself than to her. "And the pipes you saw at Cloisonné House were twin pipes, of ivory and gold. Pipes that the heir had given her, or so you were told. But broken."

"Not . . . broken, exactly," Nemienne corrected hesitantly, glad to move on at last to a different part of the story. "I mean, they were still a set—you could see they were twin pipes and not, you know, torn off a larger set of hand pipes or anything. But ruined. The ivory was cracked, and the wire twisted."

"Yes," said Mage Ankennes, seeming unsurprised by this description. "You were fortunate—your sister was very fortunate—that you heard that piping and had the ability to go after her. Or she might have followed that music to its end."

It took a moment for Nemienne to understand what he meant. Her hands moved across the table convulsively; she knocked a set of geometer's brass compasses to the floor and exclaimed in dismay at the clatter they made when they fell.

A twitch of the mage's hand made the compasses jump back to the table. He said kindly, "Your sister was never anyone's target, Nemienne. I'm sure the pipes came into her keeping by chance. She's in no danger now."

Nemienne nodded jerkily, then sat up straight. "But it was—it was *Prince Tepres* who gave her those pipes!" she cried. For a moment, dizzily, she wondered why the prince should want to murder Karah and thought he must be evil after all. Then she realized that of course the prince *hadn't* meant to do anything of the kind, how stupid she'd been to think that even for an instant—no, somebody else—a foreign lord, hadn't Leilis said so?—had given the pipes to the prince, and he'd given them in turn to Karah.

So that foreign lord had tried to murder the *prince*. Wait, wait, had the foreigner *succeeded*? She asked with trepidation, "Was...was *Prince Tepres* the...the other person I thought was there, at first—there in the dark? The one who went on after I stopped Karah?"

"Regrettably, no," Mage Ankennes said absently. He appeared lost in thought, gazing out the four large windows that lined the opposite wall. The windows looked out today over blowing clouds, a view so high that only the merest glimpses of mountain peaks could be seen far below. Nemienne kept catching elusive glimpses of insubstantial dragons in the movements of the clouds: The slow uncoiling of a white streamer around an ominous bank of clouds looked to her like the sinuous body and long tail of a white dragon swimming through the high currents of the air, and the flat sweep of white barely visible on the other side of the cloud tower looked like a vast reaching wing. Nemienne had often seen dragons in the movements of clouds and mist, but now such visions seemed so much more...fraught.

"No," the mage repeated. "That was not the Dragon's heir. Who would have expected him to give those pipes away? He seemed to appreciate them...Well, your sister is charming," he added dispassionately, and went on, "No, Nemienne: The man you glimpsed was an acquaintance of mine, in fact. No one of great importance, though it's true his death is inconvenient."

Inconvenient? "But—" said Nemienne, and stopped.

"I believe I would like to examine those pipes," Mage Ankennes said abruptly, as though he hadn't heard her. "Perhaps you might fetch them for me."

"What?" Nemienne said, and immediately felt a fool. She added quickly, "The pipes, yes. You want me to get them for you."

"Mmm, yes," the mage said. "Though they have been, mmm, used up, there may yet be some interest in examining the, hmm, interstices where the spellwork used to lie. I have not had the opportunity to study many examples of true bardic spellwork." He tapped the fingers of one powerful hand on the surface of the table, seeming any moment in danger of oversetting a pile of books on which a glass goblet stood. The goblet held several dozen brass marbles and three polished black beads of hematite.

Nemienne leaned forward, ready to try to catch the goblet if it fell, but it didn't.

"It's your sister who has the pipes," Mage Ankennes added, not seeming to notice Nemienne's alarm about the goblet. "They're no good to her in the shape they're in, hmm? She ought to give them to you if you ask."

"Well, yes, I'm sure she will..."

"Go today, then. This afternoon. I should be able to acquire the pipes of horn and silver merely for the asking," the mage added absently, clearly thinking about something else.

"There's another set of pipes? Oh, for the other victim, the man who died?"

Recollecting himself, the mage smiled at Nemienne. "Indeed. You're quick to understand, young Nemienne." He gave her a brisk nod. "You may go on. There's script and hard coins in a jar on the kitchen table. Take enough for a conveyance and, oh, whatever small necessities may come up. There is no particular need for haste, however. After you get the pipes, you may go visit your sisters, if you wish. Return here in the morning. I shall see about persuading my door to open for you."

"All right—yes—good," stammered Nemienne, and retreated, since she could see Mage Ankennes wanted her out of the way. That unexpected permission to *go see your sisters*—she would be happy to, of course, but it was also clearly a polite way to say *Go away and don't bother me for a while*. She wondered what he could possibly mean to do while she was gone, but couldn't think of any way to ask. And, anyway, she longed to see Karah again and make *sure* she was all right. She went out to find the coins and a conveyance.

There was no conveyance handy to the Lane of Shadows, so Nemienne walked on foot toward the more traveled areas of the city. She didn't mind. It was cold, but she wanted time to think— time to herself, out in the open air.

The image of the Dragon of Lonne kept coming before her mind's eye, though she didn't want to think about it. Or at least, not about Mage Ankennes destroying it.

Nemienne badly wanted to tell someone else about the Dragon of Lonne, if not about Mage Ankennes's plans for it. She felt that if she did, she might find a way to understand it better herself. "Leilis," Nemienne whispered. She didn't know why, but she felt that Leilis would understand the dragon—maybe better than Nemienne did herself.

Not that *that* would be difficult.

Cloisonné House was awake and beginning to be lively when Nemienne arrived in late afternoon. But it was sufficiently early that the flower world still belonged almost entirely to itself. A girl came to the door in answer to Nemienne's tentative rap, but her faint air of surprise said plainly that it was early for outsiders to arrive.

But the surprise on the girl's face cleared at once when Nemienne gave her name. "You're Moonflower's sister, of course," she said confidently. "My name's Birre. You're welcome, of course. Moonflower is busy dressing for the evening—she's going to attend a small engagement. Rue will be with her, don't worry about that."

"That's fine," Nemienne said, wondering what she ought to have worried about. "Actually," she added, since the opportunity presented itself, "I was hoping I might see Leilis? If she's free?"

"Oh," Birre said earnestly, "I'm so sorry. Leilis isn't in Cloisonné House this evening. She went out early and I know she hasn't yet returned because Mother was only just asking for her. We really can't imagine what might have taken her away so long." She looked a little worried, but then added with more cheer, "But then, Leilis always has good reasons for everything she does, and I'm sure she'll be back soon. But it is too bad, with first that foreign lord and then you both looking for her. She'll be sorry she missed you both, I'm sure."

"Oh," Nemienne said faintly, and then rallied and asked, with some trepidation, "What, um . . . the foreign lord? You don't mean . . . not the same foreign lord who gave Prince Tepres a set of twin pipes? That the prince later gave Karah? That lord?"

"Why, yes." The girl looked wistful. "The prince is in love with your sister, everyone in the House says so, and anyway it's obvious. I saw him when I was carrying platters during his private engagement with your sister—he's so splendid—and that foreign lord, so gracious, do you know he gave out a gratuity for all the servants? It's a shame Leilis was already gone when he came by today. She ought to have been the one to accept it on our behalf, really—"

"Yes, I'm sure," Nemienne said almost at random. "You mean

the foreign lord was here today looking for Leilis? But she was already gone then?"

Birre gave her a mystified look. "Why, yes."

"Um." Nemienne hesitated. Leilis's absence seemed important, but she was not really sure why. She asked after a moment, "Well, then, do you know when Karah will be free? In just a little while, you said? I think I really need to talk to her. Could I wait in her room? Or where would be convenient?"

Karah, of course, shared Rue's room—Nemienne had forgotten. But Rue politely excused herself and left the sisters in privacy, only reminding Karah that she'd expect her to be ready for the engagement in half an hour.

"And I mustn't be late, Nemienne, though of course it's wonderful to see you," Karah told her sister warmly.

Karah looked wonderful herself. She was wearing blue robes embroidered with dusky rose and white, and a strand of beads wound through her hair: black glass and hematite, white and black pearls, with three lapis beads neatly arranged where they would show to best advantage. She had her silver kitten on her knee. The kitten, amazingly, was not batting at the beads. With her hair up, Karah looked all grown up and every bit a keiso. Nemienne, despite the urgency driving her, paused for a moment in astonishment. She had somehow never thought of her sister as *really* a keiso, and Karah's glamour startled her.

But it wasn't just the glamour. Robes and beads aside, Karah just seemed to glow, somehow. A private smile curved her lips; her gaze was warm and happy and a little unfocused. If Prince Tepres *was* in love with Karah, the sentiment was obviously returned. Nemienne had no doubt about that, now. If the prince and Karah... well, that should have been exciting and wonderful, but in fact it added a new worry to the pile that seemed to be accumulating.

"What's wrong?" Karah asked, a trace of worry entering her eyes. Even distracted, she couldn't help but notice when somebody else was anxious or upset.

"Oh." Nemienne hesitated, and then asked about the pipes instead of the prince.

"Oh, I don't have them anymore," Karah said, sounding a little surprised. "Leilis showed them to me—it's so strange what happened to them, and really too bad, after Prince Tepres"—her voice softened a little on his name—"was so kind to give them to me!" She stroked her kitten possessively, smiling down at this other gift from the prince.

"I suppose Lily did something to them," Karah added. Her tone here went a little doubtful. She added quickly, as though trying to justify such an unpleasant supposition, "Lily is jealous, Rue says. But Leilis said she'd find out for me if a similar set could be made, so the prince won't be disappointed. Leilis is very kind, really, though she tries to hide it," Karah added, happy again once she could think of Leilis's kindnesses rather than Lily's jealousy. "But why ever did *you* want them, Nemienne?"

"Mage Ankennes wants to look at them. He said he can learn things about them even though they've been ruined."

"Yes," Karah said artlessly, "that makes sense. I remember: Your Mage Ankennes was so impressed by the pipes when Lord Chontas first gave them to Prince Tepres and Lord Miennes. Of course, we all were."

Nemienne was startled. At first she did not understand what Karah had said to startle her. Then she did, and she was at once dismayed as well as shocked. Mage Ankennes had been at that banquet? Yes, she remembered now he'd said he was going to a banquet at Cloisonné House. He'd seen the foreign lord give Prince Tepres those pipes. And he'd seen the other set given away, too.

Could he have failed to realize right then the instruments were enspelled?

But Nemienne knew, even as she wondered this, that Mage Ankennes hadn't missed that ensorcellment at all. Horrible pieces fell into place with appalling smoothness.

"Sympathy between similar objects," she whispered. *Unfortunately the necessary sacrifice appears to have failed.* That was what the mage had said. "The Dragon of Lonne—the Dragon of Lirionne," she said aloud. "Sympathy between similar objects."

"What?" asked Karah.

"It's a principle. Iasodde explains it in his codex. Oh, sea and sky. I wrote an essay on this..."

"Did you?" Karah was plainly mystified.

Nemienne shook her head. "This can't be right. I must be mistaken." But she knew she wasn't. For the first time, she really *understood* Iasodde's principle. She felt cold right down to her toes...She whispered, knowing it was true, had to be true, "Mage Ankennes wants to kill *Prince Tepres* in order to, to destroy the dragon. The sympathy between similar objects. He can destroy the dragon if he murders the prince. He *said* it was unfortunate it wasn't the prince who...who died. *That* was the sacrifice he meant."

"Wait—what?" Karah stared at her, horrified and frightened. "What are you saying, Nemienne?"

Outside, the descending sun must have begun its plunge into the western sea: The light had shifted from the gold of late afternoon toward the shadowy violets and sapphires of dusk. Nemienne felt like similar shadows were stretching out in her heart. "I think," she whispered. "I think—"

But before she could complete the thought, the whole of Cloisonné House, maybe the whole city, abruptly went *thump*, as though caught in an earthquake. It felt like the whole House jerked sharply to one side and then the other before returning to rest.

Nemienne cried out, a thin sound that seemed to vanish in suddenly thick air. Karah gasped. Other exclamations, the crash as somebody dropped a tray, and a burst of startled laughter came from elsewhere in the House and from outside on the streets. The kitten, its little tail lashing in alarm, leaped off Karah's knee, crouched on the floor, glared around at the room, and hissed.

And yet, Nemienne realized, in fact neither Cloisonné House itself nor the city had actually been shaken by any physical tremor. None of the little bottles or mirrors or combs on Rue's table or in the cabinets had even trembled. There had not been a real earthquake at all.

Nemienne had an uncomfortable conviction that she knew, at least in broad terms, what had actually given Lonne that twisting not-quite-real sideways shove.

CHAPTER 13

The Laodd was imposing enough from the candlelight district. When one actually stood before it, with its powerful walls rearing above and the afternoon sun blazing in its thousand windows and close at hand the roaring Nijiadde Falls drowning speech and sense as it thundered down the cliffs into its lake... "imposing" was not an adequate term. Leilis had almost changed her mind at that point, almost gone back to Cloisonné House. But pride, or stubbornness, or simply the habit of making careful decisions and then holding to them, had stiffened her resolve. Thus she had not turned away, but instead approached the guards.

Now she waited, alone, in a great echoing chamber with walls as thick as those of a tomb and no amenities to soften its stark chilliness. In its own way, this room was as intimidating as the Laodd's outer ramparts. It was meant to be, she knew: the intimidation as much a calculated effect as Cloisonné House's warm welcome. Common people were supposed to wait in this room, and while they waited, they were supposed to think again about why they had come here. If their reasons for approaching the court were trivial, they were expected to slink out quietly and go home. The guards at the Laodd gates wouldn't question them. For most people, leaving the Laodd was much easier than entering.

Leilis could leave. Indeed, she hadn't had to come here at all. She could have gone to Mother right away, let Narienneh be the one to approach the court. Narienneh knew everyone. She could have approached the right person, someone powerful who would know what to do about a Kalchesene sorcerer who'd had the temerity to enter Lonne. But, no. Leilis had told herself she'd meant to keep her House clear of any entanglements, but now she suspected it had merely been pride that had prompted her to venture the cliff road herself. Misplaced pride. Whom did *she* know?

She hadn't really been thinking clearly, she acknowledged now. Or at least, she hadn't let herself recognize everything she'd been thinking. Because even more than leaving everything to Mother, she'd been tempted simply to take no action whatever. Because she knew—she *knew*—the foreign lord must be a sorcerer. A Kalchesene sorcerer. Why else would he have tried to murder the Dragon's heir? Why else would he have tried to do so with enspelled *pipes*?

But, even knowing so much, she hadn't been able to stop herself from wondering what else a Kalchesene sorcerer might be able to do that Lonne mages couldn't. Might a sorcerer, for example, be able to remove strange curses? Hadn't the foreigner even implied as much? And seemed willing to do it?

And, after all, Prince Tepres hadn't *actually* been harmed by whatever magic had been in those pipes. In a way, that made it almost as though the foreigner had never given them to the prince, didn't it?

She couldn't quite persuade herself of this, although she wanted to. Besides, if she told no one about these pipes and then the Kalchesene finished what he'd come to Lonne to do—if the prince or anyone else died at his hands—it would be her fault. That was an obvious conclusion, and wishing it had never occurred to her didn't make it vanish from her mind.

Leilis hadn't, in the event, been able to persuade herself to anything so immoral as complete inaction. But she hadn't gone to Narienneh, either. She'd come to the Laodd herself, in a sort of compromise between inaction and efficiency.

She'd first intended to approach the prince himself, but that had clearly been foolish. Then she had thought of Jeres Geliadde.

Surely *he* would be interested in what she had to say. But the dour bodyguard frightened her. So then she had thought of the prince's left-hand friend, Koriadde. Surely Koriadde, himself keiso born, would listen to a woman from the flower world.

So she had come to the Laodd and asked to see Koriadde. And now she stayed, and waited, and would not give up and go home. She stood instead by the room's one window and looked out at the late sun turning the spume from Nijiadde Falls to glittering diamond, and though she wanted to run across the room to the door and then down the echoing hall and out of the Laodd and back to the candlelight district, she didn't.

She turned restlessly and paced around the perimeter of the room. She had done this twice, now. Each circuit took a long time, if one walked slowly, for the room was quite large. She told herself that when she reached the window again, if someone hadn't yet come to escort her to Koriadde, she would leave the Laodd, but she could tell that this wasn't a firm decision because as soon as she told herself this, her steps slowed even further. Maybe if she delayed long enough, she would never reach the window. Or maybe Koriadde—

But it wasn't the prince's friend who interrupted her slow circuit of the room.

Lord Chontas Taudde ser Omientes looked like he'd been hurrying, and the big man with him was clearly a hired thug. They could only be here looking for her—and the door through which they had entered was also the only way Leilis could leave. She froze, momentarily panicked. When she'd thought of bracing the sorcerer, it hadn't been here, like this, with the pipes in her pocket and no way to defend herself.

Lord Chontas looked relieved, as well he might be, finding her here—clearly she hadn't had time yet to speak to anyone— undoubtedly he meant to ensure that she wouldn't speak to anyone ever again—she said quickly, "I'll scream. Guards will come if I scream, you know! They'll come right away—stop there!"—as the foreign lord seemed inclined to approach her.

To her surprise, Lord Chontas did stop, one hand a little extended toward her. He said, his tone an odd mix of caution and certainty, "Leilis. You won't scream." And then, with a jerk of his head for the other man, "Benne."

The large man retreated back through the door—to watch for the threatened guards, Leilis understood. She said sharply, "He had better not try to fight Laodd guardsmen. They're all King's Own, you know. They'd kill him."

"He won't," answered the foreign lord. "He won't have to, because you aren't going to scream. Leilis, I don't wish to harm you. I don't *intend* to harm you."

"I'm sure you don't." Leilis couldn't quite manage to keep the scorn out of her tone. "You just want your pipes back. Here, then—" She took the ruined pipes out of a pocket and showed them to the foreigner. Then she pretended to throw them across the room, but really she threw a comb that she'd palmed when she got out the pipes. The comb clattered across the floor, and as the foreigner turned to follow its path, Leilis darted past him and toward the door.

She almost reached it. But the foreigner spun back, took two long strides, and caught her by the wrist. The curse flared to life. Leilis, better accustomed to the silent clash of dissonant magework, wrenched herself free from the foreigner's suddenly lax grip and jumped for the door again, and this time she made it.

But the foreigner's servant was there, looming just outside the doorway, his broad, stupid features more alert than Leilis had expected. Certainly he was quicker than she'd guessed: His arm came up to block the hall. He could effectively block it all by himself; he was that big. Leilis, frustrated, slid to a halt.

"Don't scream!" Lord Chontas said behind her.

The foreigner spoke with a kind of quick force that stopped her even as she drew breath. Sorcery? Leilis wondered, and suspected it was, of a sort. Besides, unfortunately, no guardsmen were in sight. Leilis turned back to face Lord Chontas instead.

The foreigner met her eyes. "You've guessed already that I'm

Kalchesene. A bardic sorcerer. Of course you have. Surely it has occurred to you that I might remove the mageworking that is interfering with the smooth extension of your, your...own immanent self."

Leilis said nothing. If Lord Chontas wanted to offer a bribe rather than a threat, she was more than willing to let him.

"It had occurred to you. And yet you are here. Well." The Kalchesene looked like he wanted to shout at her, but he didn't. He said quite reasonably, "Leilis, I will try to, um. Resolve your problem. If you permit me. All I ask is that you have enough hope to let me try." He waited.

Leilis said drily, "And all you'd ask in return is these pipes."

"Well, yes. Is that so much to ask?"

"I saw those twin pipes when you gave them to Prince Tepres, and I saw them when he gave them in turn to Karah. And I saw them this morning, all cracked and ruined, and I think I'm not the only one who ought to see them. So you tell me: how are you not a threat to me and to everyone else in Lonne, Lord Chontas, if that is your name?"

"Because I don't wish to be," the lord said patiently.

"You're Kalchesene. Here because of the coming solstice—you intend to murder our prince—maybe our king, too, I don't know—"

"I swear to you, Leilis, I did not come here to murder the prince, or anyone else in Lonne. I was grieved to know I might have done harm to that little keiso, and greatly relieved to find I had not. I swear to you, I never meant to harm her. Nor would I harm you. I'll help you if I can. And I think I can."

Leilis could think of no reason in the world she should believe a word of this, and yet somehow this assurance sounded true. More than true: honest. Lord Chontas was a Kalchesene sorcerer: He must be doing something to make her believe him? But he wasn't using any instrument...

"Then why did you come to Lonne?" she asked at last. "If it was not to murder our prince—but it was, of course it was, what other reason could have possibly brought you here? Everyone knows blood will wash across the land like the tide across the shore this spring, when the Treaty of Brenedde expires. You *must* have come to assassinate the prince—or his father."

At first she was sure the Kalchesene wasn't going to answer. He turned away and went across the room to look out the window, though Leilis didn't know whether he was looking out at the darkening sea or only into his own thoughts.

He said after a moment, not turning, "The sea goes out forever, doesn't it? Sweeps in with the tide and washes endlessly out again, iterations on a single unfathomable theme...One could imagine the setting sun drowning out there in the far west. The sea seems more powerful even than light..."

Leilis wondered where this was going.

"I used to dream of the sea. I love the high mountains of Kalches, but I dreamed of the sea. The deep music of the tides has pulled at my bones for as long as I can remember...I have lived in Miskiannes as well as Kalches, and traveled through Enescedd to get from one land to the other. My uncle told me I was a fool to enter Lirionne, especially this year. But if I did not come to the coast this year, when would I come? This was my only chance. My grandfather begged me to be content with the countries behind the mountains and leave Lirionne to the Dragon of Lirionne, but he is also a sorcerer and did not call me a fool." He turned back to face her. "I swear to you, I did not come here to strike at your prince. Indeed, I swore to my grandfather I would not attempt personal vengeance. But then there was Miennes. So I was a fool, after all."

Leilis said nothing. Dreams alone hardly seemed adequate reason for a Kalchesene sorcerer to dare the Seriantes ban. Until she remembered the goading power of her own dreams. Though *those* had been thoroughly crushed. And this man swore he could restore them? Probably he meant to murder her, too, and drop her body into one of Lonne's rivers.

But, though she couldn't have explained why she doubted this, she honestly didn't think so. "Then why did you give those pipes to the prince?" she asked him, trying to think.

The foreigner bowed his head a little. "Lord Miennes discovered my nationality and commanded me to cause the prince's death. I immediately resolved to destroy Miennes, if I could. But I knew there must be a foundation of truth in my actions if I were to deceive him."

Leilis tried to think through this. If Lord Miennes had tried to get the foreign lord to murder the prince in the first place, it did seem reasonable for the foreigner to strike at Miennes in turn. Leilis had never liked Miennes; none of the more acute keiso liked him. She knew personally of two who had rejected his offers to become their keisonne. *That* said something, as wealthy as he was. Had been.

But if she hadn't liked Lord Miennes, still Leilis had respected his cleverness. It would indeed have been difficult to deceive him. But Leilis also realized she hadn't asked the right question—hadn't yet even approached the right question. She tried again. "Couldn't you have done something else? Evaded Lord Miennes's demands somehow?"

"I should have tried," the foreigner admitted at once. She thought he spoke honestly, and *knew* there was no reason for such a feeling, but still she thought so. "There were other reasons why I . . . thought I was justified to . . . do what I did. I think now I was wrong. I was glad to find I had done less than I meant to do."

Leilis hesitated. She said carefully, "But Lord Miennes did die."

The foreigner lifted an eyebrow, suddenly disdainful. "And I'm glad I didn't fail of my entire aim. I don't care to have such things required of me." His tone was edged with remembered anger and something else. Injured pride, Leilis thought. And something beyond that, less identifiable still.

How had Lord Miennes missed this man's pride? Perhaps Miennes had protected himself against magecraft and thought that would suffice against sorcery as well. Leilis, in contrast, was under no illusion that she could protect herself.

Lord Chontas added with more humility than she would have expected from him, "The prince lived because he gave the pipes away. I was relieved, though I could hardly blame you if you don't believe me now. I . . . I had been willing to destroy the heir of Geri-odde Nerenne ken Seriantes. But then I found that outcome less desirable than I'd expected, after all. Particularly after the enchantment went astray. I'm very glad it landed nowhere else to ill effect."

There was a deep sincerity in his tone that compelled belief. This was part of his bardic skill, Leilis understood, and yet she felt that beyond the deliberate sincerity lay, well, genuine sincerity. She heard both: deliberate earnestness layered over truth like a descant line above a melody.

She said after a moment, "I think perhaps that is even true. But you might have been more careful, then. Or do your enchantments often go astray, Lord Chontas?"

The foreigner relaxed a little. He even almost smiled. "My name is Taudde, if you will. 'Lord Chontas' is several of my uncles and a handful of my cousins, and we may be less formal, surely, under these circumstances? I grant you may not believe this on the evidence you've seen. But no. Not often."

Leilis found she did believe him. "Then why did Karah live?"

"Truly, I do not know. I understand that her sister is an apprentice of Mage Ankennes? I don't *know* that her sister saved her, but it seems likely." Now there was a note of—shame, Leilis was almost sure—in the man's voice. In the deeper part of his voice, the part she thought was most true. He bowed his head and spoke slowly, one word coming after the last as though each took a physical effort to pronounce. "You need not say it: I know perfectly well I should never have made a sorcerous weapon that mischance might so easily turn to harm the innocent. Like a fool, I never considered that the prince might give away those pipes. My grandfather would call me a hasty, ill-tempered, arrogant, unthinking fool, and I could hardly deny any of that."

There didn't seem much Leilis could add to this. She said nothing.

"You might give me those pipes," coaxed Lord Chontas. Lord Taudde. "At least go back to Cloisonné House without showing them around. Let me try to remove that strange half-magecrafted curse that's wrapped itself around you. I swear I'll deal with you honestly and not harm you in any way. Or anyone else in Lonne, except perhaps Ankennes, though that may be beyond my power."

Leilis understood the unspoken message: *Don't you become an obstacle.* But she was so surprised by the mention of the mage that this barely registered. "Ankennes?" she exclaimed.

"Didn't you know? He constrains me. I can't leave Lonne until he is distracted. I merely hope a distraction will prove sufficient."

"But Mage Ankennes is one of our close clients and friends!" Leilis protested.

"Whatever his relationship to Cloisonné House, he was also conspiring with Lord Miennes," Taudde told her. His voice was soft, but the certainty in his tone was compelling. "You may blame me for those pipes, Leilis, and I am to blame, yes, but you should look closer to home for the ones who wanted them made and then brought them to life."

Leilis found that she believed this, too. She hesitated.

Then the big man, Lord Taudde's servant, suddenly came into the room and gestured urgently for their attention.

Lord Taudde turned in alarm, but so did Leilis—uneasy, now, at an intrusion that half an hour earlier she would have welcomed gladly. She was aware, even at that moment, of the irony. Besides, there could be no real reason for alarm. Probably there was a guardsman there, maybe one of the King's Own, come to escort her to some minor functionary so she could make the accusation she'd come here to make. She would simply tell the guardsman she'd changed her mind—*had* she changed her mind? All her priorities and fears and hopes had been thoroughly disarranged—

But it was not just guardsmen who followed the servant into the room. It was Lily. She wore her black deisa overrobe with its tracery of keiso blue, and there was no need to wonder why her three guardsman escorts looked dazed: She was stunning. Fine boned and effortlessly poised, Lily was graced by a wonderful fall of straight black hair, a soft pouting mouth, lovely sapphire eyes, and a commanding presence. At the moment, her beautiful eyes were alight with satisfied malice.

"Why, Leilis!" she exclaimed in her soft childlike voice, and laid a hand delicately on the arm of one of the men with her. The guardsman smiled down at her and then glowered at the rest of them. The other guardsmen looked envious of their fellow.

"Rue told Bluefountain," Lily said softly, "that something had happened to Karah's pipes, the pipes Prince Tepres so generously gave her, and then you'd gotten all worried and taken the pipes and disappeared. Isn't that strange, that you'd get all fussed about those pipes? And Bluefountain told Featherreed, and Featherreed happened to mention something about it to Seafoam, and Seafoam told Meadowsweet once everyone started wondering where you'd gone, and Meadowsweet, clever child, thought perhaps I'd be interested to hear the tale. Which I was."

Leilis didn't say anything. She had never thought Lily was stupid.

"I'm not stupid, you know," Lily added in her sweet little voice, childlike and yet, to Leilis's ear, sparkling with malice. She turned to the guardsmen. "It's obvious—the man there must be a spy from Kalches, perhaps even an assassin. And this servant of my House is clearly in his employ."

The problem was, Leilis thought, that when a girl as lovely as Lily said something, even something outrageous, she just naturally *sounded* credible. Her beauty and her keiso-trained manner made her believable. And this winter, well, nobody would be surprised at a flood of spies and assassins from the north trying the Dragon's defenses.

The three guardsmen, after the first startled instant, clearly took Lily's accusation seriously enough. The one who'd been escorting Lily shook her hand off his arm and put his hand on his sword. The other two also reached for their swords, casting wary looks at Lord Taudde and his big servant. The servant only gazed at them blankly, either too stupid to recognize the implicit threat or at least playing the role persuasively. Lord Taudde did nothing. He might be a sorcerer, but perhaps it would be asking too much to expect him to do something sorcerous here in the Laodd itself.

Since no one else seemed ready to do anything, Leilis straightened her shoulders and looked down her nose at the younger girl with her best keiso manner, her plain slate-blue robe notwithstanding. "Lily," she said coolly. "Skipped out on your kinsana lesson, have you? Avoiding your assignment for this evening? Planning to whip up a bit of excitement? You'd best reconsider. Practical jokes in the Laodd itself won't please Mother." She turned regally to the leader of the guardsmen, distinguishable by his manner and because he'd been the one escorting Lily. "You must pardon the child," Leilis told him. She borrowed a keiso's regal disdain for an uppity deisa and continued with kind superiority. "The deisa have lately been overcome by tedium, and I'm afraid that Lily has a tendency to enjoy flights of fancy. Normally she confines herself to pranks within the House, however."

Lily, lovely eyes glittering, said with silken fury, "Such airs you have, Leilis, for a servant."

Leilis sighed tolerantly. She added to the guardsman, in the tone one adult would use to another in the presence of a pettish child, "The Mother of Cloisonné House will certainly assure you, captain, that I am definitely not a spy nor in the employ of spies. Lily's imagination has run away with her—if this is not, in fact, a deliberate prank. To which, I fear, deisa are rather inclined." Her tone suggested, *Girls will be girls*. She turned slightly to include Lord Taudde in the circle of presumptive adults.

The foreigner had, thus far, seemed content to let Leilis speak for him. But now he stepped forward and, following her lead, said smoothly, "I shouldn't like the girl to get in any trouble, you know, guardsman. But I'm afraid she's speaking rather wildly. I can easily produce documents proving that I'm from Miskiannes, that I'm in Lonne on business for my uncle, and that my uncle has long-standing business acquaintances in Lonne and in the rest of Lirionne."

None of the guardsmen had relaxed, although all three were now looking a little doubtful. Men had such touchy pride. They could just imagine a pretty girl trying her hand at inventing a story, and how long they'd hear about it from their fellows if they fell for a prank like this.

"Nonsense!" Lily's voice was taut with anger, her confidence only a little shaken. "What of those pipes?"

Leilis tried to look impatient rather than nervous. "Lily, really," she said, in her kindest tone. "What pipes? I came here to meet, well—" she cast a glance of womanly appeal through her eyelashes at the senior guardsman "—a friend. Lord Chontas merely happened across me here, and as we are acquainted, of course he stopped a moment."

"A 'friend'! You!" Lily said scathingly. She turned in pretty appeal to the guardsmen. "Search her, and then let's see if there are or aren't pipes!"

"I am, of course, a foreigner in your city," Lord Taudde murmured. "But that suggestion hardly seems proper."

"Sea and sky! I only mean, check her pockets!"

"If we might speak to Jeres Geliadde—" Leilis suggested, since it was clear the guardsmen were going to pass this problem along to *someone*.

The senior guardsman rolled his eyes. "I don't get paid enough to handle you lot. Geliadde, eh? Come along, then, and just let's all be calm."

Jeres Geliadde listened to the guardsman's rather garbled account with an expression of dour patience. "Now, let me see if I understand," he said eventually, tenting his hands before him on his desk and gazing at them all over the tips of his fingers. "This foreigner, Lord Chontas Taudde ser Omientes, ostensibly from Miskiannes, is accused by this deisa, Lily, of being a Kalchesene assassin who has aimed sorcerously at Prince Tepres's life. An ineffectual assassin, evidently, as the prince was perfectly well when I last saw him, a scant hour past. This accusation owns no evidence save the set of twin pipes originally given by Lord Chontas to Prince Tepres and subsequently given by the prince to the young keiso Moonflower. Moonflower, notwithstanding possession of these pipes, also currently enjoys good health."

Lily drew an angry breath to speak, but at a calm look from Jeres closed her mouth without saying a word.

"Meanwhile, Lord Chontas maintains that he is an ordinary man of business and a nobleman of Miskiannes. Tarre," he added to a waiting guard captain, "please send someone to Lord Chontas's house and bring me the papers we are informed exist. Lord Chontas, does your servant know where these papers are located? Tarre, have the servant accompany your guardsman. Lord Chontas, if you will indulge me by accepting the hospitality of the Laodd for an hour or two while we examine these papers?"

Lord Taudde inclined his head graciously, and Jeres Geliadde said, without a trace of irony in his tone, "Thank you, my lord."

Then the prince's bodyguard transferred his attention to Leilis. "Also, the woman Leilis, staff of Cloisonné House, is accused of having been suborned by Lord Chontas. As it happens, the woman is known to me. As well as the regard in which she is held by the Mother of Cloisonné House. Also, I am familiar with the keiso and deisa of Cloisonné House."

He gave Leilis a small nod of acknowledgment. Of course, Leilis realized: The prince's senior bodyguard would have carefully studied the personnel of Cloisonné House after the prince had become infatuated with the House's newest keiso. It hardly sounded like Jeres Geliadde meant to take Lily's accusation seriously.

The prince's bodyguard continued, "This accusation is certainly irregular. I should have expected a young deisa to make her suspicions known to the Mother of her House, not directly to me." The look he turned on Lily was not sympathetic. Then he transferred his gaze, now neutral, to Leilis. "However, I will inquire as to your purpose in coming to the Laodd today. You asked first for Koriadde, and then for me, I believe? Koriadde is not here, but as I am here and attentive to this matter, we may as well examine these pipes. Do I correctly surmise that you are able to produce this instrument, young woman?"

Without hesitation, Leilis extracted the pipes from the interior pocket of her robe.

"You said—" the senior guardsman began, and stopped, looking embarrassed. Lily was plainly outraged. Lord Taudde maintained an inscrutable neutrality.

"I wouldn't have wanted to have them disappear into the court bureaucracy," Leilis excused herself blandly, and Jeres Geliadde gave her a grave, faintly amused nod.

"I think—I'm certain—Mage Ankennes is responsible for these," Leilis told him.

"A serious accusation," the prince's bodyguard murmured.

"I've reason to make it." Leilis realized this was true even as she spoke. She knew now what had been bothering her about, well, everything—something Lord Taudde had said had made things fall clear in her mind. She explained to Jeres, afraid she would sound incoherent but trying to be clear, "Moonflower's sister Nemienne is Mage Ankennes's apprentice, did you know? Nemienne must have told Mage Ankennes everything about hearing the pipes. Of course she told him. It's a strange story, but Mage Ankennes must have heard it almost as soon as I did. Why didn't he come to see us? He should have come to see that Moonflower was all right and look into what had happened. I know it may not seem like a good reason—perhaps I shouldn't have come to the Laodd—I must sound like a fool—"

"Hmm." Jeres tapped his fingers gently on his desk. "No. I quite understand your reasoning, young woman. Your conclusion seems sound to me, if hardly definitive. As it happens, I am also recently in receipt of a letter that makes much the same accusation." He laid a thoughtful hand gently on a black-bound scroll, which Leilis hadn't previously noticed among the clutter on his desk.

"Tarre," the prince's bodyguard continued after a slight pause. "Please send a man to find Mage Ankennes and deliver my request that he attend me here when he next finds himself at leisure."

This was a polite way of saying *at once*, Leilis knew.

"And a similar message to one of the King's Own mages, please," Jeres added. "Preferably Mage Periannes, if he can spare a moment. Thank you." He returned his calm gaze to Leilis, who was still holding the ruined set of pipes. Then he turned to Lord Taudde. "Lord Chontas," he said after a moment. "May I ask you to examine this set of pipes and identify them as the set you originally gave Prince Tepres? And perhaps you would describe for me the process by which they came into your possession?"

Lord Taudde turned his head, and his eyes met Leilis's. His expression was remote, thoughtful—not worried in the least. Was it a mask such as keiso learned, Leilis wondered, or was he truly so calm? And if his coolness was a mask, where had he learned to wear it?

The Kalchesene sorcerer reached out his hand to take the ruined ivory pipes from Leilis. Unusually for a man who had once touched her, he made no effort to avoid brushing her fingers, but for a moment held both the pipes and Leilis's hand.

And at that moment, the shadows in the room all rose up and choked the light. The world tilted and swung, and suddenly all the air in the room seemed to press inward with tremendous pressure. Leilis bit back a cry and clung tightly to Taudde's hand; indeed, that hold dragged her hard toward him and after him, and she thought, *Oh, he's doing this, he's taking us both elsewhere.* To Kalches, she guessed. But then Leilis saw that his eyes—almost the only things she could still see—had widened, and she realized that he, too, was surprised and alarmed, and that was bad, because if the expanding darkness were not his doing, then—then—

And then they both fell into the darkness, thought and awareness vanishing along with light and air and everything familiar.

CHAPTER 14

Nemienne wondered whether anybody else realized that there had been no real earthquake. Everyone did realize, at least, that nothing had been damaged and no one had been hurt, and so the candlelight district was already settling back to its customary calm pleasure in the coming night. But such calm had never been further from Nemienne's grasp. She seized Karah's hands, demanding urgently, "You love Prince Tepres, don't you?"

Karah stared at her, shocked.

"Don't you?" repeated Nemienne, with some urgency. "Because the only reason I found you in the dark was because I love you! I don't think *I* could find the prince, not if he follows the wrong path into the dark. But *you* might—if you love him."

"What in the world do you mean?" Karah asked, bewildered.

Nemienne hardly knew how to explain anything. She said rapidly, "That wasn't a real earthquake, was it? And Leilis is missing, *and* those pipes—and the foreign sorcerer came here this morning, but he didn't find her, or you, or the pipes, did he? And Mage Ankennes gave me the evening off—and the prince is heir to the Dragon, which means he's a similar thing to the real dragon. Karah, *do* you love him? Because if you do, I think we haven't much time left—"

Karah still looked confused, but she didn't argue, just nodded, scooped up her kitten, and followed her sister. Nemienne caught her hand and dragged her, nearly at a run, up the stairs and down the fourth-floor gallery to the last bedchamber: Leilis's room.

The room was just as Nemienne had remembered: small, austere, and dominated by the large fireplace with the cracked stones in its hearth. But this time, Nemienne recognized the jagged patterns of the cracks. They were clear kin to the sharp, angular patterns carved on the music room door in Ankennes's house. She only wondered how she could have failed to recognize that relationship before.

"Leilis isn't here," Karah began.

"I know. The foreigner from Kalches went after her because she had his pipes, I expect," Nemienne explained quickly. "What I don't know is whether the foreigner is working *with* Mage Ankennes or against him. I'm sure Mage Ankennes knew about the pipes, but what I don't know—oh, everything is so *confusing*! I don't *know* who's on whose side—only if *you're* in love with Prince Tepres, it *can't* be right to make him a sacrifice—" She was conscious of Karah's intake of breath, and stopped. But whatever exclamation or question her sister might have thought of asking, Karah closed her mouth again and was silent.

Nemienne was grateful. She needed to find a way into the mountain—she was almost sure she *could* find a way—the fireplace *was* a door into and out of the darkness. She crossed the room and knelt down by the fireplace, tracing the crack in one of its hearthstones with the tip of her finger. It was a rune, she knew, or a letter in some strange angular alphabet. Whoever had long ago set these stones in place, these runes brought Cloisonné House under the shadow of Kerre Maraddras. One house of shadows should do as well as the other to find the way...Nemienne closed her eyes and recalled the spell Mage Ankennes had taught her, the one to let you read a language you had never learned. She lifted the spiky cracks from the hearthstones into her mind and let them rest there, illuminated by remembered light.

At first, the letters refused to reveal themselves, but only rested like stones in her mind. Then Nemienne, driven nearly to distraction by the sense of time rushing past them into the vanishing past and inspired perhaps by necessity, called to mind instead the pale greenish light of the caverns under the mountains. This sprang not only to her mind, but, unexpectedly, to her hands. The light gathered like water in her palms and spilled between her fingers to run across the hearth. It pooled in the kitten's eyes, lambent green, and the little animal crouched down with its ears back flat against its skull. The light poured into the cracks in the hearthstones and filled the fireplace itself with a green light that was nothing like fire. The lines seemed to swim and rearrange themselves. They *were* runes, Nemienne saw. She knew because her spell told her, that the first was a rune of summoning, the second a rune of traveling, and the third a rune of breaking—summoning what or breaking what, she had only the sketchiest idea. But she had a pretty solid guess about the one connected to traveling.

"Come here, hold my hand," she said to Karah, holding out her hand for her sister to take.

"What *is* that light?" Karah asked, hesitating. "What did you do?"

"Do?" Nemienne had hardly *done* anything, yet. She said instead, still feeling the press of passing time and still carried along by the quick stream of inspiration, "Quickly, quickly, come *on*, Karah!"

"You *do* know what you're doing, don't you?"

"Yes," Nemienne promised recklessly. She only wished she did know more specifically what it was she *was* doing, or might do, or ought to do. But she felt strongly that there was no time now to hesitate; that they had to move *now* if there was to be a chance of saving anything from this night. She caught her sister's hand in hers and, with the hand she still had free, traced the rune on the middle stone.

The cracks in the stone split wide. Light spilled into the fractures in the stone and darkness spilled out of them. Around Nemienne and Karah, the room seemed to twist, turn itself inside out, and stretch out—and up—and out again. When the world steadied, they found themselves standing close together in the moist chilly air of the caverns. The greenish light showed them the beautiful, strange, stone formations of the caverns. Far away, seeming to echo from every direction, there was the resonant sound of water drops falling from high above into the fathomless black water of the dragon's pool.

Nemienne had no idea which way to go to reach that sound.

Then twin lights like miniature green lanterns caught her eye, and she made out the dim shape of Enkea, sitting statue still among the shadows. The cat's eyes were fixed on the girls—no, on the kitten that clung to Karah's shoulder.

The kitten leaped to the ground and bounced toward Ankennes's cat, only Enkea wasn't really Ankennes's cat, was she? Nemienne studied the green light of the caverns that folded so smoothly around the slim creature and wondered how she had ever mistaken Enkea for a tame house cat. It was clear enough now that she was a creature of shadows and dim light, and nothing tame.

Karah's kitten paused to stretch her nose toward Enkea's face, her whiskers arcing forward—then skittered past and dashed away into the far reaches of the caverns. Enkea rose to her feet and followed sedately, her white foot flashing in the dimness.

Nemienne drew Karah after the cats. She recognized nothing. Without guidance she knew they might have wandered for hours or days...forever, maybe?...through the endless dimness and never found the dragon's chamber. She hadn't thought of that when she invoked the rune, and her blood chilled now at the thought. But Enkea never outpaced them, and the kitten dashed forward and back. And very soon she found she could hear, ahead of them, the sound of voices, not quite interpretable. One was light and quick, a voice that Nemienne did not know. The other belonged to Mage Ankennes. Nemienne bit her lip.

"That's the foreign lord, Lord Chontas Taudde ser Omientes," Karah whispered in her ear. "And the deep voice is your Mage Ankennes, of course. He sounds very...very *confident*."

Nemienne nodded, and swallowed. She wished fervently that she found the mage's voice reassuring. She would have, mere days ago—she *should* have, even now—he had to know what he was doing, didn't he? He was the mage, and she only a girl who'd barely begun to learn from him.

But she was uncomfortably aware that she didn't trust the mage at all. No matter how horribly presumptuous she was to doubt him, Nemienne couldn't help herself. She knew that doubting Mage Ankennes was probably going to ruin her whole *life*. She'd loved being his apprentice—she'd longed to be a mage—if she acted against him now, he'd never forgive her. But she couldn't be loyal to him and to her sister both. And she was terribly afraid that what her master wanted to do, sacrificing Prince Tepres to destroy the stone dragon, was just *wrong*. How *could* it be right?

She bit her lip again, hard enough to hurt. She could still retreat back to Cloisonné House. Take Karah with her—they'd both be so much safer if they slipped away again and nobody ever knew they'd been here. Karah might think she loved Prince Tepres, but how often could she even have *met* him, yet? Once, twice? Karah couldn't really *know* him. He was a prince—not just some court noble's left-hand son by a keiso wife, but a *prince*—not just *a* prince, but *the* prince, the heir—Nemienne bit her lip till it bled and told herself that her sister would even probably be better off if Prince Tepres was gone. She would meet somebody else, somebody less exalted, somebody safer to love.

But even while Nemienne was telling herself they should simply creep away again and flee back to Cloisonné House, she and Karah were quietly following the cats instead.

The voices became louder as they pressed ahead, but no more comprehensible. The weird echoes of these caverns kept layering words on top of words, until the constant rippling sound blurred to a meaninglessness like the sound of the sea.

The light that illuminated the caverns before them was different here. It was magelight, Nemienne knew. It seemed out of place here beneath Kerre Maraddras—harsh, almost offensive somehow. The stone was meant to shine under a gentler luminosity. Nemienne shuddered. She wanted *so much* to like Ankennes's brilliant light, but she couldn't. She wanted so much to trust her master, to believe that he knew what he was doing, that he was right. But she couldn't do that, either.

The two girls picked their way toward the hard magelight through a sweeping cluster of fragile needles and spires. At last they emerged to find the voices much louder and more intelligible.

"...needn't be so delicate," Mage Ankennes was saying. His deep voice broke through the silence of the caverns like a stone dropped into water, and echoes came back and back again, some with a clear and rounded sound and others hissing and sibilant. "Do you think I'm unaware why Miennes died, or how? You weren't so reluctant there, I believe."

"And yet," replied the lighter voice, "I find I have no wish to lay out a path to sorcerous death a second time to suit the whims of you ruthless Lonne conspirators. You might well consider again what happened to Lord Miennes." It might have been Nemienne's imagination that this voice, while sharp, produced echoes that wavered.

"That won't happen to me," Mage Ankennes said with assurance.

Nemienne was sure he was right. She might not know exactly what had happened to Lord Miennes, but she was absolutely certain that her master was far more clever. She wondered if the foreign sorcerer realized this, or if he'd been misled by Ankennes's brawn into thinking the mage dull. She edged around the final curtain of stone, drawing her sister after her, and then at last the girls were able to see into the dragon's chamber.

The black pool was unchanged. Everything else was different. Mage Ankennes had not carried simple lanterns into the dark, not this time; instead, he had set balls of harsh magelight here and there around the chamber. The white light glared mercilessly off the dragon's sinuous form, making it look somehow more like stone than ever, flatter and less real.

Mage Ankennes stood nearest to the pool, his back to it and to the dragon. He held a staff in one hand. The staff was heavy and black, nothing Nemienne recognized. The mage looked tensely exultant. It was easy to see him as a man close to achieving his life's great ambition.

A circle of light blazed on the stone before the mage, and within the circle stood Leilis and the Kalchesene sorcerer. Nemienne knew the man must be the foreign sorcerer because he was with Leilis, but he didn't at all resemble the image Nemienne had had in her mind's eye. She had imagined an old man, at least Ankennes's age, with a scholar's fine-drawn intensity. This man was young, not much older than Leilis. He possessed an unusual, long, sharp-featured face that instantly proclaimed him foreign, but he didn't immediately *look* like a sorcerer. Leilis looked far more stern and proud than he. The Kalchesene only looked frustrated.

Within a separate circle, this one smaller and not so brilliant, stood another young man. Even without Karah's intake of breath beside her, Nemienne would have known this man for the prince, for royalty was in the haughty set of his shoulders and back. He had pale hair caught back with a clip of jet, dark eyes that at the moment snapped with outrage, and a thin, arrogant mouth. He was standing very straight, his arms crossed over his chest and his jaw set.

"He looks so alone!" whispered Karah.

This, although she supposed it was true, would not have been Nemienne's first thought. She hissed, "Shush!"

"Fulfill my requirement," Ankennes said in a reasonable tone, "and there's no reason you shouldn't return to Kalches with perfect liberty and health. I may be a ruthless Lonne conspirator, but why should that matter to you? A Kalchesene bardic sorcerer surely hasn't any deep concern for the well-being of the Seriantes, head or tail."

The foreigner shrugged. "Perhaps I've little concern for the Seriantes, but less interest still in accommodating the murderous whim of a Lonne mage."

Prince Tepres tilted his head to one side and said in a quick fierce voice, "Yes, Ankennes, do explain your odd *whim* to us all.

I'm certain we are all passionately interested to know your purpose."

Mage Ankennes completely ignored the prince. He said to the young sorcerer, "I would prefer to harness your peculiar magic to my ends, but, believe me, there are other ways. You'll play death for the Dragon's heir and return unharmed to Kalches, or you'll die first and he'll still follow. Well?"

"Taudde, you can't," Leilis said in a low, passionate voice to the sorcerer. Her tone was odd: She spoke to the foreigner as though she had not only an interest in the outcome of this decision but a right to dictate it. She said, "It doesn't even matter whether Ankennes can really murder the prince without you or not, and I'm not so sure he can or why would he complicate everything by forcing you to do it? But it matters to you, just you—as well as to, well, everybody else. It would be worse if you murdered the prince than if Mage Ankennes does it."

The sorcerer tilted his head toward Leilis and listened to her as though he really cared about her opinion.

Mage Ankennes said with exaggerated patience, "The romance of the young! I assure you, Lord Chontas, the prince will be just as dead whoever kills him. So why not live? Play his death for me."

The young sorcerer gave Ankennes a look of disdain. "You've made pipes of your own, then? But even if I would play one set of pipes, do you believe the prince is so foolish as to play the other set? Under any compulsion?"

"Oh, I'm sure he wouldn't," Mage Ankennes said drily. "Fortunately, his cooperation isn't required."

"Aware or unaware, the cooperation of the one to be ensorcelled is always required," the foreigner began, and then stopped.

Mage Ankennes was holding a thin white flute out to him. Nemienne knew, with a creeping horror even though she didn't understand why she was so sure, that this flute had been made of bone. She guessed further that it had been made from old, brittle bone—from *Seriantes* bone, though how the mage would have come to possess such a bone she could not begin to guess.

"He went to the tomb on Kerre Taum," Karah breathed next to her. She sounded sickened, at least as sickened as Nemienne felt. "He stole a bone from one of the Seriantes kings—from Tepres's great-great-grandfather..."

Nemienne had not even known there was a tomb of kings on Kerre Taum, but the idea of Mage Ankennes slipping into a tomb to steal bones was horrible. But horribly believable. If Ankennes *had* stolen a bone from the first Dragon of Lirionne, that would be... well, besides horrible, the flute he'd made would probably be *far* too suitable to the mage's current purpose.

"This," Ankennes was saying, "is not an instrument that requires the cooperation of anyone but a bardic sorcerer. I might even be able to play it myself. But I would prefer to use my strength elsewhere. You will play it."

"You made that?" The foreigner sounded appalled, as well as shocked. "*You* made it?"

"Did you assume Kalches had a monopoly on bardic sorcery?"

"We have a monopoly on bardic training." The foreigner sounded dismayed. "Is that flute grounded? Did you obtain permission of the, the donor?"

"It was a little late to ask permission, don't you think?" Now Ankennes sounded almost amused. "I'm not entirely untrained, however. I am acquainted with the limitations with which you Kalchesene sorcerers hedge yourselves about. Charming, to be sure, but unnecessary when you use sea magic and good solid magecraft to compensate for the inherent limitations of bardic sorcery. Take it!" He threw the bone flute through the circle of light that surrounded the foreigner.

The sorcerer, apparently quite by reflex, caught it. Then he quickly tried to snap it in two, arms and shoulders flexing, but he didn't seem surprised when the slim flute resisted his effort. After a moment he looked back at Mage Ankennes. His expression was neutral, but Nemienne thought there was fury behind the neutrality. He said, "You think I'll play this dead-bone pipe? For you?"

"Oh, come." In contrast to the young sorcerer, Ankennes

sounded simply matter-of-fact. "You have already demonstrated your willingness. What difference if you do away with the young prince for Miennes or for me?"

Prince Tepres said steadily, "Lord Chontas Taudde ser Omientes, I swear I will forgive any previous acts of yours in Lirionne if you will work on my behalf tonight."

"Play, and I will see to it that no one suspects your hand," said the mage. "Or do not, as you please, and I'll play that flute myself, and then give it to the Dragon of Lirionne as evidence of your guilt. What do you suppose the Dragon will do," he asked impatiently, "when he believes Kalches sent a sorcerer here, despite the Brenedde Treaty, to murder his last legitimate son? Kalches will look back on the war Geriodde Nerenne ken Seriantes ended fifteen years ago as on the mere breeze that precedes the storm."

There was a silence. The Kalchesene straightened his shoulders and began, "You may be surprised at what the Dragon will believe—"

"He's going to play it," Karah whispered, with an agonized glance at the prince.

Nemienne wasn't so sure. She thought that the foreigner might be proud enough that he would continue to refuse, no matter what threat Ankennes might make. As the pause lengthened, she found herself becoming more and more sure of it. But she also thought it would all go wrong if he did—Mage Ankennes was *prepared* for that refusal. "Look," she whispered back, "If he does—if he *does* play that flute—Karah, *you* be ready to hold the prince in this world. We'll get you into that circle, and whatever you do, don't let go of the prince! You have to be his anchor—you have to hold hard to what you love, but remember I'm here, too! I'll try to hold you, but you have to hold onto me, too! And be sure you give that kitten to the prince, all right?"

"What? Nemienne—"

"Just be ready to hold the prince! And don't forget about the kitten!" As the foreigner drew a breath to speak, Nemienne caught her sister's hand, scooped up the kitten herself, and pulled a startled Karah after her into the light. Enkea curled her tail around her feet and sat behind them like a statue in the dimness.

Their sudden appearance got everyone's attention. The young Kalchesene looked mostly at Karah, and he seemed furious. Leilis looked momentarily horrified, then went expressionless, as though she'd donned a mask. Prince Tepres, drawing a shocked breath, took a step toward the edge of his prisoning circle and put out his hands as though he meant to try to push through the light. But he stopped without touching it.

Mage Ankennes was not pleased to see the girls. "What is this?" he demanded of Nemienne, visibly trying to decide whether to be furious or merely annoyed.

"I had to, to come. To see," Nemienne explained awkwardly, trying to sound young and ignorant. This was not at all difficult.

"*How* did you come?" Ankennes asked next.

"From Cloisonné House," Nemienne explained, glad to have a ready excuse for bringing Karah. "Cloisonné House just, just echoes—all through—with ties to these caverns, you know. You can walk out of Cloisonné House right into shadow. Didn't you know?"

Ankennes frowned at her, but now he seemed more interested than angry.

Karah, behind Nemienne, had tried at first to shrink into Nemienne's shadow. But now she abruptly straightened her shoulders and stepped out in front of her sister, looking outraged, but in a surprisingly adult, elegant, keiso sort of way. "How dare you!" she exclaimed. "Don't you have any shame? Trying to make somebody else do your murder for you!"

Mage Ankennes snorted, a rough sound that was almost a laugh. "Ignorant child! You would do better to be silent until you know whereof you speak." He turned away dismissively, back toward Nemienne. "Come over here," he commanded her.

Nemienne hesitated. "And Karah? She wants to be with the prince, she says—"

"Your sister's presence doesn't matter. She can't interfere," the mage said shortly, and added to Karah, "You may certainly join Prince Tepres, if you wish."

Nemienne put the kitten into her sister's hands and gave her a little shove toward the prince's prison. Karah lifted her chin, gave Ankennes a scornful look, and walked gracefully across the uneven floor of the cavern toward Prince Tepres. Her kitten climbed to a perch on her shoulder.

"No!" the prince said sharply, lifting a warding hand toward her. "Ankennes—"

"The girl won't be harmed by your death," the mage assured him impatiently. "I don't pursue the deaths of innocents."

Karah reached the prisoning circle and stopped, trying to decide how to enter it.

"Don't touch it—it will burn through all your bones," Prince Tepres warned her in a low voice, and put out a hand almost but not quite to the circle. Karah bit her lip and matched his gesture from her side.

"How many innocents do you think will die if the Seriantes are destroyed?" the foreigner inquired of Ankennes, his tone of academic inquiry underlain with contempt. "That is your intent, is it not? To use the prince's death as a wedge against the family entire? And when the Seriantes are destroyed, what then? Do you care nothing for Lirionne?"

Ankennes waved a dismissive hand. "I hardly expected a Kalchesene to be dismayed at disorder in Lirionne. In any case, the side effects will be unfortunate, but they are unavoidable. Negative effects must sometimes be accepted to accomplish a great good."

"How comforting to us all," Leilis said tartly, "that a great man such as yourself should see so clearly the path we should all be compelled to take. I'm sure that the survivors of the wars and riots will sing praises to your name."

The mage glanced her way and said simply, "I do not care for the opinions of the ignorant." His tone was perfectly matter-of-fact. He was not trying to insult Leilis, Nemienne realized. He genuinely did not care about her opinion, no more than if she had been a horse or dog.

Prince Tepres said sharply, "How can you think it right to do what you are about to do? Are you not a man of Lonne? What has my family done that is so terrible that you would wreak vengeance on your own country?"

Ankennes, harassed, snapped, "Vengeance is not my aim— nations and families are all ephemeral—I do not expect a Seriantes scion to understand greater necessities that overwhelm the transient welfare of his own small country." He added, to Karah, "Join your young prince, then. You may have a moment to make your farewells." At his gesture, the circle of light around Prince Tepres suddenly flickered and expanded to encompass Karah. She gasped and shrank back, and the kitten hissed, but the movement of the circle had been very quick and was finished almost before either of them had time to be frightened.

The prince put a hand out toward Karah, but then hesitated, looking uncharacteristically uncertain. He drew a breath, but then let it out again without speaking. But, though she did not say anything either, Karah took a step toward Prince Tepres, looking both shy and somehow confident at the same time. She took his hand in hers, turning to face Mage Ankennes at the prince's side in a mute declaration of support and alliance. For what good that might do, which they both probably believed would be none at all.

Actually, Nemienne had some hope the gesture might prove more than merely symbolic. She herself walked slowly across the cavern to join the mage.

"Well?" he said to her.

Nemienne tried not to flinch under his severe gaze. "I had to come," she repeated. Even to her own ears this sounded weak. She added, trying for a firm tone but not able to tell whether she managed it, "I dreamed of the Dragon." This was even almost true; she felt in a way that she'd seen nothing else, waking or sleeping, since she'd first gazed upon its long sinuous form in this cavern. She added, which was not true at all, "And of the *other* Dragon," and glanced significantly at Prince Tepres.

"And found your own way here." The mage sounded thoughtful. "I would not have expected that. Well...well, very well. Perhaps it's as well you came to this place, since evidently you were so strongly drawn. And as you were drawn to be here, I am interested in your further impulses. However, now that you *are* here, you may do nothing without my permission, no matter how strongly you feel drawn to do it. Do you understand?"

"Oh, yes," Nemienne assured him earnestly. She felt ill, and didn't even know whether this was due to generalized terror of what would happen in this place, or because she lied so easily and yet she didn't even know—not even yet—what if Ankennes was *right*, had been right about everything? What if Prince Tepres and all the Seriantes were irrevocably corrupt, and the stone Dragon of Lonne the creature of darkness and evil that had corrupted them? She did not *know*, even now that this wasn't so—how could she dare do anything to stop Mage Ankennes when she didn't even *know*—

"Very well," said the mage, and turned back toward his Kalchesene prisoner.

The Kalchesene drew a breath, bracing himself visibly to refuse any demand Ankennes might make. Ankennes, though he didn't move, seemed to gather himself— Whatever he meant to do when the foreigner refused him again, he was ready to do it—

Behind the mage's back, Nemienne shook her head sharply at the Kalchesene. She held out her hands and waved at him urgently: *Go on, go on!*

Neither the foreigner nor Leilis exclaimed, *But what do you mean?* and so at least Ankennes did not turn and see Nemienne's insistent gestures. The foreigner seemed uncertain. It dawned on Nemienne at last that whatever signs they made in Kalches to mean *go on* were different from the crossed-wrist palm-down gesture of Lonne. Her heart sank. But then Leilis leaned forward and spoke quickly to the young foreigner, and he arched an eyebrow of his own and said slowly, to Ankennes, "And you will free me if I do this?"

"I will swear to it. I do swear to it. This is the only task I demand of you."

"Well," said the foreigner, and glanced at Leilis and then back at the mage and past him to Nemienne. He turned his gaze last toward Prince Tepres.

The prince, too, had seen Nemienne signal the foreign sorcerer. He gave Karah an indecisive glance, bending his head down to listen as she whispered to him. She put the kitten into his arms, and he lifted it absently to his shoulder. Then, as the foreigner turned toward him, his face stilled into an arrogant mask. He said nothing.

The Kalchesene sorcerer lifted the bone flute to his lips and began to play.

The flute had a soft, breathy tone, not quite pure. It was a sound that reminded Nemienne of the moist chill of mountain mist, of the bitter taste of wood ash, of the way the air smelled before a storm. The melody the bardic sorcerer played first rose up as a prisoned bird, freed, might fling itself skyward; then, as though the bird had struck the limits of a chain, it fell back again, descending with dizzying swoops through strange minor keys. The melody swirled around the cavern, and then seemed somehow to fade— absorbed, somehow, into the darkness under the mountain—the darkness that, underlying Ankennes's brilliant light, was somehow still there. On the far side of the black pool, the Dragon of Lonne slept, impervious to the human folk who played out their small dramas in its cavern.

The light dimmed. Not the light of the circles that trapped Prince Tepres and Karah on the one hand and the foreigner and Leilis on the other. Those stayed bright. But the rest of the light in the caverns faltered. The waiting darkness crept forward on all sides, while the music of the flute spun a fine pathway through the dark. It was a path meant for the prince. It held his name and his heart. Within his circle, the prince's expression passed from hard-held arrogance to openhearted wonder. He took a step along that path, and another.

Karah clung to the prince's hand. For a moment, the prince hesitated, held by that grip. He half turned, looking back toward Karah, but the bone flute called, beckoning, seductive. Prince Tepres turned again toward the pathway it showed him, trying absently to shake Karah loose. But she would not let go, and the prince, even enspelled, wouldn't use violence to make her.

Beside Nemienne, Mage Ankennes exclaimed impatiently and made a sharp gesture. The circle of light suddenly contracted, exactly as it had previously expanded to include Karah. This time it excluded her, slicing between her and Prince Tepres, cutting through the dark where their hands were joined.

Both Prince Tepres and Karah cried out as the circle divided them, convulsing as the light burned through their bones. Their hands sprang apart. Karah took two stumbling steps backward.

The Kalchesene sorcerer hesitated in his playing, but the melody he had drawn from the eternal darkness somehow lingered. And Prince Tepres, no longer held by Karah's grip, followed it. He passed through the magecrafted circle as though it was not there. But of course, Nemienne realized, he was not really moving forward—he was moving sort of sideways to the rest of them, at a slant to the familiar world. Even as she understood this, the prince blurred.

Karah gave a little cry of distress and alarm, and for a moment Prince Tepres wavered in their sight, looking back over his shoulder, held by the sheer force of her will even though their hands were no longer joined.

"Play!" snapped Mage Ankennes. "Or I will turn all her bones to fire, and we shall see if she can hold him then!"

"Oh, you can't! You can't!" Nemienne cried, but Ankennes disregarded her, and she knew he would do it.

The sorcerer stared at Ankennes, his expression remote. Then he lifted the bone flute back to his mouth, and as the disturbing melody slid through the caverns again, the prince turned away from Karah and faded from sight. Leilis bit her lip and looked urgently at Nemienne.

Mage Ankennes gave a grunt of satisfaction, hefted his staff, and turned toward the quiescent dragon, striding rapidly through the shallow black water of the pool toward its head.

Karah gave another sharp little cry and ran suddenly into the dark, following the prince down the slantwise path that led through darkness and into death.

Nemienne cried out. She had meant her sister to hold the prince and draw him back to life, not lose her hold and then run after him toward death. She could still see Karah, but only faintly. The kitten was with them, Nemienne reminded herself—there was still hope, because if anybody could walk the pathways between the ephemeral world and the eternal dark, it was the cats.

The sorcerer continued to play. Nemienne hesitated for one moment longer and then ran for the path that led into the darkness. If she could follow that path herself—if she could only bring Karah back—if Karah could reach ahead and bring the prince back as well—then Ankennes wouldn't be able to use the prince's death to bring death against the true dragon the prince symbolized and everything would still be all right. But the path eluded her. When she tried to put her foot on it, it wasn't there after all, but somewhere else, somewhere slantwise of any place Nemienne could enter. She screamed in frustration and tried again while her sister faded from her view, but with no greater success, and then ran instead to the edge of the black pool and stared in terror across it toward Mage Ankennes.

Ankennes had paused for a moment at the dragon's head, gazing up at it with—what, satisfaction? A last moment of reluctant awe for the thing he was about to destroy? The top of its head, resting on one great clawed foot, was many feet higher than the mage's own head; each of its long curved talons was as long as his leg, and its closed eye as large as his chest. Enkea had somehow crossed the pool with no one seeing her, at least without Nemienne seeing her, and was sitting upright and still beside the dragon's foot. She seemed impossibly tiny beside those huge stone talons.

If Ankennes saw the cat, he didn't find her presence reason to hesitate. He turned down to stride along that huge head toward its neck, beginning to lift his staff as though he meant to swing it like a sword. He called out in a deep, rolling tone, "The dragon is departed! The dragon is dead! The dragon is destroyed!" Then he whirled his staff over his head and brought it down toward the relatively slender area where the dragon's head joined its long neck.

Nemienne almost expected Enkea to do something to prevent that blow, but of course the cat could do nothing. No more than Nemienne herself. Flinching from the blow as though it was aimed at her, Nemienne fell to her knees at the edge of the pool. The water lapped over her fingers, not like water but like embodied shadow, with green light glimmering at its heart. She gasped and pulled her hands back.

The staff struck—

Above them, everywhere around them, there was a vast, terrible noise as the mountain trembled. Some of the more delicate stalactites and needles shattered with a terrible crystalline chiming like breaking bells, and great cracks ran through the smooth curtains and walls of the cavern. One crack ran with a grinding sound across the smooth stone of the floor from the far side of the cavern nearly to where Nemienne knelt. In the pool before her, ripples disturbed the surface of the water. The pale greenish light natural to the caverns wavered and flickered, like the light of a lantern somebody was shaking. But, though this seemed impossible, the dragon itself remained undisturbed. Not the faintest crack disfigured its neck where the mage had struck it.

Ankennes, looking nonplussed, stepped back and leaned on his staff, studying the stone dragon. Enkea had not moved. Her green eyes rested on the mage, not tame at all. She blinked, once. Above her head, a drop of water made its way down the curve of the dragon's wing and fell, gleaming faintly green, into the waiting pool: *plink*. Nemienne stared down into the water after it. The mage also turned his head at the sound, but then he turned slowly back to stare at the gray cat. One of his eyebrows lifted.

Around them, the melody the Kalchesene sorcerer was playing suddenly altered. Everyone, Ankennes included, jerked around to stare at him.

The sorcerer was standing with his legs braced and his flute to his mouth, playing a rippling melody so delicate that it was barely audible—but he had switched the bone flute Ankennes had given him for a plain wooden flute of his own. The bone flute lay discarded at his feet. The sound of the wooden one, if one listened closely, was purer. Cleaner, somehow. Leilis stood with her hands gripping the foreigner's arm, but she stood like one lending support, not one being supported.

Nemienne looked for and found the thread of music the bardic sorcerer was holding. It led slantwise into the dark, but dimly, far along that path, she could once again see her sister. And beyond Karah, a still dimmer form that had to be the prince. Both of them brightened as she watched.

Mage Ankennes leaned on his staff while he peered along the dark path Taudde's skill was pulling from his flute. The mage's eyes widened. He turned sharply toward the Kalchesene. "What is that flute? Stop playing!" he commanded.

The foreigner looked across the pool at Ankennes and nearly smiled behind his wooden flute, which he did not lower. The melody he was playing changed again, it seemed to Nemienne. There was something about it that coaxed, that urged...

Ankennes, face contorted with anger, began to wade back across the pool toward the sorcerer. He still held his staff like a weapon, and Nemienne, thinking of how he'd made the mountain tremble with it, swallowed.

The bardic sorcerer backed away to the far side of the circle—a few steps only—and played on. His eyes, wide and wary, went swiftly from the dragon to Ankennes and finally to Nemienne.

"Oh, where is your sister?" Leilis cried to her. "Nemienne, can't you bring them back?"

Nemienne was impressed that Leilis had understood so quickly, but she could only answer helplessly, "Yes, I'll try, I meant to, only now I'm not sure—I'm not sure how far they've gone, how far they have to come back. But they *are* coming. Look, they *are*—"

Nevertheless, she bit her lips until she tasted blood, and stared after her sister as though she could, by sheer force of will, force her faster back to them along the flute's path. She reached out, meaning to take her sister's hand as she had done once before— she would draw Karah out of the dark, and Karah would bring the prince with her—

Mage Ankennes lashed out with his staff, striking right through the brilliant circle of light; his staff came down with frightening force against the sorcerer's guarding arm. The young man did not cease playing, but his face contorted with pain and he staggered and would have fallen against the burning circle except that Leilis caught him. She flung herself between the mage's next blow and the young sorcerer.

Ankennes swept her out of the way without using his staff, with just a wave of his hand that sent her staggering. She hit the circle of light and cried out, a high-pitched agonized sound that made Nemienne press her hands to her own mouth to block a scream. But Leilis was not dead. The woman staggered back to her feet, and though she was weeping, Nemienne thought it was as much with rage as with pain.

But the mage punched his staff through the circle a second time, and this time Leilis was not there and the sorcerer could not block the blow. The staff struck at his face, and the wooden flute flew across the circle, struck the barrier of light, and crumbled instantly to dust.

The young sorcerer made a short, hoarse sound and went to one knee, reaching a hand out to the little flurry of dust that was all that remained of his flute. Leilis scrubbed her hands across her face, straightened, and glared with desperate fury at Ankennes.

The pathway the music had laid through the shadows faded, and Nemienne, who had almost thought she could feel her sister's fingers in hers, suddenly lost her again.

"Let the death of the fledgling Seriantes Dragon summon the

true dragon of Lonne down the path of mortality," Ankennes cried. He turned back toward the black pool and the stone dragon.

Nemienne had never hated anyone before, but as she searched in vain for some fading echo of her sister and found nothing, she found she could hate Ankennes. At least she knew, now, that she was right to fight him. Not that she even *could*. She had a sudden, vivid hope that the dragon would suddenly lift its head and bite the mage in two. But it remained quiescent. And she could think of nothing at all to do.

Mage Ankennes took a step into the black water, hefting his staff once more.

A gray cat dashed suddenly into the dragon's chamber. For an instant, Nemienne thought it was Enkea, but this cat was larger and darker: smoky black but with white showing beneath the black as it moved, like smoke veiling white mist. It ran across the cavern and leaped without pause onto a high ledge, spinning around to stare out at them all with a fierce wild gaze. Nemienne saw that one of its eyes was green and the other gold. With a thunderous rush, a crowd of men exploded out of the far reaches of the caverns, following the path the smoke-colored cat had laid down.

Mage Ankennes spun, not only startled but, by all appearances, also alarmed. As he had reason to be, evidently, for the leader of the newcomers flung out an arm and a dozen of his black-clad followers headed toward the mage, faces grim.

The leader was a tall man, with harsh, angular features. He had high cheekbones; a narrow, high-arched nose; and a thin, severe mouth. His hair, caught back with a heavy ring of island jade, was pale as sea-dragon ivory; his eyes were a frosted gray as cold as a high mountain winter. He wore no gold, but, on the first finger of his left hand, a single ring of black iron that glinted with twin rubies. Though all his followers were armed with swords or long-hafted jagged-bladed nikenne, this man carried no weapons. Nemienne could not imagine he would ever need a weapon, because she couldn't imagine anyone having the nerve to defy him.

And yet, Mage Ankennes did defy him. The mage strode toward

the stone dragon, lifting his staff and at the same time laying a bar of fire across the black pool behind him to block pursuit.

The black-clad men hesitated before that fire. But their leader flung out a hand and brought the chill darkness of the caverns falling down upon the fire to smother it. At once the men leaped forward. One of them threw his nikenne. It was not a weapon made for throwing, but it flew as smoothly as an arrow and skidded across the stone so close to Ankennes's feet that for a moment Nemienne thought it had hit him. Sparks scattered behind the blade where it scraped across the stone.

Ankennes hesitated, but then lunged forward. For a moment, Nemienne thought he would manage to take the few remaining steps that separated him from the dragon and strike at it again. But Enkea stood up, no longer sleek: Every hair on her body had fluffed up and she seemed three times her ordinary size. The cat hissed, and Ankennes hesitated again, and then the cold-eyed leader of the newcomers set the weight of the mountains dragging at Ankennes's heel, and at last his men closed on the mage, tearing the staff out of his hand and casting it away.

"Bring him to me," the cold-eyed man commanded, and demanded of the mage when his followers had done so, "Where is my son?"

So this was the *king*, Nemienne realized, and was at once amazed she hadn't known immediately, for he looked exactly as she would have imagined him. This was Geriodde Nerenne ken Seriantes—the Dragon of Lirionne, who was a "similar thing" to the stone dragon. Nemienne thought he definitely looked similar enough to the dragon.

Ankennes did not answer.

The king turned his head to regard Lord Chontas Taudde ser Omientes, where the Kalchesene sorcerer knelt panting on the stone, still imprisoned by the circle of light. The king's gaze went for a moment to Leilis, then came back to the sorcerer. One ivory eyebrow rose, profoundly skeptical. He asked again, with stark patience, "Where is my son?"

To Nemienne's astonishment, the sorcerer caught up the bone

flute that had lain discarded near his hand and held it out toward the king. "Give me leave to play this!" he said in an urgent tone. "Give me leave, before the path is irretrievably lost!"

Mage Ankennes said, "No!"

The king did not even look at Ankennes, but gazed steadily at the sorcerer. "Play it," he said—not so much granting permission as issuing a command.

The sorcerer lifted the bone flute to his mouth. The flute still had that strange off-tone quality; it still sounded like ash and rain. But the melody that spun out from it had a compelling beauty to it now that had previously been lacking. The melody, deceptively simple, drew back out of the dark the glimmering path down which the prince and then Karah had traveled.

Nemienne rose to her feet and peered as hard as she could down that pathway of music and light. She said helplessly, "I don't see her—" But then she did. Far away, veiled by shadows and by a light that seemed itself a kind of shadow. But she thought her sister was going the wrong way, despite the new melody. She was becoming less clear, fading farther away before her eyes. Of Prince Tepres, Nemienne saw nothing at all. She bit her lip. They would both be lost...In a way the flute made it worse, because they could watch Karah fade from their reach...

Geriodde Nerenne ken Seriantes strode past her suddenly, straight into the pathway the bone flute had reopened. Like his son and like Karah, he was swept away at once down that shadowed path. But unlike the others, the king remained clearly—almost blindingly—visible. He trailed a greenish brilliance that unraveled behind him to leave a strong, clear trail overlaying the tenuous path the flute had created.

"No!" Mage Ankennes repeated and, in the absence of the crushing power of the king, summoned fire. The men holding him leaped back, cursing. One of them lifted a sword, but a blaze of fire and power sent him sliding across the stone. Ankennes brought both his hands together with a sound like a crack of thunder and lifted them—the fire did not expand, but it intensified—

Nemienne, who had never been able to summon fire into the peculiar heavy darkness of these caverns, found in her heart an understanding of shadows and darkness and black water that had never known the sun. She held in her mind the heavy smothering darkness, knelt on the stone, dipped a finger into the black pool, and drew quickly on the white stone the rune for summoning that she had seen on the hearthstone of Leilis's fireplace. What she summoned was the patient darkness that lay beyond the reach of any light, the endless heavy shadows that could smother any fire.

Before her, Mage Ankennes's magefire went out like a snuffed candle. All the light in the caverns vanished—all the light and fire that men had made or brought: not only Ankennes's powerful fire but also the prisoning circles of light and all the torches the king's men had carried with them. Through all the caverns, the only light that remained was the light that somehow wasn't quite light at all: the odd greenish glimmer that seemed a part of the stone, that seemed to rise from the black pool without disturbing its blackness; the pale light that slid along the long elegant head and sinuous neck of the stone dragon and lit the pathway that Taudde had made—or found—with the music he drew from a dead king's bone.

Mage Ankennes stopped, staring at his own empty hands and then, with an expression of furious amazement, at Nemienne. She couldn't meet his eyes. The black-clad men caught him roughly by the arms. One of them forced the mage to his knees and another set a blade at his throat. Nemienne didn't feel triumphant, but rather ill and near tears. She thought the king's men might kill Ankennes right where he knelt, but they didn't. She was glad of their restraint, but also wrenched by a guilty wish that they *had* killed the mage, because she was terrified of him now. But the wish seemed somehow worse than the fear. Nemienne lowered her gaze and stared into the black pool.

The music of the bone flute continued, untouched by any of this struggle. Each note fell into the air like a drop of water into the black pool. The melody slid down a haunting, uncomfortable scale where every note edged toward an unrecognizable minor key, then rose again in repetitive swoops where every phrase seemed to build toward something that could never be reached, that *should* not ever be reached... The Kalchesene sorcerer had closed his eyes and played by feel or instinct. Leilis stood behind him, her hands on his shoulders. Her eyes were open. She stared with calm intensity into the shifting path of light that the sorcerer had lain through the shadows.

Geriodde Nerenne ken Seriantes was returning along that path, following the melody. The silver kitten rode on his shoulder. Behind him he drew, evidently by sheer force of will, both Karah and his son.

But the king did not walk easily along the path of light. As he became more visible, it became evident that he was forcing his way through the shadows that tried to drown the trail he had left. He leaned hard forward as though he breasted a ferocious wind; he struggled to lift each foot as though he waded through sucking sands. His eyes were open, but his stare was fixed and blank. Nemienne thought he saw nothing of any of them, but only shadows and the desperately faint glimmering of the path.

"*Help* him!" one of the black-clad men snapped at the foreign sorcerer. He was their senior, a man with a seamed, experienced face, gray streaks through his short-cropped dark hair, and a harsh mouth. His voice cracked across the dragon's chamber with authority.

"Can't you see that he's doing everything he can?" Leilis snapped back. "Are you fool enough to interfere with the only one who *can* help him?"

The man looked at the sorcerer and said nothing. It was perfectly clear that Leilis had spoken nothing but the truth. The Kalchesene sorcerer looked, indeed, almost as strained as the slowly approaching king. His face was as white as the stone that surrounded them all. The foreign stamp of his face stood out starkly in his drawn exhaustion. He had closed his eyes and now played blind, scattered notes that sometimes seemed random and sometimes resolved into a strange melodic line that never seemed to go in any expected direction. Each phrase he played coaxed the trail of light into brief clarity, and yet it would fade again between one moment and the next.

Geriodde Nerenne ken Seriantes now seemed in one way close at hand, his features clearly distinguishable; yet though he strove continually along his path, he grew no nearer. His attitude was one of set endurance. Shadows broke like water before the king and eddied behind him; currents of darkness tried to force him first one way and then the other, so that all his effort was bent on keeping to the path of music and light that lay before him, narrow and tenuous as a ribbon. Yet there was an air of solidity about the king as well. Nemienne could not imagine either his strength or his will failing. If anyone failed here, it would be the sorcerer and not the king. Nemienne thought the king might hold with unchanging force to that uncertain path for uncounted days or years, until everything but that strength and will had been burned away, and he would still in the end win free of the dark. And he would bring his son out with him, too, because he would never let himself fail.

Both Karah and the prince were always partially hidden by the shifting shadows and rippling light that trailed them, but they were there, in the king's wake. Safe, Nemienne thought. She could see that they were struggling, that they clung to one another, that each of them sometimes hesitated as though to turn back into the shadows. She could see that it was the king's will that overrode theirs and not only gave them a way forward, but compelled them along it.

"Can he make it through?" asked the senior of the black-clad men. But he didn't speak as though he addressed anyone in particular, nor as though he expected an answer. He was simply driven to speak by his own desperate uncertainty.

Nemienne understood that very well. She whispered, "I think he will. I think he has the strength to walk it all the way. Surely he will! He's his *father*."

The man glanced down at her. He asked her quietly, as though she were someone who might know, "Is there nothing we can do to help him?"

"No—" Nemienne said uncertainly, and glanced over at Leilis's sorcerer. The Kalchesene was now sitting on the stone floor of the cavern, leaning back against Leilis. His eyes were still closed, his face tight and strained. He let notes fall one at a time into the air, left each lingering as long as possible before playing the next. Nemienne looked up at Leilis and asked, "There isn't, is there?"

"Should I know?" said the woman, but then she leaned down and said softly in the sorcerer's ear, "They have almost won back. You have held the way almost long enough."

There was no sign on the young man's face that he'd heard her. But he drew a shuddering breath and began a series of long, sweeping phrases: one note after another that blurred into another, higher pitched, that gave way in turn to another that rose higher still. Like waves running against a gentle shore, Nemienne thought. No. Like the tide coming in, where it rose higher and higher and drowned the sand...in the bone flute, she thought she could hear the sea.

And, following the strong pull of the flute's melody, the king heaved himself through the clustering shadows and strode at last out of the paths of shadow and light and back into the dragon's chamber.

CHAPTER 15

Rightly was Geriodde Nerenne ken Seriantes called the Dragon of Lirionne, Taudde thought. The king's brief, profound journey had pared him down beyond mortal flesh to essential will, and indeed, though white and profoundly exhausted, he now seemed very dragonlike.

Once he had broken through the paths of the dead and back into the world of the living, the king turned and stared back through the dark moving shadows among which Taudde had laid his path. Taudde was no longer playing, but there was no longer any need. The king merely put out a hand and, with the force of his own stark resolve, pulled his son and the young keiso out after him.

Prince Tepres, though not as worn as his father, also had a strange look about him. He had gone farther along the path of death than the others, and this showed in a lingering remoteness, a darkness that still inhabited his eyes. The prince glanced around the cavern. His gaze paused on Taudde's face, unreadable, and at last met his father's. The prince's expression, from vague, became guarded.

The little keiso's response was different. She came out into the cold moist air of the caverns, gasped, laughed, burst into violent tears, and fled across the cavern to her sister, who embraced her. The two girls clung together in mutual comfort and anxious inquiry: *Are you all right? Yes, but are* you *all right?* They looked very young.

Geriodde Nerenne ken Seriantes, in those first moments, had

attention only for his son. His face, pale and set, showed very little: long experience of court diplomacy had no doubt taught the Dragon of Lirionne parsimony of expression. But he reached out, oddly tentative, and took his son by the shoulders. Prince Tepres stood passively at first, merely allowing this near embrace without returning it. But at last he lifted his eyes to his father's face and slowly brought his own hands up to grip his father's arms. The two of them stood that way for a long moment, neither of them speaking. They looked very like, the Dragon and his heir, both worn with fright and exhaustion and the dawning awareness of reprieve.

While they were caught up in the moment, Ankennes acted. The mage, balked at every turn at the very cusp of success and blazingly furious, disregarded the blade at his throat and smashed one hand down on the stone where he knelt.

Thirty feet away, by the edge of the black pool, his staff exploded.

The force of that explosion slammed through the caverns, cracking stone and smashing delicate formations. A thousand bells, of iron and brass and crystal, shattering all at once, might have sounded like that.

Taudde was not on his feet, so unlike the rest, he didn't fall. He rolled to put himself between the girls and the jagged fragments of rock that crashed down all around. Except he had lost the bone flute and truly could not protect anyone. A piece of stone larger than his head hit the floor not an arm's length away, sending sharp missiles in every direction. Beside him, one of the girls, he thought Nemienne, cried out and he knew she'd been cut.

Geriodde Nerenne ken Seriantes flung out his left hand, the rubies of his black iron ring blazing up like sparks of fire. He might have meant—Taudde thought he meant—to draw on the dark power of the mountain. Even so, he was smashed back against the wall of the cavern and pinned there. And Prince Tepres, also flung back and down, slammed into stone with such force that Taudde could hear the impact of body and bone against unyielding rock even through the other clamor of destruction.

Ankennes alone had gained his feet amid the devastation he had wrought. He reclaimed his staff, which somehow was once more whole and undamaged in his hand, and spun around to fling that staff straight as a spear at the stone dragon.

Beside Taudde, Nemienne snatched at the beads wound through her sister's hair, leaped to her feet, and threw three beads one after another in a high arc toward the dragon. Somehow there seemed plenty of time to watch them fly and fall. They caught the pale light and fell like sparks of darkness through the air: a glass bead, and one of hematite, and a black pearl. They fell into the pool, one after another, but not with the sound of beads falling into water. Each one struck with a clean, clear, chiming sound, three notes that spanned a chord, as though three harp strings had been plucked. The notes were amazingly pure and sustained, audible through everything.

At almost that same instant, the mage's staff struck the dragon. Its blow gave rise to a low, powerful note that answered the chiming of the fallen drops of darkness-infused beads. The carved stone shattered beneath that blow, but the three notes of the beads rose up under the sound of breaking stone, and Taudde saw that beneath the stone lay something else, something that was not stone and had not broken.

In the cavern at the heart of darkness, a dark eye slitted open.

Everywhere through the caverns, stone flowed and smoothed out damaged areas. Water that was not water—none of it was precisely *water*, Taudde thought now—trickled and dripped and gathered into streams that were made of shadows. Or of a strange kind of light. Amid that light and those shadows, the Dragon of Lonne lifted its head.

Ankennes stood mute and amazed.

Geriodde Seriantes got slowly to his feet ... slowly, like a man of waning strength trying to make the failure of his body seem merely like considered dignity. He wore a stern, ungiving expression as he turned with slow reluctance toward his son, dreading, Taudde understood, to see too clearly the ruin Ankennes had made of blood and bone. But pale light and strange shadows flowed like water across the prince as well, and around him, and under that influence the prince's body was visibly repairing itself, just as the caverns were. The king's attention was fixed on this. He began to step toward his son, then caught at a stone pillar to support himself and stayed where he was.

But Prince Tepres rose to his feet, levering himself away from stone stained with his own blood, and came over to his father on his own accord. This time, it was the prince who reached out first, his gesture constrained and almost shy, to touch his father's hand.

The king's expressionless mask cracked like stone, and his hands closed around his son's arms with the force of mountains shifting. It was a profoundly intimate moment. Taudde looked away, ashamed to have witnessed it. Deeply ashamed, now, that he had tried to strike against the king in the person of his son. He looked at the dragon instead, and then found himself unable to look anywhere else.

The stone opened to free the dragon and closed behind it once it was loosed. Subtle colors washed across it as it emerged from the wall of the cavern. Pale green and silvery blue and delicate lavender ran down its neck, the colors deepening to brilliant jewel tones as moments passed. Its elegant head was lapis and amethyst, with shadings of garnet around its nostrils and at the corners of its long mouth. Its antennae, flexing and extending above and around its head, were a deep sapphire that shaded to aquamarine and then to emerald. The emerald ran down its long sinuous neck in a wash of color that shifted as the dragon moved, to sapphire and then amethyst and then back to emerald. Its nearest wing, sapphire traced with gold, opened a little and then relaxed. Its eyes were black, containing all the darkness that lived beneath the mountain.

"What did you do?" Taudde whispered to Nemienne.

The girl, her gaze wide with wonder, shook her head a little. "Glass for the ephemeral," she whispered, but almost more to herself than to him. "Iron for the eternal, and pearl for the immanent...I wasn't sure it was right..."

But the girl had evidently guessed exactly right. The dragon turned its huge head and studied each of them in turn. Taudde experienced its gaze as pressure and heat, or perhaps as a noiseless clap of thunder and cold. He wanted to look away, to lift his hands to block that terrible gaze. But he couldn't move. When the dragon looked away, dismissing him, the shift of its attention was like being released from physical bonds.

Last of all, the dragon turned its attention to Geriodde Nerenne ken Seriantes and his son. The prince still stood with his father. They looked much the same, for each wore the same stern mask. They both gazed at the dragon, and there was something in their eyes that was akin to what Taudde had seen in its gaze.

The dragon's nearest foot shifted across the cavern floor. Its talons, each longer than a man was tall, tore gouges across the stone. But the stone flowed in again afterward and was left unmarked.

Then the dragon spoke. Its voice was dark and slow as a dirge, powerful and somber as the tolling of iron bells. "**Blood and magic you have spilled into the deep shadows, O king. Glass and iron and pearl you have cast in tribute into the darkness. Is it then time to bring down the heights and let in the great sea?**"

Geriodde Nerenne ken Seriantes gazed speechlessly at the dragon.

The dragon shifted restlessly, opening its wings to the farthest extent allowed by the caverns, which suddenly seemed small. "**Is it time?**" it repeated.

The king closed his eyes for a moment, visibly gathered his strength, and stood up straight with an effort almost painful to witness. He put back his shoulders, lifted his chin, and said in a tone that just missed matter-of-fact confidence by a hair, "This disturbance was a...a mischance, O Ekorraodde, Dragon of Lonne. No one meant to disturb you. It is not time."

"**No one?**" said the dragon. "**Would one reach through the ephemeral shadows and the eternal darkness to wake me...by mischance? Do you say so, O king?**"

The powerful, rolling tones of the dragon's voice were completely unfamiliar to Taudde, and yet he knew it spoke with irony. Or perhaps with threat. Or possibly with humor. Its black gaze rested on the king, and yet he was certain that its attention was on Ankennes. And, Taudde felt, on himself as well. He stayed very still.

Mage Ankennes, blank with well-deserved dismay, was staring at the dragon.

"**It was a mage's hand that woke me**," the dragon said to Ankennes. "**Yours? What do you desire, O mage?**"

"The destruction of the darkness that underlies and corrupts Lonne," Ankennes answered, with a directness and courage Taudde couldn't help but admire. The mage gripped his staff, once more returned to him, with both hands. But if he tried to work any magery, Taudde perceived no signs of it.

"**And is it in pursuit of this desire you have worn your heart so thin?**" asked the dragon. Its tone held a strange kind of indifferent condemnation. "**You are mistaken, O mage. It is by the existence of shadows that men recognize light. Darkness does not corrupt. All corruption exists within the hearts of men.**"

Mage Ankennes began to speak.

"**For example, your heart**," added the dragon, and reached across the pool of shadows to hook the mage's heart out of his chest with one long talon. The heart was made of a sliver of black obsidian so fine and translucent that the greenish light of the caverns shone through it. The Dragon held it between the tips of two talons and observed, "**Hard and cold is the heart of the Mage of Lonne. There is nothing left of it but stone.**"

Ankennes had put a hand, in an involuntary gesture, to his unmarked chest. "Illusion," he said, but with an involuntary tremor just audible within his voice. "A play of light and shadow."

"**Of course. Also truth, for truth lies at the heart of all illusion as darkness lies at the heart of the light. It was not you who cast glass and iron and pearl into the shadow. You have not the inclination toward truth**," said the dragon, dismissing him. Its talons parted, and the obsidian heart it held dissolved into the dimness and was gone. The dragon turned its attention to Nemienne. "**It was you, young mageling, who cast the ephemeral and the eternal and the immanent into the heart of darkness, which is my heart. Was it not?**"

"Yes," whispered the girl. Her voice shook, for which Taudde could not blame her at all.

"**Your heart echoes with the rhythm of my darkness,**" said the dragon. "**I see you are not a mage, nor yet a sorcerer of Kalches, nor a spellcrafter such as the sea-folk make, nor an enchantress out of Enescedd. What are you?**" And when the girl only stared, baffled and frightened, it asked, "**What would you be?**"

"I don't know!" Nemienne protested.

"**You must choose,**" said the dragon. "**Would you be a mage of Lonne?**"

"...yes," Nemienne answered, but uncertainly, with a flinching glance toward Ankennes and away.

"I hardly think so," Ankennes said coldly. Two of the king's men had moved up beside him and held him now between their drawn swords. One of them took his staff. Though he did not seem especially intimidated by them, neither did he try to resist his staff's confiscation. And no wonder. After his last trick, Taudde suspected the men would have been happy with any excuse to kill him. He was only surprised they didn't simply cut the mage to pieces without waiting for an excuse. Probably they were afraid the dragon might be offended. That possibility would make anyone hesitate.

The dragon ignored the mage. "**It is for you to choose,**" it said to the girl. "**Do you then reject magecraft and all its strictures and precepts?**"

"...no. I don't...I don't think so. Can't I...can't I choose more than one thing? You...you're more than one kind of creature. Aren't you? You exist in the ephemeral and the eternal and the immanent. All at once. Isn't that right?"

The dragon lowered its long, elegant head across the pool toward Nemienne. The lapis and amethyst tones of its head deepened toward sapphire and rich violet as it moved; the colors were reflected back again by the black water of the pool, the light of the caverns taking on a purplish cast. The dragon's antennae stretched out in sinuous curves, reaching forward to comb through the air near the girl. What those delicate antennae perceived, Taudde could not guess. Magic, perhaps.

Nemienne had closed her eyes. She put up a hand without looking and laid her hand on the dragon's jaw. For a moment the dragon was still. Then the light surrounding them took on pale opalescent tints, and the dragon lifted its great head with a sharp, decisive gesture.

Nemienne dropped her hand to her side and opened her eyes. "I can't reject magecraft. But it's all the same to you, isn't it? Magecraft and Kalchesene sorcery and the sea magic of the islands and whatever they do in Enescedd. Because you're not really a dragon at all. Dragons are natural creatures, but you... 'Ekorraodde' means 'indwelling darkness,' doesn't it? Kelle Iasodde wrote about glass and iron and pearl, but he said if a mage wants to see the eternal darkness, he has to be ready to cast his heart into the darkness after those elements. Only... only, he didn't write about what would happen after that."

"**The gift of the ephemeral drew me into the ephemeral world**," said the dragon. "**Did Iasodde write that? Much of what he wrote was false, but that was truth. You have indeed offered me your heart, little mageling: I have it already in my hand.**" Talons closed, with a gentle clicking sound, and opened again to reveal a heart like a delicate rose-and-pearl jewel. "**It was your gift. What would you have of me in return? You may ask one boon. Perhaps I will grant it. Shall I bring down the mountains? Do you wish the eternal sea to cover the bones of this transient city of men?**"

The king's hand closed hard on his son's shoulder. Prince Tepres's mouth tightened.

"No!" Nemienne cried in horror.

"**No?**" To Taudde's ear, the dragon sounded amused. He thought it had never expected the girl to agree to anything of the sort, but what it expected her to ask for, or wanted her to ask for, he could not begin to guess. "**Then ask a different boon**," said the dragon. And, relentlessly, when the girl did not answer at once, "**Ask.**"

Taudde more than half expected Nemienne to ask for everything to be back the way it had been the previous night, or for something else equally impossible. She bit her lip and glanced quickly at her sister, but then she straightened her back and said steadily, "O Ekorraodde, how should the ephemeral know what boon to ask of the eternal? I don't ask for anything, only...only," this time she glanced at the king, flinching slightly at his hard, impassive face. "Only, if it does not offend you, and if you think it wise, O Ekorraodde, I would like...I would like the transient cities of men to prosper and not be...not be covered by the sea."

Geriodde Nerenne ken Seriantes closed his eyes briefly, letting out a breath. His expression eased.

The dragon tilted its head, regarding Nemienne out of one black eye. It began to speak.

Mage Ankennes, moving suddenly, stabbed to either side with knives fashioned out of darkness. Both his guards cried out and fell back—one clutching his stomach where the knife still stood and the other stumbling to avoid a second blow.

Ankennes dropped his shadow knives, deftly caught his staff as the first guard dropped it, raked the end of the staff through the blood still pooling on the floor where the prince had lain, raised the staff an inch from the stone floor of the cavern, and brought it down. The sound of that blow was like thunder, but like thunder that did not end: like an avalanche, like the sound of a mountain falling. All around them, the mountain trembled and cracked.

It had honestly not occurred to Taudde that Ankennes might still challenge the dragon. That despite its vast size and terrible power, the dragon might still be vulnerable. But at once it was obvious that he had merely suffered from a failure of imagination, because Kerre Maraddras itself was cracking open. And when Ankennes threw his staff, it flew like a spear straight for the dragon's own heart; and this time, Taudde knew that when it struck, carrying with it Prince Tepres's mortality, it would strike deep.

The dragon whipped its long neck back and around, but despite its speed, Taudde knew it was not going to be fast enough to block that flung staff. So, in the only instant that remained, Taudde set the bone flute to his lips and called out of it a note pitched to echo the dragon's own powerful, resonant voice. So small a flute should have been unable to produce such a note, but it did. The deep, powerful sound found Ankennes's staff in its flight and flung it aside from its course to spend its force slashing harmlessly across white stone. The mage turned, furious. Taudde pitched his second note high, to match tides and chill currents and subtle greenish light, and cast music like a flung knife across the cavern.

Like Ankennes's own shadow blades, Taudde's weapon of music and sea craft was hard to block. Though the mage flung up his staff, Taudde's attack struck straight through Ankennes's defenses and found his heart, which, despite the dragon's illusion, was still in his chest and not made of stone. The mage had time to look surprised. Then he fell, not all at once, but crumpling slowly first to hands and knees and then at last to lie in abandoned disorder on the cavern floor.

Everyone stared at the fallen mage, and then turned, almost as one, to stare at Taudde. Geriodde Nerenne ken Seriantes turned slowly, but with the power of the mountain in his pale eyes. The dragon itself tilted its head and regarded him from one vast, unreadable, black eye.

Taudde was glad he was still sitting on the floor, for if he'd been on his feet, the force of that combined gaze would surely have thrown him down. He stared into pale human and dark dragon eyes, each containing the same powerful depths. He thought, rather desperately, of the brilliant, windswept heights of Kalches, so unlike these caverns of shadows. If he played a melody of traveling and distance, a melody that recalled the cold heights of distant Kalches and called to them across all the miles that lay between... There was so much power loose in this cavern, he knew he could gather merely the smallest part of it, wrap himself up in his song, and drop right out of the sky to land on his grandfather's doorstep. He could take Leilis away with him. He thought she would not object—hoped she would not object, because he had no time to ask her. He lifted the flute again, reaching after power.

But there was, after all, no time to play a second enchantment into life. The king's power came down on Taudde like the weight of the mountain. Crushed by that weight, Taudde fell into the dark, down, gone.

CHAPTER 16

For a long moment after Taudde crumpled to the cavern floor, Leilis thought his collapse was an aftereffect of the strength he'd spent on all his foreign sorcery. Certainly he'd spent himself without stint this night. She'd watched him wear himself down to bone making that path for the king, and that was before the...dragon. Just bearing the weight of the dragon's immense gaze would surely be enough to exhaust a man.

Then she saw the weary satisfaction in the king's eyes, and the glance he shared with his senior officer, and understood. At once she was so angry she couldn't speak. Or dared not speak. She was already kneeling beside Taudde. She lifted his head to rest on her knee and hid her anger carefully behind a keiso mask.

"**This mage of yours called mortality into his staff**," said the dragon, putting out a saber-long talon to gently nudge Ankennes's body. Its somber, powerful voice continued with slow condemnation, "**But once released, the mortality he sought claimed him instead, as is only just.**" It folded its talons around the mage, and when it opened its long, strange hand again, the body was gone.

"Ekorraodde," the king began, and stopped. The dragon swung its head around and locked its gaze on the man's. There was something frighteningly similar about the depths in their eyes, Leilis thought, but she could not have begun to describe what it was.

"**King of Lonne**," said the dragon. "**Give me your name, O king.**"

"I am Geriodde Nerenne ken Seriantes," answered the king.

"Great-grandson of Taliente Neredde ken Seriantes, whom I think you knew." His voice was steady, but his hand on his son's shoulder was white knuckled with strain and exhaustion. He lifted his hand to show the dragon, Leilis suddenly understood, his ring. The iron was cast in the shape of a dragon, she saw; the rubies were its eyes.

"**Yes**," said the dragon. "**I remember Taliente Seriantes. You are much like him. Also, little like him. He offered me his heart. Will you give me yours?**"

"It is yours already, O Ekorraodde."

"**Yes.**" The dragon opened its hand. The king's heart gleamed dully against the dragon's brilliance, a thing of black iron and stone, of smooth powerful lines and sudden sharp angles. "**It is not the heart of a dragon. Would you have a dragon's heart, O king? That is what Taliente Neredde ken Seriantes desired. I could give you the heart of a dragon. It would be impervious to harm.**"

Geriodde Seriantes looked, beneath his calm mask, subtly horrified. "... That is not my ambition. No."

The dragon tilted its head. Leilis thought it was amused, but not with any familiar human amusement. "**No?**" It closed its hand again, and the iron heart vanished. "**Then where lies your ambition? What would you have of me, O king?**"

The king made a little gesture of negation. "Nothing. I would never have ... called you into the ephemeral. I ask nothing of you, O Ekorraodde." He hesitated, then continued carefully, "What should I dare ask: I, who was blind to the heart of the mage?"

"**And to your own heart?**"

Leilis glanced from one dragon to the other, trying to understand the undercurrents that lay beneath their words. She felt that she was missing half the exchange, but if the dragon was baiting the king, he did not rise to the bait. He said merely, "Perhaps."

"**And to mine?**"

But at this, surprisingly, the king shook his head. "No. Yours, I recognize, O Ekorraodde."

The dragon tilted its head, regarding the king from one great black eye. **"What would you have of me, grandson of Taliente Neredde ken Seriantes, King of Lirionne, in exchange for your heart? Ask."**

The king bowed his head. "My heart was always yours. But as you ask me, O Ekorraodde—I, too, would be pleased to see the transient cities of men prosper."

"Then see to it that they do," said the dragon, and sank its long head down to rest on one taloned hand, regarding the king almost from his own level.

After that there was at last a discreet, relieved withdrawal. Several of the King's Own guards carried Taudde, carefully, but with an air of bearing a prisoner and not merely a wounded man. Leilis watched them with covert anxiety. She had attached herself as by right to Karah's company, and thus by implication to the protection of Prince Tepres. It might have been this that prevented any guardsman from laying a hand on her. Or they might merely have thought her held safely enough without going to the trouble, as was clearly true.

Karah walked hand in hand with her sister, both girls quiet and strained. But Karah's other hand was laid on Prince Tepres's arm, and there was no mistaking the possessiveness with which the prince regarded the young keiso. But the prince also cast one and another distracted glance back toward the dragon's cavern. His father had not left the cavern with the rest but had remained to speak further with the Dragon of Lonne. Leilis wondered what they would say to one another, the king and the dragon, but was not sorry to have been dismissed with the others. The big smoke-and-silver cat had stayed behind with the king, but the little gray cat with the white foot walked before their little company and Karah's kitten perched on her shoulder, guides and guards and whatever else they might be. They were a comforting presence in the dark places of the mountain.

The caverns scrolled out before them and around them, graceful curtains and spires of white stone barely revealed by the simple lanterns of men. For a while their path lay beside a swift rivulet of opaque water. The sound of it running across the stone made Leilis realize that she was desperately thirsty. She saw some of the King's Own guardsmen also glance wistfully at the water, but no one was rash enough to drink from *this* stream.

At last they crossed a narrow arching bridge of stone, barely a handspan across at its narrowest width—Prince Tepres looked worriedly at little Karah, but there was no room on the bridge for him to give her his hand. But the girl simply walked across with matter-of-fact grace and no sign of fear. Soon after the bridge, they found themselves at the base of a long, steep stair of rough-carved steps. Water glistened on the stone walls and dripped from thin needles overhead, but even so, Leilis fancied she could already feel a draft of warm, ordinary air coming down these stairs to welcome them back to the places of men.

The stair let onto a wide landing with a small door of iron-bound oak, now standing open. More King's Own guardsmen stood on the landing. They greeted their companions with first relief and then anxiety when they found the prince but not his father in the company. The senior officer murmured to them, increasing both their evident relief and their unease. "Derente, you and yours will stay here to wait for the king," the officer said then, brisk and assured. "Keredd, take your man—" he nodded toward the unconscious sorcerer two of the guardsmen carried between them "—to the upper east prison, and send for Mage Sehennes to see he stays there. Be swift. We do not know how soon he may wake." He glanced at Leilis and the girls while his men murmured acknowledgment, and then looked finally, warily, at his prince.

"They may stay with me," Prince Tepres said firmly. "They are my guests, Neriodd. I will not have them frightened or offended."

The officer bowed his head in acquiescence. But he also said, "Eminence. Your guests, if you will have it so, but still your father's to dispose of as he sees fit. I will send Jeres Geliadde to you, and I will ask you to keep your guests secure. You might escort them to . . . the lower east suite, perhaps. If you will, eminence."

The prince's mouth tightened. But he inclined his head, accepting this...command, Leilis thought, was an accurate term, for all the deference with which the officer had delivered it. Karah gazed trustfully at Prince Tepres, but her sister—more sensibly, to Leilis's mind—looked exhausted, frightened, and quite wretched.

Leilis allowed herself one quick glance after Taudde as the guardsmen carried him away, and then lowered her eyes and went obediently with the girls, as she was directed.

The lower east suite proved to be a large, airy apartment halfway up the face of the Laodd, with three wide windows and a generous balcony. It was a beautiful morning. Sunlight poured down through the chilly air, shining on the frost that lay across the rooftops of the city. Not a thousand feet away, the Nijiadde River Falls poured down the cliffs, its thunder muted by distance. Shattered fragments of rainbows glimmered in the mist around the lake far below, where the waterfall crashed into spume.

There was a basin with brass taps for hot water; there were scented soaps and warm towels and pins for their hair. Clean robes were brought, keiso blue for Karah and Leilis, the white of magecraft apprenticeship for Nemienne. Nemienne looked almost as uncomfortable with her robes as Leilis felt with hers. Neither of them protested.

Prince Tepres, in black and saffron and with his hair tied back with a fresh black-and-gold ribbon, had sent for breakfast: perfumed tea and warm rolls with butter and honey, rice porridge with chicken and shrimp, poached eggs floating in broth. Jeres Geliadde arrived with the breakfast, his face set in hard lines, ashamed to have so nearly lost his prince to unsuspected enemies.

"Not so grim," the prince told him firmly. "Nothing of this was your fault."

"I never liked him," muttered Jeres, not comforted in the least. "But I don't like anyone. I should have seen the black treachery in his eyes. But I had no plain suspicion, not of him nor of Miennes, until suddenly I received warnings from every direction. And trusted none of them. I should have—"

"I can't think why you should have seen so much more clearly than the rest of us," Prince Tepres said, still more firmly. He gripped the man's arm and gave him a little shake. "Don't take on guilt that isn't rightfully yours. Do you hear, Jeres? Well, then. Have you had breakfast? Stop glowering and eat something." He glanced around at Leilis and the girls, with a special smile for Karah. "We are all still half frozen with the memory of cold—at least, I am. Have some tea."

The fragrant tea was welcome, but Leilis had no appetite for the food. Nor did Nemienne, who only stirred her porridge without tasting it and nervously tore a roll into shreds. Jeres Geliadde ate an egg to please his prince, but he didn't look like he enjoyed it. Prince Tepres buttered rolls for Karah and drizzled them with honey, and the girl blushed and tried, not very successfully, to keep from smiling. Leilis tried to appreciate the resilience young love gave to the pair, sorely tested as they had been, but she found it hard. Well enough for them, yes, but what of Taudde? He had been harder used than even those two, and she doubted anyone had brought him hot tea and buttered rolls.

The senior officer—Neriodd, wasn't it?—came in, then, frowning. Karah glanced up in mute alarm, and then at the prince in equally mute appeal. He gave her a reassuring nod and Neriodd a cool look, which the officer did not seem to regard.

"Your father asks for you to attend him, eminence," the officer said, and then, in the tone of a man reprieved, "Ah, tea!" He hooked a chair out from the table with his foot and sank into it with a sigh of relief and without waiting for leave. "Your father has not stopped for tea," he added to the prince. "You might see what you can do along those lines."

"Neriodd—" began the prince, but then shook his head and stood up. Karah began to rise as well, but he patted her hand and she sank into her chair again. Nemienne crept closer to her sister, and Karah put an arm around the girl and smiled down at her in calm reassurance.

"I shall see that your guests receive everything they desire," the officer assured Prince Tepres, and bowed with an ironic air that suggested the prince probably should be on his way. Leilis thought the prince might be angry at the informality, much less the implied dismissal, but he didn't seem to be. She could see there were undercurrents to this relationship not visible to any outsider. The prince murmured to Karah and went out. The officer stayed behind, and Leilis, who might otherwise have liked to speak plainly with the girls, veiled her eyes behind the steam from a fresh cup of tea and said nothing.

After the prince, a man came to take Karah to the king. Nemienne looked white and nervous, and shredded another roll. Leilis touched her shoulder in sympathy for their mutual situation and wondered what in the tangle of magecraft and terror and treachery had made the girl so wretched. There seemed so much to choose from. She did not dare speak to Nemienne about anything important, not with the officer keeping his ironic eye on them. But she made the other girl eat a roll rather than crumble it. "You can't be fainting from hunger," she pointed out, and Nemienne shuddered and obediently ate the roll.

After Karah, Nemienne was summoned. Leilis followed her own advice and made herself eat a plain roll and a little rice porridge, hoping to settle her nerves and stomach before her own turn came. It seemed a long time coming, but at the same time, Leilis would have been glad to wait longer still. Days, if possible. She had no idea what she was going to say to the king when she was finally brought before him. So much seemed difficult, now.

Her summons came at last, as the sun stood for its little time at noon and began its slow westward slide toward the sea. A long day, following an unspeakable night, and a long time yet to finish it...Neriodd himself escorted Leilis down a long stair and along a complicated path through interior hallways. Leilis had expected some sort of starkly formal reception chamber, or perhaps a grim prisonlike room. Instead, she found Geriodde Nerenne ken Seriantes waiting for her in a small, warm corner room much like one of the parlors of Cloisonné House. There were comfortable-looking chairs and small tables scattered in two groupings, one by each window, and rugs of blue and gold, and a writing desk with a dozen books on a shelf above it. A fire burned in a tidy fireplace, with a single chair drawn up before it. The king occupied this chair. His big cat sat on the hearth, its fluffy tail curled neatly around its feet, glints of underlying silver showing beneath its black fur when it turned its head. It blinked its odd-colored eyes slowly at Leilis and then looked away, disinterested.

Whoever had prevailed upon the king, he had a pot of tea on a table by his elbow, and a steaming cup in his hand. The heavy iron ring on his finger gleamed dully as he set the cup down on the table. He did not look exactly rested, but the strong bones of his face no longer stood out with quite the stark exhaustion Leilis remembered from those last moments in the dragon's cavern. The pale eyes he turned her way were calm and cold, the line of his mouth ungiving.

Leilis, for all her years in the flower world, could not guess what he might be thinking. Nor had she imagined that she would ever stand before the King of Lirionne—but keiso manners came to her rescue. Though she was no keiso, still she glided forward and sank down with deliberate grace to kneel before the king, her right leg tucked in and her left foot arched so that her robes would drape elegantly. She bowed her head, hiding behind her still face.

"You may stand." The king's voice was not as cold as his expression had led Leilis to expect, yet its very impassivity was somehow more alarming than open suspicion or even anger would have been. "Look at me, woman. Your name is Leilis? You are of Cloisonné House, yet not a keiso?"

Leilis admitted all this.

The king touched a summoning cord, and Neriodd reentered the room. This time, to Leilis's surprise, the King's Own guardsman escorted Narienneh—and, far less welcome, Lily. And behind them both, Jeres Geliadde. The prince's bodyguard was expressionless. Narienneh's manner was surprisingly similar, but behind her regal keiso mask, the Mother of Cloisonné House looked weary, almost as worn as the king himself. Lily, in contrast to them both, glittered with beauty and malice.

"This deisa of your House has described to me your treacherous dealings with the Kalchesene sorcerer Lord Chontas Taudde ser Omientes," the king told Leilis. "I understand that you were suborned by this man and aided him in his designs against me and against Lirionne."

For a long moment, Leilis said nothing. A wild flurry of denials clearly would not serve, but what would? At last she said merely, "The deisa is mistaken. The only such designs of which I was ever aware were owned by Mage Ankennes. And I think by your cousin, eminence—Lord Rikadde Miennes ken Nerenne—but I do not know his role with certainty."

"One might wish," murmured the king, "to know anything whatever with certainty." For a moment, before he recovered his cold neutrality, his harsh face showed stark weariness. He asked, "You maintain you did not know Lord Chontas Taudde ser Omientes and were in no way in his employ?"

"I was not. We had hardly conversed five minutes altogether," Leilis said firmly.

"She's lying—she's a deceitful, treacherous creature—she's—" Lily began to protest. Then she stopped, collected herself, and said much more smoothly, "I assure you, eminence, Leilis would have done anything and betrayed anyone for a promise to remove her curse. I know Mother—" she slid a sideways glance at Narienneh "—always trusted her, but truly that only shows the smooth manners Leilis learned. Mimicking her betters, never knowing her place—"

"Lily," Narienneh said. Only that, but it stopped the deisa in midsentence, almost in midword.

The king lifted an ironic eyebrow at Leilis. "So?"

Leilis drew a slow breath, and let it out again. Then she said, "You were in the dragon's cavern, eminence. What can I add to what you saw there?"

"You see!" Lily said triumphantly.

"Yes," said the king. "Thank you, deisa. You may go. Jeres—"

The prince's guard, professionally bland, escorted Lily from the room and then returned to resume his place next to Neriodd, behind the king's chair.

"Well?" said the king.

Leilis bent her head to the king, but she spoke first to Narienneh. "I'm sorry."

The Mother of Cloisonné House shook her head, looking tired. "Leilis, you were not the only one of my many children to try to tell me about my one child."

Leilis touched Narienneh's hand in sympathy. To the king, she said, "What shall I tell you, eminence?"

Again, a pale eyebrow rose above an eye as cold as the gray winter sky. "Everything," said the king.

Leilis had both dreaded and expected precisely this. She had hoped that if—when—this moment came, she would suddenly know what to say. But the moment had arrived, and still she did not know. Next to the king's cool command, Lily's viciousness shrank to something obviously childish and petty.

She could tell the king nothing but truth and yet leave out any hint that she had ever known—before the cavern—that Lord Chontas Taudde ser Omientes was Kalchesene. She knew she could tell a smooth tale to cover her encounter with Taudde and then Jeres Geliadde in the Laodd. She dismissed without even consciously thinking of it any fear that Taudde would give her away when he himself was questioned. Without any clear reason for her confidence, she simply knew that he would not.

Yes, Leilis could reach for her own safety. She doubted the king would question her story very closely. Lily's accusations were nothing, or close to nothing. The girl's vindictiveness was too obvious to be a threat. With his son infatuated with Karah, the king would wish to maintain a good relationship with Cloisonné House.

But only if she told the king *everything* could she tell him also the things Taudde had said to her. *I think now I was wrong. I was glad to find I had done less than I meant to do.* And, *I swear to you, I did not come here to strike at your prince. Indeed, I swore to my grandfather I would not attempt personal vengeance. But then there was Miennes. So I was a fool, after all.*

Leilis believed the Kalchesene. Now she wanted to make Geriodde Nerenne ken Seriantes believe him as well. But she had no faith in her ability to persuade the king of anything.

But in the end, she tried. Narienneh and Jeres Geliadde and the king's own bodyguard and the king himself all listened to Leilis's careful attempt to explain what she had thought and guessed and seen and surmised of the Kalchesene's heart. All four listened with nearly identical neutrality, yet she knew she must at best sound like an impressionable girl, and at worst like exactly what Lily had accused her of being: a treacherous fool concerned with nothing but her own advantage.

At last, finding herself at the end of her ability to express herself, Leilis simply stopped. There was a pause that seemed to scroll out for a long time.

Then the king leaned his chin on his fist and said, taking Leilis utterly aback, "Do you know, young woman, you resemble your father amazingly."

Leilis simply stared, for once utterly forgetful of elegant keiso manners.

"He was a close, mmm. Not friend. A close ally of my father, and then of mine. He, too, could see through all duplicity to the indwelling truth at the heart of a man." This did nothing to resolve Leilis's amazement, but Narienneh seemed enlightened. "Oh," she murmured. "Yes. That was Nasedres Perenedde. Yes. He was a faithful client of Cloisonné House, and so fond of Coralberry."

"And a fine mage," murmured the king. He continued to gaze at Leilis, his chilly eyes thoughtful. "As you noted earlier, young woman, I was indeed present in the dragon's chamber."

CHAPTER 17

Taudde woke into silence.

At first he thought he had been made mute. Then, as he realized that more than his own voice had been silenced, that there was no sound anywhere, he thought he had been made deaf. The horror of these thoughts was so great that when it finally dawned on him that he was merely imprisoned in a soundless prison, the realization came as a relief. He traced the lacy edges of the muting spellwork with sideways glances—the spellwork could not be seen straight on—traced them again and again, compulsively, not because he hoped to break the spell, but simply as evidence that sound still existed in the world, that only his own prison was soundless.

Aside from its silence, the prison was not terrible. It was the sort of apartment a guest of rank might be given. The bedchamber where Taudde had awoken was small, but it boasted a bed that, though narrow, was well supplied with good blankets and coverlets. There were two other rooms. The first of these was a private bath, where the basin possessed six taps that ran with fresh water. One of them offered hot water, one cold, and the other four warm water that had been perfumed with musk or floral scents. Clothing had been laid out on a chest. His own clothing, Taudde observed with a tremor of disquiet. This was the gray outfit he had purchased himself...how many days ago? That trip to the Paliante seemed far in the past.

The water ran soundlessly from the tap and splashed equally soundlessly into the basin. When Taudde tapped his fingernails against the porcelain, there was no resulting sound. He bathed and dressed in total silence. His clothing did not rustle, his soft boots did not whisper against the floor. Taudde set his teeth against a desire to shout, to scream: He could not have borne proof of his own voicelessness. He went out into the final room with deliberate calm.

This room was the largest of the three. It held two small tables, a desk, and several chairs, all of polished wood inlaid with lapis and pearl. It was also the only room with a window. The window, of course, was barred—but the iron bars were chased with silver. Or no—he saw on closer examination that what he had first taken for silver decoration was the lacework of the muting spell. So outside that window, sound existed: voices and music, the simple calls of birds and the whisper of the breeze... Taudde went to the window and stood looking out at the world beyond. Rugged cliffs and a glimpse of the city, and beyond both, the endless sea. Below him, waves climbed the shore and broke into froth, but he heard nothing.

The bars were too closely spaced for him to reach a hand through to the outside air. Though that would avail him nothing, even if he could. This was a good prison. It might easily hold a bardic sorcerer for a hundred years, Taudde concluded. Exactly as he had been warned. He put a hand on the windowsill and leaned his forehead against the cold bars, closing his eyes. If Geriodde Nerenne ken Seriantes left him in this prison for so long as a hundred days, he knew he would go mad.

Geriodde Nerenne ken Seriantes left him there for three. They were the longest days Taudde had ever known. Well-prepared food was delivered at intervals, but he had no appetite for it. Clean clothing—his own, mostly—was delivered as well, and Taudde kept himself neat out of habit and pride and the hope that eventually he would find his respectable appearance useful in persuading someone that dramatic measures were not necessary to keep him imprisoned. But he also slept as much as he could, trying to drown the silence of the world that surrounded him with the remembered sound and music of his dreams. By the third day he found, to his despair, that sound was leaching out even from his memory, leaving his dreams as silent as his days.

On the third day, he was again standing by the window, gazing out at the soundless world. When a hand landed on his shoulder, Taudde leaped and whirled, his heart pounding. He had, of course, heard nothing of the man's approach. Three black-clad men had entered his prison. Two stood near the door, and the other, of course, had come to get his attention with a touch, since a word could hardly do so.

This one was, he saw, the same senior officer of the King's Own guard who had been with the king in the dragon's cavern. The man didn't look amused by Taudde's startlement. The man's hard face did not lend itself to expressions of amusement, but even accounting for this, he looked grim. He looked like he thought Taudde was dangerous. Taudde had never felt less dangerous in his life. He bowed his head, trying to show that he intended only to cooperate.

From the ironic crook of his mouth, the officer was not convinced. He stepped back and gave a jerk of his head, and one of his subordinates came forward, drew a sword, and stepped behind Taudde. A hard hand came down on Taudde's shoulder, pressing him to his knees, and the sword was laid against his throat. For one dizzying moment, Taudde thought that despite the elaborate prison, he was simply going to be killed out of hand. But then the door of his prison opened again.

This time Geriodde Nerenne ken Seriantes himself entered, with his son at his side. Another man, a thick-bodied older man with the black overrobe and long white underrobe of a mage, trailed a step behind.

The king. The Dragon of Lirionne . . . The king was thinner than he had been before the caverns. The bones stood out starkly in his harsh-featured face. His ivory-pale hair was streaked with pure white. That, too, was new. But the king's eyes were still cold and opaque, and he still wore expressionlessness like a mask.

Prince Tepres was very like his father, if not so hard to read. His gaze flickered to Taudde's face and then away—and then, as if unwillingly, back again. The prince looked fine drawn and strained. His dark eyes had become, Taudde thought, a shade darker, as though the memory of shadows had crept into them and remained. And yet there was a sense of ease between the prince and his father that to Taudde seemed new.

The king glanced at his officer and gave a small nod, then glanced in command at the mage who had accompanied him.

The mage took a short wooden rod out of a pocket in his robe and broke it. The spell of silence surrounding the prison relaxed.

The return of sound—the *proof* that sound still existed in the world—was a relief so shattering that Taudde nearly cried out. The rustle of cloth, even the sound of men breathing, seemed loud; the creak of leather as one of the guards adjusted the sheath of his sword was a sharp counterpoint. Taudde drew a hard breath, suppressing an exclamation that might have been nearly a sob. At his throat, the sword shifted.

Taudde bowed his head again and held very still, certain that the mage could restore the muting spell as quickly as it had been eased. Even if that was not true, he would hardly be allowed to sing a note, or whistle, or tap out a rhythm. He waited to see if he would be allowed to speak.

Then the king made a small gesture. The sword lifted away from Taudde's throat as the black-clad guards eased back a reluctant step.

Taudde promptly used this new freedom to cast himself prone at the king's feet. It was a dramatic gesture, one Taudde hoped might incline the king toward clemency. He was glad the prince had come with his father; possibly in his son's presence, the king would be less inclined toward ferocity than if he had been on his own. Taudde pressed his face against the floor and waited.

The king broke the pause. His voice was quiet, overlain by harsh tones that called to mind the powerful tones of the sea. "Do you plead for pardon, Kalchesene? Do you believe you deserve pardon of me?"

Taudde rose as far as kneeling, lifting his gaze to the king's face. He might have reminded the king, *I saved your life, and your son's life, and your dragon as well.* But of course Geriodde Nerenne ken Seriantes knew that, and Taudde did not need to be told that the gratitude of kings was not merely fickle, but on occasion actually dangerous. He said instead, "I have permitted myself to hope for generosity, eminence."

The king inclined his head the merest fraction. "I wish you to explain to me, Kalchesene, why you came to Lonne. To kill my son? Despite the Treaty of Brenedde?"

At least this was a question and not a statement. Taudde answered at once, slipping subtle layers of sincerity and truth into his voice. "No, eminence. I never intended to break the terms of the treaty. I came...I came to Lonne because I found myself driven by a desire to learn the magic of the sea."

"And were discovered in this endeavor by my cousin, Lord Rikadde Miennes ken Nerenne. And were drawn by him into his schemes. Is this so?"

The king certainly seemed well-informed. "Yes, eminence. I didn't know Lord Miennes was your cousin."

The king made a slight, dismissive gesture. "A trivial detail. So you agreed to serve Miennes, but instead plotted his destruction. You made ensorcelled pipes for this purpose. You used materials stolen from Gerenes Brenededd's shop in the Paliante? Gerenes Brenededd is also my cousin, on the left," he added drily, observing Taudde's surprise.

"Well...yes, eminence," Taudde admitted. It would hardly have been worth denying, even if the king hadn't already known everything.

"And you plotted the destruction of Mage Ankennes, who stood behind Miennes. But less directly. There was a letter, I believe. Did you have any other method in mind for Ankennes's destruction? One hardly believes waking the dragon out of darkness and stone was your idea."

"Ah...Mage Ankennes represented a greater challenge than... your cousin. Eminence." Taudde was uncertain of what reaction the king expected from him. "I would have been glad to destroy him, but I merely hoped to entangle him in other concerns so that I could slip his attention and escape."

"But you moved not only against the conspirators but against my son as well." This was not a question. There was deep anger in that quiet statement.

Taudde made an abrupt, unexpected decision and said, as quietly, "It was a wrong decision, yes. But...my grandfather's name is Chontas Berente ser Omientes ken Lariodde."

There was a little pause. Then the king took a step forward and reached out, disregarding the alarm of his guards, to set his hand under Taudde's chin and tilt his face up toward the light from the window. He said, "Your grandfather has many grandsons. But I would wager that *your* father was Chontas Gaurente ken Lariodde. Is that so?"

"Yes."

"You have the look of him." The king dropped his hand and took a step back. "I defeated your father on the field of Brenedde, fifteen years past. I put him to death there, when he would not yield to me."

"Yes," Taudde said again. He glanced at Prince Tepres, who was staring at him with a strange kind of recognition: one prince to another. Though Taudde was not nearly so close to his grandfather's throne as Tepres was to his father's.

Having confessed to royal blood, Taudde got to his feet. The drama of the original gesture would have to serve; he could hardly now outrage his grandfather's dignity by willingly kneeling to a foreign king. He was relieved, and a little surprised, that no one tried to force him back to his knees.

The king half lifted a hand toward Taudde, then closed the hand into a fist and let it fall back to his side. "That was why you chose to accede to Miennes's demands. To kill my son, as I had killed your father."

"The idea had a certain compelling symmetry," Taudde admitted. "It...gave me a reason to take the easy path, I suppose. It would have been far more difficult to strike merely at Lord Miennes. I suspected that your, ah, cousin would know if I lied to him. Especially with Ankennes working behind him."

"That is very likely so," agreed the king. There was no forgiveness in his iron tone. It was merely an acknowledgment of truth.

"Yes, eminence. How much easier, then, to create a weapon that would do precisely as he demanded! I told myself that as Miennes forced my hand, and he no agent of Kalches, it was no outrage against the terms of the treaty to do as he commanded."

"Sophistry."

"Not...not entirely, I maintain, eminence." Taudde's gaze went to the prince's face. Prince Tepres returned him a level stare that gave away nothing, very like his father's. Taudde said, quietly, "Yet almost at once I regretted my cleverness."

"As soon as you discovered the death intended for me had gone so badly astray," the prince observed. His tone, too, was like his father's; his voice held deep anger.

Taudde bowed his head. "In Kalches, gifts are never given away again within the same year they are received. It did not occur to me until far too late that the custom in Lonne might not be the same. For the peril in which my carelessness placed an innocent girl, I am indeed to blame. Yet it was only when I thought my plan had gone astray that I realized I would have regretted success almost as much as failure." He hesitated, and then added sincerely, "I am sorry, Prince Tepres. Even aside from the treaty, I was wrong to strike at you in vengeance against your father."

The prince lifted a skeptical eyebrow. "My father defeated yours on the field of battle—a battle for which Kalches itself pressed. Do you then claim a right to vengeance for the fortunes of war?"

"The *fortunes* of war, do you say? That was a war *forced* on us—should we not wish to reclaim lands properly ours, wrested from us by unwarranted Seriantes belligerence?" Taudde caught himself and went on more moderately, "But even so, my father's death was, as you say, a result of his defeat in combat. I was wrong to strike at you in vengeance for his death, and I beg your pardon for the harm I tried to do you."

A little to Taudde's surprise, the prince did not cast this apology back in his face, but answered, "I swore in the dragon's chamber I would forgive the attempt. But I forgive it now because I believe you are sincere in your apology."

Taudde bowed his head, finding to his surprise that this actually mattered to him. He had known for some time that he wished the prince no ill, but he hadn't realized until this moment that he actually cared for Tepres's good opinion.

"I admit, your professed repentance still puzzles me," observed Geriodde Nerenne ken Seriantes, recalling Taudde's attention. At his gesture, one of the black-clad guards brought the king a chair. He sank down into it, making it instantly a throne. Then he steepled his hands and gazed at Taudde over the tips of his fingers. "I do not understand, now less than ever, why you chose, in the dark beneath the mountain, to oppose Ankennes and defend my son." The king put a faint stress on the *my*.

Taudde tried to think how to put an answer. He said at last, looking at the prince, "It was not so much a Seriantes I defended, but a man of whom I knew no ill and to whom I owed an act of contrition. Owed it twice over."

Prince Tepres gave a very small nod.

Taudde turned to the king and went on, "You would say, no doubt, that with the treaty set to run out so soon, any Kalchesene should surely strive to ensure disorder in Lirionne. But...eminence, in that case I should have struck at you. Not at your son. I was a fool to be misled into striking at Prince Tepres by dreams of personal vengeance. When I realized how great a fool I had been, should I have compounded the foolishness?

"Under the mountain, it became clear that Miennes—Lord

Miennes—had never been important. That Mage Ankennes had ruled the conspiracy and was far more dangerous. I could not see everything that would follow if the dragon was destroyed. But I believed Ankennes wrong in his intention."

"I think he was," agreed the king, quietly. "His treachery was evidently both constant and thorough. I believe now that he was also responsible for...pressing my elder sons toward...the dark paths they chose." He glanced at Prince Tepres, who returned his look steadily. Then he turned back to Taudde. "I will own that you protected this remaining son of my wife. Even in this year, and this season." The king lifted a skeptical eyebrow. "I continue to find this remarkable, Kalchesene. Young Lariodde."

Taudde hesitated, searching for words. At last he said, "I came to Lonne to listen to the music of the sea. And I have listened to it. I have listened to the music of Lonne as well, so entwined with the sea, for the songs of the sea are clearest where the waves come against the shore. The dragon...your dragon was a surprise to me. But I think now that the dragon's heartbeat lies at the foundation of all the music I have heard here, and what I heard in that cavern is not what Ankennes apparently heard. I heard a balanced rhythm—powerful, yes; dangerous, without doubt—but with nothing of wickedness or corruption about it. I confess I have no love for the Seriantes line. But I said I believed Ankennes wrong, and I did. Do. Wrong in everything."

"You take a great deal on yourself, to make such a sweeping judgment. Are you swayed merely by enmity?"

Taudde drew a breath and tried to find words. "Ankennes was, I suspect, possibly brilliant. But deeply mistaken. I believe he had developed an edifice of theory. I think that this theory became all he saw. I perceived nothing of the corruption in which he believed so passionately, and for which he was willing to bring down Lonne." Taudde hesitated, then added, "You may suspect me of arrogance, but if you will permit me to say so, eminence, I am not the least skilled of Kalchesene sorcerers."

The king lifted an ironic eyebrow. "From what I observed of

you in the dragon's chamber, I do not doubt it. Were all Kalche-sene sorcerers so powerful, I should greatly fear Kalches. I suspect you are fortunately exceptional."

Anything Taudde answered to that would be either presumptu-ous or insolent. He said nothing.

"You may continue."

Still off balance, Taudde hesitated. He said at last, "The destruc-tion of Lonne might serve Kalches, but at what cost? But for my country's sake, I might have supported Ankennes in what he tried to do, except he was too powerful. I believe there was no limit to his desire to force the world into accordance with his theories. And once he had destroyed Lonne...What then? Would he ever have felt himself finished? Or would he have chosen another proj-ect, equally misguided and equally destructive?" Taudde con-cluded carefully, "I struck at him then because there was at that moment so much power loose to grasp, and thus the opportunity existed. Above all, I did not want to face Ankennes later in my own country."

This time the silence stretched out. The king continued to regard Taudde steadily, his expression still unreadable. Yet Taudde thought he might have recognized truth when he heard it. Not all kings could. But, then, Geriodde Nerenne ken Seriantes was not an ordinary king. Taudde rather thought that behind the stillness of the room, he could hear the heartbeat of the dragon. He could not tell what the king was thinking.

"Thus your actions were ultimately on your own behalf, and on behalf of your own country," the king observed at last.

"All my reasons were important to me," Taudde said steadily. "Why should anything but the result be important to you?"

There was another pause. "I have several remaining questions to ask you, Kalchesene," the king said eventually. "I will have truthful answers to each. Then I shall decide what to do with you."

Taudde opened his hands to show that he would yield to the king's will. He had no idea what questions the king had in mind, or whether he himself would in turn be willing and able to answer them honestly. He wondered, rather desperately, whether any plea of his could prevent the re-imposition of the muting spell. He knew now, to his shame, that he *would* plead, rather than suffer the silencing of the world around him.

"Do you now wish harm to my son?"

Taudde almost exclaimed in relief. He was able to answer at once, with perfect truth, "I do not!" Then, when the king merely lifted an eyebrow and waited, he went on more slowly, choosing his words with care, "Do you think my apology was not in earnest? I assure you otherwise, eminence. I wish your son no harm."

The king gave a little nod. He asked softly, "And do you wish me harm? Do you wish Lirionne harm?"

These were more difficult questions. Taudde was not even certain of the answers himself. "I could wish Lirionne had different borders," he answered at last. "I could wish the treaty you imposed on Kalches had had different terms. But I think…I think I can honestly answer that I do not wish your people ill. You…when I was a boy, I dreamed that someday I would meet you on the field of battle and leave you broken in the mud."

"A natural dream for a boy," acknowledged the king. "And now?"

"Now, eminence, I think I have come to prefer that the borders between our countries be redrawn by some more peaceable means."

The king inclined his head. "I am satisfied with the borders as they are. But peace is my own preference."

Taudde found that he believed him. Fifteen years ago, the Dragon of Lirionne had been ruthless in his victory. Taudde, in his boyhood, had perceived only the ruthlessness. His grandfather had tried to explain to him the tactical uses of brutality, but Taudde had not been able to understand him. But he saw now that it was that same ruthlessness of will that had presided over the grim horror of the executions of Geriodde Nerenne ken Seriantes's older sons and, more recently, sent the King of Lirionne into the shadowy paths of death to find this younger son. And had then allowed

him to force his way out again. Geriodde Seriantes ruled according to his grim view of necessity, and spared himself no more than
his enemies. But Taudde thought he truly did not want the war to
resume.

Taudde said slowly, "That being so...I think I could bear to
give up ill will against you, eminence."

The king leaned back in his chair, regarding Taudde with no
expression Taudde could read. "Could you, indeed."

Pressed, Taudde said, "How can I know until I see what you
will do, eminence? I have hated you all my life, but now I see that
this was a boy's hatred. I think I could give it up...I *wish* to give it
up...but I don't know yet whether you intend to open your hand,
or rather lock me again into silence and...and despair." He
stopped, shaken by his own words. He hadn't intended to say so
much.

"And if I should open my hand? Would you wish to leave
Lonne? Have you finished...listening to the sea?"

Taudde doubted one could ever finish listening to the sea's
music. He thought that once one stood on the harsh shore below
the Laodd and heard the waves break against the cliffs, that sound
would always underlie all others. He answered without thinking,
"If I return to Kalches, I will miss the sound of the sea all my life.
Learning to listen to it properly would *take* all my life." Then, too
late, he realized what he'd said. He added hastily, "But of course I
would never again dare break your ban, eminence. I would go to
Kalches and never return to Lirionne. I would swear any oath you
might require of me."

There was a little silence.

"And break any oath you made, if war comes," the king said at
last. "No, do not protest. You would not be able to keep any such
oath, Prince Chontas Taudde ser Omientes ken Lariodde. There is
no point in requiring you to swear one. Answer me this: what
would you do if I asked you to stay in Lonne?" He paused, and
then went on, still quietly. "I think now that my mistrust of Kalchesene sorcery has made Lirionne vulnerable in ways I did not

expect. I banned sorcery in Lirionne—and then found that, once Seriantes blood and death had been poured out into the dark, *I* could not prevent Ankennes from destroying the Dragon of Lonne. *Your* sorcery prevented that. You have not flung that fact in my face. But you have hardly needed to. You ask me for generosity. Does it surprise you to learn that I am inclined to be generous?"

This did surprise Taudde. It did not seem politic to say so.

"I would not ask you to serve me," the king added, "but I would ask you to serve my son—though I understand your oath to him would be secondary to the fealty you owe your grandfather and your cousins, his heirs. If I ask you to remain on those terms, and continue your study of the sea, and teach bardic sorcery to those of my people who might be fit for that study, would you do this?"

Taudde realized that he was staring in open amazement. Turning, he went to the window and pressed his hands against the iron bars, trying to think. He looked blindly out over the sea. The sound of it came to him, ceaseless and indifferent in its power. He was cold. His hands were numb where they touched the metal.

At last he turned back, still not knowing himself what he would say.

The king remained patient. He folded his hands across his knee and waited, his cold gray eyes hooded and unreadable. At his side, Prince Tepres rested a hand on the back of his father's chair and gazed at Taudde with an expression not quite so closed. Taudde could see that the prince hoped he would agree but believed that he would not.

"I think..." said Taudde. "I think I showed you too much power in those caverns. Whatever you suggest now, I don't believe you could ever allow me to stay in Lonne, save as your close-guarded prisoner, held behind walls of silence." He stopped and waited for a response.

"It is true that you are a dangerous man," answered the king, calmly. "Your power concerns me. Your skill concerns me. I would fear what you might find to do, if the solstice should give way to a summer of iron and fire. I would not wish my mages to face you across a bloody field. I will be plain: I do not wish our peoples to face one another upon such a field. I would prefer a quiet summer followed by a calm turning of year into year. I would be pleased if your country and mine could reach a more permanent amicability. And you, Prince Chontas Taudde ser Omientes ken Lariodde? What would you prefer?"

Taudde answered slowly, "Eminence...now that your dragon is roused, I should hardly wish Kalches to face Lirionne across a field of war."

"Quite so." The king gave a grim, satisfied little nod. "If I were to permit you to return to Kalches...you would inform your grandfather of your opinion, would you not? Would he hear you?"

Taudde tilted his head, amused despite himself. "Oh, yes. Once he was finished shouting at me. He would certainly wish to know of your dragon."

"If you will not remain in Lonne, I shall send you back to him," Geriodde Nerenne ken Seriantes stated. "But I wish you to remain, on the terms I have outlined. I desire goodwill between us, and likewise between our countries. That you are a prince of Kalches could be useful to me, if your desire runs alongside mine."

Taudde looked at him for a long moment. At last he said, "Whatever your desire or mine, eminence, I must tell you, my grandfather will not accept the borders as they now lie. He will not and cannot permit Lirionne permanently to own lands so close to the heart of Kalches. However cautious of your dragon he may be, this will remain true. I would not try to persuade him otherwise, nor would he hear me if I did." He paused.

"Am I to understand that your grandfather desires war and will not be dissuaded?"

"No," said Taudde. "I hope he would not be displeased if I tell you plainly that he does not desire to resume the war. He will pursue that course only if he must. But which of the lands that you and your father and his father took from Kalches will you yield back, to persuade him to a different course?"

The king tilted his head judiciously. "We can discuss the matter.

You may approach your grandfather for me, when the time comes for such an approach. If you will, Prince Chontas."

Taudde looked at him. He could hear the distant sea and the whisper of the breeze. He said at last, "I confess I don't understand how you can imagine you may ask *any* of this of me."

"I would have to trust you," the king answered calmly. "Prince Chontas...other than Miennes and Ankennes, who in Lonne knew you were Kalchesene? I will go further and ask: who were your allies? Which of my people aided you?" The king paused and then went on softly, "If you will remain in Lonne as anything other than my prisoner, or if you will approach your grandfather for me, then you and I must trust one another. Fondness is unnecessary. Civility will serve well enough. But trust is essential. And because I have power here and you do not, you must trust me before I may give trust in return. I will do no harm to those you will name. But if you would remain in Lonne, you must name them to me."

This talk of *trust* was entirely unexpected. The Dragon of Lirionne, speaking of *trust*? Yet...there was no deceit in the king's voice. Taudde heard ruthlessness in it, yes, underlying every quiet tone. But no deliberate deceit. Nor any inclination toward cruelty. But then, sometimes ruthlessness was enough like cruelty to serve...Taudde shut his eyes and asked himself, *did* he want to stay in Lonne, here where the sea met the shore? Not as a prisoner, after all, but as...some sort of ally?

And could he possibly bring himself to trust this dragon king?

The answer to the first question was uncomfortably clear. The answer to the second...uncomfortably opaque. He said, "Do you know what you are asking?" and then waited, his eyes still closed so that he might listen with all his attention to the king's answer.

"The first step into trust," the king said steadily, "must always be blind."

Taudde opened his eyes and met the king's gaze. The gray stare was cold, patient, merciless...but Taudde found no deceit hidden in the king's eyes, as he had detected none in his voice. Perhaps a man who had all the power in his hand had no need of deceit.

But he knew even as he thought this that it was wrong. That the candor Geriodde Nerenne ken Seriantes offered him was an unusual and precious gift, and that if he failed to take that gift now it would not likely be offered again.

Speaking at all felt like . . . a step over a cliff's edge, when clouds hid what lay below. And yet . . . and yet . . . "My servant Benne, who was first Miennes's servant," Taudde said quietly. "He is more clever than he appears. He guessed. And . . ." Taudde nearly said *no one else*. To his own surprise, and driven by an instinct he prayed was sound, he said instead, "And a woman of Cloisonné House, a woman called Leilis. It was chance I was touching her hand when Ankennes pulled me into the dark, chance she was dragged after me. She was neither my servant nor my employee nor my ally; indeed, her first thought when she realized my true nationality was to warn the Laodd. But . . . I acknowledge that once she came to believe I posed no threat to Lonne, she then tried to protect me.

"You claim to put a high value on trust, eminence. These people trusted me. I can only hope now that I have not betrayed them to your vengeance. They are simple people and no danger to you or yours. I must hope you will keep your word and do no harm to them."

The king lifted a hand at one of his guards, who went to the door and opened it. Benne and Leilis came in together. The big man looked strained, but calm. The young woman was white as parchment. Almost as astonishing as the mere fact of her presence, Leilis carried a finger harp in her hand: his own, a harp made of pale mountain birch and strung with delicate silver wires. For one of the few times in his life, Taudde found himself utterly bereft of speech.

"I did not find either of them so simple as you would have me believe," Geriodde Seriantes said. His tone held something that was not quite amusement, but certainly included irony. "Each of them told me everything he or she knew of you, evidently believing I should be swayed by this to clemency, and begged my pardon on your behalf.

"Your Benne—I use the pronoun advisedly—came to me to intercede for you. He is an eloquent man when he holds a quill. After he confessed he had been Miennes's spy, I commanded him to write down for me all the secrets he had learned through his years of spying. He told me there were people who would die before revealing the secrets they thought they held hidden, but that of course he had no recourse if I would compel him." The king gave Benne a raised-eyebrow look, and the big man looked down, flushing. "Then he asked me how I was different from my cousin, who compelled men beyond their own choice to do murder for him. This was insolence, but I found I had no answer."

Taudde said nothing.

The king nodded toward Leilis. "Now, this woman, Leilis, was not half so shy as you have been in bringing to my attention how great a service you did for me. She asked me if I did not care for justice. I had some difficulty recalling the last person who spoke to me with so little care for her own safety. Then I remembered that my wife used to speak to me so." He paused.

Taudde still said nothing. He could see that Geriodde Nerenne ken Seriantes liked and approved of Leilis, and found himself in return wanting to like and approve of the king. This was clearly a dangerous impulse, as well as a horribly uncomfortable one.

After a moment, the king went on, "I promised them both that I would spare you if I could, which, of course, I already intended. I am aware of the promises you made to each of these people. I wish to see the art of Kalches for myself. Do you understand?"

"Yes," said Taudde. He wanted the harp Leilis held as a man dying of cold in the mountains longs for warmth. "You will, of course, require an oath that I shall do nothing with that harp save keep those promises."

"I require no such oath," said the king, astonishing them all.

Or, no. Taudde saw that Prince Tepres was not astonished. The glance the prince gave Taudde was wary, but the look he bent on his father was merely exasperated, not in the least surprised.

"Eminence—" the senior officer of the guard objected.

"I cannot guarantee either your safety or this prisoner's continued imprisonment if he touches that instrument," warned the mage, speaking for the first time.

"Peace," returned the king. "Trust must be reciprocal. If it is merely required of a prisoner, it is coercion." He lifted a finger in a minimal gesture toward Leilis. "Give Prince Chontas the harp."

Leilis's first step was hesitant, but then her brows drew down and her mouth firmed. She crossed the room to Taudde with decision and put the finger harp into his hands. She was careful not to let her hand brush his: the unconscious care of long, long practice. Taudde did not let her step back; he caught her hand in his, setting his teeth against the immediate dissonance. "I gave your name to the Dragon of Lirionne," he said to her.

Those grave eyes met his, utterly forthright, not in the least surprised. "I hoped you would."

Taudde found his mouth wanting to curve into a smile, and sternly tamped it straight again. Yet it took him a moment to discipline himself to study merely the dissonance that clung to the woman, and not the graceful curve of her lips or the smooth line of her cheek. He had to tell himself very firmly that the dissonance, too, was fascinating. It was, in fact. Taudde studied it...only for a moment. It had become, as he had expected, familiar to him. Taudde opened his eyes, surprised to find he had closed them, and let go of Leilis's hand, not quite willingly. She began to draw away, then met his eyes and stood still.

During those endless days he'd spent imprisoned by silence, Taudde had thought, one regret sharp among so many others, that he would never have the chance to break the twisted spell that bound this young woman. Now he sent one quick glance of honest gratitude toward the King of Lirionne, and bent his head over his harp.

Unraveling the dissonance that afflicted the woman proved a simple matter. Half of the spell was magecrafted, and though Taudde knew little of magecraft, he thought that this part was not even very well made. But it had tangled up in a familiar shadowy

darkness that was not quite darkness, but almost a kind of light...
Taudde said aloud, "I heard the Dragon's heartbeat the first time I
stepped across the threshold of Cloisonné House. I didn't know
what it was, then. But, Leilis, your heart beats in time with the
dragon's."

The woman gave him a wary look from her sea-gray eyes.

"It's a good thing," Taudde assured her. "I think," he added, and
then more to the point, "except when the dragon's inherent magic
tangles with the craft of a mage who knows nothing of the darkness at the heart of the mountain." He let his hands evoke that
darkness, sending delicate notes whispering through the bright
afternoon. He tuned each note to the shadows that tangled across
the spellwork that bound Leilis, and then let each slip away, back
to the living darkness from which it had risen.

Opening his eyes—he had again not been aware of closing
them—Taudde checked his own work and found it sound. "All
that's left is some fairly clumsy mageworking," he told Leilis. "I
expect any mage could remove it. Certainly he could." He nodded
at the king's mage, who looked sardonic but did so with a brief
gesture.

Taudde took Leilis's hands in his own once more. The spark
that jumped between them this time owed nothing to magic. Nor
was it at all unpleasant. He smiled at the woman, a little uncertainly, trying to decide whether she felt that spark as well. Then
she lifted her gray eyes to meet his, and he knew she did. Even
given the uncertainty of their respective positions, he found he was
glad. He looked warily at the king. "She is free? You will not harm
her? She never meant harm to you, or to Lonne."

"She deliberately chose to break my law," Geriodde Nerenne
ken Seriantes answered, his tone neutral. "But I have pardoned
her. She is free. I shall do her no harm. Nor need you inquire on
behalf of your servant. I shall save us all the time and assure you
once more that him, too, I have pardoned."

Taudde bent his head to the king in a second gesture of sincere
gratitude and looked at Benne.

The big man slowly walked forward. He had a small flat box attached to his belt and a quill thrust through his hair above his ear, in the manner of a scribe.

"You went to the king? On my behalf?" Taudde asked the man and, at the wary nod Benne returned, "I would not have expected that—nor asked it of you. I am grateful you would take such a risk, and glad of the chance to return the good you have done for me." He let his hands travel over the strings of his finger harp, smiling at the fragile purity of the notes.

Music could not restore wholeness to a cut tongue. That was not, so far as Taudde knew, within the realm of sorcery. But he had a different technique in mind, for a bard knows that sound is shaped out of minute vibrations of the air, and that there are many ways to shape a voice that do not depend on a wholeness of body.

Now Taudde created, with purity of music and clarity of intention, a voice that would not require an entire tongue. He fixed this voice to Benne's intention. Then, leaving the music of his harping to linger, persistent, in the air, he reached out and lifted the box from Benne's belt. It held small, fine leaves of paper and thin parchment and an extra quill, exactly as Taudde had expected. Taudde curved the quill into a circle and folded a bit of parchment across the circle thus formed, fixing it in place with a touch. He caught the last lingering notes of his harp in this tiny drum, and then offered it to Benne. "Touch it lightly as you speak," he instructed the other man. He infused his tone with assurance, because Benne's own trust and belief were necessary to the sorcery Taudde was still framing.

Benne slowly took the drum from Taudde's hand and brushed the parchment with his thumb. He opened his mouth, and anyone expecting ordinary speech would surely have thought his deep gravelly voice came from his throat. It was exactly the sort of voice Taudde had expected from the man. It sounded perfectly natural. But those who had seen the sorcery done knew that Benne's voice actually came from the drum he held in his hand.

"Will this restore my voice?" he asked, and paused. He went

white, and then flushed—and then paled again, and put a hand out blindly to a carved table in order to keep his feet. For a moment, Taudde thought the table would collapse under Benne's weight, but it held. After another moment, the big man steadied and looked up again.

"I know no way to restore your tongue," Taudde explained, opening a hand in apology. "I will continue to consider the problem, if—that is, I will consider it. This solution is a little cumbersome, I know."

Benne opened his mouth—then touched the drum. "It is my voice," he said, and the great amazement and joy in his deep voice was unmistakable. "You have given me this. My lord—" His voice failed, but only for the intensity of emotion that overcame him. He went to his knees and bowed to the floor in fealty, never glancing at the King of Lirionne. Taudde did, quickly, and saw the ironic look in the king's pale eyes.

Taudde bent and touched Benne's powerful shoulder. "You should offer me nothing. You owe me nothing," he said urgently.

"I think you will find he does not agree," the king said drily. "That is your servant, Prince Chontas Taudde ser Omientes ken Lariodde. I could hardly mistake it. But he is a free man of Lirionne and at liberty to take service where he chooses. Even with a foreign prince, if he must."

Taudde bowed, for once wordless. Benne rose to his feet and stepped to the side, turning to set himself at Taudde's side. The big man's steady presence was oddly comforting.

"Now," commanded the king, "put aside your harp."

Taudde looked at the king's harsh, unreadable dragon's face, and ran his thumb gently across the strings of his harp. The notes fell one by one into the room. Everyone hushed to hear them. The king's mage shifted, but the king moved his hand in quiet rebuke and his mage stilled. Taudde touched the strings once more . . . and then set the harp aside on the carved table. He left it there, coming forward several steps to stand before Geriodde Nerenne ken Seriantes. "I thought you would bring down the silence," he admitted.

"And I would have been in no way astonished if you had used your sorcery to fly for Kalches," answered the king. "But I believed you would not strike at me, and I was actually confident that you would not strike at my son. And there I was not wrong."

There was a long pause.

"You must understand, eminence," Taudde said, "I cannot possibly serve you."

"I don't ask that of you."

"And I will wish to return to Kalches before the solstice. Indeed, I must; I have a duty to my grandfather."

The king inclined his head. "You will not depart without leave. But I shall give it." Another pause fell, heavy as the weight of a mountain.

Taudde broke it. "I might speak for you to my grandfather. But if war should come—"

"If war comes, of course your loyalty must be wholly to your grandfather and to your country. Until such time, however, and while you are my guest, I will expect you to refrain from striking against my son. Or myself."

"I will swear to that," Taudde said cautiously. He winced inwardly, thinking what choice comments his grandfather would have, knowing Taudde had made such a pledge.

"I will trust you to hold to that oath."

Taudde bowed his head, then lifted his gaze to meet the king's eyes again. "I may study the magic of the sea? And I will be free to practice bardic sorcery?"

"To practice it and to teach it. I shall expect and require nothing less."

Taudde bowed again, then turned at last to Prince Tepres. Their eyes met, and held. Taudde saw the dragon's shadows move behind the prince's dark eyes, and wondered what the prince saw in his own. He bowed once more, this time to the prince. "I think I may even owe you service," he said quietly, lifting his gaze to look into the prince's face.

Prince Tepres shook his head. "No, you have repaid that debt in full, Prince Chontas Taudde ser Omientes ken Lariodde. I hold you free of it." The Seriantes prince sounded so like his father that Taudde blinked, but then he went on, his tone lighter, "I will have your service, but freely offered, not from the constraint of obligation. And I will return trustworthiness of my own, and no base coin. If you will believe it of a Seriantes."

Taudde found he had very little doubt of it. Glancing around the room, he found wary distrust in the faces of the guards, cautious interest in the mage's expression, grim wariness in Benne's coarse face, and real pleasure in Leilis's sea-gray eyes. Geriodde Nerenne ken Seriantes rested his chin on his hand, his mouth crooked in irony and satisfaction. His face was overlain, to Taudde's sight, by the elegant, dangerous lines of the dragon's face.

CHAPTER 18

After looking in the kitchen, the workroom, and both libraries, Nemienne finally found Taudde, as she ought to have expected, in the music room. He was seated at the room's only table, a heavy, ornate piece with carved fishes spiraling around its legs and sea dragons inlaid in lapis and pearl head-to-tail around its edge. At the moment, leaves of paper were scattered across the table, each one covered with the complex spidery trails of music notation. Each leaf had been weighed down with a glass bell against the spring breeze that wandered in through the open window. In this house, a spring breeze coming through a window did not necessarily imply that it was actually *spring*, but, in fact, at the moment the window's view matched Lonne's true season.

The tall floor harp with the black-eyed dragon carved down its face stood beside Taudde's chair, and the sound of a single, deep, pure note lingered in the room. The young sorcerer held an ivory plectrum in one hand and a writing quill in the other.

He glanced up as Nemienne leaned through the doorway. "Yes?"

"I'm sorry to interrupt, but there's a new door in the hall," Nemienne told him. "It's made of pine and granite, and it opens onto high cliffs where there's snow blowing in the wind. You can see a road curving around an angle of the cliffs near the door. I suppose it's a road. It looks terribly steep."

Taudde put down the quill, laying it neatly across the topmost leaf of paper. "Kalches," he said, and sighed.

"You've been expecting it, you said," Nemienne reminded him. "You said you wanted this door to appear before the solstice. Well, it has, hasn't it? What's wrong with having the door appear now?" She had thought he'd be happy about the new door to Kalches. He didn't look very pleased.

"I did expect it." The Kalchesene sorcerer stretched his long legs out under the table and tapped the plectrum absently against the surface of the table. He sighed again. "I'll have to ask leave of Prince Tepres to visit my grandfather. He'll give it, of course." He didn't sound as if he relished the prospect. "It's true I'd hoped to have that door before the solstice. It's also true that I don't look forward to using it. I imagine Grandfather will have several choice comments to make about, well, nearly everything that's happened in the past six months." He brightened slightly. "Perhaps I'll ask Leilis to come with me. Let Grandfather try to sharpen his wits on *her*. He'll find he's not the only one with an edge to his tongue."

"She may be too busy to go with you. Or Narienneh may not want her to go, now that she's made Leilis her heir to Cloisonné House. Or—"

Taudde held up a hand. "Let's not borrow trouble against the wretched day, shall we? What time is it? All right, there should be time before the candlelight district wakes for the night. Please step over to Cloisonné House and ask Leilis whether she might find a moment for me this evening, would you, Nemienne?" He bent a stern look on her. "Take Enkea with you, mind. None of this solitary wandering through the dark."

Nemienne hadn't known he'd been aware of her slipping from one house of shadows to another of an evening. She could feel a flush creeping up her cheeks. "I do know the way, now," she protested.

"Through those caverns?" The Kalchesene sorcerer's tone was mild, but unyielding. "I doubt anyone could. I'm glad of your skill and confidence, Nemienne. But let's not exceed good sense. Do you wish to accidentally trouble the dragon now that it is awake? Take Enkea with you."

"Yes, all right," Nemienne agreed hastily, wanting all the more urgently to drop the subject because she knew he was perfectly right. "It's only, she's not always handy when you want her—"

"Patience is a virtue in sorcery as well as magecraft," Taudde said mildly. "If I can't expect you to act with reasonable prudence, Nemienne, I'll go myself. Only I should first attend upon the prince."

"I'll take her, I'll take her!" Nemienne promised.

"Attend upon me?" The prince's voice, faintly edged with the fierceness of the dragon, made Nemienne jump; she hadn't heard him enter.

But Taudde glanced up with no sign of surprise, then rose and bowed, a brief gesture. "Ah, eminence, welcome. It seems this house has at last seen fit to offer us a door that leads into Kalches."

"I see." The prince's dark eyes rested on Taudde's face. After a second, the pale brows lifted. "You don't doubt I'll give you leave to go? No, of course not." The light, fierce voice gentled. "And is that such a burden?"

Taudde moved his shoulders uncomfortably. "It's not a burden I ever expected to bear. Forgive me if I sometimes find it weighs heavily."

The prince inclined his head without comment. He said after a moment, "And you are concerned about your grandfather."

"I fear his initial reaction to . . . all this . . . will be, um. Intense."

The prince did not smile. "You will have to persuade him, then."

"I know. I will." Taudde lifted a hand toward the door, inviting the prince to accompany him. "Shall we find out whether you are able to perceive this newest addition to the house's complement of extraordinary doors?"

The young men left the music room together, Taudde politely stepping aside to allow Prince Tepres to precede him.

Nemienne didn't entirely understand what either of them had

meant. Sometimes she felt that the ten years that lay between herself and the young men might as well be half a lifetime. She thought about the exchange as she ran down the stairs to the kitchen, collected Enkea—fortunately the cat seemed in an accommodating mood—and then headed through the infinite darkness beyond the black door to emerge in the cellars of Cloisonné House. In Lonne, as had eventually become clear to her—she was sometimes slow, but Taudde was patient—quite a number of houses hid a way into the shadows. The gallery of her father's house, the cellars of Cloisonné, the dungeons of the Laodd, more than one shop in the Paliente, many a shadowed warehouse corner, almost anywhere where the sea came up under the docks—half of Lonne, it sometimes seemed, lay under the dragon's shadow.

The kitchen staff greeted her absently as Nemienne emerged from the cellars into the warmth and light. They were in a desperate flurry. Clearly some massive event was planned for this evening, which wasn't good because it meant that Leilis was probably extremely busy.

Nemienne found the other woman still in her room, however. Two little girls were helping Leilis dress in elaborate robes of sea blue and slate gray; spume broke around the hem of her overrobe and white gulls flew from knee to shoulder. Leilis wore a gull of pearls and hematite in her hair. She looked beautiful, calm, and remote as the sea. She greeted Nemienne with an abstracted nod.

"Your sister is attending a dance at the House of Butterflies," she told her. "You would do better to look for her tomorrow. Or better still, four days from now. I believe there's a break in her schedule at noon. She's terribly busy. Or were you looking for me?"

"Oh, for you," said Nemienne, rolling her eyes at the idea of trying to catch up with her keiso sister. Karah's flower wedding to Prince Tepres was still more than a year in the future, but from the pace of preparations anyone would think that merely days remained. All of Karah's sisters had resigned themselves to seeing very little of her until the ceremony was over.

Nemienne explained why she'd come, and also related the

exchange between Taudde and the prince. "I knew you'd understand what they meant," she concluded, and folded her hands in her lap, looking expectantly at Leilis.

The woman inclined her elegant head. "I know you're an apprentice mage, Nemienne, but do try to think like a keiso for a moment. They were speaking of the burden of Seriantes trust, of course. Poor Taudde."

Nemienne didn't understand what Leilis meant. She blinked.

"There are two edges to this knife," added Leilis, with a slight air of explaining something obvious in words of one syllable. "Taudde has to explain to his grandfather how he has become almost a friend of the son of the man who killed the son of his grandfather—"

Nemienne unraveled this only because she already knew the story.

"*And* Prince Chontas Taudde ser Omientes ken Lariodde *also* has to explain to the King of Kalches how he came to be in service to the heir of the Dragon of Lirionne. And this on the eve of the solstice. The King of Kalches cannot be pleased at any suggestion of divided loyalties in a prince of Kalches. I wonder whether he will understand how Geriodde Nerenne ken Seriantes forced Taudde's choice?" Her expression had become calm and even more distant. Despite her youth, she looked every bit a worldly, experienced keiso. "It would be a pity if Taudde loses his grandfather's trust because of the Seriantes Dragon. We shall need the King of Kalches to listen to his grandson. Perhaps I would like to go to Kalches, after all. Travel broadens the mind, they say."

"And strengthens the will" was the rest of that saying. Nemienne tried to think of someone whose will needed strengthening less than Leilis's, but failed. And Seriantes trust…Nemienne had never thought of trust as a burden, either to give or to bear. But she understood that it might be, for Taudde. In fact, thinking about it made her flinch a little. She asked instead, an easier question, "Will Narienneh let you go?"

"I should think so, if I put it to her properly. Almost anything can be managed if one simply goes about it properly." Leilis slipped three silver bangles over her left wrist and turned to study the effect in the new and expensive full-length mirror that stood next to the fireplace.

She looked beautiful. And intimidating. Her mood did not seem precisely confiding—Leilis was never in a confiding mood, as far as Nemienne knew. And the sharp side of her tongue was nothing Nemienne wanted turned her way. But Nemienne asked anyway, cautiously, "I have wondered...I know it's nothing to do with me, but I have wondered—what sort of proper management..."

"Led to the rearrangement in Cloisonné House's line of inheritance?" Leilis glanced over her shoulder. Her tone was dry, but not offended. "In fact, that was hardly my management. Lily removed herself from the line by her own efforts."

"Oh."

Leilis gave a brief, matter-of-fact nod. "Mother knew well enough that her daughter would never make an acceptable successor for this House. She had known for years, of course, though she hadn't wished to know it. I was actually sorry when she was forced to admit the truth. It was hard on her." She sounded distantly sympathetic.

"Oh," Nemienne said again.

"I didn't expect her to name me as her heir," said Leilis, but added without a trace of modesty, "but it was a good decision, so I wasn't actually surprised."

Nemienne doubted anyone had been.

Leilis glanced absently about the room and added, "You might hand me those slippers. Thank you. You might go to Kalches, too, if your sisters could spare you."

Nemienne hadn't thought of going to Kalches herself. She didn't answer right away, for she hardly knew what she thought of the suggestion. She had hardly been out of Lonne; she had never really imagined leaving Lirionne itself. And to go to Kalches, of all countries! She wondered what her sisters would think of the idea.

Well, she knew, really. Ananda and Enelle and Tana would

worry for her, but Ananda was too wrapped up in her marriage and Enelle in the stone yard and Tana in running the house for any of them to protest very much. Liaska certainly wouldn't worry; far from worrying, Liaska would fight passionately to come along. Jehenne and Miande were the ones who would miss Nemienne the most: not just worry about her, but miss her. And she knew, as she would not have been able to guess half a year ago, that she would miss them both quite bitterly.

Leilis said calmly, "I believe Taudde would agree with me that a Lonne mage with a heart tuned to the darkness under the mountain ought to learn something useful from listening to the wind in the heights."

"Anyone with a heart tuned to those shadows might," Nemienne agreed. "Anybody who managed to tangle up magecraft with the magic of the dragon, for example. Especially anybody whose father was a mage." She didn't quite dare say, *Or anybody who's fallen in love with a mage.*

"Why, yes," said Leilis, in an extremely bland tone. She turned back toward the mirror, adjusted her silver bangles, and said to her reflection, "Yes, I rather think that might be true."

ACKNOWLEDGMENTS

Thanks to my fabulous agent, Caitlin Blasdell, without whose critical insight every one of my books would be the poorer; and to the whole Orbit team, especially my editor, Devi Pillai, who tells me I'm "awesome." Always good to hear!

extras

orbit

meet the author

Hastings' Creative Images, Inc.

RACHEL NEUMEIER started writing fiction to relax when she was a graduate student and needed a hobby unrelated to her research. Prior to selling her first fantasy novel, she had published only a few articles in venues such as *The American Journal of Botany*. However, finding that her interests did not lie in research, Rachel left academia and began to let her hobbies take over her life instead. She now raises and shows dogs, gardens, cooks, and occasionally finds time to read. She works part time for a tutoring program, though she tutors far more students in math and chemistry than in English composition. Find out more about Rachel Neumeier at www.rachelneumeier.com.

interview

You have three main characters in House of Shadows—
*but do you have a favorite? Is there a reason you wrote this
book with three main characters who are all about equally
important?*

If you twisted my arm, I might admit to a slight partiality to
Taudde. I like the big problem with conflicting loyalties that
he has to deal with. But I like Nemienne's earnestness and
Leilis's bitterness as well.

There's no big thematic reason I wrote this story with
three main point-of-view characters. It happened because I
started the book three different ways—or you might say I
started three different books—and then I liked all three and
came up with a plot to tie them all together.

*Many writers characterize themselves as "character" or
"plot" writers—from the above, we might guess that you
would say you belong to the first camp. Is that right?*

Definitely! As far as I'm concerned, characters just walk on
stage and then drive the plot because of who they are and
what they need. The plot itself is first suggested by the characters and the world, and then plot details get bludgeoned
out of the ether by brute force.

*So is that the aspect of writing you find most challenging—
plotting?*

Yep. I often know practically nothing about where the story
is going to end up when I start—or else I may know the ending but have no idea about how to get there. Actually, when I
started writing the climactic scenes of *House of Shadows*, I
wrote about forty pages, then completely changed my mind
about what was happening, threw them away, and came up
with something that worked much better.

About the only book where I had the basic outline of the
full plot in my head from the start was *Law of the Broken
Earth*—because I had to know something about the third
book of the trilogy so that I could write the second.

*The keiso of Lonne are clearly based on the geisha of Japan.
What inspired you to create the keiso?*

Actually, I'd just read *Memoirs of a Geisha*, by Arthur Golden,
and then the nonfiction *Geisha*, by Liza Dalby, so the keiso had a
very direct inspiration. I was intrigued by the roles that geisha
have played in Japanese society and, when I created the keiso,
decided to emphasize their roles as artists and high-status women
and completely separate them from common prostitutes.

*Do you often draw ideas for a new book this way—from
books you've just read yourself?*

Absolutely—all the time. Nonfiction. For example, reading
Self-Made Man, by Nora Vincent, made me want to write a
girl character who disguised herself as a boy (in *The Floating
Islands*). And it would never have occurred to me to write a
character like Tehre (*Land of the Burning Sands*) except that
I'd read a book on materials science by J. E. Gordon called
Structures: Or Why Things Don't Fall Down.

I draw on fiction, too. Mienthe was based on a very minor character in a historical novel—the character appealed to me and I gave Mienthe a similar background, which is the part you see in the prologue of *Law of the Broken Earth*.

You've written both adult and young adult fantasy—do you read both, and do you have a preference? Who are a handful of your favorite authors on both sides of the line?

I definitely read both, and I have no preference. I do think there are a lot of very good writers in YA right now, but that's been true for ages. I've loved Diana Wynne Jones's books all my life; she and Patricia Wrede might be two of my favorite YA authors. And Robin McKinley. And Sharon Shinn. I recently read the Tomorrow series by John Marsden and it is incredible.

On the adult side, there are too many to name, but definitely Patricia McKillip and Guy Gavriel Kay. And, more recently, N. K. Jemisin—her books are some of the best I've read this year.

Do you find it difficult to switch back and forth from adult to young adult?

Yes, it can be. If I've recently been working on a YA book, then it can be hard to switch to adult, and vice versa. I think it's harder for me because I tend to write on the edge, where a book might go either way, so it can be hard for me to write a book that is decisively on one side of the line or the other.

I had this exact trouble with *Land of the Burning Sands*, because I'd just finished *The Floating Islands*, which is YA. I kept thinking of characters and plots that would be fine for YA but not really okay for adult fantasy. Finally I declared that the main character would be forty-two years old, and that got me away from YA at last.

What are your writing plans for the future? Any new titles we should look for?

No specific titles, but I am currently revising an urban fantasy/paranormal story to drop it more firmly into the YA camp. Other than that, we'll see. I've been reading all these books about the Ottoman Empire, so that may turn into a wonderfully exotic setting for a book in the near future.

introducing

If you enjoyed
HOUSE OF SHADOWS,
look out for

THE GRIFFIN MAGE

by Rachel Neumeier

Kes woke as the first stars came out above the desert, harder and higher and brighter than they had ever seemed at home. She lifted her head and blinked up at them, still half gone in dreams and finding it hard to distinguish, in that first moment, the blank darkness of those dreams from the darkness of the swift dusk. She was not, at first, quite sure why the brightness of the stars seemed so like a forewarning of danger.

She did not at once remember where she was, or with whom. Heat surrounded her, a heavy pressure against her skin. She thought the heat should have been oppressive, but in fact it was not unpleasant. It was a little like coming in from a frosted winter morning into a kitchen, its iron stove pouring heat out into the room: The heat was overwhelming and yet comfortable.

Then, behind her, Opailikiita shifted, tilted her great head, and bumped Kes gently with the side of her fierce eagle's beak.

Kes caught her breath, remembering everything in a rush: Kairaithin and the desert and the griffins, drops of blood that turned to garnets and rubies as they struck the sand, sparks of fire that scattered from beating wings and turned to gold in the air . . . She jerked convulsively to her feet, gasping.

Long shadows stretched out from the red cliffs, sharp-edged black against the burning sand. The moon, high and hard as the stars, was not silver but tinted a luminescent red, like bloody glass.

Kereskiita, Opailikiita said. Her voice was not exactly gentle, but it curled comfortably around the borders of Kes's mind.

Kes jerked away from the young griffin, whirled, backed up a step and another. She was not exactly frightened—she was not frightened of Opailikiita. Of the desert, perhaps. Of, at least, finding herself still in the desert; she was frightened of that. She caught her breath and said, "I need to go home!"

Her desire for the farm and for Tesme's familiar voice astonished her. Kes had always been glad to get away by herself, to walk in the hills, to listen to the silence the breeze carried as it brushed through the tall grasses of the meadows. She had seldom *minded* coming home, but she had never *longed* to climb the rail fence into the lowest pasture, or to see her sister watching out the window for Kes to come home. But she longed for those things now. And Tesme would be missing her, would think—Kes could hardly imagine what her sister might think. She said again, "I need to go home!"

Kereskiita, the slim brown griffin said again. *Wait for Kairaithin. It would be better so.*

Kes stared at her. "Where is he?"

The Lord of the Changing Wind is . . . attempting to change the course of the winds, answered Opailikiita.

There was a strange kind of humor to the griffin's voice, but it was not a familiar or comfortable humor and Kes did not understand it. She looked around, trying to find the lie of country she knew in the sweep of the shadowed desert. But she could not recognize anything. If she simply walked downhill, she supposed she would eventually find the edge of the desert . . . if it still had an edge, which now seemed somehow a little unlikely, as though Kes had watched the whole world change to desert in her dreams. Maybe she had; she could not remember her dreams. Only darkness shot through with fire . . .

Kereskiita—said the young brown griffin.

"My name is Kes!" Kes said, with unusual urgency, somehow doubting, in the back of her mind, that this was still true.

Yes, said Opailikiita. *But that is too little to call you. You should have more to your name. Kairaithin called you* kereskiita. *Shall I?*

"Well, but . . . *kereskiita*? What is that?"

It would be . . . "fire kitten," perhaps, Opailikiita said after a moment. And, with unexpected delicacy, *Do you mind?*

Kes supposed she didn't actually *mind*. She asked, "Opailikiita? That's *kiita*, too."

Glittering flashes of amusement flickered all around the borders of Kes's mind. *Yes. Opailikiita Sehanaka Kiistaike*, said the young griffin. *Opailikiita is my familiar name. It is . . . "little spark"? Something close to that. Kairaithin calls me by that name. I am his* kiinukaile. *It would be . . . "student," I think. If you wish, you* may call me Opailikiita. *As you are also Kairaithin's student.*

"I'm not!" Kes protested, shocked.

You assuredly will be, said another voice, hard and yet somehow amused, a voice that slid with frightening authority around the edges of Kes's mind. Kairaithin was there suddenly, not striding up as a man nor settling from the air on eagle's wings, but simply *there*. He was in his true form: a great eagle-headed griffin with a deadly curve to his beak, powerful feathered forequarters blending smoothly to a broad, muscled lion's rear. His pelt was red as smoldering coals, his wings black with only narrow flecks of red showing, like a banked fire flickering through a heavy iron grate. He sat like a cat, upright, his lion's tail curling around taloned eagle's forefeet. The tip of his tail flicked restlessly across the sand, the only movement he made.

You have made yourself acquainted with my kiinukaile? the griffin mage said to Kes. *It is well you should become acquainted with one another.*

"I am *not* your student!" Kes declared furiously, but then hesitated, a little shocked by the vehemence of her own declaration.

She is fierce, Opailikiita said to Kairaithin. *Someday this kitten will challenge even you.* She sounded like she approved.

Perhaps, Kairaithin said to the young griffin, *but not today.* There was neither approval nor disapproval in his powerful voice. He added, to Kes, *What will you do, a young fire mage fledging among creatures of earth? I will teach you to ride the fiery wind. Who else will? Who else could?*

Kes wanted to shout, I'm not a mage! Only she remembered holding the golden heat of the sunlight in her cupped hands, of tasting the names of griffins like ashes on her tongue. She could still recall every name now. She said stubbornly, "I want to go home. You never said you would keep me here! I healed your friends for you. Take me home!"

Kairaithin tilted his head in a gesture reminiscent of an eagle regarding a small animal below its perch; not threatening, exactly, but dangerous, even when he did not mean to threaten.

He melted suddenly from his great griffin form to the

smaller, slighter shape of a man. But to Kes, he seemed no less a griffin in that form. The fire of his griffin's shadow glowed faintly in the dark. He said to Kes like a man quoting, "Fire will run like poetry through your blood."

"I don't care if it does!" Kes cried, taking a step toward him. "I healed all your people! I learned to use fire and I healed them for you! What else do you *want*?"

Kairaithin regarded her with a powerful, hard humor that was nothing like warm human amusement. He answered, "I hardly know. Events will determine that."

"Well, I know what *I* want! I want to go *home*!"

"Not yet," said Kairaithin, unmoved. "This is a night for patience. Do not rush forward toward the next dawn and the next again, human woman. Days of fire and blood will likely follow this night. Be patient and wait."

"Blood?" Kes thought of the griffins' terrible injuries, of Kairaithin saying *Arrows of ice and ill-intent.* She said, horrified, "Those cold mages won't come *here*!"

Harsh amusement touched Kairaithin's face. "One would not wish to predict the movements of men. But, no. As you say, I do not expect the cold mages of Casmantium to come here. Or not yet. We must wait to see what events determine."

Kes stared at him. "Events. What events?"

The amusement deepened. "If I could answer that, little *kereskiita*, I would be more than a mage. I may guess what the future will bring. But so may you. And neither of us will *know* until it unrolls at last before us."

Kes felt very uneasy about these *events*, whatever Kairaithin guessed they might entail. She said, trying for a commitment, suspecting she wouldn't get one, "But you'll let me go home later. You'll take me home. At dawn?"

The griffin mage regarded her with dispassionate intensity.

"At dawn, I am to bring you before the regard of the Lord of Fire and Air."

The king of the griffins. Kes thought of the great bronze-and-gold king, not lying injured before her but staring down at her in implacable pride and strength. He had struck at her in offended pride, if it had not been simple hostility. Now *he* would make some judgment about her, come to some decision? She was terrified even to think of it.

She remembered the gold-and-copper griffin, Eskainiane Escaile Sehaikiu, saying to Kairaithin, *You were right to bring us to the country of men and right to seek a young human.* Maybe that was the question the king would judge: Whether Kairaithin had been right to bring her into the desert and teach her to use the fire, which belonged to griffins and was nothing to do with men? Escaile Sehaikiu had said Kairaithin was right. But she suspected the king would decide that Kairaithin had been wrong. She gave a small, involuntary shake of her head. "No . . ."

"Yes."

"I . . ."

"*Kereskiita.* Kes. You may be a human woman, but you are now become my *kiinukaile*, and that is nothing I had hoped to find here in this country of earth. You do not know how rare you are. I assure you, you have nothing to fear." Kairaithin did not speak kindly, nor gently, but with a kind of intense relief and satisfaction that rendered Kes speechless.

I will be with you. I will teach you, Opailikiita promised her.

In the young griffin's voice, too, Kes heard a similar emotion, but in her it went beyond satisfaction to something almost like joy. Kes found herself smiling in involuntary response, even lifting a hand to smooth the delicate brown-and-gold feathers below the griffin's eye. Opailikiita turned her head and brushed Kes's wrist very gently with the deadly edge of her beak in a caress of welcome and . . . if the slim griffin did not offer exactly friendship, it was something as strong, Kes felt, and not entirely dissimilar.

Kairaithin's satisfaction and Opailikiita's joy were deeply reassuring. But more than reassurance, their reactions implied to Kes that, to the griffins, her presence offered a desperately needed—what, reprieve?—which they had not truly looked to find. Kairaithin had said the cold mages would not come here. *Not yet*, he had said. But, then, some other time? Perhaps soon?

I have no power to heal, Kairaithin had said to her. But then he had taught *her* to heal. Kes hesitated. She still wanted to insist that the griffin mage take her home. Only she had no power to insist on anything, and she knew Kairaithin would not accede. And . . . was it not worth a little time in the griffins' desert to learn to pour sunlight from her hands and make whole even the most terrible injury? Especially if cold mages would come here and resume their attack on the griffins? She flinched from the thought of arrows of ice coming out of the dark, ruining all the fierce beauty of the griffins. If she did not heal them, who would?

Kairaithin held out his hand to her, his eyes brilliant with dark fire. "I will show you the desert. I will show you the paths that fire traces through the air. Few are the creatures of earth who ever become truly aware of fire. I will show you its swift beauty. Will you come?"

All her earlier longing for her home seemed . . . not gone, but somehow distant. Flames rose all around the edges of Kes's mind, but this was not actually disagreeable. It even felt . . . welcoming.

Kes took a step forward without thinking, caught herself, drew back. "I'm *not* your student," she declared. Or she *meant* to declare it. But the statement came out less firmly than she'd intended. Not exactly like a plea, but almost like a question. She said, trying again for forcefulness and this time managing at least to sound like she meant it, "My sister will be worried about me—"

"She will endure your absence," Kairaithin said indifferently. "Are you so young you require your sister's leave to come and go?"

"No! But she'll be *worried*!"

"She will endure. It will be better so. A scattering of hours, a cycle of days. Can you not absent yourself so long?" Kairaithin continued to hold out his hand. "You are become my student, and so you must be for yet some little time. Your sister will wait for you. Will you come?"

"Well . . ." Kes could not make her own way home. And if she had to depend on the griffin mage to take her home, then she didn't want to offend him. And if she had to stay in the desert for a little while anyway, she might as easily let him show her its wonders. Wasn't that so?

She was aware that she wanted to think of justifications for that decision. But *wasn't* it so?

Come, whispered Opailikiita around the edges of her mind. *We will show you what it means to be a mage of fire.*

Kes did not feel like any sort of mage. But she took the necessary step forward and let Kairaithin take her hand.

The griffin mage did not smile. But the expression in his eyes was like a smile. His strange, hot fingers closed hard around her hand, and the world tilted out from under them.

LP408   165

7/12